Praise for Sam Llewellyn and His Captivating Mysteries . . .

"Llewellyn writes so well. . . . His characters are never too perfect and his plots never too simple, which makes for a refreshing read—one never knows what to expect. . . ."

—*Washington Times*

"Mr. Llewellyn is a graceful writer with a sharp feeling for his subjects and characters. . . . May he sail on for a long time. . . ."

—Newgate Callendar, *The New York Times Book Review*

BLOOD KNOT

A prize-winning reporter returns home to unravel his tangled past—and solve a very current murder. . . .

"The best seaborne thriller in many a tide . . . exciting and unusually well written . . . A cunning blend of suspense, adventure and whodunnit."

—*Daily Mail* (London)

"Good reading for any mystery fan . . . even if you don't know starboard from port or stern from bow."

—*Lincoln Star Journal*

"Extensive nautical lore, a taut plot, and copious helpings of dirty politics help distinguish this adventure. . . ."

—*Publishers Weekly*

BLOOD ORANGE

In a storm off the Irish coast, a frayed cable nearly cost James Dixon his life. But investigating this "accident" has an even higher price. . . .

"A riveting thriller that will captivate mariners and landlubbers alike . . . Llewellyn's deftly navigated story is a winner from start to finish."

—*Publishers Weekly*

DEADEYE

A divorce lawyer is in too deep when the wreck of his racing yacht reveals a lethal web of international intrigue and corruption. . . .

"Terrific pacing, clear, muscular writing, and action scenes that leave you holding your breath . . . riveting."

—*San Jose Mercury News*

DEAD RECKONING

A boat of his own design takes down Charlie Agutter's own brother. Now he sets sail on a personal mission: to track a murderous saboteur. . . .

"A most satisfying tale . . . Thrilling in its depiction of yacht racing, involving in its slow, masterly revelation of envy and violence."

—*Booklist*

DEATH ROLL

Off the coast of Spain, a world-class helmsman rides a treacherous obstacle course of deception and murder. . . .

"Skulduggery sails south from England to Spain . . . Fast and slick . . . thrills."

—*Kirkus Reviews*

Books by Sam Llewellyn

Dead Reckoning
Blood Orange
Death Roll
Deadeye
Blood Knot
Clawhammer
Riptide

Published by POCKET BOOKS

RIPTIDE

SAM LLEWELLYN

POCKET BOOKS

New York   London   Toronto   Sydney   Tokyo   Singapore

An *Original* Publication of POCKET BOOKS

POCKET BOOKS, a division of Simon & Schuster Inc.
1230 Avenue of the Americas, New York, NY 10020

ISBN: 0-671-89307-6

First Pocket Books printing November 1994

10 9 8 7 6 5 4 3 2 1

POCKET and colophon are registered trademarks of Simon & Schuster Inc.

Cover design by Shultz Design

Printed in the U.S.A.

To
Dave Burnett

RIPTIDE

1

*O*utside, the sun was shining down from an empty sky, and the Pulteney Silver Band was playing selections from Gilbert and Sullivan by the slipway. Inside the workshop it was hot, and the sweat was running into my eyes and down behind the dust mask as I hacksawed at the unopened bottle of Moët et Chandon in the woodworker's vise on the bench.

Mary, my secretary, stuck her thick and grizzled head around the door. She said, "The French Ambassador's here."

I pulled off the mask, stepped out of the white overalls, straightened the tie, knocked glass dust off the blazer and the shiny black moccasins that boatbuilders wear on big days. I took the champagne bottle gently out of the vise, and walked into the daylight.

There were flags everywhere, fluttering in the small easterly breeze blowing around the bottom of the July high-pressure system. There were people, too. There was the usual bunch of Pulteney worthies, standing as far as possible from the band, chewing at yachting-village gossip. There was a gaggle of men with leather jackets and cameras and microphone booms, from French television and *Paris-Match,* clustered around a long black car, which would be carrying the Ambassador. And there was a ragbag of boat journalists and rubberneckers, eddying in an aimless manner, waiting for the boring bit to be over and the drinking to start.

Clutching the champagne bottle, I wove quickly through the crowd, heading for its focus at the top of the slipway: a yacht, mast towering into a cloud of swallows, hull a sleek black fish's body of black plastic with a gold-leaf coving line. *Arc-en-Ciel*, latest product of Savage Yachts, my boatyard, and the reason for all the fuss.

I went up the steps of the dais at her bow, tied the sawn Moët bottle to the ribbon, and stood it in the little box provided.

Below the dais, the crowd swayed like a cornfield, parted. Two men and two women were coming toward the tower, preceded by three cameramen and half a dozen photographers walking backward, shutters rasping. There was the Ambassador, in a dark suit, and his wife, a dark woman in a bell-shaped dress that managed to look cool and neat and sexy all at once. Talking to her, making her laugh, was my old friend Thibault Ledoux, new owner of *Arc-en-Ciel*. Thibault was a small man with wide shoulders. He looked like a blue-eyed gypsy, or a pirate, or a circus performer. He had been all three in his time. Talking to the Ambassador was a woman with bobbed dark hair, and eyes that were green when you got close to them. She was wearing a linen suit. She looked as cool as the Ambassador's wife, but not as sexy. She was Mary Ellen Soames, and on our good days we were a married couple.

They came up the steps to the dais. I pasted on the grin, observed a large grease stain on my right hand, and rubbed most of it off on the railings. I switched on the microphone. I shook hands.

"Speech," said Mary Ellen out of the side of her mouth. She was a great prompter.

I walked up to the microphone, looked around at the crowd, the huge corrugated-iron shed, the pennants fluttering in the breeze. I said that Savage Yachts was proud to have built a lot of fine boats in its time, and that we were pleased and proud to have built *Arc-en-Ciel* for my old friend Thibault Ledoux, who would win races in it, and that

I was handing them over to M. de Peyrefitte, the French Ambassador.

The Ambassador started his speech. The population of Pulteney stopped listening, because the Napoleonic Wars have never properly ended in southwest England by the sea. The Ambassador said that Thibault was one of France's favorite sons, a hero of the bounding main. Thibault grinned and nodded and looked noble. He was used to this sort of thing. After some time, the Ambassador stopped. His wife picked up the champagne bottle. "God bless this sheep," she said, and swung the bottle. It broke along the grooves I had hacksawed in the glass. I ran sweat. Bottles that do not break are common, and unlucky, and I was in need of luck.

The band started to play the Marseillaise, only slightly out of tune. Alf, the yard foreman, knocked out the wedges holding the trolley. *Arc-en-Ciel* trundled down the slip into the gray-green waters of the harbor, bobbed twice, and settled over her reflection like a swan. There was a rattle of applause. Then the crowd headed for the blue-and-white-striped marquee, which contained the bar. And I stood there, weak-kneed, because it had all gone well, and at the moment I was not used to things going well.

We all chatted, us big shots, and drank champagne. Mary Ellen's chauffeur appeared and told her it was five o'clock, and she had a seven o'clock meeting in Bristol. And I was left with Thibault.

"Lovely," said Thibault. "You managed this beautifully. Last time, the bottle did not break. Listen. There's a problem with the delivery. I'm tied up. So's the team. Can you arrange this? You can borrow Yann."

I looked at *Arc-en-Ciel*, sails on, ready to go. I looked at the sheds, where Savage Yachts were built. The sheds were empty, like the order book. And I looked at the wide blue sea, rolling up to the horizon. Over that horizon was the emptiness where I belonged and felt at home. "I'll manage it somehow," I said.

"Thanks." He banged me on the arm. "Christ, look at us," he said. "Fat cats, now. D'you remember the *Kraken?* Not so fat then, huh?"

I grinned at him. He was a fat cat, all right. My old pal Thibault. "I remember," I said.

Then the press descended in an ugly roar of questions, and that was that.

A week later, I was over the horizon, and it was midnight on Biscay. There was a wind, howling out of the black west with a sound like a choir of chainsaws. There was a moon, hanging on by its fingernails among flying rags of cloud. And there was, for the moment, the boat.

The boat had looked big on the slipway. There had been twelve steps up to the dais. But just now, when you were strapped into its cockpit in the yelling black night, it felt the size of a peanut shell.

The deck moved under my feet with an ugly, twisting wrench. Up there in the moonlight the mast was canted twenty degrees out of the vertical by the press of the wind. It was the angle of heel you expect from a yacht under full sail, racing around the cans in the Solent during Cowes Week. Just at the moment, the angle was being produced by the tiny triangle of storm jib we had hoisted to give us a sense of direction in this wet, directionless world.

It was a big night, all right. But I had sailed four times around the world, and I had seen bigger.

There was a rumble and a slam as the cabin hatch went back. A head appeared. In daylight, the hair would have been a sun-bleached stubble, the skin mahogany brown, the neck thick as a wrestler's thigh. The moonlight turned it all dead gray. It belonged to Yann Lebayon, the one who could be spared from Thibault's team.

Yann shouted something. The wind tore it out of his mouth and smeared it over the stone-black sea.

I bellowed, "Come again?" Salt water slammed into my eyes.

He stuck his mouth close to my ear. This time, it was plain as a knife in the guts. "Sinking!" he yelled.

For a moment, the clock of the world ceased to tick. Then I trod on the autopilot button and tumbled down the hatch.

Below, *Arc-en-Ciel*'s cabin was a seamanlike blend of hi-tech and traditional. That was what the people who wrote the brochure called it, in the days when it had been worth printing brochures. It was an arch-topped cave of farmed mahogany, with a navigatorium like the cockpit of the space shuttle, now gleaming sullenly in the bluish light of the emergency lamps. The deck itself was maple inlaid with holly, as per purchaser's specifications.

Just at the moment you could not see the deck. Where it should have been was black, oily water. As *Arc-en-Ciel* rolled, the water sloshed heavily.

"Pumps?" I said. My heart was knocking like a diesel.

"Electrics not working," said Yann.

I did not bother to argue. *Arc-en-Ciel* carried four pumps. Two of them were electric, and two manual. It was not possible that both the electric pumps were up the spout at the one time. I slid into the leather navigator's chair.

The pump switches were in the ON position. There was fifty horsepower of electric motor in there. The boat should have been whining and throbbing like an aggravated cat, spouting water back over the side.

Except for the lash of the seas and the howl of the wind, the boat was silent.

"Water in the switching," said Yann.

There were manual pumps, backup for the electrics. We yanked handles out of their clips and locked them in their sockets, and pumped. The pumps were big. We were both sweating, the breath harsh in the throat. The yellow lights slid in the black water. The water lapped at the tread of the bottom step of the companionway. I kept my eye on it, marking. Two minutes later, the water was over the tread, creeping toward the second step.

"Checked the *toilette*," said Yann. "Checked the hull. It's in the engine."

Boats' engines need water to cool themselves. *Arc-en-Ciel* has a big intake on her bottom under the engine, starboard side.

When I undid the clips, the engine cover floated off. On the starboard side, under the cylinder block, my fingers found a solid rod of running water, thick as my arm. I groped for the seacock, the tap that cuts off the flow. I had designed the layout myself. *Everything on* Arc-en-Ciel *is*

*designed to be simple, and practical, and safe, so a single-
hander can run a big boat in a big ocean, a long way from
technical assistance.* The brochure again.

What my fingers should have found was a bronze tap,
screwed into the hull, with a fat plastic hose double-clipped
to it. They found the bronze tap, all right. It was no longer
screwed into the hull. It was hanging free on the end of the
hose. There was rough, broken metal where it should have
joined the hull. On the hull itself all that remained of the
seacock was a metal-lined orifice, three inches across,
through which the Bay of Biscay was pouring like the jet of a
fire hose. I was beginning to hate the smartasses who had
written the brochure. In these circumstances, the only use
for their work was as something to stuff into the hole.

"What you got?" Yann was still pumping, his face shining
with sweat and diesel.

I could have said something clever, like trouble. But there
was no point in saying anything. What we had was a jet of
water violent enough to strip paint, coming aboard in a
force-nine gale, a hundred miles off an evil and shelterless
lee shore. There were other problems, too. But for the
moment, they disappeared behind the main problem, which
was to stay alive.

A sea thundered against the hull. I said, "Seacock's bust
off. Get a plug."

We had been through this on our pre-delivery checks, for
the sake of form. Yann went for the locker and came out
with the state-of-the-art remedy for broken-off seacocks: a
bag of conical softwood plugs and a heavy rubber mallet.
The boat lurched as it fell off a wave. The emergency lights
flickered and dimmed.

The plug would not go in.

Every time we got its nose into the hole, the water
pressure blew it out. We were wearing ordinary oilskins,
jackets and high-waist trousers. The water had flowed in at
neck and wrist, and it was running around inside. We were
beginning to shiver. If you shiver for long enough you begin
to lose heat, get hypothermic, tired; badly tired, so you
cannot move or think. While you can still think is the time
to make hard decisions.

"Sails," I said.

"Sure about that?" said Yann. As far as I could tell above the slam and crunch of the seas, his voice was elaborately casual.

I did not bother to answer. The water was up to the second step of the four leading up to the hatch. As I pulled the hatch back, compressed air wheezed past my ears and into the screaming wind.

We clipped on the lifelines and climbed out. The cockpit was a sink of darkness. I took out the autopilot and hauled the wheel. *Arc-en-Ciel* carved a circle head to wind, sluggish with the water slopping in her belly.

Yann's wide fisherman's shoulders jerked over the winch as he hauled up the mainsail. Sailcloth drummed furiously. The wind hesitated like a rough-house fighter winding up for a big punch. A gust of air clouted the sail over sideways.

Stop it, shouted part of me. Full rag in this, and you'll have the mast out of her.

"Jib," I said, as the deck steepened underfoot.

Yann pulled the sheet. The sail came off the roller with a slap and a boom and filled, pale as a ghost in the howling night.

I spun the wheel, so we were taking the wind on the beam, all forty knots of it slamming against the kind of spread of sail you would use to trap a summer breeze in Pulteney Harbor.

Arc-en-Ciel tried to come upright, staggered as the wind smacked her over again. I dived below, and slammed the hatch behind me.

The boat went on heeling, shoved flat by the weight of wind in the sails. The black lake sloshed down to the lee side. The floorboards were floating. The emergency fluorescents bathed the cabin in a hellish blue glare.

Everything that had been vertical was now horizontal. *Arc-en-Ciel* was lying on her side.

I groped for the mallet and the bungs, and tried not to think about what lying on her side might mean.

Arc-en-Ciel and her sisters were broad in the beam. That was why they had eight feet of keel to keep them stable. When they turned turtle, skeptical folk had whispered, they

7

were stable the wrong way up. It was whisperers like them who had made sure that Savage Yachts had an empty shed.

Now was not the time for such thoughts. I clambered on to the side of the engine, tugged the fat deal plug out of my pocket and groped for the hole where the seacock had been. The fire-hose jet of water had dwindled to a flow like a slowish cold tap. I located the plug, whacked it in with the mallet. The flow stopped. I gave it another whack, for luck. Then I crawled aft in the corpse-light, and hammered on the hatch, and waited.

Jam-cleats banged as Yann let off the sheets. Waves were smashing and walloping on her hull. *Arc-en-Ciel*'s eight feet of keel should be levering her upright.

She stayed on her side.

I was shivering violently in that corpse-lit cabin. It was hermetically sealed in there. I could hear waves breaking against the hatch. If I opened it, they would break into the cabin, and it would flood, and that would be that: curtains, endsville; glug, glug. If she turned over, it would be slower, but the same in the end. If we were lucky, we would get to the life raft. But I had spent a year building this boat, and now I was delivering my year's work to Thibault Ledoux in La Rochelle. Thibault Ledoux was interested in his new boat, not life rafts. And so was I.

So I waited in the cabin, and wondered whether she would roll the right way or the wrong way, while the sweat ran down the inside of my jersey with the sea-water.

Yann was cranking a winch up there. The jib winch. Rolling the big sail around and around its stay like a flag on a stick, making it smaller. A wave came under. Click, click, click, said the winch, winding the sail shut inch by sodden inch. Another wave. The boat stirred, rocked. My heart lurched. Here we go, I thought.

Another wave. Another lurch of the heart. I felt a quickening. Slowly at first, then with increasing momentum, she came upright.

She came upright with a bang that flung the soup of water and diesel and broken VDUs hard at the other side of the boat, and broke them all into smaller, more expensive pieces.

But she came upright.

I walloped the hatch open and hauled myself into the pitch-black cockpit and took big, hungry gulps of clean wind.

The sea was making noises like an infuriated animal. We smashed the mainsail down, made it fast. Then I spun the big wood-rimmed wheel until the little green glow of the compass sat on 116°. At the bottom end of a couple of hundred miles of 116°, give or take the distance the tide washed us sideways and the wind blew us backward, was the Pertuis Breton, the stretch of water that funnels down to the port of La Rochelle.

We knocked the autopilot back in. We went below and found the pump handles. Braced against the bronco bucking of the cabin sole, we began to pump. An hour later, she was dry. After that we began to clear up.

It was like trying to soak up an oil spill with a dish mop. In specifying *Arc-en-Ciel*'s beautiful interior, Thibault Ledoux had kept one eye firmly on his public image as a man of impeccable taste. Anyone could win races in a plastic bathtub. It was Thibault's whim to win them in a real boat. Naturally, the boat was plastic. But on to the plastic was superimposed . . . *le style Ledoux*.

In the United States, everyone loves a tennis player. In England and Brazil, they go for footballers. The French love a yachtsman, and Thibault had been one of their favorites for five years. He was lean and dark, with a grin like a toothpaste commercial, and a spurious air of shyness that made women want to ruffle his hair. He was a brilliant seaman and a ferocious competitor, with a personality that had made him the focus of a tribe of other seamen, *l'equipe Ledoux;* the Ledoux team. He liked things that were excellent, and neat, and well-organized.

So did his public. The proof of it was in the photographs in the copy of the *Nouvel Observateur* macerating in the bilge. There was picturesque Pulteney, beautiful women. There were Saint Laurent blazers, and television cameras. There was Thibault's big white grin, and Mary Ellen's pleased-I-came smile. And a man standing head and shoulders above the others, with dark-red hair sticking out of his head at peculiar angles, a big, broken nose peeling with sunburn, separated from a big chin by something that might have been a grin or might have been a grimace of agony.

An analyst of grins would have had a hard time deciding which, unless he was familiar with the grins of people who are wondering what the hell to do next.

People like me.

Yann heaved his bulk into the navigatorium, squeezing a stream of water from the foam upholstery of the pilot's chair. I fished in the pile of cans we had rescued from the debris. It was cold, and dark. The wind yelled in the rig. I said, "Want some soup?"

He did not answer, because he was asleep.

I do not need a lot of sleep myself; single-handed sailors are dedicated insomniacs. I ripped the top off a hot-can, and drank the contents, which tasted of paraffin, as hot-cans do. Then I blew waterproofer into the electronics that seemed near enough intact to be worth the trouble, and scrabbled my way on deck.

The wind smelled almost sweet out there. The moon trailed a cold gray radiance over the sea. There were no other lights, which was a relief. The Bay of Biscay was crawling with ships with defective radars and worse lookouts.

So *Arc-en-Ciel* tore through the silver night, gale on the quarter, squeezing plank-hard sheets of spray from her flanks as she rode down the front slopes of the huge waves, heading for her new owner, who was not going to be pleased.

I gave myself over to grim thoughts. Thibault's boat was by no means the grimmest.

When I had left Pulteney the day before yesterday, the desk in my flat overlooking the quay had been covered in a two-inch layer of letters. Some were from creditors. But most of them bore the colophon of a fish with sails on the top left-hand corner of the paper, and a Marblehead, Massachusetts postmark on the envelope. They were from Art Schacker, coordinator of the Flying Fish Challenge for the America's Cup. Art wanted me to sign on as his shore manager. He had spent three months pursuing me with flattering vigor. My friends and family had pointed out that boatbuilders went broke, and shore managers lived like Swiss bankers. They were right; Schacker would have taken care of the creditors more or less at a stroke.

But Art Schacker's teams were run like banks. And as Mary Ellen had pointed out, while I would probably have

made a reasonable bank robber, as a bank manager I would
have gone crazy, and the bank would have collapsed.

So the idea of spending two years ministering to the needs
of boy racers with beautifully creased shorts and egos the
size of zeppelins was by no means a seductive one. The
letters had remained unanswered.

The dawn turned the sky astern paler gray, and put
ultraviolet glints in the dirty teeth of the waves. The sun
rose. The sky turned from gray to a mesh of blue creeks
separated by headlands of cloud. My eyes were sore with salt
and lack of sleep. The mind trudged to and fro.

At five A.M., the hatch rumbled back. *"Bonjour,"* said
Yann, knuckling the sleep out of his eyes. "Listen. I was
thinking. This seacock shouldn't have broken, yes? It was
new, no? Weird, huh?"

He passed me a cup of coffee and sat down, breathing
deep to get the diesel fumes out of his lungs. The wind had
come down to force seven. *Arc-en-Ciel* moved among
rocking-horsing inshore fishing boats toward the invisible
towers of La Rochelle.

I paid no attention to any of it. Because I had been
thinking what Yann was thinking.

New seacocks do not break off.

Weird was the word.

2

When you have been awake for forty-eight hours, it is hard
to summon up the energy for serious worrying. So I gave up.
I rolled up in a sleeping bag, lay for perhaps five seconds in
the wet, bucking bunk, and nodded off.

When I awoke, I could tell from the movement of the boat
that the wind was up again. I stuck my head out of the hatch.
A wave hit me, and water ran down my neck. Must put a

better coaming on the next boat, I thought. Then I realized there would be no next boat, and it all came back, and I started to feel depressed again.

Savage Yachts of Pulteney was a yard that had employed craftsmen. Seacocks are well known to be front-line items. No craftsman was going to fit a clapped-out seacock to any boat, let alone a brand-new one. Suddenly I had a powerful urge to go home and find the employees of Savage Yachts, wherever they might be, and ask them some hard questions.

But first, I had to deliver to Thibault Ledoux his new, shiny boat. And explain to him why the engine was not working, the electronics blown, and the lockers full of seawater.

It was not an enticing prospect.

I had met Thibault ten years ago. I had been sitting under the stepped gables on the quay at Hoorn, on the IJsselmeer, sipping a beer before I went to see an oil trader who had expressed an interest in sponsoring me in my fifth circumnavigation.

A big ketch had nosed into the narrow harbor. It was an old ketch, with a figurehead, and the name *Kraken* on a gold board surrounded by scrollwork.

The figurehead represented a female sea-monster with gigantic fangs and the breasts of a young woman, extraordinarily well carved. As it passed, it turned its head and winked at me. Then it lit a large pipe, fondled its by no means wooden breasts with its taloned hands and dived into the canal.

My shirt was cold, because I was pouring beer down it. Somewhere in the bowels of the ketch, a motorcycle started. A man in leathers rode out of a hatch, skidded on the deck, raced forward and out along the bowsprit. At the end he plucked a line from the rigging, clipped it to his back wheel, twisted the throttle and shot eighty feet to the top of the mainmast, where a girl in suspenders and leather underwear was awaiting him, standing on one hand.

An iron voice from the deck bellowed, *"Circus Kraken is arrived!"*

The ketch tied up. I ordered another beer. I stayed in my seat. Night fell. Spotlights illuminated the ketch. The circus began. The performers courted death by fire, death by drowning, death by falling. They turned *Kraken's* rigging into a Big Top. Next day, the honest burghers of Hoorn sent them packing, as an outrage to public decency. I never got to see my sponsor, because I went with them.

There were about twenty of them: acrobats, motorcyclists, general-purpose maniacs. The one who knew about boats was the ringmaster, a twenty-two-year-old ex-Olympic dinghy sailor from La Rochelle by the name of Thibault Ledoux.

Circus Kraken lasted five years. Then Thibault had got serious, and gone back to racing, assisted by some old *Kraken* hands. I had gone back to Pulteney and started the boatyard. Thibault had remained a friend. When a friend has held you on the end of a length of monofilament fishing line sixty feet above a sea covered in burning petrol, a trust tends to develop.

So I trusted Thibault. I trusted him to pay for his new boat. He had asked to delay the final payment. Savage Yachts had been in difficulties; we had needed the work.

Yann said, "I hope he's paid you already?" He grinned at me. It was merely a form of words. If you have ordered a boat, you pay in stages. No boat leaves the yard until the final stage has been paid. "Sure," I said, and grinned back.

It was a hollow grin. Trust works two ways. Given the state of the boat now, it would be hard to blame Thibault if he was less than enthusiastic about paying over the final third. And if he did not pay over the final third, and if I did not get it into the bank, the troubles of Savage Yachts would quickly become terminal.

We reached down the coast all afternoon. The sea had moderated to a long blue swell under a sky of Atlantic sapphire. Somewhere astern, there were a lot of other sails. Most of the South Coast of England seemed to be heading down for La Rochelle this week. With a spot of luck I would be on my way home before they could come barreling up and ask me whether we had had a good trip.

The green line of Île de Ré slid by to starboard, close enough for us to see the white slash of beach at its foot. If the echo sounder had been working, the readings would have been shrinking fast, as the seabed rose toward the flat beaches where the mussel and oyster growers fattened their produce. But the echo sounder was out, like the rest of the electronics. So we groped our way from buoy to buoy until the grain elevators of La Pallice lay across the skyline ahead, passed under the Île de Ré bridge, moving left into the funnel of the harbor, past the hayfield of masts in the new marina at Port des Minimes to the towers at the entrance to the Vieux Port. Astern the sky became red and streaky, like blood leaking into a puddle. Red buoy lights pricked the dark.

I was not looking forward to going ashore.

A ghost of breeze pushed us past the narrow entrance, Tour Saint-Nicolas to starboard, Tour de la Chaine to port. Without engine, *Arc-en-Ciel* drifted into the basin toward the mass of yachts moored at the pontoons. The stink of the mud under the stone arches of the quay was flat and rank. We turned to starboard, through the open lock gates of the Bassin à Flot, and slewed alongside in the Thibault Ledoux slot. Yann was a former *Kraken* rigger. He bounced on to the pontoon like an eighteen-stone cat, and tied us up. Sounds of cars and voices spilled down across the water from the high black quays.

Suddenly my heart was beating too fast, driven by the consciousness of the land, the millions of people mixed up with each other, backs turned to the big emptiness of the sea. I grinned at nothing, stretching the muscles you had to use on the land.

The last time I had come to La Rochelle, I had been Savage the star boatbuilder, the international nautical hero popping over for discussions with his old friend Thibault, with whom he had sailed the La Baule–Dakar two-handed race. That had been a year ago. We had drunk an *apéro* at the Café du Nord with the fishermen. And Thibault had shown me his new restaurant, on the other side, the fashionable side. The only decent restaurant in the whole bloody tourist trap, he had said. The restaurant he had wanted since he had been a child.

My boots made big, doomy drumbeats on the pontoon. I climbed the ramp, and came into the world.

There were people. There were cars. They whirled by in a big, dizzy fairground of lights and noises. I stood there and clung to the quay railing, and waited for it all to stop spinning.

Coming ashore always brought back a whiff of the feeling I had had when I had been ten, at school in England, the kid from Ireland, in the under-elevens boxing. Standing there in the lights of the ring, before the bout started, not aware of anything except that I had crossed an invisible line into a new world, where the rules were different. What you had to do was shut out the faint, hostile murmur of the crowd, and go your own way.

The spinning stopped.

I shoved my hands in my pockets and strolled up the quay toward the lights of the restaurants.

The tables on the pavements were full. The wind had dropped flat, and the evening was warm. I could feel the quick sideways glances of the waiters, the scorn on their faces. In a window by a café I saw a hulking shape dressed in dirty oilskins lit by the café lights. One leg of the oilskin trousers was torn, flapping over the seaboot. The hair stuck out like a porcupine's quills, stiffened with salt and diesel. The face was mostly a sunburned nose and a big jaw masked with reddish stubble. Two red lights burned in the eyes.

The window was a mirror. The figure was me.

I walked on over the cobbles, struggling out of my coat, toward the jumble of signs on the front. ANDRÉ, they said. MIX GRILL, WEST BURGER. At the far end, a red neon CHEZ ran across the horizontal of an aquamarine T. I strode through the pavement tables and went in.

There were white tablecloths. The tables were full of expensive-looking diners. The clock on the upright piano at the far end said ten to nine.

A stocky man in a blue jersey slid out of nowhere toward me, brown hands hanging like Christmas tree baubles at the ends of his blue arms. He was smiling a smile that did not reach above his high cheekbones; browner than his hands, the face, because of the sunlamp. He purred, *"Bonsoir?"* He had the cash-register eyes of a *maître d'hôtel,* flicking left and right at the tables on either side.

I said, "Good evening, Gérard. Boss in?"

The dark man stopped as if he had walked into a

plate-glass door. "M. Savage," he said. "Mon Dieu!" The hands fluttered up to his mouth.

I said again, "Is the boss in?"

"A minute," he said.

The Savages are Anglo-Irish, and earlier generations had married freely in Continental Europe, seeking money and urbanity. Drumcarty, the family headquarters, had been five miles upstream from the dingy little house where my mother lived. When I was a child I was the family linguist, so the Drumcarty cousins would ask me up to keep the wide-eyed foreigners busy while they filled their innocent beds with frogs and icing sugar. And of course French had been the language of Circus Kraken.

"A minute," he said.

Thibault had been brought up among the fishermen in La Rochelle. Even in the first days I had known him, when a square meal meant a slice of toast, he had fixed views about his restaurant. It would be on the quay at the Vieux Port. There would be tables outside, for the tourists. There would be tables inside, for serious eaters. And at the back, for sailing people and locals, and for the winter, when the tourists were elsewhere and the westerlies were bringing the cold rain lashing in off the Atlantic, there would be a bar, with booths, pictures, and a stove. The food would be good, with plenty of shellfish, but only the oysters eaten raw, not the whole lot, in the disgusting manner of the new gastronomy. The shellfish would be brought in from the Ile de Ré and the flats of Marsilly and Esnandes to the north of the town, by the people Thibault had grown up with, and who were still his friends.

It had all worked out as planned, for Thibault. There were the tourists, and the diners. And there was the bar.

The walls in the bar were thick with framed photographs. Thibault, wavy-haired, blue-eyed, with his famous wide grin. Thibault sailing boats, launching boats, winning races, inspiring loyalty and affection. Very little about Circus Kraken; people expected him to take himself seriously nowadays. There was a barograph beside the clock on the piano. The bar was made from a slab of elm. There were stools with people sitting on them.

There was a girl behind the bar. She was wearing the blue jersey that was Chez Thibault's uniform. She had long cat's eyes, reddish hair yanked into a ponytail, the remains of acne at the corners of a letterbox mouth that managed to be generous, lipsticked brilliant red. My heart lifted at the sight of her. She was staring at me as if I were a ghost.

"Cognac," I said, in English. "Big one."

She did not move. She kept staring. I looked down at my hands. They were spadelike as ever, and the salt-cracks made little red smiles in the oil-blackened skin.

I said, "You going to hang around all night?"

"Bloody hell, Dad," said the girl behind the bar, also in English. "What have you been up to *this* time?"

I waited until she gave me the cognac. Then I gave her a purified version. She sat there and gazed at me while I talked. She had Mary Ellen's eyes, the quiet green Canadian eyes that said, all right, I understand, but do not expect me to sympathize.

Waiters came and went. Frankie dealt with the orders efficiently, hauling bottles out of the fridges labeled MUSCADET and GROS PLANT, giving the waiters just enough of her attention not to drop anything. The cognac warmed me, and so did the fatherly pride. Frankie was off to Oxford in the autumn, to read modern languages. Thibault had offered to take her on for the season so she could improve her French. There had been no need to worry about her. She could look after herself.

When I had finished she sighed, and smiled, her mother's wide-open Canadian smile, as reasonable as a Toronto bus transfer.

Cretin, said the smile.

"So the boat's a wreck," said the daughter.

"Thibault won't be all that delighted," I said.

She said, "I don't expect he'll be too worried." Her eyes had an inward look, calculating. That came from her mother, too. It was her mother who had brought her up, while I was trying to make a living racing around the world and carrying the hat for Circus Kraken. Upstairs, a telephone was ringing faintly.

She said, "He's got other things on his mind."

There was the sound of running feet on the stairs. The door marked PRIVÉ burst open. Thibault Ledoux came in at a half-run. When he saw me he stopped dead. Then he smiled his white smile, and flung an arm around my shoulders. He had to stand on tiptoe, and even then he could hardly reach. "Mick!" he said. "What a surprise!"

There was no reason for him to be surprised. He knew the plan. "I've brought your boat," I said. Now the moment for explanations was at hand I was tired, and the cognac slopped uneasily in my head, and the explanations sounded lousy.

"The boat!" he said. His voice was higher than usual. "Good. Trip OK?" He was standing under a photograph of himself steering our big trimaran into the finish of the La Baule–Dakar. I was beside him in the cockpit. His hair was blowing off his forehead. Neither of us had slept more than an hour in the previous three days. I looked like a heavily bearded representative of the living dead. Thibault looked like an advertisement for a health farm.

The Thibault in the bar was a ghost of his photographic self. There were black hollows under his eyes. He grabbed me by the arm and took me to the back of the bar. He said, "Thank Christ you have arrived." He sounded short of breath. "I need someone I can trust here. To look after the restaurant."

"Listen," I said. "There are some things I have to tell you—"

"Later," he said. "I've got to go." His eyes were shifting from me to the plate-glass window at the front of the restaurant. "It's fantastic you are here. The manager has left. Gérard and the chef take care of everything. But Gérard panics. All you do is referee, OK?"

We were walking past the bar. He said, "Maybe I don't get back tonight. Any problem, Gérard will help. He is a genius." He turned his smile on Frankie. "Like your daughter." Frankie, I was amazed to see, blushed.

It had been the same at Circus Kraken. It had nothing to do with sex. Jutta, a gigantic lesbian biker from Antwerp whose specialty was snorting broken glass, used to make him nightly hot-water bottles in winter, and knitted him woolly hats. When you were around Thibault, you were part of the family.

I said, "We've had trouble with the boat. It'll be needing repairs."

He said, "Well, take it down to the yard. Yann'll tell you." He waved his hand, dismissing the subject. We had thought about *Arc-en-Ciel* for a year, spent weeks on the telephone, sent dozens of drawings back and forth. Now his new toy had arrived, he seemed not to want to know. He gripped my hand in both of his. "Please. I need someone I can trust. Look after the restaurant, yes?"

I said, "I don't know anything about restaurants."

He laughed. "No problem," he said. "You're an organized guy. That's all you need."

That had always been his line. It was mostly true, as long as things went smoothly. As far as Thibault was concerned, keeping the public happy was part of being organized. I had always found public relations different. The reason for Savage Yachts' empty order book had nothing to do with the quality of the boats. It was merely that I had ignored the press, so the press had ignored me back, except when they chose to mention that my boats were fast, and speculate that they might therefore also be dangerous.

But Thibault was extremely persuasive. It had been the Circus way. I had been bosun, sailing master and keyboard player with the band. After a month, Thibault had asked me if I could do a bit of knife-throwing. And three days later, I had found myself under the lights on the waist deck, dressed in a pair of leather jeans and a bandolier of six throwing knives, taking aim at the empty space between the spread legs of Spanish Rita, and never drawing a drop of blood.

After which, restaurants would be no trouble at all.

Thibault snatched a red oilskin off the rack in the bar. Suddenly the front door was closing on its spring, and diners were craning their necks after the great man. A big engine started outside. Tires squealed on cobbles, and a Lamborghini shot past the *vitrine*.

"There he goes again," said Frankie, with resignation. "Do you want something to eat?"

It had started raining, a warm, soft rain. I trudged back to the pontoon. Yann was on deck, coiling lines. I told him to leave it, and we went back to the restaurant. Frankie looked hard at my face. She sat us at a table, brought a couple of steaks and a good roughish burgundy. Yann ate in silence for perhaps twenty minutes. Then he sank back in his chair, and glared from under his heavy brow-ridge at the necklace of square-cut diamonds on a nearby diner.

I said, "Where's a yard for the boat?"

Yann said, "Georges. At the Minimes. Chantiers Albert." He took a gulp of wine.

I knew Georges already. I said, "I thought Thibault had a yard of his own?"

"Closed down," said Yann. "Use Georges. What about the seacock, then?"

I said, "We'll ask." I had the feeling that he had changed the subject.

The bar at the back had filled up with people, some of them English.

"La Rochelle," said Yann. "Used to be a nice town."

"Lay off the customers," I said. "I'm the manager."

He grinned at me, and ran his hand over his blond stubble. *"Exploitateur,"* he said. "I go to see my girl. If you need me, my number is behind the bar."

I said, "Thanks for your help."

"It has been a privilege to assist the manager." He drained his glass, and stumped out into the rain.

I gazed at the expensive people putting shellfish down their throats at the tables. A couple of them waved. The bigger boats from England had arrived, and the quay was crawling with their crews, seeking oysters and Muscadet. Chez Thibault was where you came for your oysters, if you were a knowledgeable yachtsperson.

I grinned at the wavers. None of them came over, which suited me fine.

So I tipped more wine into my glass, and watched Frankie pulling bottles out of the fridges with both hands, and did some wondering. What I wondered was why Thibault had not only forgotten his new boat was arriving, but remembered an urgent appointment elsewhere as soon as I had walked in the door. It was as if he was not pleased to see me. The way people who owe money are not pleased to see the people they owe it to.

Rubbish, said the part of Mick Savage that wanted to fall on to a bed and go to sleep for three days. You trust Thibault. He is one of your few old and loyal friends.

But there were other parts to Mick Savage, which had been trained in a hard and skeptical school. Despite the cognac and the tiredness, these parts of Mick Savage were now detecting on the salt Atlantic breeze a very faint odor of rat.

Stupid, I thought. Habits of a lifetime. Body poisons act on brain, due to lack of sleep.

I dragged myself to the back of the restaurant. Frankie took me through the door marked PRIVÉ. At the top of the stairs there was a hallway, with bedroom doors off to the sides and a kitchen and living room at the far end. In the restaurant's early days, this had been Thibault's principal residence. Now, the place had a half-lived-in, half-disused feel. She pointed me through a door at a bed. "Yours," she said.

I fell down on it.

"Problem?" she said.

I was too tired to keep up the mask it was politic to wear in front of Mary Ellen's side of the family. I said, "Sort of."

She gazed at me with the Canadian look. Tch, tch, it said, when will he ever learn? "Messing about in boats," she said.

Story of my life.

3

I was born twenty yards from the brown margin of the river Barrow, in the bottom right-hand corner of Ireland. It was a river covered in boats. There were double-ended canoelike cots, rowed by one man, built to a design unchanged since the Bronze Age. There were rusty timber ships, wheezing up the tortuous channel between the mud-banks, heading for the yards at New Ross. There were sailing boats and muckboats that belonged to my rich cousins, the Savages of Drumcarty Castle, three miles upstream from our dirty-gray house in Carthystown. And there were the salmon boats.

I was an only child. When I was very young, there were three constants in my life. There was my father, who had a grim face with a thick, porous nose over a gray-and-red beard. There was my mother, who was pale, with hair that had once been blond, straggling out of the army of combs she packed into the bun on the back of her head. And there was the argument between them.

The argument was a live thing. I would lie in my bed and hear it wake as they woke in the morning. It prowled the air between them all day. Sometimes it fed on messages from Uncle James, who lived at the Castle. After it had fed, it became noisy and savage, and my father drank whiskey.

I hated the argument even before I knew what it was. When it was prowling, I would stare out of the window, across the nettle-green thicket of garden to the river. There was a slip next to the garden, where every day three men in thigh waders and mud-crusted oilskins launched a long, four-oared salmon boat, net piled in the stern. One day, I must have been five, a letter arrived from the Castle.

"The bastard," said my father, reading it. "The *bastard.*"

My mother said, "Not in front of Michael."

22

"Damn Michael!" said my father. "Damn us all. Damn you, you whey-faced English fool!"

My mother's already pale face turned the color of milk, and her lips disappeared. Oh, no, I thought. Not again. I can't bear it.

The window was open; it was June, and not yet raining. Through the window came the voices of the salmon boys, heading down for the boat. I slid out of the chair. My father was getting ready to bellow. Neither of them noticed as I reached up for the door handle and crept out into the musty hall. Out, my mind was telling me. Out.

I ran down the path, through the green smell of wet nettles. The men were pulling the boat in off its mooring. John Tinnelly turned to look at me. He was barely five feet tall. I came up to his belt buckle. The sun was shining through his bat ears, turning them an extraordinary pink. I swallowed the dryness out of my mouth, and said, "Can I come with you?"

He frowned. He said, "What about your mammy?"

I said, "She says can I come with you?" I held my breath, waiting for the lightning that strikes liars.

"Whyever not?" said John.

Someone sat me on the net. The oars dipped. The boat glided out on to the brown satin river. The dirty-gray house, full of arguments, dwindled, became insignificant across the great sheet of water. A peace descended, the like of which I had never known.

From that moment, I was doomed.

I had met Mary Ellen in the Caribbean, when I had been seventeen. We had worked in Venezuela. Mary Ellen had fallen (as they say in Carthystown) pregnant. We had sailed back to England from Venezuela in a boat I had built myself, with Frankie as ship's baby. The weather had been bad. When we had arrived in Southampton, Mary Ellen had left the address of an English friend on the chart table, and gone straight to London.

I had gone after her. We lived in Earls Court, in a flat that stank of other people's cooking when the windows were shut, and petrol fumes from the Warwick Road when they were open. In the daytime Mary Ellen worked for an insurance broker, I sold wine at Harrods, and Frankie staggered around the small, evil-smelling flat of Fat Jen, the Cathcart Road child-minder.

By the end of three months, my hair was falling out, and I was getting into fights in pubs. Mary Ellen suggested I took a break. So I went down to Pulteney, refitted the boat with the help of friends, and entered for the Observer Single-handed Round-the-World Race. They came to wave me goodbye. Frankie did not know what goodbye meant. But I did, and so did Mary Ellen.

We stood on the quay at Millbay Dock, in Plymouth. The backwater was full of old vegetable peelings. She said, "Be careful."

I said, "Will you be here when I get back?"

She said, "I don't see why not." She smiled, her practical Canadian smile, and squeezed my hand, and kissed me, quietly and without passion. Then she walked away, without looking around. The day before, she had made me sign up for a mortgage on a first house in Islington.

During the race we talked on the radio a few times. She said she had got a job at Lloyd's, the world's biggest and best insurance bazaar, and things were going fine. The job had had a lot to do with making tea, and very little to do with insurance. But Mary Ellen had plenty of things that she wished to prove to herself and the world. She had swiftly lost touch with the tea trolley. By the time I had done a couple more circumnavigations, she was well on her way to becoming a big wheel in McMurdo Syndicates.

A syndicate at Lloyd's is a group of underwriters who assess risks and accept premiums to insure those risks. Behind the underwriters sit thousands of "names," private citizens who provide the financial underpinning for the bets taken by the underwriters. In a good year, when the sum of the premiums paid exceeds the sum of the claims against the underwriters, the profits are divided up among the names. In a bad year, when the claims exceed the premiums, the names dig deep to make good the losses, for which they are liable to the last gold tooth in their heads. Underwriters who run efficient syndicates spend their lives under siege from brokers, whose job it is to find insurers for people wanting insurance. Brokers can be clever and not at all scrupulous.

Good underwriters have to be sharp as knives, and very reliable, and not given to irrational acts.

So Mary Ellen was a natural.

She had been on the quay when I got back that time, and the time after, and the times after that.

She had borne the brunt of bringing up Frankie, and gone to the theater, and kept herself organized to the point where she could blot out intrusive memories of Caracas and transatlantic sailing.

One afternoon, seven years ago, I had arrived at Mary Ellen's flat in London. She had moved from Islington to Butler's Wharf, a big place full of light reflected from the silver Thames beyond the balcony. Circus Kraken had been refitting after someone had thrown a cigarette into a petrol tin without emptying it first. My idea had been to persuade Mary Ellen and Frankie to come down to my flat in Pulteney for a week, for a bit of sea air and relaxation in the company of the boat folk of the village, a couple of whom we had known since our days in the West Indies. Normally, Frankie needed no persuading. But Mary Ellen was so wrapped up in her work that getting her out of her flat on Butler's Wharf was like prizing a conger out of a cannon.

So I had let myself in with my keys. I was suffering from slight burns, with the regulation Kraken heavy-metal haircut, dressed in jeans that had suffered from contact with battery acid. The Butler's Wharf flat was decorated with great care. There was a Benin bronze head on a block of Carrara marble, walls that were clear, mottled, seashell yellow, and a big Louis Seize sofa in the window, in front of the file-stacked coffee table on which Mary Ellen did her work.

The coffee table was more heavily piled than usual. There was a man in the Gothic iron armchair. Mary Ellen had looked up. Her dark hair was back from her face, where she pushed it when she was working. She had fine bones, a narrow, slightly hooked nose. She smiled, a quick ray of sun from behind preoccupied clouds. "Busy," she said. "Mick, this is Justin Peabody."

The man on the sofa smiled. He had big shoulders. What little hair he had was blondish, cropped close. His handshake was hard, the grip of a man who does things with his hands. "Mary Ellen's told me about you," he said. "How's the circus?"

I scrutinized him narrowly. People who dealt in generalizations thought I was mad to desert Mary Ellen for six months at a time and run off sailing boats, and throwing knives, or whatever the hell it was that I insisted on doing instead of real work. But Justin had intelligent blue eyes, and a way of asking questions as if he was really interested. So we talked. And after a bit Mary Ellen stopped working and joined in. And we went out to dinner downstairs at Manzi's, off Leicester Square, a fish joint where the service is brusque and the food good. All three of us had a good evening that was not far off uproarious. It became clear that this was not the first time that Justin had dined with Mary Ellen, but Mary Ellen and I had an agreement about that. I would not ask questions about what happened when I was not around, and nor would she, vice versa. If either of us got serious about anyone else, we would speak up.

Neither of us had spoken up, yet.

With the Armagnac, Justin made what he called a business proposition. He worked as a broker. Brokers love information. Normally, this is provided by a network of Lloyd's agents around the world. Sometimes, he said, an insurance deal can go badly enough wrong for the syndicate concerned to call in someone who is not necessarily known to be in Lloyd's employ to ask the right questions in the right places. Justin was a sailor, with an expensive boat on the Hamble, at the expensive end of the Solent. He had heard about me, and not only from Mary Ellen. As far as Justin was concerned, the things that disposed Mary Ellen to think ill of me operated in my favor. He wanted me to keep my ears open. Specifically, he wanted to know about a repair bill for a Dutch coaster.

"Bastard at the yard's been padding it," he said. "Kicking back the skipper. Damned unsporting." That was the way he talked, to hide the diamond-sharp machinery between his ears. "Could you have a look at it?"

I had a look. I found a disaffected clerk at the yard, who made a statement. I sent the statement to Justin, and returned to Circus Kraken. He sent a check, and Frankie got a pony, which lived on a farm in the hills behind Pulteney, where she rode it when she came to stay.

I did a lot of work for him after that. He called me his cloak-and-dagger division, but that was his little joke. The investigations he asked me to do usually concerned overclaims for repair bills, or bits and pieces of stolen cargo. They did not involve false beards and physical violence. It was merely that most Lloyd's people wore their pinstripe suits at all times, and pinstripe suits tend to excite comment in Southampton docks, particularly if the people inside them are asking a lot of questions.

Personally, I had a very poor dress sense, and an Irish accent that came and went at will, and a knack of asking questions so they did not sound like questions. So in my flat above Pulteney quay, by the desk on which I ran the affairs of Savage Yachts, I had a filing-cabinet full of letters from grateful underwriters.

And all for messing about in boats.

Frankie was still by the bed.

I said, "What's wrong with Thibault?"

"Wrong?" said Frankie.

I said, "He looks bloody awful."

Frankie was not yet of an age to be too curious about the actions of thirty-two-year-olds. She said, "He looks all right to me. Bit tired, maybe. Haven't seen much of him, actually."

"I thought he was managing the restaurant."

She started looking tolerant again. "There's nothing to manage. Once a week, you have to stop the chef fighting the washer-up."

I said, "I'm the new manager."

She raked me with her cool eyes, top to toe. "Made for the job," she said. "You will be wanting to go to bed."

I nodded. The brain was slopping in my head. "You staying here?" I said.

She smiled. It was an awkward smile. "Sure," she said. "I must get back to the bar."

I dropped into the kind of half-sleep that hits you when you are exhausted, and half a steak and one belt of cognac over the line. Dimly, I was aware that the traffic was getting quiet, and the hum of voices from below had diminished. I waited for Frankie's feet on the stairs, just as I waited when she came to stay in Pulteney during the school holidays. Much later, they came; up, then down. On the quay outside the window a motorbike engine started, howled like a dog, faded into the night.

It took some time to nod off again. My mind gnawed away at problems that kept changing shape. One of the first, best rules of being a boatbuilder is: don't hand over the boat until you've got the money. I had broken the rule. I wanted a nice quiet chat with Thibault, so he could tell me everything was fine.

But the Thibault who had sprinted out of the restaurant had not been a Thibault who seemed in the mood for nice quiet chats.

I fell into an edgy sleep.

Frankie woke me the next morning with a cup of coffee so delicious she had obviously brought it up from the restaurant downstairs. She looked well scrubbed and fresh. The saddle of freckles across her nose contrasted oddly with the catlike knowingness of her eyes. I said, "Any sign of Thibault?"

She shook her head. "I've only just got back." Her eyes shifted away from mine.

I said, "Back?"

"Jean-Claude brought me on his bike."

I said, "Who's Jean-Claude?"

"A friend."

I looked at her. She looked back at me. I was eighteen years older than her. I opened my mouth to ask her what kind of friend.

She knew very well what I was going to ask. She said, "Your bath's overflowing," and left the room.

I had just been in receipt of a declaration of independence. I got up, and staggered forth into the designer paradise that was the apartment above Chez Thibault.

By daylight, it had a distinctly Earls Court feel. There was a corridor with bedrooms, a sitting room with a cubby-hole of an office at its end. There were dog-eared boat posters on the walls, and the furniture was mismatched odds and ends, as if nobody lived here for long. The bath was not overflowing, because she had not turned it on. I shaved, and squeezed a shower's worth of hot water out of the flatulent plumbing.

As usual, I had to stoop to see my face in the mirror. It was a big face. There were large, reddish eyebrows, a large, reddish nose, badly sunburned, and a jaw that Mary Ellen called aggressive. I pulled a comb through the dark red thatch, ignored a streak of gray that was trying to make itself felt, and made my way into a set of clean jeans and a Greenpeace T-shirt.

Arc-en-Ciel sat lightly on the water, mast towering above the rest, beside the dour gray fortresses of the harbor entrance. The sight of her reminded me that there was more to worry about than the sleeping habits of my daughter, particularly a daughter past the age of consent.

So I went down to the restaurant.

My plan was to sit at a table in the sun and eat a croissant, then call Georges at the yard to arrange slipping, examine seacocks, and undertake repairs. By then Thibault would be back, and he would hand over the completion check.

It did not turn out as easy as that.

When I came through the door at the back of the bar, Gérard was talking to two strange men. His hands were floating in front of his chest like butterflies. The men were stocky and solid-looking, dressed in overtight gray suits, out of place in the carefully staged clutter of bar and piano and nautical pictures. One was wider than the other. The narrow one carried a fat black briefcase with combination locks. There was an old woman perched on a stool, wearing tremendous false eyelashes. Her hands walked to her coffee like spiders. Despite the eyelashes, she was blind.

Gérard gave me the kind of look drowning men are meant to address to straws. I summoned up my French, and said, "Can I help?"

The men in suits swiveled their little black eyes at me. They did not look impressed by what they saw. The narrower of the two said, "Who are you?"

Recent experiences at Savage Yachts had got me well used

to the world of fat black briefcases. I pretended not to hear. "Can I help?" I said again. My lips felt numb with apprehension.

The wide man said, "We are seeking an interview with M. Ledoux, or his representative."

I said, "If you leave your number, M. Ledoux will call you back."

"Who are you?" said the narrower of the two, again.

"I am a friend of M. Ledoux, temporarily looking after his restaurant," I said. "And Gérard here is merely an employee. M. Ledoux has left me in charge because he has had to go away on business. He did not tell me where. Perhaps I can offer you something to drink?"

They said, "Thank you, no," both at once, as if I had offered them poison.

The wide man handed me a card. It said "Jacques Arnaud, Banque du Charente." Oh, bloody hell, I thought. Bloody hell, Thibault. "We had an appointment," he said. "Perhaps M. Ledoux has forgotten."

"This is often the case, with people in the situation of M. Ledoux," said the narrower of the two. He had a disbelieving twist to his mouth. I found myself disliking him. "I bid you good morning."

They left. Gérard began to twitter like a linnet. The noise he was making did not penetrate. I felt as if I had swallowed a five-pound block of ice.

Since he had left Circus Kraken, Thibault had got well on the way to being a national hero. People he had never met called their children after him. I had assumed he was as solid as the Banque Nationale de Paris. That, and the fact he was an old friend, was the reason I had let him have the boat before he had paid for it.

But M. Arnaud and his cynical friend looked very much as if they meant money trouble. It looked as if I had been right last night. Thibault had suddenly turned from being a rich friend into someone who had ordered a boat he could not pay for.

I ate a croissant, without much enthusiasm. A black-bereted fisherman arrived in a Citroën truck. Two *écailleurs* in green PVC aprons helped him unload plastic mesh bags of oysters. I went and dug Frankie out of the bar, where she was polishing glasses.

She gave me an uneasy look. She might have been worrying that I was going to start asking awkward questions about her friend Jean-Claude. I would have liked to. Instead, I said, "Where does Thibault live when he's not upstairs?"

"He's never upstairs," she said, none too reverently. "It's not posh enough for him. He's got a house. The Manoir de Causey."

"Where is it?"

"Out toward Surgères. Ten miles, maybe. You'd better take the van."

"The van?"

"Belongs to the restaurant. Could you be back by lunch-time? Gérard gets a bit fussed on his own. And you can help lay up for lunch."

"Can't wait," I said.

I rang Chantiers Albert. Georges greeted me as an old friend, which was what he was. I said, "I've got some work for you."

"Wonderful," he said. "Come now. No, come later. Let's eat lunch."

I said, "I can't get to you. I'll be down this evening, on the tide."

"Still in a hurry," he said.

"Still in a hurry." I put the telephone down.

In the bright glare of the quay, the *écailleurs* had finished unloading. Now they were shelling the oysters, banging them on to a mountain of crushed ice in a perspex vivarium. The van had a big red-and-blue CHEZ T printed on the side. Sweating with heat and fear, I plunged into the traffic.

4

*T*he Manoir de Causey was not the kind of house generally associated with yachties in trouble at the bank. It had a mansard roof, and wrought-iron balconies, and a pepperpot turret at each corner. The drive lay straight as an arrow, shimmering in the morning light between an avenue of horse-chestnut trees. From the parterre at the south front an ornamental canal ran to an obelisk.

Drumcarty Castle had its share of canals and obelisks. But even two hundred years ago, when my Savage ancestors had owned most of the bottom right-hand corner of Ireland, Drumcarty had never been as smart as this. Bigger, maybe; but no Savage would have bothered to expend this much effort simply on keeping things tidy, even if he could have afforded it.

I drove the Citroën under an arch of gilt wrought-iron and into a stable yard. A man in a blue jersey was raking the impeccable yellow-white gravel. Even by international superstar standards, this was serious stuff.

The chill in my stomach intensified. Perhaps the Manoir was precisely the kind of house associated with a yachtie in trouble at the bank.

I climbed out of the car, crunched across to the door and tugged the bell-pull. There was a yellow motorbike parked by the door. Far away in the recesses of the house there was a faint, hollow jangle. Nobody came.

I pulled again. Still nobody. Behind me, the courtyard was empty. The man raking the gravel had disappeared. Swallows whipped overhead, chirping.

Someone started shouting.

It was a woman's voice, hollow with distance. A man took

32

over. He sounded clipped and southern. The voice was sharp with violence. I turned the handle of the door.

Inside, a flagstoned passage stretched away far enough for its sides to start to converge. The voices rolled and boomed on the hard surfaces. The woman's was full of terror. I began to run.

At the end was a flight of stone steps. A plain door opened out of what must have been the servants' quarters into a white-and-gold hall with a double staircase curving lyre-shaped to the first story. The noise was coming from a room off the hall. The man was swearing. There was the crack of a palm on flesh. *"Ah, bon,"* the man was saying. *"Ah, bon,"* in the sort of growl a dog makes when it has stopped barking and moves in for a bite.

There was a crash of iron on stone. The woman started to scream. I opened the door.

It was one of those little salons that run endlessly inter-connecting around grand French houses. There was a big chimneypiece with a big, not very good modern picture above it. Under the chimneypiece, despite the heat of the day, a fire of logs was smoldering. There was a woman in the fire, struggling on the logs.

The man was standing over her. He was short, with the narrow hips of a disco king and the face of a spoiled Greek god, the nose too straight, the lips too fleshy, a three-day stubble on his square jaw, a raven-black forelock flopping into his eyes. He said, "Come on, Bianca. Where is he?" Then he heard me and looked around with the quick, ugly reflex I recognized from the boxing rings of my schooldays.

I went past him, gripped the arm of the woman in the fire and pulled her out.

She stood on the hearth, beating the hot ashes off her leather trousers.

"Are you all right?" I said.

She nodded. She looked like a Goya gypsy, with long black hair and brown, transparent skin, pinkened at the cheekbones. Her eyes were dark blue and glittering with anger.

The pretty boy said, doggedly, ignoring me, "Where is he?"

I did not know who was meant to be there and who was not.

The girl came over and stood beside me, and a little behind. She said, "This animal says he is looking for M. Ledoux." She frowned. "Aren't you Mick Savage?"

That sounded good enough. I picked up the telephone. She started to say, "No," changed her mind.

The pretty boy said, "Put it down."

I dialed 17, emergency.

The pretty boy's right hand went to the side pocket of his leather motorcycle jacket. The telephone said, *"Allô?"* The hand came out of the pocket. It had grown a long steel thumb that glittered silver in the light streaming through the high windows. The telephone said, *"Allô?"* He said, "Put it down." His eyes were hot, with a thick speedfreak glaze.

The air was suddenly cold. I put the receiver back, gently, not doing anything sudden. He walked toward me. He smelled faintly of sweat. He wrapped the telephone cord around his fist and tugged. It came out of the wall with a pop.

There was a poker in the fireplace, the size of an iron boathook. The woman picked it up and threw it. It spun end-on-end and whacked him on the shoulder. He went down, sprawling on the gleaming parquet. He began to roll, hand still clenched on the knife. Five years with Circus Kraken teaches you not to mess with knives. I stamped on his fist.

He made a sound halfway between a yell and a croak. His fingers opened. The knife clattered out. I kicked it. It spun away across the floor and thudded into the gilt-topped skirting. I dived after it. Somewhere a bell was ringing, the hollow ring I had heard when I had tugged the bell-pull. My fingers closed on the knife. The door slammed. I scrambled up, clutching the hilt, heart thudding.

The pretty boy was gone. His big boots were pounding across the hall and down the passage. The woman was leaning against one of the pillars of the chimneypiece. The anger had left her, and her face was gray. I said, "Are you burned?"

She stretched out her right arm. It was slim and brown

and muscular, with a gold plaited-rope bracelet on the wrist. Above the bracelet was a broad stripe of shiny, puckered skin. "Not bad," she said.

"What did he want?"

She shrugged. Her eyes were innocent as an empty sky. Somewhere at the back of the house, a door slammed. I said, "Sit down." Her hand was shaking.

"No," she said.

There were a lot of footsteps in the hall. The door opened. A dapper man with a mustache and a suit stood in front of three other dapper men in suits. The man in front was holding a fat, legal-looking envelope protectively against his chest.

He looked at the knife in my hand, then at me. He had hard, button-black eyes. He said, "Where is M. Thibault Ledoux?"

"Not here," I said. I folded the knife, and put it in my pocket.

"It is useless to pretend," said the mustache man.

I said, "Who are you?"

"Jean Lomas. Banque de Cahors."

"And your business?"

"This is private between the bank and M. Ledoux."

The woman shoved her hair away from her face, and put her chin defiantly in the air. She said, "As monsieur has told you, M. Ledoux is not here. Please leave." My stomach was as hard as corrugated iron, waiting for what was going to come next.

A grim little smile stretched M. Lomas' mustache. He said, "I much regret that it is I who must ask you to leave." He tapped his envelope. "By virtue of this writ, I have come to take possession of the Manoir de Causey."

Next to me, the woman said, *"Merde."* So here it goes, I thought. Farewell, Savage Yachts. Thibault, you bastard, where are you?

Lomas said, "So if you would do me the honor of leaving?"

The Banque du Charente was looking for him at the restaurant, and the Banque de Cahors was looking for him at the Manoir. Men with knives were looking for him wherever they could find him. When banks and men with knives are forming queues at the carve-up, boatbuilders go hungry. I felt a hundred years old.

I said, "Show me your documents."

He said, "English?"

"Irish."

He showed me.

"So," he said, in English. "All is OK, yes?"

I shrugged. "Fine."

"And me," said the woman. She stood alongside him, close, and looked over his shoulder. "It can't be true," she said, in a new, softer voice. She was frowning, the frown of a puzzled innocent.

"I'm afraid it is." M. Lomas looked grave. He had registered the fact that he was in the presence of a beautiful woman.

"Bon." She took my arm, leaned up against it. It was a surprisingly intimate gesture. I looked down at her. Her left eye, the one furthest from M. Lomas, flickered in what might have been a wink. "This blasted Thibault. He asks us to stay, and the bailiffs arrive. Well, I guess we should pack."

I climbed aboard. I said, "I guess so. Is that all right?"

M. Lomas allowed his black gaze to settle on the woman like the hands of a bishop. Her color had returned, but the remnants of anger still brightened her eyes. M. Lomas realized that he was not only in the presence of a beautiful woman, but in a position to do her a favor. He ceased fractionally to be a banker, and remembered he was a red-blooded citizen of France. "Of course," he said.

She said, "I will pack for you also, *chéri.*"

I smiled at her. I said, "I suppose we'll have to find a hotel. Really, this is too much." She shrugged, walked quickly out of the room. M. Lomas' eyes followed the sway of her hips in the close-fitting leather trousers. Under his mustache, his mouth was slightly ajar. I was afraid he was about to order one of his sidekicks to go after her. I said, quickly, "Did you see a man leaving as you arrived?"

He swallowed, and became once again a functioning member of society. "A man came out of the door, and left on a *moto.* Now, if you will permit, you and I will assist madame with her packing." We heard the woman singing as we climbed the stairs. It was a pleasant, husky noise. It led us to a vast room with a gilt ceiling painted with scenes of Diana the Huntress. She had piled shirts on to the gilt bed. There was a David Inshaw painting of Silbury Hill on the wall, a large and complicated telephone, a chromed BMW motorcycle engine. It looked as if it might have been Thibault's room. I found a suitcase in a hanging cupboard, and loaded in a couple of suits, trying to look as if they were mine.

M. Lomas glanced at the David Inshaw, then at the expanses of mythological flesh on the ceiling. His tongue ran around his lips. Behind his back, the woman had opened a drawer in a pot-bellied bureau and was moving two fat folders of papers into her suitcase, spreading a layer of shirts over the top. She nodded at me.

"That's it, *chéri,*" she said. "All yours, monsieur."

M. Lomas bowed a chivalrous bow.

The woman zipped up her suitcase. She turned the dark-blue eyes on M. Lomas, gave him a million candlepower smile. M. Lomas' tongue scuttled around his lips. By now, his mind was definitely not on suitcases.

I took a case in each hand.

I said, "You'll be taking the restaurant, too?"

Lomas said, "The restaurant is a company. We cannot touch it, alas."

"Alas," I said.

One of his men walked us to the van.

I loaded the suitcases in, climbed into the driver's seat.

The woman hissed, "Take me somewhere." She was shaking again.

We drove down the chestnut avenue. The Manoir shrank in the back window like a splendid doll's house, the dark-suited figure stark against the pale gravel.

The woman said, "Phew!" She turned to face me. "Thank you very much, my dear husband. My name is Bianca."

I shook her hand. It was warm, slightly damp. There was a tight nervous edge to her smile. I said, "What was all that about?"

She said, "Thibault has some problems. You are a friend of his, right? I worked with his team, organizing his boats, other things in his life."

I said, "Why did that man put you in the fire?"

"Because he is a pig." She spoke in a matter-of-fact voice, as if she had met plenty of pigs. We were out of the park now, passing through a village. "Stop at the pharmacy, please."

I stopped the car in front of the green cross. She bought a tube of Combudoron cream. "Thank you," she said, as if she was used to people doing what she wanted them to do. "You know, it is just as well I was wearing leather pants, or I would have been barbecue."

I said, "Who was that guy?"

She shrugged. "Someone who wanted to find Thibault," she said.

I said, "Odd way of going about it."

She said, "When you are a big shot, you can't always choose your friends."

She was making conversation. Suddenly she turned to me, as if she was going to say what was on her mind. "Listen, will you take me to the works?"

"Works?"

"I'll show you."

She dabbed the cream on her burn, tongue clenched delicately between her front teeth.

I said, "What's going on?"

"Thibault owes money," she said. She made an ironic face. "As you have maybe guessed. The banks want his possessions. There are others, who, well, who knows what they want?"

I had worked that much out for myself. Hearing someone else say it did not make it any better.

I said, "You seem to know your way around pretty well."

"I lived in the house," she said. "Many of us live in the house."

I said, "You weren't with *Kraken?*"

"No," she said. "I was otherwise engaged." She was hyping the mystery. She looked as if she might have been too young. "But you were."

I nodded. I said, "What happened?"

"I've been away," she said. "When I come back, everyone's gone from the house. And this cretin with the knife thinks I know where Thibault is. So to make me tell, he puts me in the fire."

I said, "So Thibault called you, told you he wanted stuff collected?"

"Last night," she said.

"What did he say?"

"Collect those things I collected." Her head went down. "I don't believe it." She was crying. She pulled a blue scarf from her pocket, and mopped her eyes.

I said, "What were those things?"

She shook her head, face buried in the scarf. I could not see any wet marks on the silk.

She directed me back into La Rochelle, past the Vieux Port and into a desert of boxy steel-framed buildings. Outside one of the buildings, a sign over a glass office door said ÉQUIPE LEDOUX. A catamaran lay on a patch of yellowed rye-grass, heeled over by a frame of girders under its uphill hull. The car park was empty, except for a pile of rusting steel beams.

The color had faded from Bianca's face. She was looking pale and worried, gnawing at a thumbnail. She said, *"Moment."* I cut the engine. The heels of her cowboy boots clicked on the tarmac as she walked across to the glass door and tried the handle. It was locked. She pulled a bunch of keys from her bag, fitted one in the hole. Pulled it out, tried another, then the big steel workshop doors. The place had a blank, shut-for-good look that I recognized from my own sheds. None of the doors opened. I remembered Yann changing the subject last night.

She came back. The click of her heels was slow and dragging. She climbed in and clasped her hands in her lap and stared down at them.

I said, "Problems?"

She turned her whole head to look at me. The tears were real now, sticking her black hair to her cheeks. She made no effort to push it away. "They have changed the locks," she said. "Everybody has gone."

I did a three-point turn and pulled the van's nose around toward the Vieux Port.

"Fifteen people," she said. "The team. All gone." She was

crying again, properly now. "I don't have anywhere to go. Bastards."

"Bastards?"

"He had riggers, shipwrights, his crew. All working. Then the bastards."

"Bastards from the banks?"

She scrubbed her eyes with her scarf. She said, "You should ask who is behind these bank men." I slid the van between two giant articulated lorries and down the turn that said CENTRE VILLE, ignoring the blare of horns. "It is not the fault of Thibault that it has all collapsed."

I said, "So when are you going to hand those papers over to Thibault?"

She said, "He'll collect them from the restaurant." She bit her lip. "Listen, I have nowhere to go. Is there room in the apartment above the restaurant?"

"Sure," I said.

She said again, "It is not Thibault's fault."

I have worked no-cure-no-pay for Lloyd's, built boats and raced them around the world, hung suspended over lakes of burning petrol. These are all dangerous corners of the commercial universe. In none of these corners have I ever met anyone who went bankrupt through his own fault.

Except, it now seemed, me.

5

Johnny Tinnelly was a kind man. Every day they were fishing, I would creep away from the dark house, and ride the piled net on to the domed water of the Barrow. Johnny and Mick, Pat and Andrew told me how to fish for salmon with the seine: how to lay out the net so the corks dotted in an even parabola on the water, never spanning more than half the river, because that was the law. Then the hauling, the current narrowing the parabola of the net into a shrinking bag. I had good eyes, better than the men's. I would see the first jump of the float that meant fish. And the end of the net would plow in through the water, the fish in the bag, kicking. Johnny would say, "Leadline first, boys," as if the other men had not been pulling in the leadline first for twenty years. Then the fish would be in, thrashing bars of silver held down in the mud, whacked on the head with the long stone and slid into the bag. And I would carry the bag, unless it was too heavy. Quite often, it was too heavy. Then I walked in front, as if I had done it all myself.

And sometimes, on a day of rain or fog, when nobody could be watching, there was the Long Net. The Long Net lived under a rock, and it was illegal, because it was long enough to span more than half the river. Not that it caught any more fish; but it had a superstitious value, as an emblem of freedom for John Tinnelly. Andrew, a dark-haired, gray-skinned man, did not like using the Long Net when I was with them. But Johnny would bash me on my by then seven-year-old shoulder, and say, "Sure it's the boy that makes the boat run." And out went the net.

One lunchtime in March, my parents and I were sitting in the dark dining room. There was a tureen of Irish stew that smelled like wet wool, and the faint petrochemical smell of whiskey from my father's glass. We were not talking, and there was no chance of escape, because the tide was too low for fishing, and the rain was lashing the gray-green fields outside.

There was a banging on the door. My mother got up. When she came back, there was a letter in her hand.

"It's for you," she said.

"Open it," said my father, from behind his beard.

The argument stirred, began to exude tension like an eel exuding slime.

My mother opened her mouth, then the letter. She read it. She fixed her pale blue eyes on me. Without looking at my father, she passed it over to him.

He read it. He drank from his glass. He said, "The *bastard*. How bloody dare he? Does he know what year it is? The world's been changed since 1916—"

"Not in front of the child," said my mother.

"I'll tell him, then," said my father. "Your Uncle James says you've been aiding and abetting the poaching of his salmon. He says he should have expected it, from the child of a Bolshevik and an Englishwoman. He says that next time he'll have the Guards on you."

I watched his wild blue eyes with my mouth open. My body had turned to mud, cold and heavy. "No," I said. "I wasn't."

"Leave him alone," said my mother.

The argument flexed its claws, launched itself into the air above the dining-room table, started to tear at them both. I crept away.

When there was no fishing, the salmon boys sat in the Cruiskeen Lawn, absorbing pints of bottled Guinness in tiny sips, like big, evil-smelling hummingbirds. Johnny Tinnelly was by the coke fire. I shoved my hands in the pockets of my shorts, marched over, and said, "Wet for fishing, Johnny?"

He looked up from the fire. His face was gray, swollen with heat and stout. His hand came out. It swung, cracked me on the ear. The pain rang in my head. Tears were sliding out of my stinging eyes. He said, "Fuck off, ye big-house tout."

It was the Long Net. Someone had found it, and taken it to Uncle James. Tinnelly was out of the salmon boat. So was I. But Tinnelly was in the Cruiskeen Lawn, and I was away to school in England.

Before I left, I was summoned to the Castle. Uncle James was sitting under the full-length Angelica Kaufman portraits in the drawing room, telephone at his elbow, writing a letter. "Ah," he said, looking up. "Do you know why you are here?"

"No," I said. I did not like Uncle James, because my parents did not like him. He had a long nose, and a scaly bald head, and pale blue eyes that goggled.

"Because I am paying your school fees," he said. "I am the head of the family. I am responsible."

I did not know what I was supposed to say. I said, "Thank you."

He said, "Don't thank me. We want to be rid of you, here. Get you out into the world. You are troublesome." He waved his yellowish hand. "So go."

I went. I walked down the drive, under the dripping trees, feeling different, and separate, and very sad, because of Tinnelly. Next week I was put on the boat over to England, out of there.

The restaurant was empty. Frankie was polishing glasses in the bar. There were tourists on the pavement, drinking away the hour before lunch. There were a couple of old men in the bar, and the blind woman, her fingers laced around a Pernod. Frankie said, "You're late for laying up," and flicked a calculating look at Bianca. Another of his floozies, said the look. Mary Ellen and I might have made our agreement, but seventeen-year-old daughters could not be expected to be party to it.

The old men turned their rheumy gaze on Bianca, mumbled *"Bonjour,"* and returned to their study of the way Frankie's breasts disturbed the surface of her Living Rainforests T-shirt.

I said, "I've got to find Thibault."

She shook her head. "Tried his house? And the works?"

I nodded.

She dried a glass and banged it into the rack over the bar. As far as she was concerned, she was a practical person and I and the floozie were getting in the way. She said, "I'm afraid I can't help. And for your information, Gérard's not feeling well, and there's a problem in the kitchen because André doesn't like the oysters—he's the chef—and Giselle, she's the washer-up, her brother Christophe brought them, and he says they're fine, and she's backing him up. They won't talk to me, because I'm too young. You're supposed to be the manager, so I wonder if you would mind being a bit of a help?"

I said, "Frankie, this is Bianca. Bianca's in a bit of difficulty. Is there any room in the apartment?"

Frankie forgot about peak efficiency. The calculating look disappeared. Beneath her efficient exterior beat a heart of warm treacle, ever ready with an old-fashioned welcome for the waif and stray. "Sure," she said with a big, wide-open grin. "I'll go and stay with Jean-Claude."

I remembered the motorbike in the night. I said, without any enthusiasm at all, "If you're sure it's quite convenient?"

Her eyebrows rose a notch, and the calculating look returned. She was learning subtlety. *You bring in your fancy woman. I go with my fancy man.*

But it was my fault, not the floozie's. She said, "Come on, Bianca. I'll show you."

Bianca followed her. I took a deep breath, and shoved through the double doors and into the kitchen.

André the chef was a broad, pale man with a walrus mustache and close-set, curranty eyes. He was sweating over a big gas stove, hissing to himself like a serpent. I introduced myself to him and his four athletic-looking assistants. Giselle the washer-up was at the back end of the kitchen. She was a wrinkled old woman with a scarf knotted under her chin. She was standing with her forearms in the sink, staring blindly at the white-tiled wall.

She looked as if she was in shock. I said, "What is the problem?"

She turned her head. Her face was creased and brown, the creases splashed with drying tears. "Christophe," she said.

"What about him?"

"He is an old friend of M. Thibault. Since M. Thibault was a child. Would he deceive M. Thibault in the way this man suggests?"

I said, "Of course not." I was not merely humoring her. It was the loyalty again.

"Shellfish," said André, "are shellfish."

This was hard to disagree with.

I said, "We shall see. Bring me these oysters." I seated myself at the stainless steel sink with what I hoped was the air of a Michelin inspector.

It was a frugal but excellent luncheon: a bottle of Chablis and a dozen of the offending oysters. I ate with as much ceremony and deliberation as I could manage.

Giselle hung over me, breathing hoarsely and passing me slices of lemon. She said, "It is not a good year. Really not a good year. The weather has been difficult. And Christophe is not as young as he was. But he continues to deliver oysters of high quality, in spite of everything."

She spoke with great vehemence. André looked up from a fillet of bass, and said, "Let him eat in peace." The oysters

44

were fine, and I said so, upon which Giselle stuck her chin in the air and looked triumphant. I then passed the opinion that they were smaller than they should have been, which brought the fire back to André's eyes. I poured them each a glass of wine and returned to the bar, leaving behind me a scene of grudging harmony.

The lunchtime clients were beginning to trickle through the swing doors as I climbed the stairs to the apartment. I sat down at the desk in the little office off the sitting room. There was a filing cabinet, and one of the complicated telephones that Thibault liked. It must have done duty as an office for the restaurant, because it was littered with bills. I piled them up and shoved them into a corner.

Then I picked up the telephone, and dialed England.

Mary MacFarlane answered. She was my secretary, widow of old Henry, who had run the South Creek Boatyard, down the coast from Pulteney. Henry had died, and she had sold up. Nowadays, she fielded my telephone calls, wide as a barn door in a blue jersey and a tan canvas skirt behind her desk in the drawing office. "Oh, hell*o,*" she said. "You got there."

"Sort of," I said. If I told her what had happened, she would have considered it her duty to be sympathetic. I was not in the mood for sympathy. "Any word from Thibault Ledoux?"

"None," she said. My heart sank. "Two calls. The bank. They want the final check on *Arc.*"

They were not the only ones. I said, "That's in hand. Who else?"

"Art Schacker. He's got to have an answer in two weeks. He has to speak to his backers."

"Yes," I said.

"That's good," she said. "The Flying Fish Challenge, I mean. Rather exciting."

"Yes," I said, trying to sound excited. "Do me a favor. Can you dig up the worksheets on *Arc-en-Ciel?*"

She said, "There are about two thousand of them."

"The fitout sheets," I said. "Engine seacocks. Check suppliers and installers."

I gave her the restaurant's telephone number and rang off.

Bianca was sitting in one of the armchairs next door, watching me with hot blue eyes. When she saw I was looking at her, the eyes slid away.

I said, "What were you doing at Thibault's house?"

"Six or seven of us from the team lived there."

"And he didn't tell you where he was going, or what he was doing?"

Her lower lip had a sullen jut. "I am his assistant, not his mistress. I was away. I came back this morning. He called, asked me to bring some papers. I found what I found."

I remembered Thibault's face the night before, the skin papery, stretched too tight over the bones. I said, "I do not understand a guy with a knife who throws you into the fire."

Her eyes slid away again. She said, "Thibault runs a big team, to build boats, to win races." Her mouth twisted wryly. "I guess that where there is big money, there is also big dirty business."

I said, "Are you ready to get stabbed for the sake of his business?"

"He asked you to look after his *resto,*" she said. "And so you do it. He has a way of encouraging people, Thibault. Anyway, I don't know where he is."

I said, "What were those papers you took away?"

"I don't know." There was a stubborn set to her jaw. And if I did, I wouldn't tell you, said the jaw.

I said, "Where are they?"

"A man collected them." Her eyes were a most peculiar blue, deep as an evening sky, bright and intense against the olive skin of her face.

"What man?"

"I left them in the restaurant for him. I didn't see him."

She was suspicious of me. I was suspicious of her. I did not believe her, but she was not going to tell me anything.

I went upstairs. She came after me. In case I went looking for folders in her room?

I said, "Thibault's team. Where are they?"

She said, "I called just now. Gone since three days. They said Thibault said go, it's all finished."

"Was there a business manager?"

"Thibault was the business manager."

Outside the window, the sun was rolling west. The tide was high. Little puffs of breeze ruffled the inner basin. If Thibault had known he was going broke three days ago, he must have had an inkling at the launch, when he had asked me to deliver *Arc-en-Ciel*.

Trust is a two-way street.

I twitched my dirty oilskin off the hanger.

"You are going on your boat?" said Bianca.

"It won't be much of a trip," I said. I wanted solitude. She was already pulling on her coat.

Downstairs, Frankie was sitting on a bar stool, eating a sandwich. I asked her if she wanted to come. She looked at Bianca, then at me. The pattern was establishing itself. When Bianca was with me, she ceased to be a waif and stray and became a floozie again. "Nope," she said. Her mouth looked tight and efficient. Perhaps it was the sandwich.

I grinned at her, to show there were no hard feelings from my side of the family, and stumped off down the quay.

Arc-en-Ciel did not look too bad, from the outside. I clambered from the jetty on to the side-deck, turned to give Bianca a hand up. She was already aboard.

"Can you steer if we tow her?" I said. "Engine's out."

She looked at the shadows of breeze on the water. "Why don't we sail?" she said.

"Not enough wind," I said. There was wind, but only a little. The gap between the Tour Saint-Nicolas and the Tour de la Chaine is narrow. Under sail, everyone would need to know what they were doing.

Bianca said, "There's no tide. We'll do it nicely." She was stuffing her black hair efficiently into a salt-stained red baseball cap. It looked like a familiar routine.

"You sail before?" I said.

"A bit," she said. She was leaning on the boom, hands in pockets, eyes creased against the sun on the water. And I knew where I had seen her before.

I sat down. I could feel the blood come to my face. I said, "You're Bianca Dufy."

"Once I was," she said.

Bianca Dufy had been the maritime equivalent of Joan of Arc. For five years, she had sailed rings around all comers in the Olympics, multihull regattas, even the Captain's Cup. I do not read sailing magazines, but even I had seen her picture on the front. She had rapidly acquired a reputation as a tough egg who liked to keep herself to herself. Then one day she had walked off her boat and vanished into thin air.

"We'll sail," I said.

It was not much of a sail, at first. Bianca set a few rolls of jib, and we drifted between the towers and into the blue funnel of water outside.

Out in the channel, the breeze blew steady. We pulled out all the sail *Arc-en-Ciel* had. The wake tore a long, bubbling gurgle from the dirty sea. The red can-buoys began to slide by.

"Nice," said Bianca. Her face had lost its drawn look. Her eyes were moving around the boat, testing, prodding, seriously interested.

I began to feel a small itch of pride. *Arc* was my baby. It was possible to forget that she was the property of a bankrupt, wrecked below, kept afloat by a wooden plug. She had a lovely hull, and an efficient rig. She went like a train.

"Over there," said Bianca, pointing.

Over there, where the sun was floating down at the molten line of the horizon to the south of the Île de Ré, a set of white sails heeled. "Go on," I said.

She took the wheel. I put my glasses on the sails.

It was a ketch, an eighty-foot monster carrying a tennis court of sail controlled by winches big enough to play tug-of-war with elephants. There was a big white deck on which people crawled like ants. It had a serious racing look to it, but the coachroof and dodgers said that someone had converted it for cruising. Rich man's toy, it screamed.

The ketch saw us coming. What he was seeing was a tall, narrow main and a big genoa over a sixty-foot hull much too wide and much too flat for simple cruising. He would also be seeing two little figures in the cockpit, instead of the swarm you might expect on a boat the size of *Arc-en-Ciel*. His sails rippled as he hung pitching gently on the swell, spilling wind.

Bianca brought us down on him like a ton of bricks. A puff darkened the water blue-black. *Arc*'s mast dipped like a poppy in a cornfield, the wake hissing from the sweet curve of her back end. Bianca said quietly, in English: "I go up on him." She was hard on the wind, port tack. The ketch was close-hauled on the starboard tack, crew lined out along the uphill rail like shags on a rock, slicing a rasher of white water from the fat blue swells under its bow. We were on what would have looked like a collision course, to anyone who did not know *Arc* as well as me.

If it had been me on the wheel, I would have known how to squeak across his nose. Bianca was not going to be that brave, I thought. Nor would I have been, helming a strange boat for the first time.

I gave the genoa a twitch, looked up at her. She was sprawled along the cockpit seat, hand light on the wheel's spoke. Her eyes were invisible under the long peak of her cap. A couple of blue-black tendrils of hair had escaped into the wind. She had lost her nervousness. She looked relaxed as a sleeping cat. Ahead and to starboard, the ketch's hull was a claret-red stripe buried deep in the waves, carving its way confidently to windward.

"Tack when you want," I said.

The other boat was a hundred yards off, now. Someone was hailing. "Starboard!" they yelled. Asserting that they had right-of-way.

Bianca held her course.

The ketch was a forty-ton blade of steel-hard composites, driving forward at the best part of fifteen miles an hour. I could hear the click of a winch on her deck, the cry of a gull, the roar of the water under her nose.

Bianca held her course.

Arc-en-Ciel slid straight and true, leaving the merest ripple of wake. The ketch's crew were all yelling, now. We were ten yards clear. Five. I could smell the zinc cream on the foredeck man's nose. I saw him turn and run aft to the mast, lock his arms in a halyard. Then the ketch's high red bow and stainless-steel pulpit came between me and him.

And we shot under his nose with four feet to spare.

"Tacking," said Bianca, and swung the wheel. The boom clacked over. I ground the genoa winch. And we were sitting ten yards upwind and ahead of his nose, and his sails were fluttering in the eddies of dirty air spinning back from our sails, and the foredeck man was swearing hard. I realized that it was about a minute since I had last breathed.

Bianca swore back over her shoulder, a machine-gun burst, letting go the tension. Then she eased the wheel, bore away and ducked under the bigger boat's stern. The ketch's crew watched us go. They had hard brown faces, smeared with white zinc warpaint against the sun. Their shorts were navy-blue and sharply pressed. Their polo shirts were claret-red, to match the hull, with WHITE WING in white script over the heart.

One of the men was not in uniform. He was older than the rest, beginning to be jowly, sucking a cigar. His blazer and white trousers yelled *owner*. His eyes were not so much unfriendly as downright hostile. They were fixed on Bianca. Bianca laughed, too loudly. She put her arm around my shoulder and kissed me on the cheek. Her eyes stayed on the man with the cigar.

White Wing's sails shrank astern. I had been watching those sails as we went under the ketch's nose. They had been trimmed to a hair. She had made no effort to slow down.

If we had been racing, it would have been understandable. But we had not been racing. *White Wing* had been ready to cut us in half and bend herself just to punish a bit of cheek.

I said, "Did you know that boat?"

She smiled at me, a peculiar inward smile of triumph.

"No," she said.

She was lying.

"Helm's a-lee," she said, and turned *Arc*'s bow for the land.

6

Chantiers Albert was in the Port des Minimes, the vast cement marina that waits, according to French custom, in the approaches to the Vieux Port. There is an aquarium for the tourist, a selection of yacht brokerages for the fantasist, and a variety of yards, chandlers and insurance salesmen for the serious yachtsman. Chantiers Albert was the most serious of the yards. It consisted of a grubby shed inside a chainlink fence at the top of a slipway. Inside, the shed was full of the usual howl of sanders and the stink of resins. It had the surprising tidiness which is the mark of the serious craftsman. Georges was a sallow man with a dark-blue boiler suit, a Gitane stuck in the corner of his glum mouth, and hammocks under his eyes big enough to sleep the crew of a ship of the line. He had inherited the yard from his father, who had built wooden fishing boats there. His heart was still in wood, but he knew what side his bread was buttered, so nowadays he built in plastic. He had finished a couple of boats for me. He was a good craftsman, straight as a ruler.

He had visited me in England, to discuss the fitting-out of a boat. Mary Ellen had been down that weekend, and Georges had brought Titine, his wife. We had had an evening that started good and ended riotous, with Georges walking the bar while I played "Feets Too Big" on the piano in the Mermaid. Mary Ellen had thawed to the point where she had actually taken my arm on the way back to the flat, and Georges and I had been friends ever since.

When he saw me he uncoiled from his chair, grinning, the cigarette bobbing at the corner of his mouth. Then he saw Bianca. The grin cooled several degrees, and he sat down again. I was surprised by this. A couple of years ago, when I had last seen him, Georges would have spent a lot longer on a beautiful woman than on a boatbuilding acquaintance. He asked me how things were.

"Fine," I said, lying. "And you?"

He told me things were very busy, pointed out of his scummy window at the boats piled up on the slip. I nodded and tutted, and let him go through the usual maneuvers of a boatbuilder establishing a favorable atmosphere for a good price.

Bianca wandered off to the chandlery down the road to buy a pair of boots. Georges began to look happier. We walked down to the pontoon. *Arc-en-Ciel* was lying alongside, stirring gently to the last echoes of the swell. "Nice hull," he said. "Fast?"

"Faster than you think," I said. "Who's got a ketch called *White Wing?*"

"Oh, shit," said Georges. He flicked his butt into the harbor scum, and lit a new one with his Zippo. "That lot."

"What lot?"

"They're driving people crazy," said Georges. "Part of the Mediterranean invasion. Owner's a guy called Crespi. Bought a lot of businesses here. Telling us how to sail boats, make money. What about him?"

"We wiped his eye." I told him what Bianca had done.

Georges said, "And the guy didn't give way?"

"Nope."

Georges said, "That's the boys from down south for you."

I said, "What do you mean?"

Georges said, "We're nice guys, in La Rochelle. We had a pedestrian city before pedestrian cities were fashionable. We're good old ask-the-people democrats. But this Crespi guy, he plows in, starts acting like Ivan the Terrible, doesn't care who gets hurt. And he's just one of them." Georges scowled. He had been a staunch Communist in his time. "There are others. There's bloody Alphonse Feuilla, sticking up his blocks of flats behind the beach down on the Île d'Oléron. Someone told him he couldn't build there because it's some kind of conservation site. Feuilla started waving banknotes at the bureaucrats, kept on pouring concrete. Then he acted all surprised when they shut the site down."

Georges shook his head. "Bloody gangsters, the lot of them."

I grinned at Georges. He used gangster in its Stalinist sense, to signify anyone not actually working in a collective. I said, "Gangster yourself. Also Fascist lackey."

He shrugged. "All right," he said. "That girl, though. What are you doing with her?"

"She helped me bring the boat down."

"And nearly got you rammed."

That was true, if one-sided. I said, "What have you got against her?"

"Me?" He looked amazed, except around the eyes.

"You."

His face split into the big grin. "OK," he said. "Look at her. Too pretty. She'll cost a lot. She's a hysteric. But I'm not twenty-two anymore. With Titine you are safe and happy. Or you with Mary Ellen."

Georges had brought his wife to England on a weekend when Mary Ellen had worked herself to a standstill, and wished for a few days in the company of people who knew nothing about insurance but a lot about music. She and I had these honeymoons perhaps four or five times a year. Georges had never seen us different, so he would assume that honeymoon was the usual state of affairs. "Anyway, she's with you. No chance for me. Let's look at this boat."

We went over *Arc*. In the clear evening light, the inside of her looked as if someone had been working it over with hand grenades. Georges sniffed the diesel-scented air, pitched his cigarette overboard. He scratched with a horny thumbnail at a patch of tar on the varnish.

I said, "The main engine-cooling seacock broke off."

He frowned. "Broke off?"

"Take a look."

We pulled the cover off the engine. He lay down, took a flashlight from his dungarees pocket, stretched his arm into the bilges. "You're right," he said.

"I want to know why."

"Of course you do," he said. "I'll put someone on it tomorrow."

"Sooner the better."

53

We climbed out of the smell of diesel and into the cockpit. He said, "This boat is Thibault's, right?"

"That's right."

He looked at me with his sad, deeply pouched eyes. He said, "Who's paying the bill?"

"Thibault's insurance."

He pulled out a new cigarette. "You're looking at a big work," he said. "Engine overhaul. New seacocks. Fix up electronics. Refinish cabin interior."

I thought of the bailiffs, and the changed locks on the works. "He insured the boat," I said.

The eyes became sadder. "Mick," he said. "Insurance or no insurance, nobody in this town will give Thibault Ledoux any credit anymore."

"What happened?"

He shrugged, screwed up an eye against the smoke from his cigarette. "Dunno," he said. "I'm not sure he does either. I've known him since we were kids. Did you know he was signed up with that Feuilla bloke?"

"Feuilla?" I said.

"The builder. Developer, what you call him. Six months ago. Feuilla was having his problems on Île d'Oléron. So maybe he thought he'd buy up a local hero. So he turns up as main sponsor for Thibault. Spending a lot of money, sure. But he's miscalculated down here. He's lost a packet. I told you, they won't let him build. So maybe he's cutting back, suddenly. He's building an America's Cup challenger down south. It all costs money. Maybe he couldn't afford Thibault anymore."

"Oh," I said.

"And that girl," said Georges. "She arrived nine months ago. Just when Thibault bought that Manoir, started acting like a couple of millionaires." He shrugged. "Anyway, last time I saw him, he said he was getting squeezed. Running three boats. He's got an old sixty-footer he can't sell. He's been building a big trimaran down south, and then *Arc-en-Ciel* with you. That's a lot of pressure. He wasn't laughing like he used to."

He had seemed fine at the launch. But then I thought of the final payment. It would have been in his interest to seem fine. I remembered the pale, stretched skin of Thibault's face last night. The lump of ice was back in my stomach.

"So," said Georges. "There's our old mate Thibault, offshore racing's premier hippie, living like one of the Princes of the Church with a team of fifteen guys; sailing races, building boats, fitting out in their own yard. Then . . . pouf!" He made an explosion with his long, resin-stained hands. "No more nothing. Now, he doesn't even get a newspaper unless he's got cash in his hand."

I said, "So I've got a problem."

There was a silence. Finally, he said, "Leave the boat here. I'll look at that seacock, put a couple of guys on it for a week, cost price. Get it cleaned up. Maybe you can sell it somewhere else." He seemed improbably interested in the Zippo's wheel.

There are laws about boatbuilders. Successful boatbuilders do not make good offers, even to their old friends. Successful boatbuilders look on the grim side of things, to avoid disappointment, and are nonetheless often disappointed. This was a good offer.

Georges looked up. "And watch the girl," he said. He started to hum a song. He was an old R and B freak, was Georges. That was one of the two things we had in common. The song he was humming was "Poison Ivy." *You can look, but you'd better not touch.*

I said, "I wasn't planning to."

Bianca wandered in with her bag of boots. We got a taxi back to the restaurant. I pushed a path for her through a busload of Japanese tourists who were settling like a flock of starlings on the pavement tables. The old men and the blind woman were in the back bar. I went behind the bar, slapped a couple of glasses on the *zinc* and poured.

Bianca said, "Now you are going to ask me again where is Thibault. Well, I still don't know."

I took a mouthful of wine, and leaned my elbow on the bar. The burgundy was big and round and raw, and it did not help the tiredness. I said, "I did you a favor this morning. Do me one."

"What do you want?"

"Where does Thibault keep his records?"

Her face had become stony, impenetrable. "Of what?"

"He told me he had insured the boat I was delivering. I would like to know with whom, so I can claim on the policy and pay for the repairs."

She stared at me for perhaps ten seconds, biting her lower lip. Then she said, "Sometimes it is difficult to remember what a friend is." She pulled a bill-pad across the *zinc* and scribbled something on it. "This is the broker who has done the insurance. Maybe he will help you."

There was a braying of voices in the restaurant. "The English have arrived," she said. "I go."

"Do you want some dinner?" I said.

She smiled, a softer smile than she had ever given me before. I was suddenly aware of her perfume, and another sensation, as if she and I were on the same side against the cold, hostile world. She put her hand on mine, and left.

The English people who had come in parted to let her through. She passed through them with the grace of a deer among cattle. I folded the paper she had given me and slid it into the back pocket of my jeans.

The English consisted of a woman and three men dressed in too-short red-tan trousers, too-long Guernseys, and down-at-heel blue Docksiders. The man in the middle said, "Good God! It's the Irishman!"

This was the kind of thing you had to put up with if you wished to be friends with Justin Peabody. I pulled my eyes resolutely away from Bianca, put my hands on the bar, and said, "Good evening, lady and gentlemen and Justin. And phwhat is your pleasure?"

Justin opened his slot of a mouth and began to laugh the asinine laugh he used on holiday. In the suits he wore to work, he looked big and smooth, like a seal. His sailing clothes made his footballer's shoulders wider, his neck thicker. His forehead was scorched red by the sun, and his blond hair stood on end, blasted by the wind. He looked like a Viking on a particularly enjoyable raid. "Mikey!" he cried. He was the only person who ever called me Mikey. "What are you doing here?"

"Working," I said.

They asked for gins and tonics. Justin said, "Where's Frankie?"

"Here soon," I said.

He was over in *Ariadne,* his boat. We talked sailing. He seemed faintly embarrassed that as barman I was the servant and he was the boss. In his rigidly conventional view, there was a hint that this was too close to the truth to be comfortable.

I gave everyone more gin. The private door opened and Frankie came in, trim and bouncy in a blue guernsey and red microskirt. She was wearing lipstick, and kohl around her cat's eyes. She smiled when she saw me, and managed to hang on to it when she saw Justin. She might affect to regard me as a wild man, but she knew who she had fun with.

Justin introduced her to his crew. "'Strornry thing," he said. "Told her she could come and crew on *Ariadne* for the summer. Prefers to work in a, er, waterfront dive." More letterbox grin. "Looking jolly pretty, tonight," he said. "Must be a chap in it. Feller. Eh, Frank?" Hwa, hwa, went the personnel.

Frankie turned away and polished some already sparkling glasses at the back of the bar. I looked across the restaurant's white tables, through the window, beyond the crowds drifting on the quay, at the night. It was cool out there, chilled by the big Atlantic. Lamps wobbled in the ink-black harbor. Buoys blinked from the open sea. The smoke stung my eyes.

A *moto* whined over the cobbles and stopped with an artistic back-wheel skid that left it facing the way it had come. The rider strutted into the restaurant.

He was a small, athletic-looking man with a boxer's shoulders and narrow hips. He was wearing a black leather jacket, jeans, and big black lace-up boots that hit the floor with the authentic crunch of hobnails. He had the face of a spoiled Greek god, the nose too straight, the lips too fleshy.

I opened the flap in the bar and pushed my way toward him. The man in the leathers stalked down between the tables. His eyes were poking into corners, looking for someone.

I said, "Evening." I said it nice and quiet. My mouth was dry. I had seen him before. He was the pretty boy who had thrown Bianca into the fire at the Manoir de Causey.

He was peering into the back of the room, at the bar. He

was too cool to look at waiters. He said, "Where is Frankie?"

My heart seemed to roll in my chest. I said, "Who shall I say is here?"

He lit a Marlboro, the way he had seen the guys light the cigarettes in the gangster movies, and looked at the bar through the smoke. "Jean-Claude," he said. Cool as a mortuary freezer.

"Right," I said. Frankie, you bloody fool.

The door into the bar opened and closed. Frankie was there, suspended in mid-stride, eyes brilliant with happiness. She smiled. The pretty boy smiled back. It was a wide, sunny smile, full of the warm south. He looked as if he was really pleased to see her.

I could hear my blood humming with anger. I said, "Have you come to see Frankie, or do you want your knife back?"

He looked at me then. He recognized me. He turned and started to leave. I was too angry to think straight. I put out a hand and caught the collar of his leather jacket. "So you're my daughter's boyfriend," I said. "Tell me all about yourself."

7

*H*e hit me. There was no wind-up, no preparation. There was just the bang of his fist landing on my right cheekbone. It was not a big punch, but it hurt enough to make the eyes water. I had not hit anyone since I had last stepped out of the boxing ring at school. Should have hit him first, I told myself. His boots crashed on the scrubbed wood floor, kicked over a chair. He was getting away.

Somewhere a small, prudent voice was saying, *careful, Savage, he carries a knife.* But old reflexes were working and I was too busy to listen to small voices. I bounced off a waiter and barged open the glass swing doors. The kid was straddling a yellow Suzuki, jumping up for the kickstart. A frieze of Japanese faces watched with polite interest from the terrace. I waded through a tin table covered in drinks and leapt on him. I caught his neck under my arm and yanked him sideways. We hit the cobbles with a *whump* that knocked the breath out of me. The bike's engine was howling by my ear. He stank of patchouli. He twisted away, grabbed my left hand. He was strong. My grip on his neck was slackening. He was pulling my arm. I could not understand why. He was screaming in my ear. "Frankie say you play the piano!" I got my head around. I saw that the bike was in gear, the back wheel whizzing around, spokes a silver blur in the café lights. The reason Jean-Claude was pulling my arm was because he wanted to stuff my left hand into the spokes and cut all the fingers off.

The sound of Frankie's name in his mouth sent the blood through my veins like rocket fuel. I let go the headlock and rolled away, wrenching the hand. I felt my boot go into something soft. He grunted. There were people shouting now, and somewhere a whistle blowing. Suddenly he let go of me, jumped to his feet with an acrobat's roll and kicked me in the chest. I took a step back, tripped over a bollard and went down on to the cobbles. Somewhere in the red dark, a motorbike was howling. The howl receded, losing itself in the night-noises of the city.

I pulled myself up on the bollard. There was a policeman trotting toward me. There was Gérard outside the front of the restaurant, hands raised as if he was about to take wing. There was a crowd, melting away. There was me, shaking with reaction, because for five seconds I had wanted to kill someone.

I said to Gérard, "Deal with the police." I grinned and bowed at the Japanese whose table I had knocked over. Waiters were swarming around them like antibodies rushing to the scene of an infection. I pushed open the restaurant door.

Frankie was standing inside. Her arms were hanging at her sides. Her mouth was a bloodless line.

She said, "Where's Jean-Claude?"

I took a deep breath. "He had to go," I said.

"You hit him."

"He hit me first."

"You grabbed him," she said. "I saw. He's my *boyfriend.* You're *jealous.* So you *hit* him. You're *pathetic.*"

Oh, bloody hell, I thought. Unfair, unfair. I said, "Let me explain." But it was Mary Ellen's place to be the voice of sweet reason. According to the version Frankie had been fed since infancy, Daddy was sweet, but wild, and you never knew what he was going to do next. So have fun with your daddy, darling, but never, ever trust him an inch.

She said, "You've come to mess things up. Mummy said you would. She told me I was crazy to work for a friend of yours."

Justin came up. He said to me, "Are you all right?"

Frankie said, "He's a *bully.*"

"Oh, come on," said Justin, not sweet, but not at all wild either. "That young man did hit him. Have a drink."

"Gin and tonic," said Frankie, not looking at me. She knew I hated her drinking spirits, and so did Mary Ellen.

I stood there. There were no ribs broken. I avoided the eye of Justin, and the embarrassed glances of *Ariadne's* crew. I sucked my knuckles where I had skinned them on my daughter's boyfriend's designer stubble. I said, "Your boyfriend threw Bianca into a log fire. He tried to cut off my hand in the wheel of his motorbike."

She said, "I'm sorry he missed." Then she burst into tears and ran through the bar to the stairs. The door slammed. I stood there, bleeding from the knuckles and the soul. You blew it; you lost control; you did what people expect of you.

Savage, I thought, your life is a mess.

Justin said, "Bad luck. I would have done the same." I was not consoled.

Someone cleared his throat at my elbow. It was Gérard. He said, "You're hurt?"

I shook my head.

"There's a problem."

"The police?"

"We have arranged the police. M. Thibault said . . . well, he said you would arrange everything in the restaurant while he was away." His doe eyes were anxious. I nodded. He said, "The woman who does the washing-up. She has gone."

"Giselle?"

"She telephoned. She can't come. We have no wash-ing-up."

"Why not?"

"Her brother has a problem. She must help him." He sighed. "It often happens."

I sighed back. "Where are the aprons?"

"Pardon?"

"The aprons." Tonight, washing up was all I was fit for. "Until you find someone else."

Justin said, "Well, we'll be off. Dinner on the boat. Pop down, any night." The Ariadnes paid, awkwardly. One likes peanuts with one's gin, not brawls.

I elbowed my way through the swing doors into the steam and clutter of the kitchen, stationed myself in front of the big sink, and poured myself a water-glass of the chef's cooking burgundy. The clock said seven-fifty-five. I found rubber gloves for the knuckles, and began washing up.

The anger receded. Give Frankie time to cool off, I thought. Find Jean-Claude, and ask him why he wanted to see Thibault.

At nine-forty-five, the big burst of main-course plates was over. My scarred knuckles were stinging, in spite of the gloves. Gérard appeared at my elbow, and said, "Someone to see you."

"Tell 'em I'm busy."

He said, "It is M. Feuilla. M. Thibault's sponsor."

I said, "It must be M. Thibault he wants."

Gérard shook his head. "It is to you he wishes to speak," he said.

I dried my hands, took off my apron, and went into the restaurant.

A small man was sitting at one of the tables. There was a glass of mineral water in front of him. He had white hair, longish, swept back like a lion's mane from a face the color and texture of a shelled walnut. He was leaning back in his chair, gazing at the pictures of Thibault in the bar with black eyes like twin bradawls. People were looking at him: not, you felt, because they knew who he was, but because there was an atmosphere about him you could no more ignore than you could ignore a lightship.

When he saw me, he got up. He came toward me, hands out. "M. Savage," he said. "I have heard so much about you." His accent was harsh and southern. "Listen, I have a problem, and I want your help. Come."

"Come?"

"I want to show you something. I need one hour of your time, no more." His small hand gripped my arm. He piloted me toward the restaurant door. "Thibault rang," he said. "He must go away, he said."

"Did he say where?"

"Of course not. This is Thibault." A long black car gleamed illegally in the middle of the pedestrian walkway. A policeman started to shout. "Peace, my son," said Feuilla. A chauffeur opened the door of the car. "In, in," said Feuilla.

"Wait," I said. "I've got work—"

"Won't be long," said Feuilla. "I have news for you."

The smell of expensive upholstery surrounded me. I was in. The car purred, heaved itself off the pavement and into the road, and started to skirt the Vieux Port.

"This Atlantic," said Feuilla. "A people so cold, so organized, they do not recognize leadership, commercial leadership, when they see it." We turned right at a sign that said PORT DES MINIMES. The buildings thinned out. There was a sound outside the limousine: a helicopter engine. The limousine drew off the road on to a square of concrete that might have been a basketball ground. In the middle of the ground, a small helicopter was screaming like an electric wasp.

"In, in," said Feuilla. He trotted briskly across the cement, climbed aboard. I ducked my head and went after him. If anybody knew what had happened to Thibault, it would be his sponsor.

There were three seats. We did up the seatbelts. The chopper's engine-note wailed up. The lights of La Rochelle fell away below. To the left the land stretched away, spotted with clusters of light. To the right was the empty black sea, with the occasional flash of a buoy. We were heading south, down the coast.

Something cold touched my hand. Against the light I saw the silhouette of Feuilla's hand, with a bottle. Champagne. Ten minutes ago, I had been washing up. I wanted to laugh. But Feuilla did not look like a man who enjoyed being laughed at. So I nodded, and wet my tongue with the little cold needles, and held my peace until the world became quiet enough for the asking of questions.

Below, the lights became fewer, except for one cluster in the middle of a thick black cushion of darkness. The chopper stood on its side and descended. It landed, light as a moth. Beyond the windows were gray floodlights, big concrete mixers, bulldozers in a clearing in a pine forest. Beyond the machinery were slabs of concrete, reinforcing rods projecting from their ends like toothpaste from the tube. The reinforcing rods were rusty. The rotors slowed, and stopped.

Feuilla said, "Welcome to the Royaume des Phares."

The Kingdom of the Lighthouses. Georges had spoken of it as a joke. Now we were here, in the clearing in the trees, it did not look like a joke. It looked like a lot of money rotting in the woods. It looked like a stuck project. It looked like a disaster.

"Come," said Feuilla. He led me to the only finished structure in the clearing, a concrete box thirty feet high. We went up a flight of steps, until we were standing on top. "Café des Phares," he said. "There they are."

He waved an arm. The floodlights went out.

We were standing in the center of the Île d'Oléron, on a forested rise of ground that must at some point have been a great dune. My eyes began to get used to the dark. Beyond the pines, the moon shone on a distant sea. And out on the sea, three-quarters of the way around the horizon, were lighthouses, speaking to each other in cryptic glow-worm blinks.

"Well?" said Feuilla. "Here, you drink the aperitif."

"Fine," I said. It was fine, if you were the kind of person who liked to drink aperitifs and watch lighthouses.

"Yes," said Feuilla. "But they will not let me start."

"They?"

"The government," said Feuilla. "These people with vichyssoise instead of blood. I have bought the land. Now they tell me it is only for trees and little birds. I have plans for ten swimming pools, four hundred apartments. I am kind to these bureaucrats who grant the permissions. I will look after them, the way I look after the people who work for me at home. But they will not listen. They say no building. Because they are suspicious of me. Because I am a foreigner."

I said, "I'm sorry to hear that."

"Yes," said Feuilla. Obviously, he had taken that for granted. He raised his hand. The lights came on again. Cautiously, he walked down the steps. He was an old man, I realized. It was his energy of mind that made him seem younger than he was. "So I must raise my profile. For this, I needed Thibault. But Thibault has disappeared. So I want you to sail *Plage d'Or* for me."

"Plage d'Or?"

"The boat. The good boat I bought for Thibault."

He must have been talking about the sixty-footer *Arc-en-Ciel* had been built to replace. Thibault had bought her himself; but some sponsors like to exaggerate the size of the role they play in their skippers' lives. She was a fast boat, though crude by Savage Yachts standards. "She is in Sables d'Olonne. There is no Thibault to sail her. So I wanted you to sail her instead, in the Tour de Belle-Île."

The Tour de Belle-Île was a sort of omnium-gatherum race. Most of the year's big, beautiful boats would be there, each one a floating billboard for its sponsor. French TV would run coverage at prime time.

"I want the public to know about this," he said. His little arm embraced the clearing in a Napoleonic sweep. "Make a fuss. They will want it when they know more about it. They will pressure their politicians. Your job is to get me some column inches."

I said, "Fine."

He said, "How's business?"

I said, "Middling."

We were walking back to the chopper, through the lights. His eyes held mine a second too long. He had done his homework. He knew how business was. He said, "I heard you were considering an offer from Art Schacker."

I said, "You've got good intelligence."

He smiled. "We're building an America's Cup boat ourselves, in the south." The eyes were hard and shrewd. "Maybe we'll meet later, on different sides. But for now, please do not let me down. Yann will sail with you. He knows the water. And take who you want, for the ride. I heard Bianca Dufy is in town." He smiled, a pint-sized beacon of grandfatherly charm.

I said, "I am honored."

He said, "It is me who is honored. To prove it, I'll pay you a fee, win or lose, and a win bonus." He laughed, because we both knew we knew what we were doing and honor did not come into it anywhere. He named a fee that would cover the yard bill and pay for a ferry home. Then he became businesslike. "Get yourself up to Sables d'Olonne when you can. Or send Bianca to fetch her. There'll be a crew. And if you see Thibault, tell him I'm cross."

I said, "You don't know where Thibault is?"

He said, "No." Again the eyes hung on too long. "I think he is being stupid," he said. "In fact . . ." He looked at his hands; square, short, efficient hands. "If Thibault turns up, the two of you can sail the race. And if he doesn't turn up . . . maybe you should pretend he is on board anyway. Could you arrange this?"

"Probably," I said. "Why?"

"He's the local boy," said Feuilla. "That will have its influence. I should be grateful."

If we won, it would be Thibault who got the credit, not me. But Feuilla was an influential man, and one good turn deserves another. And just at the moment, Mick Savage was suffering from a lack of influential friends.

We climbed into the chopper.

"On y va," said Feuilla.

He flew me back to La Rochelle. As we got out of the chopper, he shook my hand. His palm was clammy. His face looked gray in the lights, his lips blue. I went back to the restaurant sink.

By the time the place was clean, it was one A.M. I poured a glass of the cooking burgundy on top of Feuilla's champagne, and went upstairs.

The exhaustion always hits you the day after a big trip. On the final flight of stairs, my knees were so far gone that I did not think I would make the door.

The apartment smelled most wonderfully of women. The lights were out. I sat down on my bed and went through my pockets. Never leave anything in your pockets, the mother had said. If it's money it will put temptation in the way of the servants, and if it's anything else, they'll throw it out, lazy good-for-nothing sluts every last one of them. Not that there had been any servants.

I put the coins in a pile, and stacked the papers. On top, I left the piece with the insurance broker's name Bianca had scrawled on the bar: Agences Giotto.

I laid my head on the pillow, and it was morning.

The telephone directory told me Agences Giotto was in the Port des Minimes.

Apart from me, the flat was empty. It was ten o'clock. Gloom weighed me down as I remembered I was not on speaking terms with Frankie, and why. I crept downstairs, looking for coffee. Frankie was helping the blind woman install her false eyelashes. The blind woman was getting her old heart started with coffee and cognac. Frankie looked at me from the side of her long eyes, stuck her nose in the air.

I said, "Your friend Jean-Claude's a thug."

She said, "You went for him."

The gloom intensified. I ignored it. I said, "Listen to me. He carries a knife. I found him at Thibault's house yesterday, and he tried to use it on me. I don't want you to see him anymore."

"Oh," she said. There was a note in her voice that made it clear what she thought of what I wanted. "Do you seriously expect me to believe all this rubbish?"

"Yes."

Five years ago, just after I had left Circus Kraken, Mary Ellen had shown me Frankie's bedroom at Butler's Wharf. There was a shelf of scrapbooks, going back over ten years. The scrapbooks were full of newspaper clippings about the maritime exploits of Michael Savage.

But that had been five years ago.

She said, "I don't believe a word of it." Her face was red. "And you know why not? Because I think you're jealous."

"What?"

"You're bloody jealous. Mummy said. She said that when I started going out with a bloke, when I fell in love, you'd get furious, because it would mean that you're not the center of the universe anymore, not that you ever have been. She says you've spent too much time on your own, on your boats, only thinking about yourself."

I said, "I'm not trying to lecture you—"

"Oh, yes, you are."

I took her wrist. "Listen—"

"Go on, then," she said. Her eyes were blazing. "Bash me one. Get it out of your system."

I let go of her.

"Thank you," she said. "By the way, who told you who to go out with when you were my age?"

That was a good one.

When I had been her age, I was running my own charter boat out of Antigua, and nobody had told me to do anything for two years.

She gave me the superior Canadian look and marched out of the room.

The blind woman's name was Annie. She told me that young people were always in love, her sightless pupils shifting restlessly inside the dreadful false eyelashes.

I said yes, of course they were, and told myself that being angry got you nowhere.

"Bad guy," said blind Annie. "It's the age. She'll grow out of him."

I said, yes, of course she would. It was just that, speaking as someone who loved her, I was anxious that she should live long enough to get the chance.

8

Agences Giotto occupied the ground floor of a building that looked as if it had been run up last week by someone who had previously designed greenhouses. Those parts of it that were not glass were navy-blue vinyl. Inside, a heavily made-up blond girl was sitting behind a vinyl desk. There were leaflets advertising cheap yacht insurance on a vinyl coffee table. Boats sailed the vinyl walls: yachts, most of them, and a couple of small ships that might have been coasters. SÉCURITÉ EN MER, said a poster. Safety at sea, with Giotto.

The advertisements smelled of hard sell, high volume, low premiums and difficult claims. Somewhere behind all this, there would be a broker with a line to an underwriter, selling his heart out and hoping nobody ran into anything. If there had to be a payout, it would take a long time, and there would be quibbles all the way to the bank. It was not the place I would personally have insured a boat like *Arc-en-Ciel*.

The blonde told me that she thought the broker might have left for lunch, and had I thought of making an appointment? I said no, and got up to march through the office into one of the inner rooms. She picked up the internal telephone, and made me an appointment, double quick, with M. Buffet.

M. Buffet had a flat-top haircut, gold-rimmed glasses above a sincere smile, and a suit made of a form of plastic tweed. He sat me in a deep leather chair, settled back into a padded swiveler, and asked me what he could do for me.

"You are the insurers of a boat called *Arc-en-Ciel*," I said.

His smile widened. He said, "We are part of an extensive chain of retail outlets throughout Europe, monsieur. We insure twenty-six thousand yachts in the west of France alone. If I can, I shall help you." Above the jolly cheeks, his eyes did not look at all helpful. "Perhaps you have a certificate of insurance?"

I had not a certificate of insurance.

"I am the builder of the boat," I said. I explained the difficulties about delivery and payment. "So in the absence of M. Ledoux, I wish to make the claim."

The smile now looked faintly agonized, as if M. Buffet had bitten a lemon. "The insurance is for M. Ledoux, and you wish to make a claim for your own benefit?"

"Correct," I said.

He said, "I regret very much that the only person who may claim is M. Ledoux. Until we hear from him, we are not in a position to help you."

"Has he not spoken to you?"

"No." A pair of chubby white hands came up and adjusted a pile of papers. They drew one off the top like a baccarat dealer slipping a card from the shoe. I was dismissed.

I was not surprised that he would not pay out. But I was surprised that Thibault had not been in touch. When you are flat broke, and your boat has been smashed up, the first people you talk to are your sponsor and your insurer. Thibault's nature was not a reticent one.

As I walked out into the reception area, a long Mercedes pulled up outside. A squat, dark driver opened the back door. Two men got out. The first was deeply tanned, with a palm-tree mop of dyed blond hair and Bermuda shorts with a design of frangipani. He looked left and right, and said something to someone who was in the back seat. The man in the back seat got out.

He had black hair oiled into crinkles. He had a handsome Latin face, thickened by prosperity, the cheeks showing early signs of sliding into the neck. He was wearing a tan linen suit. The driver and the blond man formed up behind him. He pushed the door open. They came into the office.

The receptionist looked up as if she was being electrocuted. "M. Crespi," she said.

He gave her a big mechanical smile, without breaking step. He and his henchmen went straight through into the inner office.

"Crespi?" I said.

"The proprietor." The receptionist looked pink and excited. "He makes a visit."

I said, "Ah."

The proprietor, M. Crespi, was the man who had been in the cockpit of *White Wing* yesterday evening. It had been M. Crespi who had not yielded an inch when Bianca had taken *Arc-en-Ciel* bang across his nose. The men walking behind M. Crespi might have been his private secretary and chauffeur, but they looked a lot more like bodyguards. There are not many insurance brokers who feel the need to be accompanied by bodyguards.

It was twelve when I got back to the Vieux Port, and the pavement tables were full. Gérard was standing by the door, opening and shutting his mouth like a stranded mullet.

I said, "What's wrong with you?"

He said, "Mademoiselle. She's not well."

"Mademoiselle?"

"Frankie."

A hollow developed where my stomach should have been.

I walked quickly to the back. Frankie was behind the bar, polishing glasses with her back to me. Normally her shoulders were straight. Now the blue jersey sagged, and her head seemed to droop.

I knew the posture, and my spirits sank with it. In her infancy, there had been a succession of damaged worms and three-legged mice. She picked them up and looked after them, and they died. Every time they died, Frankie's shoulders sagged, and it was the end of the world.

Mary Ellen had been of the opinion that the arrival of boys would dismantle this emotional switchback. But Mary Ellen had a strong tendency to judge the emotions of other people in the light of her own rocklike steadiness. Frankie was not yet of an age to distinguish between men and three-legged mice. Baz from the garage had been a nice enough guy, if you approved of your fifteen-year-old daughter going out with a twenty-five-year-old greaser with his name tattooed on his knuckles. She had tried to save him from himself. He had accepted her term's allowance and spent it on Sharon from the chip shop. And down had gone the shoulders.

Of course, it was always someone else's fault. This time, the fault was mine. All I could do was say it again. *He's a little crook,* I wanted to say. *I did it for your own good because I love you.*

What I actually said was, "Frankie."

She turned around.

Usually, Frankie's face was what people stuck for words called heart-shaped. Now, the left eye was blackened and closed, the cheek swollen, the lip cracked, the skin purple with bruises.

When I could speak, I said, "What happened?"

She looked at me out of her good eye, wiping mechanically at the glass in her hand. She said, "Accident." Her voice was thick with tears.

"What happened?"

She said, "I hate you."

"What did he do?"

"He said it was my fault you fought him. He pushed me. I fell over. I hit my head on a chair. It wasn't his fault. He was dreadfully sorry. He can't help how he is."

My heartbeat was a hot thump. I was having trouble breathing. I said, "Where does he live?"

She threw the glass she was holding at my head. It missed. She ran out from behind the bar, through the door marked PRIVÉ. I stood cold as ice, listening to the sobs begin as she reached the landing. Gérard oozed alongside, wringing his long beige hands. He said, *"Les femmes, c'est comme ça."*

I went and fetched a dustpan and brush and cleaned up the glass. Then I trudged up the stairs and knocked on her door.

"Go away," she said.

I turned away. Bianca was standing there. She was shaking her head, beckoning. She said, "It is no good talking to her when she's angry."

I took a deep breath, to tell her to mind her own damn business. Then I let it out. She was not interfering. She was intervening, out of kindness. There was a difference. I shoved Frankie and Jean-Claude into a compartment in my mind and shut the door on them. I did my best to grin at her. There were things I wanted to ask.

We sat in the big, greasy armchairs in the living room. She kept her back straight, knees apart, like a dancer.

"Who is M. Crespi?" I said.

She had been smiling, her Etruscan-goddess half-smile. The smile congealed. "Crespi?" she said.

"The man on *White Wing*. The man who owns Agences Giotto."

"I don't know what you are talking about."

I said, "Rubbish."

There was a silence. She said, "You do not understand anything. Not even your daughter." She looked at me through her eyelashes.

It was a primitive attempt at a red herring. I took it as an encouraging sign. I started again. I said, "You do not like Crespi. You take pleasure in making him look stupid."

She shrugged. "So?"

"Why?"

"Because he is a pig. I don't want to talk about this."

I tried a new tack. I said, "Did you look after Thibault's insurance?"

"No."

"Then how do you know about Agences Giotto?"

Her face became perfectly blank. Finally, she said, "Thibault trusted you. So I trust you. There were documents from Giotto in the papers I took from the Manoir."

I said, "So did you know Crespi was the owner of Giotto?"

"No," she said. She did not seem at all interested. "Listen, I'll show you those papers, if you want."

It was another red herring. This time, I could not ignore it. I said, "I thought someone picked them up."

"Thibault told me you are an old friend, but he owes you money. I have to protect his interests."

I said, "Thibault is on the run. Friends are people who help when you are in trouble. I don't carry a knife."

She said, "I see what you mean." She went into her room, closed the door. I watched the panels. When she came out she was frowning, one hand in her hair. She said, "They're gone."

"What do you mean, gone?"

She said, "Someone has taken them." I went into her room. It smelled of her perfume. The top drawer of the dressing table was open. The drawer was empty.

I said, "Who?"

Bianca said, "There were two folders. I put them here last night. Frankie's been in all morning. She doesn't want to talk to you, right? I'll ask her." Softly, she tapped on Frankie's door.

I stepped into my room, which did not smell of perfume. I stood and stared out of the window. The water under the towers looked flat and gray. I could hear their voices, low and confidential. I heard Frankie start to cry, Bianca's voice soothing her. I found I was warming to Bianca. She did not know me. She was loyal to Thibault. That explained everything, except why she had called Crespi a pig.

"Bon," said Bianca. "Get some sleep, OK?"

"The bar," said Frankie.

"Nobody wants you in the bar with your face like that."

I walked out of my room. Frankie saw me through her open door, turned away, closed it. Bianca said quickly, "Jean-Claude was here this morning, in the flat with Frankie. There has been nobody else."

I said, "I think I'll have a word with Jean-Claude."

She said, "He lives in Saint-Agrève."

"Where's that?"

"She didn't tell me. Not a street. I guess it's an apartment block."

I went downstairs to the bar and asked Annie the blind woman.

"Out of town a little," she said. "By the cemetery. A big building of apartments. Perhaps six hundred of them. You have a number?"

"No number," I said.

The sun came out as I walked out of town. Saint-Agrève was a square of pink-and-buff buildings, arranged around a compound of yellow gravel that glared and shimmered in the fierce Atlantic light. There was a smashed plastic chair on the gravel. Two children were fighting in a corner, swearing in high, shrill voices.

There were five lobbies with letterboxes. There were surnames on the letterboxes. I did not know Jean-Claude's surname, so I bought a *Ouest-France* from a shop next to a tombstone merchant, went back to the apartment block, and sat among a carpet of broken beer bottles in the shade of the garbage hut. All the entrances opened off the central courtyard. It was a good spot.

It was half past four. People were beginning to drift back from work. The women wore light dresses, the men overalls or sports jackets and permanent-press trousers, the uniform of minor office workers. I hoped that in my baggy jeans and T-shirt I looked enough like a workman not to be worth a second glance.

By five-fifteen, I had read the first page of the paper. There was a drought in the Charente. Working for Justin, I had done enough hanging around on doorsteps not to get impatient. The trick is to read the story one word at a time, moving your lips. That way you make it last, and passersby think you are stupid enough to ignore.

At five-twenty a motorcycle buzzed through the litter like a yellow hornet. There had been a lot of bikes, but so far not many yellow ones. The rider was wearing black leathers and a white helmet.

I held the newspaper up all the way. The rider pushed his machine into an asbestos-roofed shed, and crunched across the gravel in his hobnailed boots, pulling off his helmet as he came, flicking back his dark forelock. He had a straight nose. He was whistling through his sulky lips. The lips Frankie loved to kiss.

I stood up, folded the newspaper and stuck it in the back pocket of my jeans. My heart was beating faster than it should have been. I stepped forward, and said, *"Salut."*

I had forgotten his reflexes. He looked at me and started running, his hobnails crashing on the concrete. He ran into the building.

I ran after him.

9

*T*here was a lobby. There were five or six people, talking. At the back of the lobby was a row of lifts with gray metal doors. None of them was open. He ran straight past the lifts, barged open a door, and vanished. The inhabitants of Saint-Agrève had seen this kind of thing before. They continued their conversations, shifting casually aside as I ran after him.

There were stairs behind the door. The boots were ringing on the next flight up. I kept close to the wall, my sneakers quiet on the treads. Above, the boots stopped. I stopped, too. For a moment the only sound was the thump of my heart.

Something sailed down the narrow well and landed with a wet smack on the banisters. A gob of spit. The anger started back. I began to creep up, step by step. The boots stayed silent. Hold it, you bastard, I thought.

He coughed. The noise rang around the cement walls. Then he laughed, a gibbonlike screech. *"Te voilà, beau-papa!"* he yelled. There you are, father-in-law. He started to run.

The stairwell rang with the sound of his boots. One flight above, a door-spring wheezed. The boots no longer roared. I pounded up the last two flights, caught the door before it shut, yanked it open. There was a long cement corridor, lined with doors. Seven doors down on the left, the heel of a boot flicked around a jamb and vanished.

The blood was hammering in my head. Easy, I thought. You know where he lives. Walk along nice and easy, take the number. *The number of the flat where he brought Frankie,* yelled the voice in my mind.

I shoved my hands in my pockets. I walked nice and easy, quiet as a mouse. Get the number, call the cops. Leave it to the proper authorities. This yobbo has stolen some papers, property of Thibault Ledoux. Thank you, officer. The little voice in my mind was screaming that I was a coward. I told it to shut up. I had enough on my mind. The police could take care of this. The number on the door was 507. There was a spyhole. All right, I thought. Got you. I started to turn away.

The door burst inward. Two men came out, fast as cannonballs. One of them was Jean-Claude. I did not have time to look at the second one, because his head was coming at my nose. I turned aside and caught his skull on the cheekbone. My head rang. Somebody hit me in the stomach. I doubled up forward. Someone yanked me into the apartment. There was a low table in the way. I fell through it with a splintering crash. The door slammed. My ribs heaved as I gulped air.

They were coming at me across the white tile floor, one either side, so I could not concentrate on both of them at once. I rolled up on to my knees. My hand closed on a black iron tableleg with splinters of wood attached. I threw it at the one who had tried to head-butt me. He had a brown crewcut. The whirling end of it caught him on the top of the forehead. He crashed back into the door, blood falling across his eyes in a glossy red curtain. That's you, I thought.

But there was no time for feeling smug, because Jean-Claude had come up on the blind side and kicked me hard on the side of the thigh.

I rolled away from the table. My leg felt as if he had been hacking it with a blunt axe. Silver light flashed from his steel toeplate as he aimed one at my head. I ducked, grabbed his ankle as the boot went past, heaved. He went down. I got halfway up, tried to stamp on his leg, but I could not stand properly, and he was crawling away. There was a kitchen behind a little breakfast bar. He crawled in there. I tried to crawl after him, but my leg was still not working, and I had to keep an eye on his friend, who was groping at his face, trying to claw his way out from behind his mask of blood.

Next door, someone was singing snatches of opera. The lift whined in its shaft. Life was entirely normal in Saint-Agrève. Except that in 507, Jean-Claude and his friend were killing an Irishman.

I climbed to my feet. Crockery splintered in the kitchen. Jean-Claude came around the breakfast bar. There was a long kitchen knife in his right hand, edge up, in the disemboweling position. He was grinning now, a nasty, jumpy grin. My stomach felt weak and nervous. "I do it to you slow," he said in English. "Frankie like it slow. I do it the same way to Daddy."

The cold in my stomach went. It felt as if someone had lit a fire down there. There was a sofa. I threw a cushion at him. He stood there and laughed at cushions. I could breathe now, and the leg he had kicked was bearing weight. I threw another cushion, grabbed the curtains. He came toward me, shuffling like a crab, knife out in front. I pulled the curtains hard. They came down, rail and all. I threw it at him.

They were cheap nylon objects, covered with orange flowers. They fell over his head. I grabbed him. We spun like ballroom dancers. He made a nasty sound, lurched sideways, slashing at the fabric. The window was behind him now, a sheet of plate glass that stretched from floor to ceiling. Outside the window was a balcony. Beyond the balcony, the houses and towers of La Rochelle stretched to the blue sheet of the sea. I caught hold of his leather jacket and his knife wrist, and flung him at the window.

The glass went with a huge, jangling crash. He dropped the knife and sprawled through the frame, hit the balcony rail with a thump that shook the apartment. His feet left the concrete. The knife clattered into the yard below. I went through the hole in the window and grabbed him by the collar of his leather jacket. He was doubled up over the rail. I shoved his collar until he was just past the point of balance.

There were more children in the yard, now, playing football. The clatter of the knife stopped them. Their faces became pale disks as they looked up. *What if he falls?*

I said, "Where are those papers?"

He said, "Papers?" He was looking at seventy feet of nothing, with hard-packed yellow gravel at the bottom of it. Broken glass winked in the gravel.

I jerked his collar. He lurched further over the rail. He was all the way over now, weight on his upper thighs, head down, only my hand on his collar holding him. I said, "You stole them from Frankie's flat. Tell me. Or I let go."

Jean-Claude made a quick decision. He said, "Garbage can."

I pulled him back a couple of inches, but not far enough to make him feel safe. "Who told you to steal them?"

"Arthur."

"Arthur who?"

He did not answer. I gave him a little shove. He swung outward over the abyss. "Arthur who?"

He did not answer. Instead, he wrenched sideways, trying to get out of the grip. But he had miscalculated. He rocked forward, too far, still twisting. I felt his weight come suddenly on the collar of his jacket. His legs flew up. His boots caught the sun as they clattered over the rail. He was dangling off the balcony by the collar of his jacket. The football players screamed. So did he.

My fingers were opening.

Oh, no, I thought. I will protect myself against knives, but I do not wish to kill anyone. I reached down with the other hand, looking for a grip. He spun, grabbing for the edge of the balcony. As his arm went up, it slid out of the sleeve of his jacket, so he was hanging by a single sleeve now, groping at the balcony with the other hand.

He did not find a handhold. There was a sound of tearing

cloth. The sleeve by which he was hanging split all the way down the seam.

He fell.

The footballers screamed again. He twisted in the air, hit the balcony rail of the flat below, rolled off, fingers scrabbling for the rail. They missed. He fell on, feet first. The feet landed inside the balcony of the next-but-one down, caught.

He fell into the balcony.

There was a crash of breaking glass. The footballers cheered. Somewhere, someone was still screaming. I felt sick. *Let him not be dead,* I thought.

Behind me, a foot crunched on broken glass.

I turned.

Jean-Claude's flatmate was standing inside the threshold, balanced on the balls of his feet, gazing at me between eyelids clotted with blood. There was a big shard of glass in his right hand.

"Now I cut off your head," he said. He took a step toward me.

I still felt sick. My knees were shaking. I took a step back. He took a step forward. The balcony rail was pressing into the small of my back. I could feel the void behind me. His teeth were white in his brown face. He was keeping his distance, leading with the chunk of broken glass. My daughter's friends certainly knew how to handle their blades.

My mind told me, go forward. Go for him.

But my body had done enough fighting, and it would not do what my mind instructed.

A trickle of blood ran out of the crewcut and into the dog-brown eyes. He blinked.

I put my head down and charged.

It was a pathetic move, by the standards of advanced streetfighting. But he had an eyeful of blood, and he was not ready for it. I hit him in the stomach, thirteen stone of muscle and bone. He slammed back into the wall and slid down. The shard of glass fell out of his hand, and he started making sounds as if he had suddenly forgotten how to breathe and was trying to teach himself in a hurry.

The garbage can was in the kitchenette. I picked it up and emptied it on to the tiles. The folders were between the liner and the outside of the bucket. As I gathered them up, police sirens were howling across the rooftops. I rinsed Jean-Claude's blood off my hands, tucked the folders under my arm and went out of the door, down the stairs, and out of the back of the apartments.

Someone had planted trees out there, and put polythene around their bases to keep the moisture in the La Rochelle sand. The plastic was torn, flapping in the breeze off the sea. I limped quickly away. Tires screamed, and sirens wailed in the yard.

I turned on to the main road. There were taxis waiting like black crows in the cemetery entrance. I climbed aboard one, and told the driver to take me to the Vieux Port.

10

I slumped in the back seat of the taxi. Stonemasons' shops and little gray houses wound past in a dizzying strip. A sign said PAPETERIE PHOTOCOPIE. I banged the driver on the shoulder. "Stop," I said.

He stopped. He looked at me with disgust. Another lunchtime drunk, he was thinking.

"Moment," I said.

The girl in the shop looked at me, then looked away again, frowning. She photocopied the contents of the folders, and patted the loose leaves fussily into a brown envelope. I leaned on the counter and tried not to be sick into a display of pencils. When I paid her, my fingers did not want to hold the money. I staggered back to the cab on rubber legs.

"Station," I said.

He took me to the station. He wanted to be paid, fearful that I was getting on a train. I left my wallet with him, lurched to the left luggage, and shoved the copies into an automatic locker. He took me back to the restaurant.

I went in through the kitchen entrance and straight up the

stairs. I slammed the original folders on the table. There were bloody fingermarks on the brown card.

The face in the bathroom mirror kept going in and out of focus. The chin looked bruised under the reddish stubble, but most of the blood belonged to Jean-Claude's flatmate. I washed it off, went and sat at the table to read the folders.

I was tired and shaking. My eyes would not focus. It was hard to read. I rested my hot forehead on the cool oilcloth.

Terrible things were happening. Thibault was underwater with Frankie and Bianca, sitting around a table with a lamp in the middle. They were playing cards, except that the cards were not playing cards, but pieces of paper out of the folders. They did not seem to know the rules. One of the rules was that every time one of them put a paper on the table, someone in the dark beyond took a step closer. The boots the person was wearing made a metallic crash on the ground. *Wake up,* I was shouting.

Because the light was shining on something in the person's hands. It was a giant Opinel knife. The person was Jean-Claude.

Wake up, I shouted again.

The boots crashed again.

It was me who woke up.

It was not Jean-Claude's boots. It was the telephone.

I staggered across the room and picked it up. It seemed heavy as lead.

"Georges," said the voice. "From the yard."

"What is it?" I was having difficulty remembering who Georges was, what yard he was talking about.

"Your boat," said the voice.

"Everything all right?"

"The work goes well." His voice was cautious. "I think you must come down."

"Now?"

"It's important," said Georges. There was a note in his voice that stirred up the porridge that had replaced my brain.

"Sure," I said.

It took me two tries to get the telephone back on the hook. I kicked off my clothes, blundered into the shower, and turned on the cold water. That helped. I turned on the hot, too hot, and then cold again. Then I lurched into some clothes and walked stiffly downstairs to the bar.

Gérard peered at me, horror in his eyes. He said, "You're hurt."

I said, "Coffee." It felt like a long sentence.

The coffee helped even more than the shower. After the second, I felt almost conscious.

The restaurant van was around the back. It took ten minutes to get to the yard. Georges was in the office, face haggard and nicotine-yellow, squinting against the smoke of his Gitane.

He opened a drawer in his desk and pulled out a vaguely tubular fitting, made of yellowish metal. "Look at it," he said.

I got my eyes to focus. It was a 150mm engine-cooling water seacock. I would have recognized it in a blacked-out room, because it was the type Savage Yachts fitted to their boats. I turned it over, looked at the brand name. It was the right brand, too. The clouds began to roll away from my brain. I felt cold, and my hand was shaking. It was the same as the one in *Arc-en-Ciel*. It was broken off, the same way as the one in *Arc-en-Ciel*. But it could not have been the one from *Arc-en-Ciel*.

I said, "Give me your knife."

He passed me over a bone-handled Laguiole. I flicked it open, pared at the bronze fitting with the heel of the blade. I used very little pressure. Crumbs of metal fell to the blotter. The bronze was perhaps as strong as rotten wood.

"No zinc," said Georges.

"So?"

He looked at his cigarette packet. It was empty. He crumpled it, threw it into the bin, pulled the silver foil out of a new one that was ready on his desk. "It is from *Arc-en-Ciel*," he said.

My stomach felt as if it was full of cement. "Don't be bloody stupid," I said.

"That's what I told Guy the fitter," he said. "How can this be, on a new boat?"

I opened my mouth. I shut it again. There was no way this could be, on a new boat.

Seacocks are made of bronze, which is an alloy of copper

and zinc. Exposed to sea-water, bronze is subject to electrolysis, which means that the salt water becomes a battery solution, in which the zinc in the bronze is the anode, and the iron in the propeller shaft the cathode. If you do not put an earth wire on your seacock or your propeller, in time the zinc atoms are pulled out of the bronze and deposited on your steel propeller shaft, leaving behind a crumbling mass of porous copper.

In time. In a year, maybe. But *Arc-en-Ciel* had only been afloat for a week.

Georges said, "Maybe you use a second-hand fitting?"

I said, "Do me a favor."

He shrugged, and blew smoke. "So what the hell is going on?"

I said, "Was there an earth wire on this?"

"Yes." The earth wire is there to drain current off the metal fittings.

"Zinc anode?" The anode is a zinc ingot, sacrificial, to take care of anything left over from the electrical bonding.

He said, "The anode was new. In good condition."

My brain fizzed like an old radio with a valve loose. It was entirely impossible. I said, "Let's have a look."

He got up. The evening air was warm as milk. We threaded our way between the chocked yachts to the far side of the slip where *Arc-en-Ciel* stood on a patch of oil-stained concrete, her sleek black hull propped with balks of timber. We went up the ladder and over the side. The engine was under the cockpit floor. Georges switched on a working light. We went below.

They had taken out the upholstery and scraped back the worst of the varnish to the clean white timber. When we had brought her ashore she had looked derelict. Now she merely looked half built. It was an improvement.

He rummaged in a toolbox by the open engine hatch. "Here's the other piece."

The other piece was the ring of bronze that had lined the orifice in the plastic hull. I took the seacock in one hand, the ring in the other, fitted them together. It was a clean fracture. Clean as a whistle. First bang, and off she comes—

But there had been no bang.

I took the pieces on deck. There was an inspection light up

there. I put the broken ends under the light. The crystalline structure of the metal glittered dull gold under the filament. Here and there on the inside of the tubing, streaks of silver shone.

There should not have been any streaks of silver.

I said, "Even if it was dezincified, why would it break then?"

Georges said, "Maybe it got hit?"

Yann had been below. Yann could have hit it. But Yann would have been committing suicide. Besides, there were the streaks of silver.

I said to Georges, "You'd better fit a new seacock, check the others and the anode."

"Sure," said Georges.

"I'll keep this one," I said. "You got a metallurgist in town?"

We walked back to the office. He gave me the telephone number of a metallurgist. He was looking embarrassed, the way a boatbuilder looks at another boatbuilder who has been installing garbage on his boats.

I did not mention his bill, and nor did he.

I rang the metallurgist from his desk. His name was Docteur Kerdelo, and he was working late. I loaded my aching body into the van, booted the accelerator, and headed for his office.

It was a specialist foundry, out by the cranes of La Pallice. Kerdelo met me out of the lift. He had a brushcut and a long, shrewish nose. "More titanium?" he said. "Georges is always on about titanium."

I pulled the broken seacock from my pocket. I said, "This."

He peered at it, and muttered, looked up at me over his glasses. "Electrolyzed bronze," he said. "On the inside. In the tube, something else."

He took me into a tidy laboratory with a Formica workbench and a faint, sour smell of reagents. It was late, but he was not a man to be rushed.

He took a pipette, shook up a solution of some sort of acid, laid a drop on one of the bright streaks on the broken seacock. "Zinc," he said.

I stared at him. "What?" I said.

"The inside of the tube has been zinc plated," he said. "Look." He pulled a microscope across the bench, adjusted the objective, stood back, fingering the end of his shrew's nose.

I looked. There were several silver streaks. They looked as if they had been smeared on the inside of the seacock casting. I said, "That's not possible."

"It is, however, the case," said Kerdelo, and looked pleased with himself.

I said, "What would be the point of plating the inside of a seacock with zinc?"

He picked up one of the halves, and scrutinized it. "Mechanically fractured," he said. "It is not easy to guess. Unless, of course, someone electrolyzed the object, fractured it and galvanized the interior with zinc in order to stick the two halves together. But of course as soon as it is immersed in seawater, well . . ." He laughed. "So it is not probable," he said.

I grinned at him as best I could. What would happen if the seacock was immersed in water was that electrolysis would begin, and the plating would melt away nice and slow, over a period of a few days.

Slap in the middle of the Bay of Biscay, for instance.

Kerdelo showed no curiosity, and I did nothing to arouse it. I took the metal parts, told him to present himself and companion for a free dinner chez Thibault, and hobbled to the lift. I stabbed the button, and stared at the wall, and tried to believe what I had seen with my own eyes.

It was not easy.

Until now, there had been in the back of my mind the idea that the failure of the seacock had been a catastrophic accident, caused by a dud casting or freak metal fatigue. Now, there was no getting away from it.

In order to sink *Arc-en-Ciel,* someone had removed her engine-cooling water seacock, suspended it in a salt solution with an iron cathode, subjected it to big current until it was the consistency of rotten wood, and broken it with a hammer. Then they had galvanized its innards and screwed it back into the boat.

There was only one reason they would have done this. They wanted to make quite sure the seacock was going to fall off, leaving a hole the size of a baby's head five feet below the waterline. If the wreck had been recovered, the zinc plating would have been long gone, and Savage Yachts would have been world famous for installing dud seacocks. It had very nearly been a very neat time bomb.

Someone said, "Which floor?" I realized I was standing in the lift with the doors open. I walked slowly to the van. It felt like walking through quicksand.

I sat in the van, and thought about what could have happened. It made me feel even iller than I felt already. After a while, I drove back toward the Vieux Port, slowly.

Someone had wanted to sink the boat, and did not care whether or not the crew got drowned. Originally, Thibault had been going to make the delivery himself. I had agreed to go ten days before we had sailed.

So it all boiled down to when the dud seacock could have been installed.

We had had a survey two weeks before the launch. Everything had been fine then. After that, there had been the usual chaos of boat-finishing. Savage Yachts had no reason for high security, and a lot of outside contractors who came and went as they pleased.

Anyone could have done it.

Anyone who wanted to get rid of me, or who wanted to get rid of Thibault.

Or who wanted to get rid of the boat, and did not care who went with it.

There was only one reason for that: to turn a boat into cash, via the magic of insurance.

Bianca had said that there were papers from Agences Giotto in the folders I had reclaimed from Jean-Claude.

I drove to the station, opened my left-luggage locker, and took out the copies I had made. Then I went back to the flat.

The originals were lying on the oilcloth of the table in the flat where I had left them. The living room was dark. There was a light under Frankie's door. I shouted, "Evening!" She did not answer.

I said, "You there?"

The door opened. She came out. The bruises on her face were subsiding. There was a bag over her arm, a pair of boots. My heart lurched. I said, "Are you leaving?"

She said, "Yes." There was a pause. "I'm going to pick up *Plage d'Or* with Bianca for the race." She frowned at me. "What have you done to your face?"

I said, "I had a slight accident." I hesitated. I did not know how to say what I had to say. So I said it straight out. "I don't want you to see Jean-Claude again."

Her face froze. "I don't want to talk about it," she said.

"And your mother doesn't want you to."

"Leave Mummy out of it."

I said, "He's a thief. He's a gangster. He carries a knife."

She said, "That's just a way of saying he's had bad luck. He's had to fend for himself in life. He hasn't had any rich uncles. You and him . . . you talk different languages." She put her hands on my arm. "Try to understand him," she said. "I love you, Dad. I'd like you two to be friends."

I shut my mouth with a snap. I said, "That's not possible. I think you are being a romantic idiot. I don't want you seeing him again. That's that."

She stuck her chin out. She did not answer. Bloody hell, Savage, I thought. Why did you not learn to talk to people, instead of spending all that time on your own?

But it was too late now. I had told her the truth. I hated myself for it. She felt the same way about me.

She slung her bag on to her shoulder, and walked out.

I said, "Have a good sail."

She banged the door behind her and ran down the stairs.

I sat down in front of the folders.

I did not open them straightaway. I sat there and stared out of the window at the narrow slice of black water between the dark masses of the Tour Saint-Nicolas and the Tour de la Chaine. Out there, the buoy-lights winked their little red eyes, confidingly, as if they knew that Mick Savage was in a big, nasty mess. *He's had to fend for himself. He hasn't had any rich uncles.*

Soon after the Long Net incident, I came downstairs one morning to find a large and sinister trunk gleaming like a midget's coffin in the hall. My father was in the dingy room he used as his study. The air smelled of old drink and new Woodbines, and there were dirty papers a foot thick on the desk.

The papers, he gave me to understand, were something to

do with a book he was writing. The book was called *Heirs of Grania*. He said it was about the destiny of Ireland, and would change a lot of things, at which he frowned terrifyingly in the general direction of the Castle. The book was always about to be finished, but never was. He said, "See that trunk?" His eyes looked boiled, his nose red. "School trunk," he said. "You're off to school. In England. Bloody terrible place. It's your uncle's idea. We can't afford it."

I nodded. I had heard about the school, secretly, from my mother, who must have wanted to prepare me. Since the Long Net, Carthystown had become a place of important silences and averted eyes.

He said, "They're stealing your heritage, boy. And there's nothing I can do. It's bitter. Bitter."

I said, "I don't mind." Actually, I was excited by the idea of getting out of the dark house in the green-black valley, seeing exotic places like Bournemouth.

"I do," he said. "Oh, I do. I don't care what you think." He reached for his bottle. "Well," he said. "We can console ourselves with the notion that you are under the direct influence of the head of the family." He spoke with a twist to his mouth under his beard. Even at the age of seven, I could tell that he did not mean what he was saying.

Two days later, I went off to school.

It was not a bad spot, on the whole. It was based in a large house on the western shore of Poole Harbor. The headmaster was an old man who had been a District Commissioner in Nigeria. He treated the children under his control as if we were a good-hearted, if occasionally warlike tribe. I made a couple of friends, boxed enthusiastically, and sailed in Poole Harbor. I was not particularly good at anything except sailing. Going home for the holidays to the stifling family politics that linked Carthystown with the big house became an ordeal.

The worst part of it was that my parents had decided that since my uncle had taken over my education, they no longer had any say in what would happen. The house was boring. Up at the Castle, there were various cousins of roughly my own age, whom I was bidden to amuse. So every day I would rattle on my bicycle up the two-mile avenue that plunged through the derelict rainforest beside the river and over the bridge to the castle.

By the time I was thirteen, some of the female cousins were beginning to look very attractive. Personally, I was no oil painting. I had a lot of reddish hair, and a nose already showing signs of battering in the boxing ring. I was also nearly six feet tall.

At school, I was meant to be learning to play the piano. The music master had given up the attempt to make me the new Chopin, but the lessons were being paid for. So rather than sit in silence, he had beguiled the minutes by playing boogie-woogie, his big enthusiasm. I had picked up some licks, and practiced them on the piano in the gym. When Uncle James was out of earshot, I lammed into Pinetop Smith and Fats Waller on the out-of-tune grand in the Blue Drawing Room, where Mrs. C. F. Alexander was rumored to have composed "All Things Bright and Beautiful."

I was at it one sweltering overcast evening in August when Murphy, my uncle's secretary, came into the room. Murphy was a pale dark Dubliner with a malicious glint in his eye. He bowed with suspicious deepness to my green-eyed cousin Dervla, who was leaning on me in a fascinating manner. And he said, "Your uncle says would you ever visit him above in the solar?"

The solar was a big circular room on the first floor of the gray stone tower. There was a peculiar smell on the stairs: incense, and garlic, and hot spices. I twisted the heavy knob and went in.

There was a fire. The air was suffocatingly hot, pearly with smoke from two braziers. Uncle James was sitting at a table in front of the fire. He was wearing a red fez over his scanty gray-blond curls. The table was covered in books. He looked up at me. "Welcome," he said. His eyes were like pale blue headlamps, close together on the front of his face. "Welcome to Egypt. Your name is Achmet. Bring me my luncheon."

There was a pan of something on one of the braziers. I walked across the Turkey rug and picked it up.

"No!" he shouted. "Shirt-tails out!"

I said, *"What?"*

"Egyptians," he said. "The peasants are known as fellahin. They wear their shirts outside their trousers, you ignorant boy. It is their *salient characteristic*. My family duties will not permit my . . . physical absence. So I must voyage in the mind. So tiffin, Achmet."

"What?" I said. As far as I knew, tiffin was an Indian word, not Egyptian.

"Shirt-tails out."

I pulled out my shirt-tails. He watched with his blue goggle eyes as I placed the chafing dish between a diagram of the Great Pyramid and the memoirs of an ancestor who had reformed the plumbing system of Alexandria. "You must call me effendi," he said.

"Effendi."

"You are giving me my lunch."

I glanced up. Dervla was standing in the doorway. She had her hand over her mouth. Her eyes had a demonic glitter, and the visible portions of her face were scarlet with laughter.

"Say, 'Tiffin, effendi.'"

My shirt, I thought. And Dervla watching. Dear God, please take me away from here.

"Speak," he said. *"Speak!"*

I tried. Nothing came out. His bellows rang in the solar's vaulting. I wanted to tell him to shut up, keep quiet, stop behaving like a lunatic. But he was the head of the family, directly responsible for me, he had said. And my parents had said it, too. So it must be right. If he wanted to make his mad voyages to an Egypt of the mind, he was allowed to do it.

I said, "Here is your tiffin, effendi." There was a scornful snort from the doorway. Dervla was gone. Uncle James began to eat, his eyes gliding over the dimensions of the Great Pyramid.

Humiliated, I sneaked out of the room, pushed my shirt into my trousers, and pedaled home, away from the crumbling house, through the derelict woods.

With distance came defiance. Pharaoh, I thought. He thinks he's a pharaoh, and my parents are his courtiers and I am his slave. I hated the lot of them, with a pure, clear, thirteen-year-old passion.

* * *

I turned back to the table, and started on the folders.

I could see why Thibault had told Bianca to keep the papers out of the bailiffs' way. There were what looked like title deeds, a couple of bank books with big numbers in them, and a certificate of insurance from Agences Giotto. The name of the boat on the Agences Giotto specimen was *Arc-en-Ciel*. Two weeks ago, he had insured her for $200,000, and paid the first month's premium in advance.

The purchase price of *Arc-en-Ciel* had been £120,000, give or take the odd tenner. Of this he had paid me eighty. He stood to make a nice little profit if there was a tragedy, like the boat going to the bottom, nice and deep, because someone had done a spot of creative welding.

Hold on, I told myself. This is your old friend Thibault Ledoux, not some Greek shipowner trying to catch up with his alimony payments.

I was sweating. I got up, and walked to the window again, and stared out at the blink of the buoys. My head was aching. On the La Baule–Dakar, Jamie Arbuthnot had fallen off the boat ahead of us. Jamie would have been dead in two hours at the outside. But Thibault had sailed sixty miles off-track, done twelve hours of box-search. He had blown the race in the process, to the disgust of our sponsor. I remembered him flogging to and fro, head aching with the glare of the tropical sun on the water, looking for the dark speck, seeing only the glitter. And when we finally turned away and headed south, a new glitter, in the tears of frustration on Thibault's face.

And now Mick Savage was trying to convince himself that this same Thibault was ready to get himself out of money trouble by drowning two of his oldest friends.

I did not believe a word of it.

I sat and waited for the heart to slow down and the palms to dry. And when I had the mind steady, I rang my secretary Mary in England.

She said, "I've been trying to get hold of you."

"I've been here," I said.

"Probably. We've been having trouble with the telephone."

"Did you find the worksheets?"

"Yup."

"And?"

"New 150mm seacocks fitted by Chris Barnes, early June."

Three weeks before the launch. Chris Barnes was the son of Chiefy Barnes, coxswain of the Pulteney lifeboat, an RNLI engineer in his spare time. He would no more fit or wire a dud seacock than I would sail the Atlantic in a washbasin. The surveyor would have inspected it, passed it after fitting.

I said, "Can you do me a list of visitors to the yard for the two weeks before we launched *Arc?*"

Her voice became exaggeratedly patient. She said, "We had about five hundred people through, and you will remember that we don't keep a visitors' book. No can do."

"No," I said. Dead end.

She said, "Have you got any orders?"

"No."

She said, "I've been to the bank." Her voice sounded tight. "Bloody Lenin said there's nothing he can do."

Lenin was Mr. McLennan, the bank manager. "What do you mean?"

She said, "He's pulling the plug. The problem with the telephone was that they'd cut it off."

I knew it was happening, but I still could not believe it. I said, "Who put it on again?"

There was a silence. Then she said, "I found some money."

"Your money."

She said, quickly, "Oh, well, you can't spend it at my age."

She rang off.

I sat and looked at the insurance certificate.

Nobody would pay out to Michael Savage from an insurance in the name of Thibault Ledoux. So Thibault had to claim. But Thibault was not among those present. So I would have to get hold of him. But nobody knew where he was.

But if nobody knew, then nobody would know that I did not know.

So if I made a claim in his name, forging his signature and giving the restaurant as an address, I could intercept the check, endorse it with another of his signatures, and turn it over to Mr. McLennan.

It was fraud, of course. It was the kind of little white lie I had tracked down for Justin Peabody more times than I could remember. Cutting corners. I had never cut a corner in my life.

Just as Thibault had never in his life endangered anyone except himself.

Perhaps everyone had to start somewhere. Get practical, Savage. Forge a signature. Pay your yard bill. It makes no difference.

I took a deep breath.

I had seen his signature on a contract in the folder, as the girl in the stationer's did the copying. I flicked through the papers.

The contract was not there.

Bankruptcy is not good for the concentration, particularly when combined with a good kicking. Perhaps I had missed it, I thought. I went to the kitchen, hooked down a bracing tumbler of burgundy, and returned to the file.

Still no contract.

It had been a long, hard day. I frowned wearily at the folder. It did not help.

The girl in the copy shop had taken the papers out and laid them on the copier. When they came off the machine, she had put them face down on the table. The contract had definitely been in the folder when I had brought it up to the apartment.

And left it with Bianca for the day.

I slit the envelope I had brought back from the station and took out the copies. The contract was there, halfway down, with the signature at the bottom. I laid a thin sheet of white paper over the top, took out a pen and traced it. Savage changes his uniform to survive the war. I was a lousy forger. The signature was nothing like the real one. Still, I thought, practice makes perfect.

So I practiced, scribbling Thibault's signature on a sheet of scrap paper. And as I scribbled, I thought about pitfall traps.

If the contract had been in the file of copies, but not the originals, someone must have taken it out. They must have taken it out between the time I had left the originals on the table, and the time I had got back from Chantiers Albert.

I read the contract. It confirmed that Thibault Ledoux owned a one-third share in Transports Drenec, a company that owned a ship by the name of *Poisson d'Avril*. Fascinating.

My body ached like a tooth. So did the knowledge of Frankie grieving over her hoodlum; and Thibault, who might have conned me. And the fact that Mick Savage, who had so far made his own straight way through a crooked world, was shivering on the brink of fraud.

I poured the last of the burgundy. The second glass tasted better than the first. It oiled the machinery, and I began to think clearly. I took the folder of originals and the folder of copies, and I started to compare them, one against the other, side by side on the red tablecloth.

It took ten minutes. At the end, I had eight sheets left over.

11

They were all to do with Transports Drenec and the ship *Poisson d'Avril*. There was a three-page survey, undertaken by a Marcel Bonnard, classification society's agent at Sainte-Jeanne-des-Sables. There was a document confirming that *Poisson d'Avril* had been chartered from Transports Drenec by Lignes Étoile. There was also a certificate of insurance, based on the survey. The certificate had been issued by Agences Giotto. And there was a letter, confirming that *Poisson d'Avril* had been purchased from a Greek owner for $100,000.

I looked at the insurance certificate. The sum insured was $391,000. The purchase letter and the insurance certificate were dated three weeks apart.

Shipyards are expensive places. Even so, it is very difficult to do $291,000 worth of work on a ship in three weeks.

Last time I had heard of a repair bill that size had been a year ago. Justin had rung me up at the yard. "Funny thing," he had said in his plummy voice. "Ship called *Vida,* bound from Marseilles to Rio, gone down off Cape St. Vincent. Very sudden. Horrible old thing. Heavily insured. Would you have a look?"

So I had flown to Portugal and had a look. And in the course of a hot, nasty week among the tennis courts and lager bars of the Algarve, I had met the crew of the *Vida.*

The Angolan cook had been staying in a chalet by the beach. There had been explosions, he said. Just before the explosions, the first officer had ordered packed lunches for the entire crew. The cook, a simple man, had been indignant. There had been a rumor that the officers had booked in to the Da Gama Hotel in Faro two weeks before the sinking. In his view, this was discrimination. I checked the rumor with the Da Gama, and found it to be true. The insurance claim made by *Vida*'s Singaporean owners had not been paid. Her officers were now in jail, and the owners had changed their names.

I was beginning to understand why Thibault might have wanted these documents relating to *Poisson d'Avril* kept out of the public eye.

What was also interesting was that other people wanted them kept private. Like Bianca. And Arthur, on whose behalf Jean-Claude had stolen them from the flat. Whoever Arthur was.

I pulled the telephone across, and dialed Mary Ellen's number in London. She answered quickly. She always did. The telephone was on the coffee table, facing the sofa. There were three lines, which she used all at once. Behind her, the lights would be wobbling in the black and oily Thames. "Oh," she said. I could imagine the movement of her hands as she pushed the hair back from her fine-boned face. "It's you."

My heart sank. We had cooperated over Frankie's upbringing. During the week, she had lived with Mary Ellen. At weekends and for holidays, she came to Pulteney. It was like the rest of my relationship with Mary Ellen. Most of the time, we managed to pull in roughly the same direction. When we did not, there was no chance of compromise. I said, "Something's come up."

She said, "So Frankie's been telling me." Her voice was rough at the edges, as if it was taking her most of her strength simply to hang on to herself.

I said, "Frankie has got a very bad boyfriend. You wouldn't like him."

She said, "I wouldn't hit him. For God's sake, can't you control yourself?"

I said, "She rang you."

"She rang. Justin rang. If you didn't like the bloke, surely you could talk about it with her?"

I said, "This afternoon, he tried to cut my throat."

She said, "You should bloody well know your daughter well enough to realize that the more fuss you make the tighter she'll hang on." She paused. Then she said, in a new voice, "Cut your *throat?*"

"That's right."

"Over Frankie?"

"Partly."

She was sounding worried. She said, "Where is she now?"

I said, "Sailing."

"Without the boyfriend?"

"Without the boyfriend."

She said, "You've got some explaining to do."

"Not now. It's . . . stabilized." Jean-Claude could well be dead, or in hospital, but that was not going to be much consolation to Mary Ellen. I said, "There's an insurance matter."

"Oh?" She sounded wary and exasperated.

"A ship called *Poisson d'Avril.*"

"*Poisson d'Avril* means April Fool," she said. "It's nearly August."

I said, "Don't be stupid. This is serious."

She drew breath to tell me to go to hell. Then she let it out again. *"Poisson d'Avril,"* she said. Her voice was steady and businesslike, perhaps even faintly penitent. Insurance was insurance. "No," she said. "Never heard of it. Why don't you ask Justin?" Then she said, in a voice to which the edge was returning, "And for goodness' sake look after Frankie. I suppose you know what you are doing but I want her back in one piece." She put the telephone down.

It was a retreat, of a kind. We were back in equilibrium. I knew what I was doing, more or less.

The pain in my body and mind had come back, double strength. I gathered up the photocopies, crawled into bed, and blacked out.

Uncle James had delighted in manipulating my hopes and desires. One moment, I was the hope of the family; the next, I was a villainous gurrier. By the time I was fifteen, I had realized that he did not give a damn about me either way, and his teasing was a cruel little game he played because he had too much power and too little to do with it.

My father had gone away on some mysterious Republican errand, and been run over by a lorry. Little had changed in my mother's life; she floated through the dingy, increasingly musty rooms of the little house in Carthystown like a wraith. I had been away at school when my father died. I came back for the funeral, which had been small and dismal. He had been excluded from the family vault, and planted in a cemetery of shiny black granite stones canted on a mountainside above the village. There had been a pile of paper-ash in the fireplace, which I had presumed was the *Heirs of Grania*. The desk was clear, and the room was cold and damp. It was near the end of term, so Uncle James told me to stay and keep my mother company. But the house was cold and full of the relations who had congregated for the funeral, and my mother was not interested in seeing me. There was a sort of reception at the big house. I had dodged away early and headed for the woods with my cousin Dervla.

Dervla had taken me up into a cave, where she had demonstrated the art of kissing. She was at school in Dublin nowadays. She looked at me with her acid-green eyes. "You don't know anything," she said.

I said, "What do you mean?"

"Either you're at school in England with a lot of boys," she said. "Or you're buried down here." I did not point out that she was no better off herself. Dervla lived in Dublin, which she regarded as an advanced city full of culture.

I said, "Shut up." I kissed her again. Her tongue was a wonderful thing. Her arms were wrapped around my neck, and her breath was hot in my ear. She had real breasts. I had never held anything like her in my life.

Someone was wailing in the dark-green thicket of ponticums. It was a Carthystown voice, high and frantic. Dervla rolled away.

"Dead," the voice wailed. "Oh, Gods, he does be dead!"

"Shut up," said another voice, more controlled. It was Murphy, Uncle James's secretary. "Miss Dervla!" he said, with the coo of a calculating dove. "Michael! Are you above?"

Dervla brushed her skirt down. She looked pink and flushed, though not as pink and flushed as I felt. Murphy emerged from the thicket. He was wearing a black tie. "Bad news," he said. "Your Uncle James has fell off his bicycle. He is dead, God rest his soul."

"Oh!" said Dervla, and started to cry.

Piecing it together, I found out that Uncle James had drunk a lot of whiskey, and whimsically decided on a bicycle ride to clear his head. Wobbling through the woods, he had ridden straight over a low cliff, and been killed instantly.

I felt shocked, and solemn. Solemnity gave way to gloom. He was bound to have cooked up some form of embarrassing ritual for his funeral, and given me a leading part in it.

The relations were still crowding the house in the village, whispering about the evil of it all, two brothers in so short a time. I felt as if I were suffocating. Whiskey was drunk, and solemn statements made. Dervla would not come to the cave, out of respect for the dead. The funeral was on Thursday.

On the Thursday morning, a watery-eyed solicitor from Wicklow came to the house. I sat at the dining-room table, and listened while he told my mother that my father had left me ten thousand pounds, for my own immediate use, no member of the family to have any say in how it was spent.

To my mother, he bequeathed the house in Carthystown, and the manuscript of *Heirs of Grania*—"The which," he said, "shall be provision for her old age."

The grate was clean. The ashes were in the bin. There was

no copy. Besides which, the book had undoubtedly been very bad.

She was yellowish-pale, like old ivory. "And the rest of the money?" she said.

The solicitor cleared his throat. "The rest of the money amounts to three hundred and one pounds," he said.

There was a long, horrible silence. Then my mother looked at me down her long, high nose. "I wash my hands of you," she said, as if it were my fault. "Get away to the big house. God knows there's two tyrants dead. I'll have no more in this place."

I left. I mooched into Carthystown Street. What the *Dungarvan Leader* would have called a large and representative attendance was milling around the Protestant church. I had lost my family, it seemed. I was fifteen. I hated families.

The church bell started to ring. The crowd stirred expectantly. I marched through to the front, where a black car was spewing cousins into the lych-gate. We walked into the church. Dervla was there, in black, ignoring me. We walked to the pews at the front. They faced crosswise, placed that way by past generations of Savages who wished to study their co-religionists. My mother kept her eyes away from me, white with jealous fury. I wanted to say something to her, but I knew she would not listen.

A black door stood open on the far side of the church, in the south transept, beyond the coffin. The Dean of Clonmel began to mumble. The door was the door of the Savage vault.

A lot of mumbling later, the bearers picked up the coffin and hauled it into the vault. The family followed, and Murphy, the secretary. He was carrying a black bag, of the kind used by old-fashioned doctors.

The bearers slid the coffin on to the shelf. From the black bag, Murphy pulled a bottle of Jameson's whiskey. He peeled off the foil and placed the bottle beside the coffin. Beside the bottle he put a glass. In the glass was a key, with a label. The label said VAULT.

Uncle James had been terrified of being buried alive.

Something was happening to me. It was as if my mind were full of bubbles. They rose through the dull, dismal crowd, the rotten coffins, the whole bloody stupid charade that had been Uncle James, head of the bloody stupid charade of the Savage family. There was only one way for the bubbles to get out.

I started laughing.

The laughter bounced around the vault like a flock of parrots. Tears were squirting from my eyes. There was a horrified silence. The silence made it funnier.

I staggered hooting into the church. I walked down the aisle, through the smell of ill-dried funeral suits. I stole a bicycle from outside the Cruiskeen Lawn. I caught several buses and a train, and got to the office of the solicitor in Wicklow. There, I possessed myself of three thousand pounds in banknotes, and sent a check for seven thousand pounds to my mother. Then I climbed on a boat to the West Indies.

I was fifteen, and I had left it all behind, and I was never going to let families make me miserable again.

It was the telephone that woke me. The quay was buzzing outside, and the light that filled the room looked more like after lunch than after breakfast.

I rolled out of bed and grabbed the receiver. My mouth was gluey. The voice on the other end said, "Who's that?" A man's voice. Official.

I told him my name.

"Police," he said.

"Wha'?" I said.

"I'm sending an officer around," said the voice. "Don't go anywhere."

"Ah," I said.

He rang off.

I climbed into the shower. The aches were going. The bruises on my face had subsided, but not far enough to make it possible to shave. I found some clothes and a cup of coffee. Feet sounded on the stairs.

There was one man, in an anorak, polyester slacks and trainers. He had a around head whose roundness was emphasized by a black crewcut. His face had a tough, closed look.

"Jonzac," he said. "Police."

We sat down at the red oilcloth table. He had unfriendly brown eyes that clambered around the room as if they had

seen places like this before, and did not think much of them.
He said, "What were you doing yesterday afternoon?"

I said, "What time?"

"Between four-thirty and six," he said.

"Why?"

He said, "A taxi driver said he brought someone from the cemetery to here. An Englishman who looked as if he had been in a fight."

Irishman, I thought.

"So what are you doing, frightening nice bourgeois in apartment buildings?" The voice was light. The eyes were not.

I decided that the truth was checkable, so the truth was the best policy. I said, "There is a guy who is after my daughter."

"Jean-Claude Dupont."

"How do you know?"

He permitted himself a faint stretching of the mouth. "He's in the hospital, under guard," he said. "He seems to have fallen out of a window. Severe bruising, suspected internal injuries."

"Why under guard?"

He said, "We know the guy."

"How?"

The policeman seemed to relax. He said, "He arrived from the Midi, six weeks ago. We found stuff in his apartment. Amphetamines, mostly. Dangerous little bastard."

I said, "My daughter is of an impressionable age. Dupont attacked me with a knife."

He said, "I understand." He shrugged. "Maybe I would have done the same thing myself. But I must ask you to come to the police station."

I said, "Why not?"

He took me to a green interview room in the station and took a statement, using one finger on a manual typewriter. He had read about me in the papers, it turned out. He had a daughter of his own. He had no difficulties with me as an aggrieved parent. I told him enough to support the impression, and no more. Once I knew I was in the clear, my mind was not on making statements. I sat in that little green room listening to the woodpecker clack of the ancient Underwood, and wondered what Thibault had done to get himself hunted by small-time speedfreaks from the Midi, working for someone called Arthur.

It took all afternoon. Afterward, I bought Jonzac a drink in the Bar Pilote. He told me about his weekend sailing experiences in a fat trailer-sailer, the way people do. And I asked him, as one anxious for his daughter's welfare, to let me know if he found out anything else about Jean-Claude.

We drank up, shook hands, and parted friends. I walked slowly back along the quay to the restaurant. Gérard was there in the bar, panicking. "No oysters today," he said. "No Giselle. Where is Christophe?"

I did not know. I stood behind the bar while he yelled down the telephone. I did not believe that Thibault would deliberately drown his friends. But I did believe that Thibault had got himself into bad trouble, and that he had dragged me and Frankie down with him.

A sensible person would have forged the insurance form, and picked up his daughter, and taken the first plane home.

Blind Annie was in the bar. She was far gone, drooping over her glass of pastis, singing quietly, miles out of tune. She heard me come in. She said, "Where is the beautiful Frankie?"

"Sailing," I said.

"Everyone's on holiday," she said. "Frankie's on the boat. Christophe and M. Thibault have gone to the beach. And M. the Englishman is on holiday in the beautiful town of La Rochelle."

"Irishman," I said. "And it's not a holiday."

She grinned, cracking the paint on her ancient cheeks, and fluttered her great eyelashes in a frightful manner.

I bought her another drink because she reminded me of the barflies in the Cruiskeen Lawn in Carthystown, when things had been miserable but straightforward. Straightforwardness was in short supply just now.

At eight o'clock I left the bar and walked down the quay and on to the pontoon.

Justin's boat was an Oyster Lightwave. I heaved myself aboard and stuck my head down the hatch. Justin and his crew were below, around a beautiful sycamore table. They had been eating. Now they were drinking. Their faces were red with wine and sunburn. "Mikey!" roared Justin. "Come on down, my boy!"

The other people around the table gave me nervous looks. I was someone who had fights in bars. I climbed down the companionway, perched on the bottom step, accepted a glass of wine. "Why aren't you out there racing in that new boat?" said Justin.

"Because the bloody owner's vanished," I said. "Furthermore, someone tried to sink the thing, and it is currently on the slip. I don't want to talk about it. Listen, Justin. Can we have a chat?"

His bright blue eyes were awash with wine, but still shrewd. "Fine," he said. "What about?"

"Bit of business. I'll buy you a cognac."

He got up. He was a great cognac enthusiast. Also, he never turned down an opportunity of doing business. People who owned Oyster Lightwaves had to do a lot of business, to pay for them. "All right," he said, with a show of what I knew was mock reluctance. He told his crew to meet him in the bar at Chez Thibault in half an hour, and jumped heartily on to the pontoon.

I took him around the unfashionable side of the harbor, to the Bar du Nord, one of the last serious drinkers in the port. The barman brought us coffee and brandy. Justin snuffled around in his glass for a while. He talked about races he had nearly won. Then he said, "What's the problem?"

I said, "Have you ever heard of a ship called *Poisson d'Avril?*"

He took a sip of brandy, and pursed his lips like a chimpanzee. "Why?" he said. His eyes had narrowed. I had seen him look that way hovering behind a box at Lloyd's, when he was handing a big chunk of risk to an underwriter with a brain smaller than the knot in his Old Etonian tie. "What do you know about it?"

"I got a whisper," I said.

He rested his big red forehead on his hand, gazing into the amber deeps of his glass. "Funny thing," he said. "Sounds familiar."

"Why?"

"Can't place it," he said. "Rings a bell, though. What about it?"

"Sounds a bit odd," I said. "What if it was a nasty one?"

He looked at me with eyes that were cool and steady in spite of the brandy. He said, "You'd better look into it. See what you can find out. If there's anything wrong, collect some evidence, and I'll take it to the underwriters concerned." He paused. "And we'll split the commission, seventy–thirty in your favor."

"Fine," I said. "Can you keep your ears open?"

"Sure," he said. "Can't promise a lot. Everyone's on holiday. More brandy?"

I said no. What I had already drunk was whanging around in my head like a bat in a garbage can.

He looked at my face hard, clocked the bruises. He said, "Been doing some more fighting?"

"Only a bit," I said. "Same guy. He won't be back."

Justin put his big head back, and laughed fit to rattle the glasses behind the bar. "Well done," he said. "Come on. I insist."

So we drank some more brandy and began to talk about England, yacht racing, prospects. For three minutes, it was like sitting in a bar in La Rochelle when you were on a nice holiday on a nice yacht with some nice friends.

Then the door opened, and a thin man came in. He was dressed like a fisherman, in faded blue canvas jacket and trousers, a black beret pushed down over his nose. He said, *"Messieurs, 'dames,"* went to the bar.

It was Christophe, who brought the oysters to the restaurant. I was not on holiday anymore.

I remembered Annie, in the bar. *Christophe and M. Thibault, gone to the beach.*

I said, "Excuse me, Justin."

He said, "Better be getting back."

I went and leaned on the bar next to Christophe. He looked at me nervously. His face was leather-brown, the chin frosted with white stubble, the eyes under the beret seamed with red. He looked old and worried, and I knew why.

I said, "Will you take me to see Thibault?"

12

*H*e opened his mouth to speak. He looked frightened.

I said, "It's a big problem. It won't go away by itself. You and I are the friends of Thibault. He needs friends."

He stared at the brandy in his glass. Then he nodded. "All right," he said. "Why not?"

I said, "I'll meet you by the Casino in twenty-five miutes."

"Fine," he said.

I walked back to the restaurant.

I went upstairs to the flat, and sat down at the desk. I typed out a letter to Agences Giotto claiming the cost of the repairs to *Arc-en-Ciel,* and clipped on Georges's estimate. Then I strolled downstairs, made my way out of the front of the restaurant, under the loom of the Tour de la Chaine and along the cobbles toward the gaudy lights of the Casino.

The truck was waiting on the wide street that runs along the sea-front, a gray Citroën pickup with a corrugated cab. I climbed in. It smelled of old fish. Christophe drove very fast, swaying through the bright-lit streets, north and west, until the houses thinned into wide-spaced factories, and the factories thinned in their turn, and the cars peeled away, and we were jouncing along a flat, stone-walled lane. From time to time he looked over his shoulder. There were no other cars. The only lights came from the huddle of a village that half-remembered charts told me might have been Esnandes. To the west, the night had the luminous vacancy that comes from the coast of a shallow sea.

The lane turned into a track. At the end of the track, the Citroën's lights swept a line of boats lying in a creek beside a collection of clapboard oystermen's huts with fenced-off cement storage tanks. He parked on a patch of rammed stone, and turned off the lights.

My eyes got used to the dark. La Rochelle was a red bonfire to the south, and Île de Ré twinkled roguishly to seaward. Beyond a sea-wall of boulders, the tide was in, a rustling black sheet of water covering the stakes and cages of the mussel and oyster beds in the shallows of the gently shelving beach. The air smelled of rotting weed and dead shellfish.

Christophe began to walk along the sea-wall toward a shed on its own, silhouetted against the red glow of La Rochelle. He was thin, and he limped. Fishermen get arthritis young. Halfway to the shed he picked up a stick and rapped on a barrel.

There was a click as somebody pulled a bolt back. I followed the limping form through a dark door.

The door was low, so I had to stoop to get under the lintel. Someone closed it behind me, and for a second I was in the smell of tar and antique fish, and a blackness so intense it made red shapes float in front of the eyes.

A lighter scraped. The flame grew slowly, attached itself to the wick of a paraffin lamp, spread a yellow light over a concrete floor, nets hung tidily in rope strops, a pile of orange buoys in the corner. A man with dark hair was sitting in a deckchair beside a table made of an old door on trestles. He got up fast, grabbed a bottle off the table.

I realized I had been holding my breath. I let it out in a long sigh. I said, "Thibault."

He was wearing an old blue jersey, jeans and seaboots. He had not shaved for a couple of days. He shook my hand, in the French manner. Normally he had a hard, warm grip. Tonight it was cold and clammy. It could have been the lamplight, but the black stubble looked gray in patches, and the skin seemed to have tightened over the bones of his face. The famous white smile looked dulled and sheepish, as if he had been caught out. He said, "Mick. I should have known you'd find me. Have a seat."

I sat on a lobster pot, and thought about the gilt sofas and pneumatic ceilings of the Manoir de Causey. I said, nice and quiet, "Thibault, what the hell is going on?"

He reversed the bottle in his hand from the clubbing to the pouring position. He filled three glasses. He passed one to me, and one to Christophe. It smelled like yet more brandy.

He sat down. He made a rueful face, the ghost of the crazy Circus Kraken grin. He said, "I like to stay in touch with my roots. With the fishermen of my childhood."

I got angry. I said, "I did not come all the way out here to where you are hiding like a rat in a shoe to listen to bloody stupid jokes."

He rocked back in his chair as if I had hit him. His face turned the color of raw sea-salt. That was better.

I said, "What are you doing here?"

He said, "Hiding," as if the word was something dirty he was spitting out of his mouth.

"Who from?"

He said, "I owe people money. I owe you money."

I said, "We've known each other for ten years."

He said, "It's not you I'm hiding from." He looked me straight in the eye.

"Then who?"

"There are some people."

"You don't hide from bankers."

"Ah," he said. "You've met the bankers. No, you don't hide from bankers."

I remembered Jean-Claude, dangling from the balcony by his coat-collar. "So you're hiding from Arthur."

He knocked over his glass. "Who's Arthur?" he said.

"Someone who scares the wits out of you," I said.

He looked at his feet. He did not say anything.

I said, "What's the point of hiding?"

He laughed. I had never heard him pretend to laugh before. It was a shocking sound. "To stay alive until the money comes in."

"The money," I said. "Yes. Do you know what went wrong with your new boat?"

"Wrong? No."

"The seacock fell off," I said. "Because someone had smashed it and stuck it together again. You wouldn't know anything about that?"

He said, "I don't understand."

I explained it to him, in great detail. "So a disloyal thought occurred to me," I said. "It occurred to me that you might have bust the seacock to collect the insurance."

He leaned back and took a sip of brandy. He closed his

eyes. "I hide," he said. "And suddenly, my old friends are thinking I am capable of sinking a boat, for money. Killing them, for money." There was a silence. The wick of the oil lamp made a small, sulfurous sputtering. "So. I deserve it," he said. "But it's not true."

"So what is true?"

He opened his eyes again. "You don't want to know," he said. "I promise you that."

I said, "Thibault, this is me you are talking to." I was getting angry again. He was dodging the issue. Worse, he was betraying a trust between friends. I passed him the letter I had written to the insurance company. "Sign that."

He read the letter. He said, "No."

"Why not?"

"Because you will show the letter to the insurance agent, and the insurance agent will know you have seen me, and he will ask questions, and he will not ask them nicely."

I said, "So Arthur is the insurance agent."

"That's right."

"Arthur Crespi."

He stared at me. "How did you know?"

I said, "What's the problem with this Crespi?"

"He's a bastard."

I said, "What about Bianca?"

He said, "Bianca is a good friend. One of us. But she is on her own side."

I said, "What do you mean?"

He said, "I have known Bianca a long time. She wants you to think she's crazy, out to lunch. She's not. She does things for reasons, but I still don't know what the reasons are."

He pulled a pad of paper off the table, wrote on it with a ballpoint and handed it to Christophe, who scribbled on it himself. "Here," he said. "Instead of the insurance, for the moment. Until we can get organized."

I looked down at the paper. It said that Thibault Ledoux handed over to Michael Savage all sixty-four sixty-fourth shares of the yacht *Arc-en-Ciel*. It was signed, dated and witnessed. "So if you get a big problem, you can sell the boat, take what I owe you, give me what's left."

I did not know what to say. It was a gigantic, an outrageous gesture. I said, "Have you talked to the police?"

He smiled. It was something like his old smile, but it had a wistful quality. "I would very much like to talk to the police," he said. "But it is a bit too late."

"What are you talking about?"

He was not listening anymore. He said, "Be quiet."

Outside, the sea lapped the shingle. Somewhere in the distance, a redshank whistled. And close at hand, quiet as a cat, a car's engine was purring.

Thibault was up, moving fast. The lamp went out. A wad of salt breeze blew into the shed. Christophe said, "M. Thibault?" There was no answer.

Feet crunched in the shingle at the front of the hut. Four feet. I shoved the paper Thibault had signed in my pocket, went to the door, pulled it open. Two dark figures loomed against the sky. Aftershave floated in the night air. One of them turned on a flashlight. It was as if the sun had just risen in my face. A voice said, *"Ce n'est pas lui."* It's not him.

All of a sudden, I was as worried about Thibault as Thibault was.

"Where is he?" said the voice. It was a quiet voice, hard, without bounce or springiness.

I said, "What?" in English.

"It's the one from the restaurant," said the voice. "What are you doing here?"

Through the open door behind me I heard the soft *clonk* of an oar on a boat's side. They were breathing hard. They did not hear. I said, "What?" again, in English. "Who the hell do you think you are?"

"Watch your mouth," said the voice. A hand pushed me hard on the shoulder. I stumbled backward out of the door.

Beyond the sea-wall, someone pulled the starting cord of an outboard.

The flashlight came out of my eyes. It swept a powerful shaft of light into the black dark, settled on a boat. The boat was one of the flat-bottomed scows used for collecting oysters. It lay twenty yards off the beach, rocking in the still black water. It had a big outboard. Bent over the outboard was Thibault.

There was a sudden scuffle of movement from the men with the torch. One of them was cursing. The outboard caught. The scow's nose came up, settled on to a cushion of foam as Thibault twisted the throttle. It shrank into the distance at the head of a giant V of wake, aiming for the distant black centipede of the Île de Ré bridge.

"No," said one of the men. They were standing still now, dark and frozen against the red glow of La Rochelle. One of them was pointing a long something down the torch beam. A stick, I thought. Why a stick?

Then I caught a stray gleam of light on metal, and I knew it was not a stick.

It was a gun.

13

The man with the gun lowered it. My knees were made of jelly. *"La chasse,"* he said. Hunting. I could hear the smile in his voice.

Then the torch was in my eyes again, and the barrel of the gun was at my chest. It was double-barreled, over-and-under. Trap gun, I thought.

The barrel moved. It jabbed into my solar plexus. I went down on to the stones, lay with my face in the oyster shells and tried to remember how to breathe, and how to run. Breathing came soon, but not soon enough. It is not practical to run on shingle, particularly when you cannot breathe, and people with flashlights and shotguns wish to talk to you.

"Where did he go?" said the voice.

The breeze was small, full of salt and mud and aftershave, and it sighed a tiny sigh in the grasses of the foreshore. I was badly frightened.

"Maybe he doesn't speak French," said the quiet voice, like the purr of a mechanical cat. "He's English."

Irish, I thought.

"He speaks French," said the other one. In my mind, I heard Thibault's voice. *He will not ask nicely.*

"OK," said the one with the quiet voice. "No more amusement. Where is he going?"

I did not say anything. I was concentrating on absorbing air, a cubic centimeter at a time. Something cold landed gently on my cheek: a double ring of metal. The other voice said, "This is a shotgun. You like to keep quiet, I can oblige you. I pull the trigger, your teeth go into the beach, and the bottom half of your face, too. But you don't die. You bleed a lot, and you never kiss a woman, and you do a lot of thinking about how you eat through a straw forever. Maybe this will make you happy. I count three. One."

My insides turned to dirty water. The gun ground into my face. I said, "I don't know where he's gone."

"Two," said the voice. The cold metal seemed to have become tense, as if he had taken up the first pressure on a trigger.

I said, "I went to see him. He owes me money. How do I know where he goes?"

The first voice said something I did not hear. The man with the gun said, *"Merde."* The pressure of the gun came off my face. My heart banged like a steam-hammer in my chest. "Get up," said the man with the quiet voice. "You say he owes you money. What for?"

I got up as far as my knees. I said, "I built him a boat he hasn't paid for."

Silence. The lap of little waves on the dirty shore. "Your name?" said the voice.

I wondered why I should tell him. Then I wondered why not. "Michael Savage," I said. "What's yours?" The fear had left me at the same time as the gun-barrel. I was angry now.

The one with the gun growled like a dog. The other one raised a hand. I could smell his aftershave, like flowers beaten up in rocket fuel. "It is not important," said the shadowy figure in his soft purr. "OK." There was a smooth, metallic click. Sweat broke on my hands and back. The gunman was taking the shells out. "But we don't like you. So you leave the restaurant, OK? And you leave La Rochelle."

For a moment, I thought they were going. Then the dark

silhouette jerked against the light of the horizon, and the gun-barrel flashed quick as a snake in the starlight. It poked me gently but precisely in the solar plexus. It still hurt.

"We always hit the spot," said the smooth voice beyond the tears. Feet crunched on gravel. There was the rasp of a cigarette lighter, a tinkle of broken glass. The mist in front of my eyes glowed orange. I blinked it away.

Flame was running down the roof of Christophe's shed. It dripped off the gutters, smeared itself down the clapboard walls, crawled back up under the eaves. In its light I could see Christophe himself, frozen, arms straight out from his shoulders, as if crucified. In the fringes of the light, two figures were running. One of them had been Crespi's driver. The other had a mop of hair that shone red-gold in the jumping firelight. He had opened the door for Crespi outside Agences Giotto.

Christophe started to yell, high, despairing yells like a seabird's. Instead of going for the figures in the shadows, I went for the shed. "Bucket!" I said.

Christophe turned to me a face with perfectly circular eyes above a round mouth. Then he seemed to wake up.

He ran around to the back door, came back with two black rubber pails. The flames had moved quickly. The smoky orange of petrol was becoming the emerald-green transparency of salt-pickled wood. They were beginning to crackle.

We filled the buckets in the sea. Water slopped down my trousers. The first water hit with a hiss and a roar. The flames jumped higher. There were shouts from further down the beach. People came running, burly men in boots and overalls, carrying more buckets. I hustled them into a line from the water's edge to the hut. The water began to flow off the front of the line, pulsing like a severed artery. Someone got a hose going from the oyster tank. The flames shrank and died.

"*Bien*," said a big man, ducking his head to light a cigarette. "*C'est fini*." Christophe had turned his bucket upside down, and was sitting on the shingle. "How did it happen?"

Christophe raised his old, innocent face. "A cigarette," he said.

"But you don't smoke," said the big man.

Christophe shoved his hands in the pockets of his faded blue jacket, and got up. The shed door was open. He went in.

"Crazy," said the big man. He looked worried. Soon, he would ask questions.

"Shock," I said. I wanted it to be me who asked the questions.

The big man said, "He was lucky." We shook hands. He walked back down the beach after the other fishermen.

I watched the yellow discs of their flashlights shrink by the flat black sea. Then I went into the hut.

Christophe had lit a lamp. He stood under the black, dripping rafters in the stink of smoke, fingering a half-melted Terylene net.

I said, "Who were those guys?"

His eyes were round and innocent as a baby's. "What guys?"

"The guys who torched your shed."

The brandy bottle stood unbroken on the wet table. The neck rattled against the glass as he poured. "I saw no guys," he said.

I said, "Christophe, I am a friend of Thibault. I want to help him."

He said, "He owed you money. You told the man."

At least he admitted there had been a man. I said, "Somebody rams a gun in my face, I will tell them I am the Emperor of China."

He stared at me. He said, *"Merde.* I have been with the *Résistance."*

I said, "The war is finished."

He looked at the charred and blackened inside of the hut as if he were seeing it for the first time. He opened his mouth. There were two teeth left in his lower jaw, like yellow tombstones in front of an open grave. He laughed.

He laughed till the tears squeezed out of his deep-creased blue eyes. He said, "He owed me money, too." He looked around him at the devastated shed in which no war had taken place. He laughed so hard he bent double. "And he got away!"

After a while, he quieted down. He said, "When he was a

child, he used to come down here, help with the oysters. I built him a boat once. A real boat, from wood, with a red sail. He could almost have been my son. So he owed me money, but small sums, not the kind of sums sons owe fathers. He always spoke well of you. He trusted you." The strain had come back into his smile. Loyal Christophe, and my old pal Thibault.

I said, "Something has changed him."

Christophe said, "Since four weeks, maybe. First he is worried. Then it is the banks. Then he said, it is all finished, hide me."

"Two nights ago."

"Two nights ago. I have seen people worried about money. And I have seen people in the war, you know, frightened for their lives. Thibault is frightened for his life."

"By whom?"

He shrugged. "People from the south. I don't know." He drank brandy, not bothering with the glass. He looked old, lonely, and lost, because people he did not know were trying to kill the man who was nearly his son.

I said, "Don't worry. Old Thibault, eh?"

He grinned. "Yeah," he said. "Old Thibault."

So we sat and grinned at each other, and Christophe poured more brandy.

But both sets of grins were as false as blind Annie's eyelashes.

In the end he got up and slid the brandy bottle into the pocket of his blue smock. He gave me a ride back to the restaurant in his van. I let myself in with the key. The kitchen clock among the photographs of Thibault in the back bar said one-twenty. My stomach muscles were issuing loud protests, and my head was throbbing with brandy. I stumbled into bed, and fell asleep.

Brandy is not a good anesthetic. I snapped awake with the feeling that it was too early. Gray morning light was seeping in at the window and across the ceiling. Down on the quay someone was banging fish boxes into a truck. My watch said half past five. There was no chance of going back to sleep. I had the feeling it was going to be a terrible day.

I rolled out of bed, and mixed some instant coffee with

some water, and navigated my way through a jungle of feminine unguents to the washbasin to splash water on my face.

Someone was hammering on the door of the restaurant.

I went downstairs, hanging on to the banister rail. It was Jonzac, the policeman, pouchy-eyed in a fawn raincoat darkened by the drizzle. He said, "I hope this is not too early. I was on my way home from night shift."

I said, "Fine. Come in."

We went up to the flat. He accepted coffee; said, "About your friend Jean-Claude."

"Yes?"

"I thought I should warn you that he has escaped from hospital. We are searching for him. I imagine he will have left the town. But I thought, since it is a matter of your daughter . . ."

I said, "Thank you."

He said, "Jean-Claude Dupont is not his correct name, of course."

"Oh?"

"He is Lucas Baragouin. Born in the Midi. He has been in jail five times. Theft, assault, selling drugs. Not recently, though. It seems he has found regular employment. With whom we do not know."

I kept my face still. I knew. But telling the police would not help Thibault in his difficulties.

Jonzac cleared his throat nervously. "I saw in the newspaper that you are sailing with Thibault Ledoux in the Belle-Île race tomorrow."

"That's right," I said.

He smiled, ran his hand over his brown stubble of hair. "Permit me to wish you a good success." He did not sound like a policeman anymore. He sounded like a weekend sailor who thought he had brushed up against greatness.

"You are lucky to sail for a profession," he said. "So free, so innocent."

I smiled with a face that felt like cardboard. "Exactly," I said.

He left.

I made another cup of coffee. Then I rummaged in my

pocket for the bill of sale Thibault had given me last night. There was his signature. There was Christophe's. It was all in order.

I put it in an envelope, addressed it to my insurance broker in England, and wrote a letter, asking him to put the boat on cover. At nine o'clock sharp, I took it to the post office, and sent it to England, registered mail.

And that should have been that. Sail the race, go home, sell the boat.

Except that someone had knocked the seacock off and tried to drown me, and I had a job to do for Justin Peabody.

And my old pal Thibault.

14

I went back to the flat. There was a race to get ready for. So I pulled an almanac and a chart and a tidal atlas from the shelf behind the bar downstairs, and found a weather forecast, and started to scribble notes about tide times and streams. We were supposed to have Thibault on board, and these were Thibault's home waters, so any mistakes I made would stick out a mile. We would have Yann, of course, and they were his home waters too. But there was force of habit: *Don't leave anything to the other guy.*

Also it was a good way of calming down after someone had stuck a shotgun in your face.

Its attraction dated from the time I had arrived at the British Virgin Islands. I had landed up there with the clothes I had worn at Uncle James's funeral still in the bottom of my suitcase. I had gone to see Henry Green, a distant cousin, who had charter boats at Road Town. Henry was pleased to see me. He was a tall man, so laid back it was hard to tell whether or not he was awake. My height had made him think I was older than fifteen. He had been in need of a skipper for a yacht which had been chartered by a group of incompetents from Des Moines, Iowa. Once I had shown him that I knew how to reverse the boat out of its berth, he had given me the job. What the charter guests wanted was sun, fun and sea, in apparently random combinations. Working out these combinations called for meticulous planning. I enjoyed the planning. Skippers who believed that if they allowed things to happen it would all work out fine brought their guests back sunstruck, seasick and bored. Mine came back fit as fleas, without even a hangover.

Within a month, I had acquired a sudden but complete education in the ways of charter guests, the West Indies, and big boats. I had competitive instincts honed by years of dinghy racing in Poole Harbor. I could play boogie-woogie piano. Within six months, I had succeeded in helming the winner of the Swans race in Antigua Week. I could hardly remember Ireland, and I was convinced that I was a hero.

With the money my father had left me, I bought *Freya*, a thirty-foot ketch a couple of Danes had sailed down from the Azores. She was cheap, because she was rotten in places. I pulled her up a slipway, begged and borrowed fastenings and paint and timber. People took pity on the gangling kid with no skin on his nose and his toes sticking through the ends of his shoes. Four months later, *Freya* was back in the water, and I was running day-trips around the islands by day, and sleeping in her wheelhouse by night.

Then, a week before my seventeenth birthday, a cruise ship like a big white block of flats dropped anchor in the blue water off Road Town. I borrowed a can of diesel and motored out to see if there was any business to be done. I came alongside the towering white wall of her. High above at her rail there was a frieze of heads, black against the brilliant blue of the Caribbean sky. I had met the mate earlier in the year. He had said that for the usual kickback he would send me down a few punters for what he called the Long John Silver experience.

So I sat, and drank a Coke, and whipped a line, feeling terrific on my own boat on a blue sea in all that sun. And a woman's voice said, "Can I come on?"

She was tall, with a black Prince Valiant haircut and clear brown skin. Her eyes were grayish-blue, the whites ice-white. She had long, slim legs and a short-short skirt. She was called Mary Ellen Soames. She looked at me. She looked at *Freya*. She said, "Is this really *your boat?*"

I nodded. I did not trust myself to speak.

"Wow," said Mary Ellen. *"She's beautiful."*

Two fat women in print dresses were wheezing down the cruise ship's companion ladder, followed by reptilian husbands in white cheese-cutter caps. She gave them a look I immediately understood: desperation and loathing.

I said, "Off we go." I let go the lines, kicked *Freya* away from the cruise ship's side. I was blowing two hundred much-needed dollars, and the mate would be furious about his kickbacks. I did not care. I was in love.

Mary Ellen had graduated from McGill University six months previously. She had won her cruise in a raffle. She liked seafood, preferred wine to beer and Art Tatum to the Rolling Stones. She had never been on a small yacht before.

We snorkeled. I took her to the Baths on Virgin Gorda, then almost untouched by the hand of man. We followed the whales through the Sir Francis Drake Channel. On the second night, she said she was not going back on the cruise ship. On the third, she said it again, and meant it. On the fourth morning, I emptied my bank account in Road Town, she wrote to her parents, and we set off south down the islands.

A year later, we were in Aruba, anchored off a beach covered in the executives of dubious offshore banks. Behind the beach were the banks themselves, a white concrete forest in which prowled smooth-spoken criminals. Mary Ellen was lying with her head on my knee. Her eyes were brilliantly blue against the coffee-tanned skin of her face. She said, "I'm going to have a baby."

We drank to the baby. We made love with a depth of tenderness neither of us had felt before. Then we sailed across a black, phosphorescent sea to Venezuela, to get serious. We were married in a hot, dark church outside Caracas. I was just eighteen, and she was twenty-one. The landlady of our lodgings gave us a party, rum and wide white grins under the whispering palms. Everything was going to be fine.

After an hour and a half, I put away the charts, got up to stretch my legs, and wandered up to the flat.

I found myself in Frankie's room. There were a couple of books by the bed: Racine's *Mitridate*, and Entwhistle's *European Balladry*. University reading-list stuff. A letter from the Dean of her college was tucked into one of them. There were three floral-print dresses, her holiday dresses, on hangers hitched to the picture rail. There was a picture of Mary Ellen smiling by a bed of lupins and stocks at her weekend cottage in Suffolk.

As I turned to go out of the door, my foot caught the wastepaper basket. There was broken glass in the wastepaper basket. I looked down.

The glass was from a picture frame. The picture in the frame was of me.

There was nobody in the restaurant. When I went on to the quay, it was still raining, a slow, Atlantic drizzle. The *écailleurs* were on the pavement, smoking Gitanes and opening oysters.

I went back inside and fired up the Gaggia machine. The chef came back from the fish market. The baker wandered in with the bread. China began to clash in the kitchen. The wheels of the day were getting up to speed.

In the sky over the towers the clouds broke, and bars of sun turned the harbor milky green. I banged coffee into the Gaggia's filter, heated milk. Gérard arrived. The wheels meshed. The world began to hum. The telephone rang.

The man's voice on the other end said, "Mr. Savage? How nice to have the opportunity to speak with you." He spoke English, with a faint accent overlaid with American. "My name is Crespi."

Everything had gone still and quiet. I said, "Mr. Crespi. How can I help you?"

He said, "I have been speaking with my friend M. Feuilla. He told me that there has been a difficulty with the boat you were selling to M. Ledoux."

"Has he?"

"We should meet," said Crespi.

"Where?"

"I am in La Rochelle for the race, with my boat. I have an office in the Minimes. At Agences Giotto."

"I've been there," I said.

"They told me. Two-thirty?"

"Two-thirty." It could have been someone else saying it. Then I rang Feuilla's office in the south.

The girl who answered had a voice made of black velvet. "M. Feuilla?" she said. "Of course."

Feuilla said, "I've got some people here. Go ahead, though." I could hear them in the background. La Rochelle offices were silent businesslike places, dedicated to maintaining the appearance of things getting done. Feuilla's office would be a hot, hazy place, marinated in bitter coffee and black tobacco, where honorable men made a lot of noise while they plotted their plots.

"So," he said. "Everything ready?"

I said, "Yann and Bianca Dufy are bringing the boat down from Sables d'Olonne. Due in this morning."

"Fine," he said. "Fine. Who else is in the race?"

I had the list of entries. I reeled them off to him. It was not a serious race. There was a class of maxis, a couple of sixty-footers like *Plage d'Or,* and a scramble of second-rate one-tonners and production boats.

"Ah." There was a pause. He wanted to say something. "Can you beat the maxis?"

"Not a big problem," I said. They were mostly oldish and slowish. Nobody was going to risk their shiny harbor greyhounds to the rough-and-tumble of the eastern Bay of Biscay.

"Including Crespi?"

"We'll do our best." *White Wing* was not your featherweight harbor maxi, but she would have been at home in an around-the-world race, and she was fast.

"You English," said Feuilla. "So modest."

"Irish," I said.

"Sorry?"

"Tell me about M. Crespi," I said.

Feuilla seemed to hesitate. Then he said, "Why?"

I did not want to talk about Thibault. "I like to know the opposition," I said.

He said, "I have known M. Crespi for a while. He is a *thoroughly unscrupulous* man." The comfortable, half-amused veil had fallen away. His voice was like a knifeblade coming out of a pocket. I could imagine the bright eyes hardening under the mane of white hair. "And of course, he has upset many people up there in La Rochelle. And in his home." The humor was back. "He insists on selling insurance cheaper than his competitors. I very much want him beaten. Now," he said. "I must go. *Bonne chance.*"

As far as Feuilla was concerned, boats were billboards that won races, and skippers were a form of account executive.

I said, "I'll do what I can."

We win the race. *Plage d'Or* gets the glory. Thibault Ledoux gets the credit. Mick Savage gets the check.

Checks were what was required, just now. Checks, and information about Crespi.

I called Yann and asked him whom he knew in the town. He told me to call Yves Marchand, a journalist on *Ouest-France.* I dialed the number. The man who answered had a high, efficient voice. "Yann," he said. "Of course. And I know who you are. Nice to talk. How can I help?"

I said, "What do you know about a M. Crespi?"

"Turned up about a year ago. From the deep south. Property developer. Started with some place west of the Rhône. Twenty years ago, it was sand dunes, mosquitoes, *parcs d'huitres,* one or two tourists, not important. But sun, you know? Sun like the breath of a blast furnace. And the sea. The Côte d'Azur had put prices through the roof, and there was nowhere for the little guys to go in the *mois d'août,* on the beach with the kids. So they started to build places, like Port Grimaud but not *chic,* huge marinas, apartment complexes. Have you seen Sète lately? Well, God help Sète. I remember Sète when it was Sète, before.

"So there's a lot of money down there. Private money, government money, EC money. And big promotion. *White Wing,* that boat of Crespi's, it gets sponsorship from some town down there. And they've got a boatyard, where they build such boats. All with taxpayers' money."

"And Crespi's in the middle."

Marchand became ironic. "Guys like Crespi get in the

middle, and take advantage of the good things that pass
from all sides."

"So why does he bother to come to La Rochelle?"

"He's coming for money. He has opened a chain of
insurance shops all over France. All over the world. Nobody
can live without insurance." I thought of Christophe's hut,
burning. "Anything else you need, call again." He put the
telephone down.

I drank another cup of coffee, and wondered what were
the talents you needed for getting into the middle and taking
advantage of the good things. I seemed to be lacking in such
talents at the moment.

But not in telephone calls. I had been in La Rochelle long
enough for the world to have caught up with me.

Mary rang from Pulteney to deliver a no-progress report.

Then Art Schacker rang from Marblehead and told me he
had heard things were not going so well, and why did I not
make it easy on myself and sign for their America's Cup
campaign, subject to a golden hello that would make my
bank manager think all his birthdays had come at once. He
insisted that we meet, and discuss things. He was a persis-
tent man. I said I would think about it all, and went back to
thinking about Arthur Crespi.

Just before lunch, Bianca and Frankie came into the bar.
Frankie looked straight at me. The swelling on her eye and
jaw had gone down. Her skin was wind-pink and sun-brown
and the whites of her eyes were clear as milk. She gave me a
grin, and went upstairs. I was not forgiven for whatever it
was she was holding against me. But a grin was a grin. It
cheered me up, but not enough.

Bianca sat down at the bar. She looked like a female
pirate, her face tanned gypsy-brown, black hair in a pigtail,
gold earrings in her neat ears.

I gave her a beer, watching the door marked PRIVÉ.

She gripped my hand, a warm, encouraging grip. "She's
young," she said. "She'll get over it."

I gazed into her dark-blue eyes. She seemed to have an
idea of herself as older than she was. She smiled at me. "And
the boat's going well," she said. She was one of the team.

There are a lot of things we do not know, I thought. You
do not know that I have seen the papers about *Poisson*

d'Avril that you removed from the folders. You do not know I have seen Thibault. And I do not know what the hell your game is.

I managed to grin back. At two-thirty, I took the van to the offices of Agences Giotto for my interview with M. Arthur Crespi.

The receptionist showed me through to a workmanlike office with a trestle desk and aluminum deckchairs. Crespi was sitting behind the desk. He put out a hand that managed to be warm and hard at the same time. "Sit down," he said. "Sit down." The incipient jowls were mid-tan, the black hair carefully crinkled over the square, handsome face. There was a faint smell of talcum powder. He would have had to shave twice a day.

He said, "You have had a problem with your boat. My manager tells me it was insured in the name of Thibault Ledoux. I believe M. Ledoux had not paid you in full?"

"Who told you that?"

"My manager also." He smiled. "I have many businesses. When I come to a place to sail, I like to analyze the progress of the business, hear about . . . outstanding events since my last visit. The manager tells me you have had a meeting."

I said, "The insurance was in M. Ledoux's name. Your manager had no reason to pay me."

"But it causes you a problem." The smile did not fade. It was the genuine South of France gigolo model, all white teeth and crinkles around the eyes. He said, "I want to tell you something. I am a sailor, as you know. Not an expert like you, of course." Still the smile. "I have made *White Wing* so I can race, but in comfort. For some time now I have watched your career. And I have to tell you, I admire the things you do." He dropped his eyes, as if embarrassed.

"To build boats according to your dream is good. It is what it is about, following your dream. For me it is a privilege to facilitate the dream for people I admire. I am a businessman, not a *sportif*. I build the boats, pay people to sail for me, enable them to achieve their personal goals. This for me is more than a pleasure. It is a mission." He was leaning forward, hands flat on the desk, earnest now. The power of his personality filled the room like cheap aftershave. I reminded myself that this was the man who had driven Thibault into hiding, and whose thugs had stolen Thibault's papers and tried to frighten me to death. *Vive le sport.*

"So," he said. "It is not pleasing to me to see a man such as yourself in difficulties because he made the pardonable error of trusting his friends. Finance is about mistrust and trust, carefully balanced. Sport is about trust. If you break the rules, the sport is finished." He spread his hands. He said, "What I propose to you is this. You want this matter settled, so you can get out of here, leave, carry on with your life. We are all busy men. I understand this. So since the underwriter would have had to pay out on a claim from Thibault Ledoux, and since your boat is in the yard, I see no reason why I cannot . . . stretch a matter, and pay what is outstanding to you direct, pending M. Ledoux's claim."

He sat back in his chair. He was smiling, full of concern for my welfare. The dark eyes were watchful.

I watched right back.

Crespi had no idea that I had made a connection between him and his bodyguards. Furthermore, he took it as a basic truth that the world was full of naïve sailors who would jump at any means of getting their boats out of hock. What he did not know was that I was a sailor who had spent time investigating people who wished to become rich by making fraudulent claims on insured assets. It is a line of work in which it is hard to remain naïve for long.

What I had just been offered had nothing to do with insurance, or *le sport*. It was an attempt to buy me off, to get rid of me and my nose. And something else.

"By the way," said M. Crespi. "Have you seen Thibault? He's been very quiet lately. I'll need his signature to authorize this payment. A mere formality."

I gave him what I hoped was the grin of a *sportif* pursuing his dream. I said, "I'll see him tomorrow. He'll be racing on *Plage d'Or*. He asked me along."

"Really?" he said. "How splendid." He looked sportingly enthusiastic.

"About your offer," I said. "Are you sure about that?"

"As a matter of policy, no," he said. "But we know who

you are. We can stretch a point." He smiled. His eyes were as kindly as a couple of pools of tar.

"I'll be in touch when I get the yard bill," I said. "If you give me what you want Thibault to sign, I'll get him to do it tomorrow."

I got up. We shook hands again. I waited for the typist to knock out the release, shouldered aside the door and trudged into the rain.

So there you are, Savage, I thought. That's how it's done. The nice man wants to buy you off. So you can forge the signature on the release, and pay the yard bill, and you can get the hell out of here, and take your daughter with you.

The how of it was quite straightforward. What really interested me was the why.

15

*T*hat evening I was behind the bar when the fleet came in on the tide. Half a dozen fat aluminum masts appeared in the gap between the Tour de la Chaine and the Tour Saint-Nicolas. The tourists got up from the outside tables and drifted out to the coping-stones of the quay to watch the huge yachts, crisp-edged and gleaming in the low Atlantic light, slide down on the docks the *Mairie* had cleared in the morning. Banners rattled and flapped on the white poles along the quay. TOUR DE BELLE-ÎLE, they said. TOUTES VOILES DEHORS.

Suddenly the restaurant smelled of old tobacco and spilled drink, a mawkish smell that failed to satisfy the lungs. I went outside to get a breath of air.

Plage d'Or was on the outside berth. Yann was running a big turquoise battle flag up the forestay. It bore a picture of a crowned lighthouse, and the inscription ROYAUME DES

PHARES. Bianca came up the ramp from the pontoon. She was wearing blue canvas shorts that showed her beautiful legs. She was glowing like a stoplight with sun and wind.

She took me by the arm, and said, "Get me a drink."

It was a good evening to have beautiful women taking you by the arm. I said, "Beer?"

"Pastis," she said. There was a lightness in her voice I had never heard before. "I am a creature of the deep south. Nothing but pastis will do."

I poured. Her throat was strong and brown as she drank. There was a breeze, and a clear sky. I should have been out there on the water, not shut up in the bar. She said, "The warhorse smells blood, right?"

"What do you mean?" I knew what she meant. She had reminded me that I was stuck in a dirty world that contained too many people. I felt dull as a rubber knife.

"Tomorrow, you sail," she said. "You'll feel better."

I nodded. She understood.

I felt suddenly warm toward her. We were on the same team.

I said, "Thibault's sailing, too," and poured myself a cognac.

"That's fantastic," said Bianca. Her face was glowing with pleasure. "What's wrong with you?" she said. "Aren't you pleased?"

"Sure," I said.

Her hand brushed mine as she reached for the pastis bottle. She poured herself another shot, took my hand. "What's the problem?" Her eyes were big and hot. They would have been easy to confide in.

"Nothing."

"English," she said, with scorn.

"Irish," I said.

She ignored me. "Cold like fish." She let go of my hand, dribbled water into her pastis, watched the clear yellow turn milky. "So how come your daughter's not cold?"

I drank some brandy, fast. "Maybe she should practice being colder," I said, and immediately felt ashamed of myself.

"Ouf!" said Bianca. "Pig."

She stopped. She was looking at the door of the restaurant. A group of men had come in. They were wearing shorts and polo shirts. The shirts had WHITE WING embroidered over the heart. At the front of the group was Arthur Crespi.

I gave him the *maître d'hôtel* wave. He gave me the gigolo smile and sat down at the head of a table for eighteen. Gérard scuttled off to take the orders.

Bianca's face had lost its glow, turned cold and hard. She said, "That bastard."

"How do you know?"

"We are from the same town," she said. Her voice came from a long way away, as if her mind was not on what she was saying.

She slid off her stool. She walked toward Crespi's table, straight as a mast, so straight I forgot how small she was. The talk and laughter in the restaurant died, strangled by the sudden tightness of the air. I saw Crespi's eyes hit her. His smile faded. His mouth opened as if he were going to say something. But he found nothing to say. Suddenly he was not a handsome Provençal beginning to go to seed, but an oily little man with a tight mouth and cruel eyes.

Bianca said, in a voice clear as ice, "You haven't managed to kill him yet?"

I saw Crespi's hand clutch at the edge of the table. He said, "What do you mean?"

Bianca said, "Too much of a man for you, eh? Same old story."

Crespi's face was suddenly full of blood. He shoved himself to his feet, took two steps across the room in a silence thick enough to cut steaks off. He stood a foot away from her.

"The hero of Sainte-Jeanne," she said. "Mr. Big, but he's frightened of women."

Crespi hit her in the face. In the silence it sounded like a door slamming. Her arms went out sideways. She sprawled backward across an empty table, and hit the floor with a bang. "Whore," said Crespi. He sat down again.

I found I was running. Bianca was sprawled like a starfish on the bare boards. Her face was white as chalk, except where blood was leaking out of her nose.

She said, "It is all right." I helped her up. Crespi took a sip from his whiskey and soda, and looked as if he was about to restart his conversation.

The blood was singing in my ears. I found myself standing by the shoulder of his Thai silk jacket. I put my hands in my pockets, to stop them grabbing him. I said, "Out."

He looked up at me, black eyebrows arched on his forehead. He said, "What?"

"Out."

He made a face meant to express amused disbelief as between men of the world. He said, "I and my crew wish to have a drink. We have reserved a table for dinner—"

My hands were coming out of my pockets on their own. I said, "If you do not leave within fifteen seconds, I shall call the police and have you ejected."

He saw I was serious. He looked mean and greasy again. He said, "I am not amused by this."

"Ten seconds."

He sighed. He finished his drink. He said, *"Bien. On y va."* Then, with the big, white smile, "And like you say in English, bang goes our deal." He stood up. So did his crew. He said, in a hard Marseillais accent, "This is a restaurant of shit." He spat on the tablecloth. They filed out.

Bianca had sat down. I summoned Gérard. "Change the tablecloth," I said.

"And Thibault will be there to beat the arses off you tomorrow!" yelled Bianca. Then she sat on a bar stool and laid her head on her hands and started to cry.

I led her to a booth. The door closed behind them. Gérard and a busboy were already clearing up glass, and a murmur of conversation was spreading like scar tissue.

I was feeling happier than I had felt all day. Crespi looked big, and slick, and bulletproof. But Bianca had rattled him.

I brought her a glass of water. She drank it like a woman in a desert. In the restaurant, the talk had started up again. Her nose had stopped bleeding. She said, "Is there a bruise on my face?"

The skin was red, no more. I said, "No."

She said, "I'm sorry for the cabaret."

I said, "No problem."

She said, "And you are turning into a restaurateur."

"So what was it about?"

She said, "He gave problems to Thibault. If Thibault was here, he wouldn't let him into the restaurant. That is why he comes."

"What kind of problems?"

"Business problems."

I said, "Who was he trying to kill?"

She looked at me blankly. "Kill?"

"You asked him if he had managed to kill Thibault yet," I said.

"Thibault?" The blankness was real. "Why should he kill Thibault?" Then she started to laugh. She laughed hard enough to squeeze tears from her eyes. She hooked her arm around my neck. "Thibault?" she said. "You poor solemn man. Thibault can look after himself."

She rested her forehead against mine. I could smell traces of scent. I leaned into it, drifting away. She kissed me.

Her eyelashes were long and black, resting lightly on her cheeks. They reminded me of thistledown.

They reminded me of man-traps.

Her eyes opened, and she looked at me with a misty smile. Half of me said she was beautiful, and wanted to go on. The other half said, Savage, you are a bloody fool. Ask her why she took the *Poisson d'Avril* documents out of the folder.

The beautiful half won. She kissed me again. This time, she had my full cooperation.

Somebody walked up to the bar. Somebody put down a tray of glasses with an unnecessarily loud bang, and cleared her throat. I opened my eyes.

Frankie was standing there, arms folded. There were angry red spots on her cheekbones. "Sorry to interrupt," she said. I felt the heat rise to my face.

Bianca said, "We were just finishing," squeezed my hand, and went upstairs.

Frankie said, "My *God,*" and slammed into the kitchen.

More diners came in. It was a big night; the night before the race. I pulled out wine and served more drinks. I worked the whole evening on autopilot. When it was finished, and the waiters were leaning on the bar sipping coffee and watching out for the *digestif* orders, I went to the piano.

I sat down on the stool, and I shoved up the lid, and I rested the old fingers on the keys, and I began to play. Once upon a time I was a jazzer of some accomplishment. But I was out of practice; and anyway, tonight was no night for jazz. Tonight was confusion, and confusion calls for the blues.

So I played "Frankie and Johnny," the slow version, with the big thumping stride left hand that was nowadays about as dextrous as I got in that department. I had not played for a while, but it went all right, the way it does when you are hungover and worried, looking for a straight line in a world tangled like spaghetti. As I played, what came into my mind was Frankie.

To be precise, what came into my mind was Gino's in Caracas, two weeks after Frankie had been born. I played a lot of piano in Gino's, because the Venezuelan orangutans soaking up their whiskey with the antique whores thought they liked a little gringo blues from time to time. I was a nice gringo kid, eighteen years old, with a baby already. Mary Ellen was sitting at the table by the stage, and I was playing "Frankie and Johnny," the fast version, because I was in practice. Frankie was on Mary Ellen's arm, wrapped in a shawl, and the whores were cooing in the background, and the lights were down low, so the candle made a madonna-and-child nimbus around Mary Ellen's head. And when I got to the chorus, that Mary Ellen usually sang with me, she could not get up, because of the baby. So I sang it myself.

It was a lonely feeling. *Freya* was sold. Down there on the hard lay the boat I had built with my own hands so we could sail back to England. It was shiny with varnish, sails bent on, ready to go. And I knew we were in trouble.

> Frankie she said to her Johnny,
> "My love, Johnny, don't go.
> Gonna catch your death of cold out there
> in the terrible rain and snow."
> Them love affairs
> gettin' harder to bear.

Mary Ellen looked up, caught my eye. She gave me a long, sad look. Then she dropped her eyes back to the baby. The tears were sliding down her face.

We had already baptized our daughter Anna Maxwell. But

from that moment on, we both called her Frankie. We had sailed back to England with Frankie gurgling in the pilot berth.

It should have been just like old times, except for the weather. But part of each of us was separate, below in the neat clutter of the cabin, with Frankie. We stood our watches. We hardly saw each other. The link was Frankie.

I knew that I was stuck with the sea. But I knew too that Mary Ellen was sliding away from it. She was getting frightened, for Frankie's sake.

As we passed the Bishop Rock, she smiled for the first time in three weeks, and held Frankie up to look at the keepers on the gallery. By the time the Isle of Wight was on the horizon, she had packed her clothes and Frankie's. As we came alongside at Shamrock Quay, she put both her arms around my neck and kissed me, hard. She said, "I love you but I can't do this anymore."

Then she hoisted Frankie under her arm, shouldered her bag, and walked up the granite steps into the crowd.

The last verse came around. I found I was roaring the words, thumping big, doomy chords with both hands. I wanted a drink. I ended it on a big ninth, and got up. Some of the diners clapped and cheered.

Frankie was watching me from behind the bar. Her eyes reminded me of Mary Ellen's eyes in Gino's, all that time ago. There was wet on the upper slopes of her cheeks.

I said, "Could I have a cognac?"

She put her hand on mine. She said, "I liked that music, Dad."

Suddenly I did not want any more to drink.

She said, "What's going on?"

I looked into her clear and lovely eyes, and I wanted to weep. I said, "Nothing's going on, except we're sailing tomorrow."

She kissed me on the cheek. We trudged up the stairs, and said goodnight, and went to our beds.

16

At ten o'clock next morning there was a strong, exciting whiff of holiday in the air. In the restaurant, the waiters were wearing matelot hats with red pompoms. The trace of the barograph on the piano was high and flat, except where I had disturbed it with bass chords the previous night.

The Vieux Port looked as if a carnival had descended on to its scummy waters. There were half a dozen racing boats at the pontoon, battle flags limp in the calm. The quays were lined with tourists taking pictures of heavily tanned men stomping down the pontoons in crew shirts and deck shoes.

Of course, there was no wind. The Azores high had shoved a loop of isobar out over Biscay, and there was no chance of it shifting.

"Nice day for swimming," said Frankie, as we turned on to the finger of wood alongside the cardinal-red hull of *Plage d'Or*. She was excited this morning. She had decided to be civil to her old man because he played good piano and took her sailing. During her stays with me at Pulteney, she appeared from time to time on the trapeze of young Jamie Agutter's 505. Last regatta, they had won their class against some serious competition. As a consequence, she had appalled Mary Ellen by demanding a dinghy at Butler's Wharf. She liked big boats, too.

I squinted up at the china-blue sky. I said, "Not much good for sailing." I waited while she pulled herself aboard.

Down the jetty was a small, stocky man, deeply tanned, with dark glasses attached to his head with an elastic strap. He had a heavy walrus mustache, a thick lower lip, navy-blue Bermuda shorts elegantly faded and a Blue Arrow crew suit.

"Bruce!" I yelled.

He raised a leathery paw.

To look at, you would have thought Bruce Missing was a real salty old dog. That was what he wanted you to think. Actually, he was a photographer who got sick when he stepped over a puddle. Furthermore, he was a fearsome gossip. If Feuilla wanted the word out that Thibault was aboard, Brucie was the one to spread it.

"Hold it," he said, and blasted off at me with one of the three cameras slung around his bull neck. "Thibault aboard?"

"Sure," I said.

"Will he come ashore?"

"Bit tied up," I said. "New hydraulics. Usual problems. You know."

"Sure," he said, wisely. He did not know.

"Come for a sail," I said, grinning at him, to show willing hospitality.

"I'm on *Nabob,* there, love to, course."

"Course," I said.

When we got back he would be waiting on the quay, explaining that he had missed *Nabob* because his agent had called. *Next* time, of course. And he would spend the rest of the day explaining how Thibault had been telling him, *in person,* mind, about the hassles with those new hydraulics.

I said, "Nice to see you," and swung myself on deck. When I looked after him, he was chatting with a grinder on our sleek white next-door neighbor, jerking his head back at us. The word was spreading.

Yann was in the cockpit, bent over a winch. He looked up. "We ready to go?"

"When we get some breeze."

"We'll get breeze."

Up to Belle-Île was home waters for Yann. We had him for local knowledge, me for sailing and tactics, Bianca for helming, and Frankie for moral support and good order. Thibault had won a lot of races in *Plage d'Or.* She had been a good boat in her time. Nowadays she was looking a little tired, and she lacked the refinement and balance of *Arc-en-Ciel.* But she had plenty of brute power. And unlike most of the other boats in the race, she was designed to be sailed shorthanded. With four of us aboard, she was overstaffed. We were easily as fast as most of the IOR maxis, with their crews of twenty-odd. We had a reasonable chance of getting over the line first.

I looked down the flat gray deck, sixty feet of it, studded with winches the size of young oildrums, the mast eighty feet high, so Bianca, up there on a halyard to check the masthead, looked the size of a weathercock on a church steeple. And I felt the old familiar grip on the stomach; the grip that had taken me away from my wife and daughter and said, here we go, full rag into the big sea to blast hell out of the lot of them. I squinted across the cockpits of *Nabob* and *El Negro* at the cockpit of *White Wing*.

Crespi was there, with the men who had been in the restaurant last night. Brucie Missing was leaning on *White Wing*'s rail, chatting. I saw him look back at *Plage d'Or,* grin under his silly mustache, waddle on down the pontoon to the next boat. The man he had been talking to went aft to Crespi. Crespi looked at us sharply. I ran down the side-decks, casting off springs. Bianca came down the mast. I said to Yann, "Off we go. Quick." We did not want anyone climbing aboard to talk to Thibault.

She said, "Where's Thibault?"

I said, "Below."

The engine whirred. They cast off the bow and stern lines. For a moment, *Plage d'Or*'s hull hung between the horns of the jetties like a sword eased in its scabbard. Then I shoved the lever to ASTERN. The wheel kicked under my hands as the rudder bit. She slid out into the harbor, her nose swinging for the gap between the gray granite flanks of the towers.

Bianca went below. When she came back on deck again, she looked pale and worried. She said, "Thibault's not there."

I smiled at her. "No," I said. "But the sponsor wants people to think he's on board."

She gazed at me for perhaps five seconds, deadpan. Then her face cracked into a grin. "And you told Bruce Missing," she said. *"Oh, le petit Nelson."* She laid her head against my arm. "Perfidious Englishman."

"Irishman."

She laughed. Frankie looked pointedly over the side. If Bianca was put out that Thibault was not there, she was hiding it well.

We hummed down the channel. Astern, boats were coming out of the slot between the towers like wasps from a nest. Among the enormous spars of the maxis were the masts of lesser offshore racers like Justin. They had been piling in all week to give themselves a workout with the big boys. The Tour de Belle-Île was one of the few remaining races where amateur boats could mix it with big sponsored yachts crewed by professionals.

Beyond the Île de Ré bridge, the mussel beds were covered. Two nights ago, on that low gray-green shore, Crespi's driver had prodded me in the belly with his gun, and set fire to Christophe's shed.

The sea was smooth as satin. The sun boomed down out of a brilliant sky. It was a lovely day. On this lovely day we had to sail a two-hundred-mile race against people who used shotguns to give them that competitive edge.

We could have done with a bit more wind.

There was a boat marking one end of the line, a buoy the other. The tide was ebbing. The digital figures on the Brookes and Gatehouse timer said there were thirty-five minutes to the start, at noon. The ebb would still be there at start time. At least it would take us over the line. I said to Yann, "Anchor?"

The anchor went down with a plunge and a roar of chain. *Plage d'Or* fell back, dug in the hook, settled stern to the start line. I stopped the engine. Silence fell, except for the cry of gulls, and the gurgle of the tide under *Plage d'Or's* polished hull, and the insect drone of yachts' motors moving down from the distant loom of the city.

"Sails," said Yann. "Ghoster ready."

The main went up the mast and hung limp in the calm, a buff-and-white triangle of bullet-proof Kevlar. We all went up to the foredeck, snapped rubber bands on to a huge wisp of Mylar foresail and laid it along the rail like a dead anaconda.

Still there was no wind.

Frankie was smearing zinc sunblocker on her freckles. She said to Yann, "Hot."

"Not for long," he said.

She squinted up at the sky, which was as achingly blue as ever. "What do you mean?"

"Vent solaire," he said. "Sea breeze."

Frankie was losing interest. What she wanted was speed, and action, the kind of thing she had got on Jamie's 505, or Jean-Claude's motorbike.

No, I thought. This is not the moment to consider Jean-Claude.

The maxis came up on the line, anchored, pulled up mainsails. They were to seaward of *Plage d'Or,* six of them. The smaller boats filtered in. So did the spectators, whizzing out from the land in fast motorboats, making *Plage d'Or* roll in the washing-machine turbulence of their wakes. Helicopters came to natter overhead, looking for footage that would keep the sponsors happy. They found Frankie in her bikini, and Bianca in her shorts, and homed in like blowflies.

On the deck of the committee boat a man stooped and pulled a lanyard. The ten-minute gun banged. A pile of white smoke hung in the motionless air for a moment, then sank on to the glassy water.

"Bloody French," said Bianca. "Wind or no wind, we start."

I pushed the Brookes and Gatehouse buttons to show boatspeed. The LCD read 1.6. The boat was anchored, so the figures showed the speed of the tide running under the hull. A man on one of the maxis shouted, "Where's Thibault?" His voice came across a hundred yards of water as if he were in the cockpit.

"Down here!" yelled Yann from below decks. He had worked with Thibault for long enough to be able to imitate his voice.

I jabbed at the timer again. Eight minutes to the start gun. I said, "Let's do the anchor."

Yann came on deck wearing an anorak with the hood up. Across the shoulders of the anorak was written PLAGE D'OR— THIBAULT LEDOUX. We shuffled up to the foredeck. I pumped the windlass. The gurgle of the tide deepened as the hull moved up on the anchor.

A helicopter hung overhead, filming. That would please Feuilla.

The anchor broke out of the mud. The horizon swung across the boat's nose. I scuttled aft to the wheel. Still there was no wind. The boat drifted down the tide, without steerage way. The wheel was slack and powerless under my hands. The committee boat slid closer.

"Six minutes," said Bianca.

The boats between us and the line were creeping forward over their anchors now.

"Wind," said Yann from under the peak of the hood, and pointed.

A long way down toward the mainland, the blue mirror of the water was blurred with shadow. My mouth had dried out.

We drifted on, sideways, washed by the tide toward the line. The breath of wind disappeared. But it was an indicator that the sun had heated the land faster than it had heated the sea, and the air would be rising, pulling a stream of cooler air off the sea. The *vent solaire*.

But if it came too soon, we would be over the line early, forced to reround the committee boat, restart. In no wind, that could take all day.

"Three minutes," said Bianca.

Plage d'Or hit a flaw in the tide, turned on her axis like a toy boat in an eddy of the stream. There were other boats between us and the line, playing it safe, still anchored, stately over their reflections in the blue mirror. We were bearing down on a half-tonner, drifting stern-first, swinging gently as we went. I could not remember if he had anchored before us. If he had, he had right of way. If not, we did.

Frankie said, "You're going to hit him!"

I said, "Let's have the drifter."

Yann and Bianca did not stop to tell me there was no wind. They put their backs into the halyard. The long, elastic-trussed serpent of sail shot up to the masthead. The half-tonner was twenty yards away. There was a man on the foredeck, bending over the anchor windlass.

Beyond the deck of the committee boat, the blue mirror was hazed with wind.

I said, "Sheets."

Frankie hauled on the portside sheet. The pop of breaking elastic bands sounded almost noisy in the still air. The huge sail floated free. The half-tonner was ten feet down-tide, now. Her crew were beginning to shout. Short of starting the engine, there was no way we could miss her.

There was a rustle, and a soft *whap*. Suddenly there was a breath on my face. The drifter swelled into a dove's breast full of breeze, and the wheel tightened under my hands as the rudder bit water. The man at the half-tonner's anchor cable stopped shouting and stared. I could see the individual beads of sweat on his forehead. *Plage d'Or's* stern was still slewing toward him. But there was wind in her mainsail now, forward motion as well as the sideways yaw of her stern. I eased the wheel to starboard. The stern held off his bow. For five seconds he was so close I could have walked to the side and shaken his hand. Then we were past him, without touching.

"Gun," said Bianca at the stopwatch.

The gun banged. *Plage d'Or* slid over the line. Astern, the start area was a jostling tangle of boats. Ahead, the water was clear.

"Wow," said Frankie. She had forgotten to look dignified.

I grinned at her. *Daddy does this all the time.*

We were away.

17

A good start is a psychological advantage, but it is not an advantage you necessarily expect to last. But we had a twenty-second lead, and we managed to hang on to it.

As the afternoon wore by, the wind went on up until it was blowing good and hard from the west. The lead boats crept up on us. They stayed in a tight, level bunch. The coast was low to starboard. To port the horizon was blue, sharp as a knife.

In the evening, we sighted Île d'Yeu, a tortoise-shaped bluish hump shrugging its way above the horizon. Yann said, "Steer in close."

I let him go. Bianca put down the helm. We went jumping away eastward. The nose started to squeeze hard wedges of spray aft, and the hull drummed the way it does when you are going very fast indeed.

"They're not following," said Yann. "They think we're crazy."

The log was flicking between nine and twelve. But the group of cream-and-yellow sails alongside us was drawing ahead. I glanced across at Yann's train-smash profile. I was not so sure he was not crazy myself. Rule one of the racer's Bible says it is no good sailing fast if you are sailing in the wrong direction. I said to Yann, "Maybe they've got a reason," and felt ashamed of myself. He had been sailing these waters since he had been able to walk.

He did not answer. After five minutes, he said, "Look."

Ahead, a drift of scum and bubbles lay across the line of the green swells. "Mackerel," he said.

He was not talking about fishing. What he meant was that the little fish mackerel like to eat are to be found in the scum lining the edge of the swift rivers of tide that flow through the slower waters of the sea.

With a roar of spray squeezed from the flare of her bow, *Plage d'Or* bounced into the tide.

"Harden up," said Yann.

The winches groaned. The big airfoils of the sails creaked in.

"So look," said Yann.

We were sailing hard on the wind again. But the water on which we were sailing was moving to windward. The Île d'Yeu came out of the sea as if on hydraulic jacks. The other sails fell astern. At nine o'clock, the dusk was rolling out of the eastern sky and the lights of Belle-Île were looming beyond the steep-canted foredeck.

Things began to take a long time. The wind went north, on

the nose, freshened. We were tacking, zigzagging into the wind's eye, clawing our way northward. We were on the starboard tack, the wind blowing into my right ear. Down to starboard, the lights of Belle-Île winked like glowworms suspended in a well. We were zigging far out into the Bay of Biscay. It was time to tack inshore, make the zag that would bring us across the Pointe des Poulains, at the northern tip of Belle-Île. Once around the point we could bear away, turn off the wind, pull up the spinnaker and start to thunder home. The trick was to tack at the right moment. If we overstood, sailed too far on this tack, we would waste time. If we did not sail far enough, we would sail into the cliffs.

I said to Yann, "Tack now?"

"Not yet," he said. *"Vent solaire* takes us around."

The steering compass was on 320°, well to the west of north. I did not believe him.

Frankie's head came out of the hatch. "Radio," she said. "M. Feuilla."

Below was a dark, rackety cave, full of ghostly screens and sailbags strewn like corpses in a vault. I jammed myself into the navigator's chair. Even over the radio, Feuilla sounded as if he had been dining. "How's it going?" he said. "How's Thibault?"

"Fine," I said. On a race like this, the press got a lot of good copy by eavesdropping on VHF communications. "We're leading, as far as I know."

"Give me your position," he said.

Plage d'Or smacked into a short, sharp wave, and went over on her ear with a crunch and a roar. I prodded the Decca and read him the numbers.

"Nearest boat's half a mile downwind," he said. "Jolly good show."

I simpered down the microphone. He wished me good luck. I hung up the mike, and went on deck. Sponsors can make you feel like a poodle, if you are not used to them.

"Well?" said Yann. The wind was up even since I had been below. It was blowing hard enough to blast your breath away. Frankie and Bianca were a dark huddle on the windward side of the cockpit.

The compass said near enough 350°, ten degrees west of

due north. The wind was veering northerly, and we were following it around.

"Vent solaire!" yelled Yann. "He always go northeast. Till tomorrow morning, now. It takes us home."

I got up on the rail, had a look. Cross-waves were ripping the swell, steep black fences of water that rushed along the long Atlantic rollers and sent sheets of spray hammering into the cockpit. We were coming abeam of the blink of Pointe des Poulains. Closer and well ahead on the starboard bow was the ten-second cycle of quick white blink and darkness of the West cardinal buoy marking the scatter of rocks off the point.

The wind dipped, gusted, dipped again. It was trying to veer, moving clockwise around the compass, slipping back again. Bianca was on the helm, feeling the wind through her hands the way a horsewoman would feel the reins of a thoroughbred. Astern, the wake was curved like a ghostly scimitar where she had luffed. There was another gust. The boat shook like a twanged cello at the thump of the wind. It fell calm, and thumped again, this time from dead ahead, hard, so *Plage d'Or* buried her lee rail, and black water roared into the cockpit. Again the twang. A clod of water tumbled aft and smashed into my face like a fist.

The wind steadied. The deck tilted, and the world became quiet, except for the whizz of the wake and the bang and rush of the seas.

Aft, a green light flicked above the phosphorescent specks of the wake. Above it was a pale shadow. I shut my eyes, looked again. The light was still there. A starboard navigation light. There was the white smudge of a bow-wave at its foot, and the distinct triangle of sails. The opposition had arrived.

I said to Yann, "How soon can we tack?"

I saw his head swing at the white flicker of the cardinal buoy, and the Pointe des Poulains light. Then he jabbed the Brookes and Gatehouse with his thumb, checked boatspeed and heading. He said, "Not quite yet, maybe." He was calm as a fisherman deliberating when to shoot his nets. The reflective letters across his shoulders flared in the lighthouse's beam: THIBAULT LEDOUX. Sailing with ghosts, I thought. The wraith of a live man. In Carthystown, people claimed they met the wraiths of those about to die.

But this was not a wraith. It was Yann, in the boss's coat.

I took a couple of bearings of my own, slid down the hatch and plotted them on the chart. We were still well to the south of the West cardinal buoy. Cardinal buoys mark dangers under the sea. West cardinals are to the west of the danger. Anyone who did not know this coast would leave this one to starboard. Then and only then he would tack, turning sharp right across the top end of the island.

Unless he had spent twenty years fiddling his way in and out of the nooks and crannies. Like Yann.

In daylight, Belle-Île is a sharp-edged fortress of granite, and the green swells rumble like siege engines in its bays and gullies. Off the northwest shore, inside the cardinal buoy, fangs of black granite stud the seabed. There is a short cut between the rocks and the shore, but it is not a good short cut to take in someone else's boat.

Unless there is a race to be won.

I went back into the cockpit, wedged myself against the kick of the deck, and watched the bearing. The wind was up again. *Plage d'Or* was over on her ear, rattling through the steep seas. Astern, there were two sets of navigation lights in the inky black. We were set for the safe route, to the west of the buoy, the long way around.

The lights astern were gaining. It was too early to tack for the point, if we were taking the safe route.

Yann said, "We can go inside."

The unsafe route.

I said, "When you're ready."

Yann's teeth gleamed briefly in the shadow of his hood.

"Tacking," I said.

The boom slammed over. The winches rang. We tacked.

The green starboard lights fell away into the murk astern, still heading for the buoy. There was a burst of sound from the VHF. I ignored it. Bianca said, "You have the helm." She left her hand on the wheel long enough for me to feel the warm touch of her fingers.

Plage d'Or was roaring through the seas, straight and tight as a locomotive. I found I was thinking of Mary Ellen.

When we had come back across the Atlantic, there had been three big days in the Gulf Stream, green waves halfway up the mast, winds force ten. She had kept quiet for those three days, with Frankie penned into her pilot berth, chasing alphabet bricks to and fro with the boat's roll. At last, the weather had moderated. Mary Ellen had said, "Don't you ever do this to your child again."

Actually, Frankie had been the only one on board who had enjoyed it.

I thought, here we go again.

"This is *great*," said Frankie.

"Breakers," said Bianca.

Down to starboard, a line of white appeared, vanished again.

"Seen 'em," I said. I had suddenly run out of spit. The Pointe des Poulains light was almost dead ahead, peeping from behind the jib. "We're taking the inside track."

Frankie said, "Great."

"The father's daughter," said Bianca. Frankie laughed. She seemed pleased and proud.

Plage d'Or dipped to a gust and thundered on. We were rushing into a funnel. The funnel consisted of a fence of rock to the north, converging with the stone shores of the island to the south. And somewhere up there in the dark, just off the point, was a gap.

The breakers were bigger and whiter now. I was steering a fraction inside the lift and flutter that meant the wind was the wrong side of the sail, disrupting the smooth airfoil that was pulling us forward. Up to port, a pale something grew.

Bianca saw it too. "Sail," she said.

I squinted hard alongside it, to use the night-vision parts of the retina. The pale something bloomed like a huge white flower, died with a roar. Spray drizzled into the cockpit. "Relax," I said. "It's only a rock."

Frankie giggled. Half a million quids' worth of boat, four human lives, hurtling at a twenty-yard gap in the rocks in a sea like tumbling houses. You had to laugh, while there was time.

Time ran out.

To starboard, the breakers came leaping out to meet us. To port, geysers of white spray were bounding into the black sky. The world was full of a rumble that could be felt rather than heard. Ahead, the sea was covered in a white scum that caught the glow of the starboard light and turned mossy green.

Frankie was beside me now, her knee pressed hard against my thigh. Yann had been crouching over his bearing compass, squinting at the lighthouse. It was high above us, the light, its white glare blooming and shrinking, blooming and shrinking.

Yann shouted, "Starboard a bit!" The rumbling made his voice small and tinny. We slid around a point of rock, leaving it perhaps forty yards to starboard.

Ahead, the black loom of the headland fell into the sea. Out from the point, a line of roaring white breakers spread across the world.

"Go for the buoy!" yelled Yann.

Bianca was easing off the sheets, adjusting the sails to the new, freer angle of the wind. *Plage d'Or* liked the freedom. She was ripping strips of spray from the waves with a sound like tearing linen. I saw the North cardinal buoy, a continuous quick flash beyond the silver-white of the breakers. I put the helm down. I hoped he knew what he was doing.

We were in the fringes of the backwash now. The rocks were streaking past, bellowing with splintered water. Ahead, between us and the buoy, the sea was boiling like a huge kettle.

Yann had come aft. He shouted above the suck and roar of the sea, "That's a rock. Leave it to port."

Frankie's fingers were hurting my arm. A big wave slid under the stern. It went up and up, the stern. The nose dipped. Somewhere at about the level of my right ear, an express-train roar began. Out of the corner of my eye, I saw the top of our wave hang and topple, start to spill forward. *Plage d'Or's* sixty feet of deck took on a steep downward slope. She shot forward, fans of white water tearing out on either side of her hull. Surfing.

Surfing toward the roaring silver patch dead ahead. I hauled on the wheel, starboard. But there are times when a surfing boat is going at the same speed as the water, and has no steerage way.

This was one of those times.

The nose would not come around. Traveling at thirty knots, she kept right on going for the rocks.

Frankie had her arm wrapped tight around my leg. Over to port, the front of the wave began to explode on granite. I screamed at Bianca, *"Leggo!"*

The sheet went out with a bang. The mainsail roared. The taut genoa pulled the boat's nose downwind, the way I was steering.

The nose came around.

Plage d'Or shot across the front of the wave like a sixty-foot toboggan. Suddenly she was traveling slower than the crest. It thundered on to her hollow decks. A big, watery hand picked me up and slammed me into the side of the cockpit, roared up my nose and into my ears and tried to prize its way into my mouth and tug my safety harness loose from its strongpoint. My arms were around Frankie. Frankie was what I had to hang on to.

So I hung on, and waited for the sea to let me breathe. And after what seemed like a couple of hours, the water receded, and I breathed, and left Frankie to fend for herself.

The sea ahead had changed. The North cardinal flickered astern. Across and away in the dark, a white glow lit the cloud. Quiberon, seven miles away to the northeast.

The sea ran out of the back end of the cockpit into the soft dark roll of the swell. I counted heads. All present. I started to sweat with relief. In the middle of sweating I wound the wheel. The compass card swung. I heard myself roaring, "So where's the bloody kite?"

Yann bent over the winch. The spinnaker popped out. At fourteen knots plus the tide, an easy mile ahead of the fleet, *Plage d'Or* started for home.

Bianca took the wheel. Off the wind was where she shone. Below, Frankie was sitting by a big basket of thermos flasks. She gave me a mug of soup. She said, "Well done, Dad. This is the life, eh?" I felt a surge of love for her.

I swung my feet on to one of the pipe cots. It is not fashionable to sleep on short offshore races, but forty winks was not going to hurt. The Lokata radar detector was beeping, picking up the emissions of a ship somewhere in the vicinity. Someone had us on his screen. We were a big target, so I was not worried. Frankie was asleep on the other cot. Now that the nervous energy had gone, I was tired. I dozed.

It could not have been much more than twenty minutes later when I awoke. Someone was hammering on the cabin top. *Plage d'Or* was still thundering along at her steady lope. Something was wrong, though. There was light finding its way through the scuttle on deck. A harsh white light, that had no right to be there.

I swung my feet on to the deck and climbed into the cockpit.

18

Plage d'Or was on a broad reach under spinnaker, plowing long furrows of spray out of the shining black wavefronts. Everything in her cockpit was bathed in a bluish-white radiance. Bianca was a hooded figure on the wheel, her brown skin deadened by the glare, shading her eyes with her hand, trying to keep her night vision.

The light was coming from the starboard side. At the end of a dazzling lane of silver water, a small sun appeared to have risen. From behind the brilliant disc came the sound of engines. It was a searchlight, and a big one.

"He's been there five minutes," said Yann.

"Silly bastard," I said. I waved my arms, to tell him to get away.

The light went out. Red spots floated in front of my eyes. Out in the night, big engines throttled up.

"There he goes," said Yann. "Christ—"

Because the engine note had climbed to a throaty roar. And night vision or no night vision, out there in the black something big churned phosphorescence with its screws, and started moving. Moving toward us.

I stumbled aft, barged Bianca off the wheel. The big thing in the night surged closer. I shoved the wheel down. *Plage d'Or* lay over as she roared up to windward. There was a split-second glimpse of a high white wall of hull. Then it slammed into *Plage d'Or,* flank to flank.

I was flung flat on my face on the deck. I climbed up the wheel. Bianca was shouting.

Yann was saying, "He rammed us," as if he could not believe it had happened.

The other boat had sheered off and turned on his light. I had seen him, now. He was big. A motor yacht, maybe. The reflective letters on the back of Yann's oilskin jacket glared in the searchlight like a traffic sign. THIBAULT LEDOUX.

I said to Yann, "Forward locker. Floating warps."

Yann's face was white in the glare. The sense came back into his eyes. He dived below.

My hand snapped out the navigation lights. I dragged the wheel around. *Plage d'Or* started to leap across the water again. I said to Bianca, "This guy wants to kill us. Roll up the kite. Put on the Number One."

She was up, now, stumbling white-faced in the cockpit.

"Let it blow," I said. "Ditch it."

Bianca understood. She went forward to the mast at a fast, agile lope.

The light went out. The motor yacht came in again. I roared, *"Hold on!"* He came down on us at twenty knots. I turned away from him at fifteen, but I could not go all the way, because the spinnaker was still up, a huge cloth bag full of tons of wind. There was the hissing roar of wakes meeting. The jar of the concussion slammed me into the cockpit locker. A tall steel side scraped and juddered all the way down *Plage d'Or*'s hull.

There was a roar forward. Something flapped against the sky like a giant bat, and was gone. Yann came up the hatch, dragging two huge coils of rope, three-inch polypropylene warps for towing over the stern in big following seas. Polypropylene is lousy rope, but it is strong, and it floats.

"Over the stern," I said.

Yann laid the coil on the deck, fed an end over the stern. *Plage d'Or* went ahead slowly, spilling wind. As she went, Yann paid the floating rope off the coil.

I said, "How's the hull?"

"Not good," said Yann. One of the warps was all the way out, trailing astern. He was crouching in the bottom of the cockpit, knotting the second warp on to the first. "But no leak."

The hull was made of Kevlar. So are bullet-proof waist-coats.

The light came on again. THIBAULT LEDOUX, blazed the letters on Yann's jacket.

"Keep down," I said. I should have been frightened out of my wits. Actually, I was bloody angry. You bastard, I thought. You think you can bang us to little bits at your leisure. You are wrong.

There had been a brief moment a few summers ago when Mick Savage had been the match-race scourge of Pulteney Bay. Being angry had helped, particularly in the nasty one-on-one jousts known as pre-start maneuvers.

The motor yacht came in again. This time, he kept his light on. I said, "Panic."

We panicked. It was not difficult to be convincing, skewered on the searchlight beam, with the wind tearing at the tops of the waves and a hundred tons of motor yacht trying to smash us to the bottom of the sea.

The yacht came to T-bone us, the light on her glaring like a great eye. When she was twenty yards off, I put the helm down. I felt the tug of the rope as *Plage d'Or* came up close-hauled, heading toward the motor yacht, but sixty feet to starboard. The motor yacht could not alter course in time to catch us. The searchlight lost us, and she surged past our stern. I could smell the stink of her exhausts. She had crossed the hundred meters of warp streaming astern. Now or never, I thought.

Yann said, "I've got a bite." On the deck aft of the cockpit, what was left of the coiled warp was jumping like an electrocuted cobra.

The other end had gone under the motor yacht. Now it

was winding around her propellers in lovely great plastic fetters, thick as your wrist.

The coil bounded aft, leapt over the transom and disappeared into the black sea.

The motor yacht made a half-turn in the water, stopped, rolling. The stretch of sea between us widened. The searchlight went out.

I put the helm down, shoved the nose back on course. I said, "Trim."

Bianca trimmed. *Plage d'Or* heeled to the northeasterly breeze. She began to move southward again, toward La Rochelle.

I sat down fast, because my knees were shaking too hard to keep me up anymore. Frankie had climbed on deck. She said, "That boat was ramming us."

I got hold of her, and I put my arms around her, and I hugged her. "Yes," I said. "That's right." Then I went below to check the damage.

If the motor yacht had managed to catch us beam-on, it would have cut us in half, no worries. But what we had had were two big, glancing blows. There was a soft spot in the side, and the keel bolts might have been strained. But there were no leaks and the frames looked all right, and while you have frames, and a skin, and a mast, and some sails, there is hope.

So I checked the liferaft, and made it easy to reach. And we put up the other kite, and went on racing.

The dawn came up pink and dove-gray over a sea of marching green rollers. We breakfasted off bread and ham, and I sent Bianca and Frankie below for a doze on a sailbag. There were three other sails in sight, the closest a couple of miles astern. I put my glasses on them.

The lead boat was *White Wing*. Crespi.

I went below, unhooked the mike and called Georges at the yard. When he answered, I said I would be on the slip at eight, and told him to find a slot for *Plage d'Or*. Then I said, "Oh yeah. I'll be bringing Thibault."

He said, "What?"

I terminated the call, raised the coastguard and told them that if they went looking, they might find a motor yacht disabled somewhere southeast of Belle-Île. They told me they had already made contact, dropped a diver to clear fouled propellers. The name of the boat was *Serica* of St. Peter Port. She was making for Sables d'Olonne under her own power.

I disconnected.

There was a race to finish.

We were flying the big gold kite with the sponsor's name across it in blood-red letters. Frankie and Yann and Bianca were crouched aft. We should have been tired but happy.

Except that someone had tried to kill us all.

By the time we could see the white straddle of the Île de Ré bridge, it was a gray, foggy day, with very little wind. We hung about in the Pertuis Breton, waiting for the tide to turn and wash us over the line. There was a gun, and a couple of helicopters, and some desultory cheering. Then we motored in and dropped the boat at Georges's yard for repairs. The rest of the crew went back to the town. I stayed, had a long talk with Georges, and went back to the restaurant. At a quarter to eight I told them that I had a sponsor's meeting to go to, and strolled down on to the quay.

The restaurant's Dory was alongside. I started up, and pointed the nose out of the Vieux Port toward the Minimes.

As I buzzed down the northern side of the channel, the boats were still coming in off the race. There was a big raft-up and festivity planned in the Vieux Port, and anyone who could cram a hull into the basin was getting in while there was still time. I drove toward the Minimes, a hedgehog of masts against the pinkening sky. Around the end of the breakwater I throttled back, puttered gently through the pontoons and tied up by the aquarium.

The Minimes is a big marina. There were a lot of people, weekenders trudging down the pontoons with trolleys of food and kit. The French, unlike the English and the Americans, tend to use their boats. I pulled my oil-stained sunhat over my eyes, tweaked up the collar of my oilskin coat, and trudged across the gray concrete to Georges's fence.

On the other side of the fence was a graveyard of derelict

hulls, fallen over on their sides, cannibalized for parts. Through chinks in the hulls I could see a tall mast, a gleaming black flank. *Arc-en-Ciel.*

I pulled a pair of binoculars from under my coat and swept the slipway. It was seven fifty-five. Five minutes to my rendezvous with Thibault.

I faded back into the lee of a parked lorry. I watched. I waited.

At three minutes to eight, the office door opened and Georges came out, cigarette in his mouth, hands driven deep into the pockets of his filthy blue overalls. There was another man with him, wearing a uniform and a peaked cap, leaning back against the weight of two big Alsatians on choke leads.

Georges said, *"Allons-y,"* and coughed. The man in uniform loosed the Alsatians. The big dogs bounded away across the dirty concrete, noses down, sniffing around the chocked hulls. One of them smelled me by my lorry. It looked at me, black lips drawn back from its teeth. When it realized that I was on the wrong side of the fence, it began an accusing stare.

Then its colleague started to bark, a new, sharp bark, and it turned and ran off at a purposeful gallop. And Georges started shouting. *"Arrête!"* he yelled. Stop! Then he began to cough.

A figure appeared around the end of the boats. He was a big man, brown, with a palm-tree mop of bottle-blond hair. I could not smell the aftershave, but I knew who he was. He was running like an Olympic athlete, because there were two Alsatians behind him. He was coming straight at the fence, hands pumping high in the air, eyes white-rimmed with terror.

He was five steps away when the lead Alsatian gathered its legs under its body and launched itself at him in a long, lazy spring. It took him in the shoulders. He went down with a crash. The dog stuck its face into his and started a long, steady growl.

I turned, and walked slowly back to the Dory. I had seen what I wanted to see. I started the motor, and steered meditatively past the channel markers toward the towers of the city, sugar-pink with the setting sun.

The only person who could know of my mythical rendez-vous with Thibault at the yard was Georges. Unless, of course, someone had been listening in to the link call I had made from *Plage d'Or*.

And if someone had been listening, it was highly probable that they had been listening in to the conversation I had had with Feuilla off the northwest of Belle-Île. In that call, I had given my position. So anyone in a fast motor yacht could have picked up *Plage d'Or* on radar and tracked her to the point where a terrible accident could take place. I remembered the beep of the Lokata, just before I had dozed off on the pipe cot. That would fit.

So it looked as if the person who had arranged our rendezvous with *Serica* was M. Arthur Crespi, the employer of the bottle-blond under the Alsatian.

That night I went ashore and called Mary Ellen, and asked her to track down the owners of *Serica*. Later, there was a reception at which I accepted the line honors cup. I made Bianca and Frankie and Yann come with me. I made a speech about my pride, and the illness of Thibault which at the last moment had prevented him from sailing.

Feuilla came in. He shook my hand and crinkled the walnut-brown skin around his eyes, showing his white teeth for the benefit of the cameras. He said, "Thank you. I'll look after the yard bill." The crowd parted in front of him like ice before an icebreaker, and he was gone.

I did not watch him. I had had enough of big shots. I looked at Frankie, standing to attention, glowing with excitement in her short-short skirt and *Plage d'Or* jersey, all freckles and eagerness. She reminded me of Mary Ellen when I had first known her.

I danced with Frankie. I danced with Bianca. She danced beautifully, pliant and clinging like a vine. For a moment, I forgot Mary Ellen. But only for a moment.

Later, I trudged upstairs and rang Mary Ellen again.

She said, "Do you know what time it is?"

"Yes." She would be lying in her white cotton nightdress in her black-and-white bedroom. There would be a sheaf of magazines and reports on the oversized bedside table, passages marked in yellow highlighter by her research department. Mary Ellen thought insurance in her morning shower, worked insurance in the day. In the night, she made risk assessments in bed. The makeup would be scrubbed off, the horn-rimmed glasses she wore for reading on the end of her nose. All that was left of the Caribbean would be the rum-and-tonic nightcap on the bedside table.

She must have heard the tiredness. Her voice softened a fraction. "Your *Serica*," she said. "Registered as owned by Hope Charter, a Gibraltar company."

"Genuine charter?"

"Tax fiddle." There are a large number of tax fiddles available through Gibraltar companies. What they have in common is that Gibraltar's company law makes it impossible to trace who owns the boat, or how they paid for it.

"Too bad," I said.

"So what's this fraud?"

"More evidence required," I said. "Sleep well."

"One thing," she said. "Your *Poisson d'Avril* ship. I found out about it. There's a claim in."

The hairs on the nape of my neck began to bristle. "Oh?"

"Yes," she said. "It sank. I'm surprised Justin didn't tell you."

I said, "I haven't seen him for a couple of days."

"Got it here," she said. "From *Le Monde de Dakar*. *Poisson d'Avril*, cargo ship of five thousand tons, sank at sea off Senegal yesterday, that's three weeks ago yesterday, after explosions in the hold. Captain, officers and five crew took to the boats. A Moroccan cook and an Ivorian deckhand went down with the ship."

Bought for $100,000. Insured for $391,000. Owned by Thibault's company. Two men dead.

"You still there?" she said.

"Still here."

"Sounds like the real thing, eh?"

"Yep." I remembered Thibault sitting in the hut. *Suddenly, my old friends are thinking I am capable of sinking a boat, for money.* Thibault, a director of Transports Drenec, owners of *Poisson d'Avril*, beneficiaries of an insurance payout. I said, "I'll find us some evidence."

"Evidence is what we need," she said.

The telephone was as heavy as granite.

Thibault in money trouble. Thibault's new boat, heavily insured, with a dud seacock. *Poisson d'Avril* sunk, two dead.

Evidence was what was required.

Evidence to nail whoever it was who had been ready to kill not only Thibault, but three innocent people with him.

Arthur Crespi had wanted the folders. He had been ready to kill Thibault, presumably to stop Thibault talking about their contents. And he had been ready for Frankie and Bianca and Yann and me to drown at the same time.

If it had been Thibault they were after.

But Bianca had seen the *Poisson d'Avril* papers, and so had I.

It could have been any of us.

I sat there and felt cold and shaky. I wished to go down and have a drink with my daughter, and make a plan to get her out of this.

I rang Agences Giotto. The girl on the end said she was sorry, but M. Crespi was not there right now. I asked where he was. She said she did not know.

I rang off, and stared at the telephone. M. Crespi was not going to tell anyone anything. The home of evidence was London, because London was where I knew people.

I rang Mary Ellen, again. My ear was getting sore.

She had been asleep. I could hear the drowsiness in her voice. She said, "What is it now?"

"I want you to look after Frankie."

The voice sharpened. She said, "What do you think I've been doing for the past seventeen years?"

"I mean she's not safe in France."

"What have you got her mixed up in?" She was all the way awake now.

"I've got to come to England. On business. She'd be better off with you. Are you in London?"

"Where else?"

I said, "Can you get a message to Justin? I want to talk to him about the next step."

She said, "Probably." The business was back in her voice. "When are you coming?"

"Tonight."

She made a surprised noise. "Don't hang about, do you?"

"No."

She said, "You sound tired." There was a pause. In a new, softer voice, she said, "Look after yourself. I'll get Justin to give you lunch at Lloyd's."

I put the telephone down. I called Georges, asked him to put *Arc-en-Ciel* on a mooring when he had finished. Then I packed my suitcase. Bianca was out. I would have liked to say goodbye. Frankie came to the station without much fuss. Life was presumably empty now that her Jean-Claude was on the run from the police. We were in Paris by two A.M. At nine-thirty we climbed on to the London flight.

The Thames squirmed like an eel under the wing. Frankie had been very quiet. She said, "That motor boat, on the race. What was he after?"

"Silly bastard," I said.

She said, "You told me he did it on purpose."

"No," I said.

"You said so."

Seventeen is no age to be rolling over stones and peering at the shine underneath. "I was tired," I said. "I was angry. He was a bloody fool in a gin palace. He panicked."

She nodded, and smiled, creasing her long blue eyes. I was the father who chased her boyfriends away, dragged her home when she did not want to go. But she trusted me.

The airplane sank through a brownish haze and landed. We found a taxi. The streets looked filthy in the heat. We went to Butler's Wharf. Frankie let us in with her keys. I shaved among Mary Ellen's collection of natural sponges. Then I put on a tie, and set off for Lloyd's.

19

Justin led me down the stairs to the restaurant in the basement. Above his black coat and striped trousers, the sunset colors of his face hit you like a fist in the eye. "Saw you won," he said. "Had to get back. Sorry about the food. Disgusting place." He ordered quail's eggs. So did I. "Mary Ellen's on her way," he said.

I said "Good," without meaning it, because there were things I wanted to say to him that I did not want Mary Ellen to hear. There was a small flurry at the entrance, and in she came.

She was wearing one of her usual suits, cut so well that you did not notice the thing itself, only a sort of nimbus of elegance and smartness. Her hair was tied back in a bunch. She carried herself very straight and upright. Her skin was pale, the bones of her face fine as a ballerina's. My mind slid to Bianca's vivid Southern coloring. Next to her Mary Ellen would have looked almost washed out, unless you noticed the power in the eyes.

She smiled. It was a smile that energized her face. As with the clothes, you did not notice the person. You only felt the warmth and energy of the smile. She turned it on me, and transferred it to Justin. She stood on tiptoe, and kissed my cheek. Her bones felt light as a bird's.

"Morning, guys," she said. "I'm starving." She reached for the menu, ordered without fuss, and said, "What's all this stuff about shipping lines?"

Justin said, "Mick's found some nasty people. He thinks he can nail them."

I told them about Thibault and *Poisson d'Avril*. I said that someone was after Thibault because he was a potentially leaky partner in the fraud. I did not tell them about the sabotage of *Arc-en-Ciel,* because Justin already knew about that, and Mary Ellen was given to worrying about my health and prospects. And I did not tell them that Crespi had tried to sink *Plage d'Or* during the Belle-Île race, because Frankie had been on board, and I did not want Mary Ellen to think I had endangered Frankie's life.

Mary Ellen nodded. She looked solemn. She said, "So exactly what have you got on this Crespi?"

"What I've told you."

"Not enough," said Justin. "If you want to nail him, you have to get the whole lot. Who owns what, statements from boat's crew, all of it."

I said, "That's why I'm here."

Mary Ellen's eyes had the faraway look they got when she was working things out. "You'd better come up to the box," she said. "I'll give you a number." She sipped her Perrier. "And could you get Mr. Schacker off my back?"

"Schacker?" said Justin. "Lucky chap."

She ignored him. "He wants you to work for him, he said. There's some kind of dance at the Royal Flotilla. There will be a lot of America's Cup people. He wants to show you to his backers."

I grinned at her. Art Schacker was a clever man. He knew where to go to press the buttons. "Oh, good," I said.

Her chin was sticking out a couple of extra millimeters. "It could be a good idea," she said.

What she meant was that the yard was bust, and there were no races to sail just at the moment, and there was not much future in life as an insurance gumshoe. It was a familiar line. As usual, she had a point. And as usual, she would reinforce the point by not cooperating if I did not take it. I found her hand under the table, squeezed it. She smiled at me, her big straightforward Canadian smile. We understood each other. That had always been the trouble.

"Coffee?" said Justin.

We both started to talk to him. For a moment he had been shut out. Both of us felt embarrassed, as if we had been caught performing an intimate act in public. We drank coffee. I walked up with Mary Ellen, across the trading floor and under the twelve-story well of the atrium, threading among the boxes to hers.

The box looked roughly like one of the booths in the bar at Chez Thibault, two benches facing each other across a table, with reference books and telephones instead of bottles and candlesticks. There were a couple of underwriters sitting there, haggling with brokers, with other brokers standing waiting, staring at their feet. The box was Mary Ellen's boat in a sea of money. She spent more time there than she did at home. She slid into her seat, picked up the telephone and made a couple of calls. Brokers began to drift in, like foraging gulls. She gave me a piece of paper with a number on it. "You can use my desk at the office," she said. "Jon Green. I've warned him."

"See you?" I said.

"Sure," she said. "No room at the flat, just at the moment. Oh, by the way. That dance at the Flotilla. Art Schacker wanted me to make sure you went." She smiled, and dropped her eyes. "One said one had no control. You'll find the stiffie on the bookshelf." She was already talking to the first broker with her eyes. She was doing business, and that was that. No room at the flat meant that she was thinking about other things, and did not want to be disturbed.

I took myself off. Justin was at another box, selling. I waved. He waved back, abstractedly; like a lot of good brokers, he seemed to have all-around vision. Outside the building I turned left, and right into a crevice between two blocks of offices. Mary Ellen's desk was on the seventeenth floor, in a roomful of reference books with a complicated telephone, a picture of Frankie, and, I was surprised to see, a picture of *Freya,* the ketch in which we had drifted down the West Indies.

The invitation was on the bookcase. It bore a coat of arms, and a lot of gold leaf. It said that the Royal Flotilla was at home to the challengers for the forthcoming America's Cup round. I shoved it in my coat pocket, sat down at the desk, and called Jon Green. He was a shipping company analyst. I introduced myself.

"Who?" he said.

"Mick Savage," I said. "Mary Ellen Soames put me on to you."

"I know," he said. "The sailor, right? Of course. I've heard all about you."

"Who from?"

"Mary Ellen, course. Can't stop her. Bloody aggravating."
He laughed, to show he was joking. "What can I do for
you?"

I said, "I've got some company names. I want some
people's names, directors, owners."

"We'll try," he said. "What ones?"

I could see them as if I had Thibault's folders in front of
me. "Transports Drenec," I said. "Agences Giotto, Lignes
Étoile, French. Hope Charter, Gibraltarian."

"All right," he said. "I'll punch the buttons. Come on
over and have tea."

I made another call, to Jemima Pattison at *Lloyd's List,*
the publication that lists ships' movements all over the
world. I said, "I want to trace the crew of a ship called
Poisson d'Avril, sunk off Dakar. Can you?"

"Gawd," said Jemima, a strapping woman I had met
crewing for Justin. "I suppose I could try."

I said, "I'll buy you dinner."

"Oh, *well,"* she said. Jemima professed to admire my
exploits at sea. "In *that* case."

I put down the telephone, and headed for Green.

He inhabited a small basement behind the Farringdon
Road, full of old styrofoam coffee cups and lit by banks of
computer screens. He was small and fat, with dark skin and
a hook nose and spectacles in which the screens floated like
fish on a reef. He started talking as soon as I got in at the
door. "Mary Ellen," he said. *"So* pretty. Universally fancied
in insurance circles, though this is not what you want to
hear, being her husband. True to you, though, I should say.
Eighty percent chance any road. But you don't want to listen
to a fat git like me talking about the woman you love. You
want to hear about horrible companies, I want to talk about
human emotions. Story of my life." He remembered he had
asked me to tea, sent his secretary out for coffee. "Well," he
said. "I don't know why you want to know about these
geezers. But it's lucky you came to me, because you would
have been disappointed anywhere else." His chubby fingers
moved over the keys with a sound like distant machine-gun
fire. "I'll print it out. Basically, you've got Transports
Drenec with one visible director, Thibault Ledoux, one-

third. And you've got Lignes Étoile and Agences Giotto, owned one hundred percent by different holding companies. So it looks as if the whole works is separate. And of course Hope Charter is separate, set up to own this boat *Serica,* because it's Gibraltarian." He paused. I thought, well, hell, that's as far as we get. The secretary came in with the coffee which, though in a plastic cup, tasted of cardboard. Green watched my face carefully. "But," he said, "I have my methods. It's all on the databases. And though I say it myself, I am very, very good at databases." He paused again.

I said, "So?"

He said, "In the case of all these companies, the sole or majority shareholder above the holding companies is Atlas Industrien, of Luxembourg."

"All of them?"

"All of them. And you will be pleased to hear that I have secured a complete list of Atlas Industrien's holdings, unto the last generation." He hit a key. A printer started to buzz.

"Thank you," I said. My mouth was dry. My palms were wet. I said, "Who owns Atlas Industrien?"

"Ah," said Green. "Alas. Not easy to say. We were talking about a corporate environment where people think they are being gabby if they ask for sugar in their coffee. I'll keep trying, for the sake of the beautiful Mary Ellen." He shrugged. "But you should get used to the idea that this is the brick wall."

The receptionist at Agences Giotto had described Crespi as the owner. But the owner was Atlas Industrien. Did that mean that Crespi and Atlas Industrien were the same thing?

I asked Green to find out, if he could. Then I collected the list of Atlas's companies, and left.

I read it in the taxi that took me back to the Synge, the nasty little hotel in Russell Square I frequented when I was in London and Mary Ellen was too busy to have me at Butler's Wharf. The best thing about the hotel was its excellent telephone system, and the large, glass-scarred table in the corner. I sat down at the table and dialed Jemima.

"Ah," she said. "There you are. I have always *loved* the Savoy Grill."

"Sorry?"

"Our dinner."

I found I was grinning at the telephone. "What makes you think we're dining?"

"Spiro Kallikratides," she said. "Captain of the late lamented *Poisson d'Avril*. Shipped on the *Milgon Swan* from Dakar for Cardiff with a cargo of rainforest. Arrived Cardiff yesterday."

I was finding it hard to breathe. "You never," I said. "Who's the owner of *Milgon Swan?*"

"Danby Freight."

I ran a pencil down the list of Atlas Industrien companies. "Is that all right?" said Jemima. "Hello?"

Danby Freight was on the first page, just under Chantiers du Palmier. "Absolutely fine," I said.

"So dinner when?"

"I've left my diary in my other suit," I said. "I'll call you."

"I'll be holding my breath," she said. *"Au revoir,* darling."

I ran down the stairs, and caught the five o'clock from Paddington to Cardiff.

It started raining at Bristol, a sweltering heavy August rain that beat the inefficient air-conditioning and filled the carriage with the smell of wet leisurewear. Wales looked gray, and increasingly dirty as the line threaded its way among the grim terraces of Cardiff. But I was not here for a day's sunbathing. I was attempting to earn a living by finding out what my old friend Thibault was doing as a director of a company that earned its living by insurance frauds, and why the company's insurance brokers seemed to wish him dead.

It takes a lot of rain to damp down that kind of curiosity. I told a taxi-driver to take me to the docks. We ground out of the town, into a drab land where the puddles were black with coal dust and piles of rusting scrap sulked behind chainlink fences.

We pulled up on a quay. A small freighter lay alongside. She was red, partly with red lead and partly with rust. *Milgon Swan* was painted in flaking white letters on her stern. A brown man in a ragged black oilskin was leaning on her rail, watching the rain make circles in the puddles. I ran up the gangplank. "Lovely day," I said. "Skipper aboard?"

"No," said the man in the oilskin. He did not look interested in people making bad jokes and looking for his skipper.

"Where might I find him?" I said. I let the Irish creep in.

"You won't," he said.

"Dear, oh dear," I said, in fluent County Waterford. My hand came out of my pocket with a ten-pound note in it.

"Admiral Benbow," said the man in oilskins, and twitched the tenner out of my hand without looking at me. I went back to the taxi.

The Admiral Benbow was a red-brick pub that had once been part of a terrace. The terrace had been demolished, so now it stood on its own, amputated on both sides. The windows had not been cleaned for perhaps a year, during which time heavy lorries had flung a constant soup of coal dust out of the puddles and on to the glass. In the public bar a nicotine-yellow lightbulb was glowing under the nicotine-yellow ceiling. A fruit machine was throbbing in the corner. There were half a dozen men in there. They were all wearing navy-blue overalls, except one. He was on a stool in the corner. He was wearing a wet white shirt. There was a pile of money on the bar in front of him, beside three empty Carlsberg Special Brew cans.

I went up to the bar at his side, and ordered a bottle of Guinness in thick County Waterford. Nobody paid any attention. "Bad day," I said to the man in the white shirt.

He did not answer. His face was dark tropical brown. He had wet black hair. He had not shaved for three days.

I said, "Word in your ear, Captain Kallikratides."

He looked around at me. "Who you?" he said. The dead Special Brews on the bar had not been the first of the day. His eyes were blank and glassy.

I said, "Come over here."

"No."

I said, "I've got a proposition."

"What is it?"

The barman was watching us with eyes that had seen a lot of violence, set on either side of a nose that had been on the receiving end of more. I said, *"Poisson d'Avril."*

Something happened to Kallikratides' face. The creases

deepened, and the eyes narrowed. He did not want to talk about *Poisson d'Avril.* It had been a tactical error to mention her. I glanced at the mirror, behind the bar, checking my line of retreat. The air was thick with sweat, and smoke, and violence.

I said, quickly, "I'm from head office."

He watched me with those narrow eyes.

"Come over here," I said, and pointed to a table in the corner.

He came. He heaved himself to his feet and shuffled across the room. I sat down beside him under a blue-and-yellow tire-pressure chart someone had pinned to the wall.

I said, "I can get you immunity."

He seemed to have woken up. He said, "What you talking about?" He had a heavy Greek accent.

I said, "There will be an inquiry into the sinking of *Poisson d'Avril.* Two men died because of your premeditated action. That makes you guilty of murder."

He put his hands on the table. They were congested and thick-fingered. They gripped the stained deal until the joints turned white. He opened his mouth to tell me to get stuffed. No sound came out.

I said, "I can get you immunity."

He said, "Immunity?" He sounded as if he did not know what it meant. His face was shining with sweat. "I dunno."

"Have a drink," I said. The violence had faded. "More beer? Glass of whiskey?"

"Beer," said Kallikratides. "No drink spirits. Bad in stomach."

I bought him a Special Brew, and a Guinness for myself. I hoped he was not too drunk. I said, "So how about it?"

"'Bout what?"

"Your immunity. Think about it."

There was a gleam of something like understanding in his yellow-and-black eyes. "Who are you?"

"Acting for insurers." I pulled a piece of paper out of my pocket, scribbled Mary Ellen's number on it, and shoved it across the table at him. He crumpled it into the breast pocket of his shirt.

"Reward," he said.

"What about reward?"

"Immunity's a thing," he said. "But if I tell you things, I don't get no more job. So I need money, too."

It had been a long day. I was hot and sweaty and the Guinness tasted like ink. I could feel my patience shredding at the hem like a blown-out flag. I said, "This is your chance to beat murder and fraud."

"Reward," he said. "How much?"

I said, "I don't know."

He said, "Find out."

I said, "Ten thousand pounds."

He shook his head. "More."

I told myself, keep calm. Words are free. I said, "That's all I can offer."

There was a silence. Finally, Kallikratides shrugged. He said, "Maybe there is nothing to tell."

I leaned toward him. I had had enough. I said, "Listen, you. You are going to be found guilty of murder. You are throwing away the chances of immunity from prosecution and a big cash sum. Are you crazy?"

Kallikratides' face was like sweating putty. I could smell his sour smell. He said, "Ten thousand pounds and no jail is fine, if you alive."

I said, "You're alive."

He said, "If I talk to you, not for long." The can rattled against the glass as he poured.

I got up. "Change your mind fast," I said. "Ring the number before midnight. They'll tell you where I am. Otherwise, the law are going to be in your front yard." I pulled open the door and walked out into the rain. The air of South Wales is heavily flavored with noxious gases, but after the public bar of the Admiral Benbow, it was nectar.

I told the taxi to take me to a hotel. They showed me a room that smelled of other people's cigarette smoke. I rang Mary Ellen, told her where I was, and asked her to forward my telephone calls. Then I went out and bought some fish and chips and a couple of cans of Ruddles, and settled down to wait for Mr. Kallikratides to think things out for himself.

I sat there, and tried to think about a sensible future, in which I would go to America and work for Art Schacker and his Flying Fish Challenge. But it was not easy to conceive of a future. My mind kept slithering back into the past.

It slid back to the south of France, when Frankie had been twelve. Mary Ellen had rented a farmhouse in the Dordogne, and asked me to go there with her and Frankie. We had not been away together for at least seven years. Frankie had splashed around in the river, and brought back a three-legged dog, and made friends with some French children. Mary Ellen and I had sat on the terrace, and drunk wine, and said not much. On the fifth night, we had been out to dinner. Frankie was in bed. We were out on the terrace, watching the glow of the lights of other houses among the trees, drinking a glass of wine before bed.

Mary Ellen's face gleamed faintly between the curtains of her hair. She said, "This is a bloody stupid relationship."

I said, "Do you mean it?"

She said, "We have been married for twelve years. We've lived together for two. This is the first time we've been away, all three of us, for . . . well, for ever. Why do we do it?"

The wine was making me feel abnormally confident. I said, "Do you want to change it?"

She touched my hand with her perfectly manicured nails. "Nope," she said. "Because it's Frankie, isn't it?"

"It's Frankie," I said.

And it was. Frankie lived between us, amplifying love. If we had been a couple having rows, there would have been dislike to amplify. But we lived separate lives, and accepted each other's absence. It was probably not a conventional upbringing for Frankie, but it did not seem to be doing her any harm.

Mary Ellen clasped my hand so I could feel the engagement ring I had bought her in Aruba, a cheap emerald, nowadays sandwiched between diamonds the size of cough lozenges. "Shall we change?" she said. Her face was near under the moon. I kissed her mouth. She kissed me back gently. For a moment, we were as close as we had been in Venezuela. "Come on." She stood up, picked up the wine bottle by the neck. I followed her into her room. Our clothes rustled as they hit the floor. Moths battered the screens.

Next morning, we lay tangled in her bed in the hot stripes the sun flung through the blinds. The telephone rang. It was her office. Half an hour later, she was on her way back to England. Nothing had changed.

I finished the first beer, moved on to the second and gazed at the flock wallpaper. I wondered whether I should go down to the hotel bar, in search of lights and action. Halfway through the internal debate, the telephone rang. I grabbed it. My heart was beating too fast.

"Yo," said the voice on the far end. Captain Kallikratides' voice. "I wanna talk to you."

"About what?" I said.

"About immunity."

I let out a long, quiet breath. "Now?" I said.

"Nah. I gotta sleep on it. Seven tomorrow morning, right?"

"Right."

"Sleep good," said Kallikratides. Now we were on the same side, he was observing the social niceties.

I slept good. At six o'clock I rolled out of bed, showered, was refused breakfast by room service, and clambered into a taxi.

It was a fine blue morning. It made even Cardiff look promising. On a morning like this, it was possible to believe that Spiro Kallikratides would spill the goods on Transports Drenec and Danby Freight, and we would get the warrants and the injunctions that would let us roll up the whole filthy carpet, bent surveyors and crooked yards, and tip it into the silk-suited lap of M. Arthur Crespi.

The coal piles had glints of blue in the sun, and the scrap iron was as red as an emperor's robe. We turned through the dock gates.

"Bloody 'ell," said the taxi-driver. "What's all that about?"

Ahead, the land was flat, reclaimed coastal swamp, nailed down with towers and silos. The upperworks of ships stuck up from the docks, jewel-bright in the low sun. Above one of the ships, the clear morning blue was smudged with oily smoke. The ship was the *Milgon Swan*.

I said, "Hurry." It came out as a croak.

He hurried.

The smoke was coming from the ship's accommodation.

There were a couple of fire engines on the quay, blue lights flashing cheerfully. Two extension ladders were pouring water into the upperworks. I got out of the taxi. The smell was strong: burned paint, oil, rubber, hot metal.

A couple of crew were standing watching, hands in pockets. I said, "What happened?"

"Accommodation went up," said one of them. He was bald, and he did not look at all bothered to see his ship burning.

"Where did it start?" I said.

"Skipper's quarters," he said. "Silly bloody piss artist." Then he looked at me. "Why did you want to know, any road?"

I forced a grin. My face felt like old leather. "Everyone loves a fire," I said.

"Then everyone's fucking stupid," he said.

I walked away from him. The smoke was dying back, leaving black eyebrows above the windows. The firemen were off the ladder. A couple of men in breathing apparatus clambered on deck, awkward in their heavy boots, and disappeared through a door.

"Anyone in there?" I said to the fireman.

He turned, heavily. There were dark bags under his eyes. I knew the answer before he told me. "Skipper," he said.

"What are his chances?"

The fireman turned his eyes to the threads of smoke crawling from the windows abaft the bridge. "Not so fucking great," he said. "Not so fucking great at all. You a journalist?"

I pulled a card out of my wallet. Justin had had it made up for me. It had more twists and curlicues than a twenty-pound note. It said, "M. Savage. Special Investigator— Lloyd's of London." It was a baseless document, but it impressed people like firemen.

"He the only one?"

"Only one," he said.

We waited. The wisps of smoke thinned and vanished. A radio crackled. The ambulance by the fire engines opened its back doors. The men in breathing apparatus reappeared on deck. They were carrying the stretcher between them.

There was something on the stretcher. It was covered in a blanket. It smelled like grease and burned cloth.

"There he is," said the fireman. "Poor bastard."

The ambulancemen trotted out, took over. One of the men in breathing apparatus pulled off his mask, lurched to the edge of the quay, and vomited between the ship's side and the coping-stones. His mate had his mask off already. "Drunk," he said. "Two bloody bottles of gin he had in there."

No drink spirits. Bad in stomach.

I turned away and climbed into the taxi. My head was aching. I was glad I had not eaten any breakfast. Captain Kallikratides had got drunk and careless at a very convenient moment for the proprietors of *Poisson d'Avril.*

The day was warming up as the sun climbed behind the cranes. But I was cold enough for the hairs on my body to be standing to attention. If Captain Kallikratides had been murdered, it might have been to silence him in general.

Or it might have been to stop him talking to Michael Savage, in particular.

Suddenly my mouth was dry, and my scalp was tingling, and the world was full of black, hostile eyes. As I climbed on the train for London, I could feel the eyes. They were still there at Paddington, and as I went back to my hotel. Shut up, I told myself. Coincidence. Accident. Lies. Murder, but nothing to do with you.

There was more flock wallpaper, and a Victorian wardrobe. In the mirror on the wardrobe was a man who needed a haircut, and a shave, and forty-eight hours' sleep. There was nothing I could do about the sleep. As I was shaving the telephone rang. It was Mary Ellen.

"What happened?" she said.

"There was a fire," I said.

"What's that got to do with you?"

I did not want her to worry. She was clever enough to know that there was plenty to worry about. I said, "Nothing."

She changed the subject. "There's a dance tonight, at the Royal Flotilla," she said. "You will remember that Mr. Schacker is going to be there."

I said, "Will you come too?"

She laughed. Dance? Silly idea. "I'm working," she said. "I'd love to, of course. But I can't."

Kallikratides had been my big lead. Now he was dead. Maybe I was going to need Art Schacker's job offer after all.

I finished shaving, went out to Moss Bros. and rented a dinner jacket. I got a haircut. By teatime, I was as neat as I was ever going to be; a person with too much chin and too much nose, and, it had to be said, a certain wildness about the eyes, off to a polite ball in furtherance of his career.

Wondering who was watching.

I rang Justin and told him what had happened to Mr. Kallikratides.

"Shit," he said. "Sounds like another claim."

"Probably."

"Anything you can do about it?"

"One is very, very interested."

I asked for the loan of a car. He had three. He lent me his big BMW. He had a collection of them. I breezed down the M3 and across to Southampton where I climbed on to the Cowes ferry. By nine o'clock, I was walking through the wrought-iron gates of the Royal Flotilla.

20

The Flotilla was founded in the mid-nineteenth century by a cousin of Queen Victoria's anxious to ensure that Britannia continued to rule the waves, but not bright enough to realize that this object was not likely to be served by a yacht club for the blue of blood and thick of head. Its exclusivity was such that even my Uncle James had been blackballed (*"too* Irish"). Nowadays, it concentrated on flying its special ensign (white, with a miniature Royal Standard instead of the Union Jack) and considering itself pivotal to the splendor that is British yachting. In the opinion of many, it was about as pivotal to British yachting as a dinosaur trainer in a racehorse stable.

This notwithstanding, its clubhouse was certainly a fair spot for a dance.

It was a gray stone pile stationed on brilliant lawns, commanding the entrance to the harbor of Cowes, an ugly but crowded village on the north coast of the Isle of Wight.

This evening, the marquees were up on the lawn, and the flags of all nations hung limp on the turrets. The Flotilla was having a party for some distinguished foreign visitors.

It was a beautiful evening. The sky was clear, and the Solent was glassy. The air was warm, with a discreet whiff of mud. The Flotilla's gardeners had planted a foul anchor in red geraniums on a background of blue salvias and white alyssum. Men in dinner jackets and women in long dresses were swarming over the lawns. I pulled the bow tie straight, showed my invitation to a club retainer, and walked up the steps of the portico, keeping pace with the crowd.

Beyond the paneled hall was a ballroom with French windows. Beyond the French windows was another lawn, hedged in with escallonia against the sea breezes. A string quartet was sawing away in the ballroom.

A lot of the guests looked as if they were past sailing. The men had white hair and red faces. The women wore off-the-shoulder dresses, and were crusted with jewelry like caddis larvae.

A voice said, "Savage!"

"Art," I said. Arthur Schacker had won an around-the-world race. He was a square, hard-looking man in a white dinner jacket. He had a wood-colored face with dark circles under the eyes. The circles had been installed by the Flying Fish Challenge.

"How is it?" he said.

"Fine," I said. He had troubles of his own this evening. He did not want to hear about mine.

"Did you decide?" he said.

"Not yet."

"Inside a week?" he said.

"Fine," I said. "Who's here?"

"Everybody," he said. "They asked all the challengers."

Schacker was a Maine fisherman, and he would rather have been running a fish co-op in a bay with no road. But there were not as many fish in the sea as formerly, so the Sound Yacht Club in Marblehead had bought Schacker's shellfish co-op and turned him into their all-purpose dynamo and ambassador-at-large.

A maid in a white lace cap and apron brought us a drink. Schacker said, "Come and meet some of the people I hope you'll want to work with." In the corners of the lawn were noticeably younger groups of men. Schacker took me across to one of them. Some of its members were carrying three glasses of champagne at the same time, in case of emergency. They had big mustaches, and eyes creased at the corners by squinting into the sun, and mole-grip handshakes. They were the hard chargers of the Flying Fish Challenge, the people Savage was supposed to get along with for a couple of years. They looked young, and healthy, and immortal. But every time I looked at the hard brown faces on them, I saw the thing on the stretcher at Cardiff docks, smelled the grease and burned cloth. And the champagne turned sour as battery acid.

I drank some glasses of it anyway. I suppose I must have been talking to people. Overhead the sky went through azure to indigo, and stars began to wink bright, but not as bright as all the diamonds. I nodded and grinned while an Admiral lectured me about a self-steering gear he had designed. White-jacketed club servants lit flambeaux on the lawn, each with its own globe of moths. People talked. The talk was louder now. A woman in a red silk dress laughed. She had dark hair in a French roll, a long, elegant neck. Her shoulders glowed the color of chestnuts in the twilight, and a diamond choker circled her neck with fire.

I knew her.

The Admiral said, "And there's a bevel gear . . ."

I left him. His mouth was a black O in his white beard. At the Flotilla, when members talked, non-members listened. I walked through the smell of crushed grass and cigar smoke until I was beside her. She was wearing Chanel, simple but effective. I said, "Bianca."

She turned her head slightly, as if to greet a casual acquaintance. When she saw me she turned around all the way. Her lips were soft on my cheek. She said, "Mick! What are you doing here?" It was not a casual inquiry. There was something urgent behind it, as if she were worried.

The man with her said, "I guess I'm not the only one after your body and mind, eh, Mr. Savage?" I realized that I had been staring at Bianca. She was worth staring at. I turned. The man was narrow-eyed, deeply tanned, heavily wrinkled, with a mane of white hair.

"M. Feuilla," I said. "I didn't expect to see you here."

He smiled. "Who can refuse to come somewhere with . . . with Bianca?" There was an odd hesitation, as if he had been about to call her something else.

"Stupid," said Bianca, quickly. I got the impression she was talking to gloss over the hesitation. "Le Patron is building a boat for the Cup, of course. There is a challenge."

"And this party is the first round." Feuilla laughed, the Montecristo clamped between his improbably white teeth. "We are brought here to be impressed by how rich our rivals are, I think."

I said, "Is it working?"

He smiled. "You know our ways of doing things. The Americans like to organize their teams like a machine; buy excellent parts, lock them in with contracts, give them orders. Us, we are a family. Not a machine; a group of humans, with all our frailties." His eyes were as frail as golfballs. As head of a family, he was in the same league as my Uncle James. "No," he said, appearing to bumble. "Not the big salesmanship. We are flexible. We look after each other. I have the money, you have the talent, the Charente needs the Royaume des Phares; we work together, each contributing what he does best." His hand was shaking slightly. He pushed it into the pocket of his black silk dinner jacket. "Not like your Americans, who say, I pay, you jump, so!" He stuck the cigar back between his teeth. "Still, I shall be sorry if you accept this job with Mr. Schacker. You make a good friend, but a dangerous rival." His eyes drifted past my head. "Excuse me." I was left with Bianca.

She said, "Why did you come here?"

"Looking for work," I said.

"You're crazy." She took my hand. Her fingers were warm and dry.

I said, "Why?" In the ballroom the string quartet had petered out. There was a big crash of horns, and the old jump riff: "In the Mood." Her diamond collar blazed as she looked around, left and right. It was the movement of a kid on a street corner, not a beautiful woman at a ball. She said, "Come. Dance. There are people here. Nothing can happen," as if she were trying to convince herself.

I said, "This is England. I live here. What are you talking about?"

She pulled me toward the dance floor. I saw a couple of faces I knew from Pulteney. One of them waved. I waved back. I was thinking of the empty windows in the upperworks of the *Milgon Swan* in Cardiff, like little surprised eyes in the white steel.

A voice behind me said, "'Aving fun, Mick?"

Bianca's fingers tightened on mine. She did not look around. She hissed, *"Va-t-en."*

I turned. A man with bottle-blond hair was behind me. He was young, deeply tanned, dressed in a white tuxedo with a wing collar. He was wearing an aftershave that stank of flowers beaten up in rocket fuel. I had smelled him before. And seen him. The last time, he had had an Alsatian on his neck in Georges's boatyard. He said, "Bianca, you're looking great!" He spoke as if he knew her well. Then he said to me, "Come along, you."

I said, "Who let you in?"

He leaned over and whispered in my ear, "There is a gun in my pocket." His face had a flat, Mongolian look, but his eyes had the hundred-proof psychopath sparkle.

I said, "You won't use it."

He said, "I may be arrested, but you will be dead." His eyes twinkled like jolly little sunbeams in his big flat face. I believed him.

Bianca said, "Get out of here, Bobby."

The blond man laughed.

I said, "How do you know this guy?"

Bianca squeezed my hand. Her palm was hot and damp. There were two other men with Bobby now. One of them was short, with black hair and big shoulders bulking out his tuxedo. He had held the shotgun on the beach by Christophe's shack. The other was Jean-Claude.

Jean-Claude said, *"Salut, beau-papa."* The band was still playing "In the Mood." I felt cold as ice.

"Let's take a look at the harbor," said the blond man. "Nice and quiet down there. Bianca, if you come after us, we might kill him."

Jean-Claude said, "We might kill him anyway," and giggled.

His friends fell in, one on either side. There was no sign of Bianca. I went. There was no option.

Out of the flares, the night was dark. Something was sticking into my right kidney. It had to be a gun. My mind was the only part of me not under duress. It scuttled around, busy as a rat in a cage, and about as useful.

Captain Kallikratides had been murdered. I had been watched, because I had talked to Captain Kallikratides.

But how did Bianca know these people?

We were on a pontoon now. The clubhouse was a tower of fairy lights in the sky, the night around it reddened by the flambeaux on the lawns. The sound of the band floated tinnily across the dark grass, quieter than the slop of water against the galvanized floats. We could have been on a different planet.

"Now," said the blond man's voice from the dark bulk of his head. He spoke English, heavily accented. "Like I said that night with Thibault Ledoux, I'm afraid we've got to shut you up."

The voice was a purr. I found it deeply, horribly frightening. I said, "What the hell are you talking about?"

I saw his shoulders shrug against the lights of the club. He said, "All this must be a shock to you. I guess you could do with a drink."

For a moment, I could not think what he was talking about. Then I heard the rattle of a bottle-top and the clink of glass on glass. Jean-Claude giggled, his high, nasty giggle. Above the salty smell of the night, I caught a whiff of gin.

Jean-Claude pushed a glass into my hand. "Dreenk eet," he said. I could see his teeth, the gleam in his thick-glazed eyes.

I said, "I don't . . ."

They moved. One of them grabbed each arm and hung on. Bobby grabbed my hair from behind, yanking my head backward. I opened my mouth to shout. An iron bar came down sideways, jamming my teeth open.

I was staring at the sky. It was full of stars. A shadow blotted out an area of stars. Someone held a glass to my lips. My mouth was full of raw gin.

I tried to spit it out. You cannot spit with an iron bar jammed between your teeth. I heard Kallikratides: *No drink spirits. Bad in stomach.* Then more immediate problems presented themselves. I tried to get rid of the stuff. It ran down my face.

"Hold his nose," said a voice.

They held my nose. Something slammed into my stomach. My windpipe filled with gin. The night turned flame red. I coughed the stuff back up, swallowing, my throat full of napalm. Everything went away, except the fact that I had to breathe through organs of breathing saturated in liquid fire.

Some time later, it might have been a day or two, I got a breath. I was on my knees now, dribbling gin, the tears pouring down my face. Bianca, where are you. *If you come after us, we might kill him.*

They were killing me anyway.

"Have another, old boy," said the voice. The glass came to my mouth again. This time, I knew what you had to do. When the disgusting stuff ran to the back of your throat, you swallowed it.

"Not too quick," said the voice. "He'll puke."

So they took it slow.

The voices got remote and strange, mixed up with the sound of the band. There was the nauseating taste of the gin, and the roar of conversation that seemed to be getting mixed up with another roaring, from inside my ears.

A voice close at hand said, "Can you hear me?" Now it comes, I thought. Death. And bloody Bianca let them get away with it.

"Listen," said the voice. "These questions you have been asking. We will hear no more of this, right? You are a tough guy. Everyone knows this. But you have someone who is not so tough."

The bar was out of my teeth. I wanted to be sick. I tried to say, "Whayamean?"

"We can do this to other people," said the voice. It came closer to my ear. "And it need not stop here. Actually, it need not stop at all. We like our work. We like it even more with little Frankie."

I tore at the hands that held me. I could not see the man's face, but I knew it would be twisted up in a nasty, dirty grin, and I wanted to smash it in.

But the hands held.

"So you better pray nobody asks questions about fires on ships," said the voice. "And now we will leave you, in the hope that you have learned an important lesson, and that your daughter will not be needed to teach you the next one."

I said, "Whyncha kill me?"

He said, "This will be just as effective."

The hands lifted me up until I was horizontal, shoulder high. Then they dropped me on the pontoon. My head slammed into the deck. It rang like a cracked bell. Somewhere, a young English voice was saying, "Hey! What's all that?"

"Guy drunk," said Bobby's purring voice. "No problem."

"Good God," said the young voice. "Already?"

"Poor guy," said the purring voice.

The young voice did not sound sympathetic. "Who is it?"

I crawled to the edge of the pontoon, and was sick in the harbor.

"Savage," said the purring one. "Poor guy."

"Really?" said the young voice. "Him?"

I was sick again. I did not hear any more.

When I stopped being sick, I splashed some harbor on my face and clambered to my feet. My legs felt strangely rubbery. The sky and the masts whirled around me. I tried looking down, to see if I had been sick down my coat. The movement tripped me, and I began a sort of controlled fall toward the inland end of the pontoon, my legs keeping up with the rest of me, but only just.

I knew something completely disgusting had just happened to me, but I could not remember precisely what. There was something about Frankie. It was something so horrible that it made me want to cry, without knowing what I wanted to cry about. The effort of looking for that sad but disappearing thing made the inside of my head whirl again, so I stopped trying to find it, and started trying to concentrate on where I was going.

I seemed to be back on the yacht club lawn. By taking a window at the corner of the building as a leading mark, I found I could hold a pretty straight course, give or take the odd tack. There were people walking on the lawn. When they saw me they stopped talking, and turned their heads away, and resumed their conversations with a new, odd intensity. I waved at one of them I knew. The movement of my arm unbalanced me, and I stumbled, waltzing seven or eight steps to starboard before I could get back on course for the window.

Through the window, I could see people dancing. I went right up to it, rested my hands on the sill. I did not see anyone I knew. But there was a girl in a red dress who reminded me of Bianca. I remembered I was extremely angry with Bianca, because she had handed me over to . . . someone or other. I could not remember whom.

I felt my way around the wall of the club, kicking irritably at bushes that got in my way. The sound of the band hit me like a bucket of warm water. They were playing "Minnie the Moocher." I would have liked to play along, but the piano was too far away, beyond a flower arrangement that was going in and out of focus.

The girl in the red dress was not dancing. She looked pale and worried, talking to a dark-haired man with a heavy mustache and skin like expensive Morocco leather. She did not only look like Bianca. She was Bianca. I walked across to her, bumping into a couple of people. I said, "Bianca."

She turned around. Her mouth was a thick cushion of red lipstick against her brown face. When she saw me, she brightened for a second. Then the mouth opened, horrified. I watched it closely. It held clues. I said, "I want to talk to you." At least, that was what I meant to say. But it came out wrong, so I tried again, louder this time. People around us had stopped dancing. I told them to stop staring. The room was beginning to rotate, slowly at first, but getting faster, like a roundabout at a fair. I said, "Come on." She was staring, too. The red mouth was not a cushion. It was a stoplight in her white face. The mouth of a red-hot hoochy coochah.

Saying stop, Savage, no. I was angry. "C'mon, Minnie," I said. I made a grab at her hand, missed, and overbalanced. Oh, Christ, I thought, I am going to fall down. There were eyes everywhere, like the spider eyes that had followed me on to the Cardiff train, across London, down to the Cowes ferry. They stared at me. I stared back.

And saw two men.

They were sitting at a table. On the table was a bottle of mineral water. They were both smoking fat cigars. One of them was white-haired, nut-brown, wrinkled. Feuilla. The other was Arthur Crespi.

They had been laughing together, like good friends. Above them was a placard. On the placard was a French tricolor. The lettering said CHALLENGE LES DIGUES—SAINTE-JEANNE-DES-SABLES.

I did not understand.

A hand took me above the elbow. It was a big hand, not at all gentle. A voice said, "C'mon, old buddy." It kept me upright, that hand. The crowd swirled in front of me. I was looking at the French windows leading into the garden. The garden door came closer. "Fresh air," said the voice. It was an immensely capable voice. I made my eyes focus on its owner. He was a stocky man, brown, with grizzled hair.

"Art," I said. Art Schacker, my old friend. Everything was fine.

He did not look friendly tonight. He said, "Mick, you screwed up."

He fumbled in my jacket pocket. His hand came out with a gin bottle. There were a couple of inches left in the bottom. He said, "You and I have a problem, bo." A flashgun popped. "Oh, Jesus," he said.

I trusted Schacker. He was one of the good guys. He would understand why I was worried, once I had made a few things clear. I said, "This is not my fault." His eyes were cold above his smile. I could tell that although he was saying sure, sure, he did not believe a word of it.

He said, "I'll fix that photographer. Then we'll call you a cab." He went away, toward a man with a camera. Schacker took the camera away from him and pulled out the film. The cameraman started shouting, a cockney barking, like a

Rottweiler. I wandered out on to the lawn, drawn by the lights swimming in the dark Solent. I wanted to cry. I still did not know why.

Someone came alongside me in the dark. I could tell by the perfume that it was Bianca. "Quick," she said, and grabbed my hand.

She pulled me after her. The lights spun and blurred. I did not know where I was. A car door slammed. There was a smell of leather. Car smell, and a car seat, and her perfume. Treacherous bitch smells. I passed out.

21

My head was aching. It was a sick, dirty ache, just behind the eyes. My tongue felt two sizes too big for my mouth. I violently wanted a glass of water. When I opened my eyes, light rushed in like a torrent of razor blades. I shut them again quickly. Then I opened one at a time, slowly. That helped.

I could see a window with a net blind. Outside the window was blue sky, and a tree. In the corner of my vision was a TV, turned off. Dead ahead was a bedside table. On the bedside table was a glass of water. The water was the only thing that meant anything. I drank it. It spread through me like nectar. The room smelled good, but my brain was too muzzy to work out why. My brain was too muzzy to work out anything. When I put my head back on the pillow, I thought I could hear someone else breathing. But it hurt too much to turn and check. So I went back to sleep.

Next time I woke, the light had changed. I wondered how long it took for the human organism to dispose of a whole bottle of gin. And in remembering about the bottle of gin, I began to remember other things.

I sat up suddenly in the bed. My brain sloshed about in

my skull. I waited for it to stop. Then I began to take things
in.

It was a hotel room. There were twin beds. The one I was
not in had been slept in. There was a dress hanging from a
hook on the back of the door, made of red silk, bright
enough to drive nails into the eyeballs.

The door opened. Bianca came out of what must have
been a bathroom. She was not wearing any clothes. She was
brown all over, and extremely beautiful. I was capable of
only the simplest emotions. The one uppermost in what was
passing for my mind was dislike.

She pulled the bedspread from her bed and draped it
around herself.

I said, "So you're a dear old friend of Feuilla."

She looked straight at me. "That's right."

"And Feuilla's a dear old friend of Crespi."

She said, "No."

"What, then?"

"Business associate."

My head hurt. I felt angry and disgusted. I said, "You
know what I mean."

She dropped her eyes.

"So what's been going on? You've been looking for
Thibault so you can hand him over to them?"

She looked up again. She said, "Don't be stupid."

The anger was getting on top of me. I said, "Last night,
those people tipped a bottle of gin into me, to show me what
they would do to Frankie if I opened my mouth about what I
have found out about Crespi's insurance deals. You're
supposed to be Frankie's friend."

She said, "They didn't kill you."

"They killed the captain of the *Poisson d'Avril.*"

Her eyes were big and dark and luminous. A tear slid
down the skin at the side of her nose. She said, "I do not
want anything to happen to you."

I said, "What do you mean?"

She took my hand. "I very much do not," she said. The
bedspread fell apart. I was gazing into the shadow between
her breasts.

She held my head against her. "Believe me, please."

I started to tell her that I would not believe her if she came with an affidavit signed by the Pope. But my mind was beginning to work. Last night she had steered me away, out of trouble. When *Serica* had tried to run us down on the Belle-Île race, she had been in just as bad trouble as anyone else.

But her friend Feuilla was a friend of Crespi.

I said, "Is Feuilla Crespi's partner?"

"You have sat in the same room as Crespi yourself. Does that make you his partner?"

I said, doggedly, "They were at the same table. Under the same banner."

She said, "They are from the same town. M. Feuilla works for the benefit of the town."

"And are they both directors of Atlas Industrien?"

She frowned. "Of what?"

She did not know.

I put my arm around her shoulders. She rested her head against my head. Her fingers massaged the back of my neck. It could have gone on from there.

But there was a big thought in the front of my mind. People do not threaten other people without reason. The directors of Atlas Industrien might be buried under armor-plated Luxembourg law. But Bobby and Jean-Claude worked for Arthur Crespi.

I got up, supporting myself on the bed. My dinner jacket was on the floor. There was mud on the shoes, vomit on the coat. I stuffed the coat into the wastepaper basket. I fumbled my way into the trousers and shirt, shoved my feet into the black shoes. She was looking at me, her eyes big and midnight-blue in her brown face. I did not like being looked at. She said, "What are you doing?"

"Going," I said. *We like it even more with little Frankie.* I was going somewhere quiet, where there would be nothing to find out, where I could say nothing, and Frankie could live safe with her mother until it was time for her to go to Oxford. I picked up the telephone and asked for a taxi.

She said, soft and tentative, "Will you come back to France?"

"No."

She winced as if I had clouted her, and hung her head, so I

could not see her face. I felt a twinge of regret. The twinge passed. She said, in a soft, sympathetic voice, "Keep out of sight. Don't tell anyone where you go. That's the best way."

"I wasn't going to."

She smiled again. The tears had not stopped. "Including me," she said.

"Of course."

"I give you a lift," she said.

I said, "You don't." She kissed my cheek. I held her for a moment. I turned away and went down the stairs. It was a hot morning, with a clear sky.

The hotel was in a leafy suburban street. I said to the receptionist, "Where are we?"

"Marlow Avenue."

"What town?"

Her face was the color of dough. She looked at my filthy clothes, and sniffed. "When I last looked, it was Southampton."

I took a taxi to the ferry car park, picked up the BMW, and headed west.

I was sticky with old sweat. The inside of my head felt dirtier than the outside. I was poisoned, and exhausted, and I was covered in bruises where Crespi's friends had slammed me on to the dock.

But that was not the trouble.

The trouble was that every time I thought of what had happened last night the sweat broke on the palms of my hands, and my stomach took on an evil swooping movement, and icy shivers prickled between my shoulderblades like squalls on a boating lake.

The trouble was that I was terrified.

Keep out of sight. Don't tell anyone where you go.

Because if you look even a little bit interested in the things you are interested in, they will force-feed your little daughter gin, and then they will kill her.

I headed straight for Pulteney.

Pulteney is an easy place to feel safe. The harbor reaches its granite arms protectively around the gaggle of pot boats and small yachts that live there. On top of the western sea-wall the lifeboat house keeps a benevolent eye on things.

Above the harbor and the quay, the houses rise tier on tier, huddled together for warmth and security.

My flat is in the middle of the village, looking out on to the quay. There were lights on in the Mermaid, and a bray of laughter from the yacht club at the opposite end. I turned my key in the lock, kicked aside the drift of mail that had piled up under the letterbox, and went in.

It smelled like a flat that has had the windows shut for almost two weeks. There was one very big room, with a stove and a terrace. There was a kitchen. And there were three bedrooms, only one of which was ever used, except when Frankie came to stay. When Frankie came to stay, the place filled with her friends, drinking my wine, playing my piano and arguing on my sofas. I wished they were all here now.

They were not here. There was only my room, with the picture of *Freya,* and a bed, and a telephone, and a painting of Fats Waller. I threw my bags into that one, opened the windows, and pulled the cork on a bottle of burgundy.

Outside the windows, there was sudden death, and arbitrariness, and people who would kill your children so they could carry on making money. Outside the windows, the world was a terrifying place.

Almost as terrifying as the world inside my head.

I drank the glass of burgundy like medicine, then filled another, and drank that too. I could see my reflection in the glass: long, thin, unshaven, sunburned, black bags under the eyes, sprawled on a sofa. Picture of ease. Picture of terror. I did not want to be a picture of anything. I wanted to be nobody, so nobody would hurt my daughter. I rang Justin's flat in London. His answering machine was on. I said, "I'm off the case. I'll bring your car next time I'm in London."

I drew the curtains. Then I pulled the telephone out of the wall, finished the bottle and threw it into the fireplace. And then I went to my bedroom and crawled between the unaired sheets, damp with the salt that rises from the harbor, and slept a nervous, twisting sleep.

When I awoke, the sun was blazing through the window. Someone was hammering on the door.

I rolled over in bed, pulled the blankets over my head.

Someone was shouting through the letterbox. "Mick, is that you?"

I swung my feet on to the floor, pulled on a dressing gown, padded across the pale boards of the living room and opened the door.

The man outside was thin and slight, with spikes of dark hair over a brown face that looked as if it had not slept for a couple of weeks. He said, "Didn't mean to wake you up."

"Charlie," I said. Charlie Agutter's family had run boats out of Pulteney since before anyone could remember. Charlie was a designer of yachts, and good enough at it to be a household name in yacht harbors from Tasmania to Anchorage. He was also Savage Yachts' design consultant.

He said, "Got any coffee?"

I told him to put the kettle on. The sun was pouring in at the big window behind the balcony. Outside, the quay noises were winding up to the roaring hum of an over-crowded harbor in southwest England. It should have been familiar and comforting, balm to the ravaged soul. All it did was make the isolation worse.

I climbed into a pair of jeans and a Tresco T-shirt from the collection in the cupboard. When I came out, Charlie was in the kitchen, contemplating the coffee jug with an expression of distrust. "Milk's sour," he said.

"Black," I said.

I banged cups and saucers on to a tray, carried it on to the balcony. The sun was jumping in the water of the harbor. Windsurfers were weaving between the lobster boats. Cruising yachts were rafted up six deep on the quay.

Charlie said, "Heard you had a bit of difficulty with *Arc.*"

"You could say that." I wanted to think about Pulteney, let ordinary things fill the crevasse that had opened up under my feet.

"What happened?"

"Dud seacock," I said. "Broke off." I did not want to talk about it.

Charlie was not an easy man to divert. "Broke off?"

The crevasse yawned at me, unfillable. When I put my coffee cup back on the saucer, it clattered like castanets. "Electrolysis," I said.

"How the hell did that happen?"

I said, "Someone did it because they wanted the boat sunk, so they could make an insurance claim."

"Ah," said Charlie. His eyes were dark and clever. "And do you know who?"

I said, "Yes."

"And how?"

I said, "No." I shoved my hands in the pockets of my jeans so he would not see them shaking. "And I am not bloody interested."

He frowned. He said, "Are you sure?"

"Wheels within wheels," I said. "Wheels within bloody wheels."

"Ah."

"And now," I said, "I am a bit knackered. I am sure you have a busy day ahead of you, and that there are things you should be doing."

He finished his coffee without looking at me. He said, "What have you been doing to yourself?"

"Drinking," I said. That seemed rather clever. I had a laugh. I could taste the iron bar between my teeth. My throat was still raw from the gin. *We like it even more with Frankie,* they had said.

"Good," said Charlie. He got up. His eyes rested on me dispassionately. "Er, I don't know if you'll need anything. But if you do, you know where I live?"

I said, "Thanks, Charlie," and tried a grin. It did not convince me, or him. As he left, I picked up the letters, so it would look as if I was going to work. I shut the door behind him and chained it up. Then I threw the letters at the wastepaper basket and went back to bed.

I had known Charlie for a good fifteen years. He had turned up in the West Indies in a yacht he had designed. When we had come back to England I had visited him, and he had persuaded me to buy the flat on the quay with the last of my ready money. It was above his drawing office, and it had been a terrific investment. I had worked with Charlie, and raced with him. He was solid as a rock. If there was anyone I could talk to, it would be him.

But I could not talk to anyone, because at the first hint of it I could taste the iron and the gin, hear that purring voice: *We like it even more with Frankie.*

I lay there fully clothed in the bed, and listened to the roar of the quay going full steam ahead, and the gulls screaming. I tried to concentrate on the gulls, floating on the breeze in the clean light of the sun. But every time I thought of the gulls, the black crevasse opened under me, and I started to fall.

I slid into a half-sleep, made of tortured liver and bad conscience. In the sleep I saw myself shaking like a leaf, jumping at shadows, desperate to confide in someone but lacking the nerve. And part of me knew that I reminded myself of somebody.

I knew who it was.

I reminded myself of Thibault Ledoux, and the late Captain Spiro Kallikratides.

22

*I*t was dark when I woke. I made coffee and ate half a packet of fish fingers Frankie had left in the freezer compartment of the fridge last time she had been staying. I liked the dark better than the day. I pulled on a jersey and a baseball cap and let myself out.

My bicycle was in the shed at the back of the hallway. I wheeled it down the steps and on to the polished granite cobbles of the quay. The drinkers had spilled out of the Mermaid, and the tables on the yacht club terrace were full of people in elaborately casual clothes from the boutiques in Quay Street. I pulled the peak of my cap over my eyes, and sank my head into my shoulders, and pushed the bike past the back of the yacht club and up Yealm Hill, where there were no pubs, and there was nothing to do, and no people at this time of night. At the top of the street I climbed on to the bike and began to pedal.

I had no idea where I was going. It was simply that I could not sleep anymore, and I needed darkness and anonymity. So I let my legs take me where they wanted.

I went east, into the steep-banked lanes, the pool of light from the dynamo wobbling down the gorse hedges. A couple of dogs barked at me in a farmyard. Then I was going downhill, toward the sea, gleaming like gray metal to the horizon. Closer to, floating in a mat of nonreflecting blackness, was a cluster of mercury vapor lights. The spokes whizzed and the damp air flowed past the face. Gravity pulled me toward that group of lights, isolated out there on the marshes that line the mouth of the river Poult.

The road surface turned from tarmac to grit. A big advertisement hoarding went by on the right. It was unlit, but I knew it by heart. NEW PULTENEY MARINA, it said. A YACHT-HARBOR ENTERPRISES DEVELOPMENT. Underneath, there were some smaller placards: NEVILLE SPEARMAN CHANDLERS, DIXON MULTIHULLS. And SAVAGE YACHTS.

I kept riding. A car came past, stereo yowling Def Leppard. Yachtharbor Enterprises had bought the marina from Neville Spearman last year, and immediately doubled berth rents. Old Pulteney hands now claimed that the only people who could afford to keep their boats there were directors of the company and dope dealers. I rode past the main gates, the glare of the blue lights, and on to a smaller compound of chainlink fencing, where a big steel-frame shed loomed against the sky.

I had done this trip morning and night for five years. The next trick was to grope for the padlock with the left hand, insert the key with the right. Savage Yachts was a dead letter. I was not sure I wanted to.

But gravity was gravity. I opened the padlock, closed the gate behind me, and went in.

Then, there had been *Arc-en-Ciel* at the top of the slip, and the silver band, and the French Ambassador. Now, there was only the carcass of a Hilliard lying like a dead pig in the corner. The sound of the bicycle spokes ticked back at me from the corrugated-iron wall of the shed. It was a black hulk, the shed, radiating gloom. I opened the door and went in.

The electricity was still connected. The fluorescent tubes buzzed and flooded the space with corpse-colored light. The end of five years' work was a litter of old timber, polythene sheeting, a pile of resin containers in the corner. Once, there had been thirty men in here, and three boats being built, and you could have eaten your lunch off the floor.

I shoved my hands in my pockets and wandered across to the office. That was where Mary and I had sat and conspired about how to get more boats to build, employ more people, generate more money to plow back into better and faster boats.

Now it was two desks, and a filing cabinet, and a computer. Unlike the shed, it was scrupulously tidy: Mary's coffee cup bottom up on the dishcloth by the kettle, the chair aligned just so with the blotter. Mary was an old Navy wife.

I sat down in front of the computer and flicked the switch.

The screen came alive, amber on black. There was a list of letters and dates: letters to clients, replying to their expressions of gratitude. Then letters to prospective clients, expressing polite understanding that the boats we had discussed were not to be built after all. Then the letters changed. There were a lot to the bank. There were a lot to Thibault. The final one of the sequence was LAUNCH INV.

I put the cursor on it, tapped it up.

Savage Yachts and Thibault Ledoux
invite you
to the launch of
Arc-en-Ciel

There was a guest list. On the list were the whole of the yachting press, a lot of yachting notables, and a lot of Pulteney people and workpeople and hangers-on and members of my family. Thibault and Yann had been around for ten days, working out the last details.

Ten days during which someone had gimmicked the seacock.

The invitation list was imponderable as a worn-out tombstone. It held the ghosts of the Pulteney Silver Band, the cheers of the crowd, the creak and slither of the boat's cradle on the slip. But they were only ghosts now, and they could not communicate with the living. Beyond the hum of the computer, the shed was full of hollow silence.

The telephone rang.

The din of it echoed from corrugated steel to corrugated steel until the air was roaring.

I let it ring, four rings. Then I picked it up.

"Who's that?" said a voice.

It was Mary Ellen's voice. I said, "Me."

"Found you," she said. She sounded brisk and in control. "Tried everywhere. What are you doing there?"

"Work," I said. Maintain the fiction with Mary Ellen.

"I didn't think there was anything going on there anymore."

That was meant to reinforce the notion of Mary Ellen in control. It was a crude move. It made me think she might be feeling vulnerable herself. I said, "Clever of you to track me down."

"I was in a hurry," she said. "Justin said you might be there. Listen. Do you know someone called Lucas Baragouin?"

The telephone receiver was suddenly slippery in my hand. "Baragouin?" I said.

"Guy turned up here yesterday. Wanted Frankie to go sailing in France. Handsome little brute."

I said, "She didn't go, did she?"

"Of course she did. You can't tell Frankie what to do. Takes after her father in that respect. She said he was sweet. Said he'd met you. They'd had some kind of bust-up, but she wanted to give it a second chance. I thought that if she went off with someone else, it might help her get over this Jean-Claude, the one you said was such a creep. I told her to think it over. But when I got back from the office she'd gone." She paused. Moths were slamming themselves against the fluorescent tubes up there in the roof. "Are you still there?"

I watched the moths. I tasted the iron in my mouth, felt

the burn of raw gin in my throat. *We like it even more with Frankie.*

"Mick?" she said.

"I'm here." The words came out like the creak of a rusty hinge.

"Where might they have gone?" There was a nervous edge in her voice. For all her pretense, she was worried.

I said, "I believe they met in La Rochelle."

She said, "Are you going back there?"

If I made any noise or fuss, Jean-Claude and his friends would squash Frankie like a mosquito. I said, "I don't think so."

"Oh." Mary Ellen desperately wanted to ask me a favor. But asking for favors was my department. "Well. If you do . . . go over that way, you might visit her. See that she's . . . happy, got what she needs. You know?"

I said, "Thanks for telling me."

"Just thought you'd want to be kept informed," she said, with spurious brightness.

I tried to think of something to say. Frankie had been our main line of communication for seventeen years. Now she was fading out of our lives, moving on her own. She left a gap that needed filling. Both of us wanted to reach out across that gap. But neither of us knew how.

She said, "Will you let me know?"

I said, "Of course."

I hung up, turned off the computer and the lights, and pushed my bike back to the town. I went slowly, not because I was tired, though I was, and not because I was nervous, though I was that too. I went slowly because in the black night nothing was happening next, and I wanted to keep it that way. I wanted nothing to happen next the way a man who has been flung out of a high window might fall through the dark, quiet air, not wanting the next thing to happen.

I parked my bike, and opened my door very quietly, and walked into the flat. And I sat there in a chair, breathing as quietly as possible, not moving, hardly even thinking.

Except one thought.

Not Frankie.

It was one thing to get used to the idea that she would

move away, cease to be a child and become a separate being. That process had been going on for seventeen years. It was supposed to be gradual. Jean-Claude and his friends had made it a violent amputation.

I sat there until the night started to gray outside the window, and the quiet was dented by the clank of a pot boat's diesel. Then I must have nodded off, because next thing it was properly light. I got up, stiff as a board, and made more coffee.

And when I looked into my mind, I found Mary Ellen looking back. *If you do go over that way, you might visit her. See that she's happy, got what she needs. You know?*

For Mary Ellen to sound that small in the voice was an admission that she knew something was not right. But I was always the one who was wrong about Frankie, not her. That was the fixed point in our non-relationship.

Nothing like children to bring you close together.

I could not go looking for Frankie, or the people she was with would hurt her. I could not not go, either.

But the emptiness was filling up with something. With memories of Frankie, and being alive, and doing things. It was no good getting drunk like Kallikratides, or hiding like Thibault. Kallikratides was dead, and God knew where Thibault was. Kallikratides had left two men to drown on *Poisson d'Avril*. As a shareholder in Transports Drenec, Thibault was implicated in his death, and the death of the sailors. Thibault would also know something about Atlas Industrien, his co-directors in Transports Drenec . . .

Frankie or no Frankie, the curiosity was stirring again. The curiosity put the fear into a sort of perspective. I had introduced Frankie to Thibault. I owed it to Mary Ellen to do something. Because I was the only person with anything like a lead on Jean-Claude.

I picked up the telephone and dialed Georges's boatyard in La Rochelle.

"How's *Arc?*" I said.

He said, "In the water."

"Any sign of Thibault?"

"Nope. Listen, I need this boat out of my hair. Feuilla turned up in a Mercedes, paid the bill in cash. He's been having more trouble with his development down there in

Oléron. Tried to bribe a planner. He's being prosecuted for corruption."

I thought of the old man grinning with Crespi at their table in the ballroom at the Flotilla. I thought of Bianca, who seemed to be a friend of Feuilla, but who hated Crespi.

I said, "Have you seen Bianca?"

"She was with Feuilla," he said. He sounded as if he did not wish to discuss it further. "When will you come and get the boat?"

I said, "I'll arrange to have it collected."

I had a shower and shaved, and put on a clean shirt and some dark-blue canvas trousers, and tried to keep my mind away from gin and iron bars.

Then I rang Charlie.

He said, "How's it going?"

"Better," I said. Better was not the right word, in the circumstances, but it was the only one I could think of. "Do you know anyone who's going over to France?"

"How about the ferry?" he said.

"Don't like ferries," I said.

"Try the pub at lunchtime. See you there?"

I did not like the sound of the pub. There would be a lot of people, and a lot of eyes. But it would be hard to explain that to Charlie without him thinking I had gone crazy. So I said, "Fine."

The Mermaid is a place that has escaped the worst of the ravages visited on Pulteney by the tourist trade. Outside, there was the usual bunch of sunshine supermen in luminous windsurf suits, accessorizing themselves with exotic lagers. Inside the public bar, the motif was a cigarette-yellow ceiling, barrels on the back wall, and calf-length leather seaboots with Vibram soles. Charlie was in a corner talking to a white-haired man I recognized as Chiefy Barnes, father of Chris Barnes the Savage Yachts electrician and retired coxswain of the Pulteney lifeboat. I took over a Famous Grouse for Charlie, and a pint of Devenish for Chiefy.

Chiefy's eyes were piercing blue in his burr-oak face. "Sorry to hear about the yard," he said.

I said, "Sorry we couldn't keep on the men."

"Chris is back at sea," said Chiefy. "Best place for 'im. Them yachts is only toys, at all."

Charlie said, "Chiefy reckons you ought to start a yard to build boats out of three-inch oak on seven-by-five oak frames, with railway-line strakes to give them a bit of rigidity."

"You're taking the mick," said Chiefy, without heat. "I'll leave you to it." He engulfed his pint and sidled off into the smoke.

Charlie said, "I've been thinking. I've got a boat on sea trials. She wants a workout. Scotto Scott'll come with you, couple of other guys. Sailing tonight. Drop you off in La Rochelle. That what you want?"

I took longer than was necessary to drink a sip of beer. He watched me with cynical eyes. I said, "That would be fine."

I knew my voice sounded stiff. Because I only half meant that would be fine. A free ride to La Rochelle would get me into France the quietest way possible. But if anyone saw me arrive, they might get the impression that Michael Savage was on the snoop again.

When I took another sip of beer, I detected the lingering taste of iron bar.

"Anything else I can do?" said Charlie.

I said, "That's plenty."

"Thanks," said Charlie, as if it were me who was doing him the favor.

I went home.

I rang Georges again. I said, "I'm coming over to collect *Arc-en-Ciel* myself."

"Thank God for that," he said. "We need the space. I'll move her to a buoy off Saint-Martin-de-Ré."

I called Mary Ellen. I said, "I'm off to pick up the boat." She said, "Keep your eyes open."

I said, dry-mouthed, "I was going to."

We rang off.

I threw some clothes in a bag. I felt better. Any decision was better than no decision.

Bloody fool, said the small, thin voice inside me. Remember the iron, the gin, the terror. But the voice was getting easier to ignore.

At six o'clock I slung my bag over my shoulder and bicycled down to the marina.

Scotto Scott was a large New Zealander, swearing at a winch on a big, fast-looking cruising ketch moored on the outside pontoon. I slung my bag aboard, helped him fill up with water. A couple more people trickled down the pontoon, pushing barrows of food and drink. We could have been off on a nice week's cruise.

At seven o'clock I peeled us off the dock and drove the knot in my stomach into the wide brown estuary of the Poult. There was a breeze. Scotto and I whacked on some sail. The boat heeled, wake gurgling at her transom. The land sank astern. The night came down.

Three days later we were bucketing in the tide with the gray finger of the Baleines light blinking at the back of our heads, and the knot in my stomach was the size of a football. The ten-to-six weather forecast said gales, imminent. But we were not disturbed. Because down there to port in the milk-green water were the two inverted black cones on the South cardinal at the beginning of the approach to La Rochelle.

"You know the way," said Scotto. "Take her on in."

I swallowed the knot. And in we went.

23

"Old harbor," said Scotto. "Oysters for dins, right?"

The towers were gray stone oil drums beyond the forestay. Ahead and to starboard, the Minimes bristled masts. There were a lot of sails out, having an evening on the water before it came on to blow.

I said, "Drop me off first?"

Scotto looked at me with his big blank New Zealand face. "Sure," he said. "Where to, skip?"

We turned to port, up under the bridge striding like a

white concrete centipede between the mainland and the Île de Ré. It took the best part of three-quarters of an hour to get level with Saint-Martin.

"There she is," said Scotto.

There she was. *Arc-en-Ciel,* parked on her buoy, sitting on the water light as a feather. I picked up my bag, slung it over my shoulder. Georges's men had polished her hull so it flung back a brilliant orange reflection at the late sun. Pretty boat, I thought, despite myself. A gust of wind made her halyards ring on her mast like a peal of ill-tuned bells.

As we came alongside she looked big, and solid, and encouraging: sixty feet of physical proof that Mick Savage was not as bloody useless as he felt. I grabbed a shroud, swung myself on deck, and stepped down into the cockpit. I waved to Scotto. Then I shoved the key into the hatch lock.

The key would not turn.

I rattled it a couple of times. The hatch cover gave a little, I realized it was open. Bloody Georges, I thought. Security sense of a nursery-school teacher.

I shoved the hatch open, stepped down the companion-way and slung my bag on to the bunk.

Walking into a boat you have thought out yourself is like coming home, particularly when the boat is yours and the yard bill has been paid. I stood in the hatch for a minute, admiring the job Georges's men had done. The varnish was gleaming, the instruments neat and dry in their panels, everything clean as a whistle. They had even got rid of the smell of diesel. Someone had left a coffee pot on the stove, true; but yards were yards.

I pulled the hatch shut. A powerboat went by. The deck rocked underfoot. The coffee pot clanked on the stove. I picked it up. It was still warm. Something clonked behind me. Loose board, I thought. Then I heard the click of a latch, and I knew it was not a loose board, but the head door. The significance of the warm coffee pot hit me like a train in the ribs. I spun around.

I turned straight into something that was flying at the side of my head. It connected above my left ear in a big bloom of pain. The light from the coachroof windows turned blood-colored. My knees went. I landed on the deck with a crash. There was varnished holly gritty against my face.

My mind was emitting a powerful electric hum. The coffee pot had been warm and the deck was gritty because there had been someone on the boat, hiding in the head. I knew there was something I should be worried about, but I could not work out what it was, because the blood-red light was too bright for my eyes, and my head was aching like hell.

So I shut my eyes. The pain started to spin like a big propeller. Out in the cabin someone was saying something, but I did not know what it was, because I could not hear it above the roaring in my ears. A mistake to come to La Rochelle, said a voice in my head. I let the mind drift off into a nasty dark that was waiting for it.

Something wet hit me in the face. My eyes came open. Light rushed in, and salt water. I blinked it away. The first thing I could see was a bucket. My eyes focused on the man behind the bucket.

"You stupid jerk," said Thibault Ledoux. "I nearly killed you."

With a big, sickening effort I pulled my knees under me. They clashed together as I heaved myself into the navigator's chair. I said, "What the hell are you doing here?"

He said, "Don't worry."

Memories were clawing their way past the electric hum. Jean-Claude, and all the other people who had been looking for Thibault. They were the same people who had Frankie. There was no reason to suppose they had given up looking for Thibault. He was not in a position to tell anyone not to worry. Nor was I.

I said, "Don't be so stupid."

He said, "Great to see you. We have to talk."

"Talk, then." The hum had become a throb, as if there were a diesel in my skull.

"Not here." I was not seeing very well. He was wearing a hooded boiler suit, of the kind worn by fiberglass laminators. His face looked grayish-white, as if he had been spending too much time out of the sun. "We must go from here. Maybe somebody saw you come."

"Go where?" I said.

"To sea," he said.

I said, "There's a bloody awful weather forecast."

"No," he said. "We go. I've been sitting in a cellar on the

Île de Ré. Then I saw this thing on the buoy. Now we're off, or I go crazy." He pulled up the hood of his overalls and scuttled on deck. I was too weak to follow him.

I heard the engine start, the slap of a mooring pennant forward. He came below, stuck his head into the perspex dome, grabbed the autopilot remote control. He said, "I show you." He gave me his famous smile. I was feeling too ill and too worried to be reassured by film-star grins. I laid my head on the nice new cushion covers and shut my eyes.

When I came around, I did not know if I had been asleep an hour or a minute. But the sky outside the dome had turned from gray to black, so it must have been more than a minute. There was a rattle of chain forward, then the slide of rope through a fairlead. I felt *Arc* fall back, drifting free for a moment. Then the mast came around, and she began to pitch like a rocking-horse, the wind wailing in her shrouds. We were at anchor.

Thibault came below again. "Safer," he said. "I go out to the lighthouse, as if to sea. Then I turn off the lights, come back with no lights, anchor."

"Where?"

"Off Saint-Martin-de-Ré, further than before." The wind moaned again in the shrouds. It had the high-pitched hiss of wind that is going to be serious wind.

"Wind sou'west, going west, gale force eight," said Thibault. "No problem. We have good shelter. You want an aspirin?"

I ate an aspirin. The head was down to a dull roar. Thibault said, "What are you doing here?"

I was not in the mood for formalities. I said, "The skipper of *Poisson d'Avril*'s dead. Crespi had him killed." I watched his face.

The film-star grin went. The skin whitened, hung slack.

I said, "Did you try to double-cross Crespi? Is it him you're frightened of?"

Thibault summoned up a ghastly simulacrum of his old grin. He said, "What are you talking about?"

I held my head in my hands to stop it from falling in two like a chocolate Easter egg. "I know about you," I said. "I know about *Poisson d'Avril*. A ship owned by you and Atlas

Industrien goes down. It is under charter to a company owned by Atlas Industrien. Two men dead, Thibault."

In the overhead light, his face looked seamed and mummified. I was angry. Mostly, I was angry at myself. Because Thibault had been an old friend, I had swallowed the line he had fed me.

"Two stiffs, and the skipper. Who cares about a cook and deckie when you've got a scuttle going? Still waiting for the money, are you? You and Atlas Industrien? Because it's all a Lloyd's investigation now, and the money won't be coming."

His head was in his hands. He said, "OK."

"Not yet," I said. "You wanted me to believe you didn't mess about with *Arc's* seacocks. You told me seamen don't do things like that. Well, you did. That was why you were so surprised when I turned up in the restaurant. But the damage was done, sinking or no sinking. You insured *Arc* with Agences Giotto, another Atlas Industrien company, and the manager swallowed it whole, because they had a policy of ask no questions, hear no lies. But it didn't work. Because Crespi turned up and he did ask questions. And when he found out the answers, he wanted you dead, because you had done two fiddles where only one fiddle was allowed. Is that right?"

He did not lift his head from his hands. "No," he said.

I said, "I've believed you once too bloody often, Thibault."

He raised his head. His eyes were shocked and sunken. He said, "You don't understand."

I was on my feet. I grabbed him by the front of his jersey. I could smell his breath. It was stale and rotten, like the breath of an old man. I shook him. He was easy to shake, as if the muscle had gone from him. I heard myself yelling, "So make me understand, you bastard!"

He coughed. I let go of him. I sat down. My head was splitting. I was ashamed, as if I had found myself fighting a sick man. He said, "All right, then. Will you listen?"

I said, "I'll listen."

"A while ago I needed a new boat, a trimaran. Feuilla is saying business is bad, he's cutting down the payments. He introduces me to a guy he knows. I get a loan to build this new boat. It is a cheap loan, EC money transferred from another project, legal or illegal, it's not my problem. They get a load of money down there; political loans, you know."

I said, "Down where?"

"Languedoc-Roussillon. A town called Sainte-Jeanne-des-Sables."

Home of Arthur Crespi.

"The idea is that when they give me the loan, I give some of the money back to the fixer who gets it for me. And I build the boat in their yard."

"Arthur Crespi's loan. Arthur Crespi's yard."

"Yes. Anyway, they are building this boat, and it is coming out expensive. So I can't afford to pay the kickbacks. And my other business is not going so good. I'm bleeding money, I can't let the team go, they are loyal to me, so I must be loyal to them. We swim together, we sink together. Like in the circus. So I've got Crespi's money, but I can't pay him."

"And he says, we convert this loan into a share in Transports Drenec, because it will be a pleasure to have an honest man like me connected with the company; it will make us look good. So I sign the papers. And then he comes to me and says, the ship has sunk, he will take my share of the insurance money, the loan will be paid off. I said to him, I do not like this sinking. And he says to me, do not complain, because I can hide behind my company—"

"Atlas Industrien," I said.

"That's right. He says, but you will go to jail. And when you come out of jail, you will find that something has happened to *Arc-en-Ciel*. So I thought a bit. You know he had insured *Poisson d'Avril* through Agences Giotto, another Atlas company. I thought that if I made an insurance with Giotto for *Arc-en-Ciel*, just below the limit the area manager would have had to check with head office, *Arc* would be safe, because if Crespi sank her, the insurers would get curious about the number of accidents happening to boats insured by Giotto." He made a face. "This was a bad calculation," he said. "Crespi doesn't stop for anybody."

I thought of Bianca, sailing across the bows of *White Wing*.

"So he puts the word out on me, and I go into hiding. And

then I hear that already they have sabotaged *Arc*, nearly killed you and Yann. Crespi has thrown me out of the family, and he wants me killed. He is not a man you can reason with. You cross him, you die." He grinned, a shrug-your-shoulders grin. I had seen him grin like that when someone had accidentally let go of the trapeze on which he was hanging from *Kraken*'s crosstrees. He had gone into the water, missing the deck by half an inch. If he had hit the deck, he would have been killed. He had come up grinning, and no more had been said.

Then I thought of the boat that had come after us on the Belle-Île race, because Crespi had thought Thibault was on board. And I thought of the taste of iron bars, and gin, and Frankie with Jean-Claude. We had had a lot of second chances with Crespi. It would be unwise to expect any more.

I said, "How did you discover they were coming for you?"

He said, "They went to the Manoir the night you arrived, tried to frighten Bianca. She telephoned the restaurant."

I said, "You trust Bianca?"

He said, "Of course I trust Bianca."

"Why?"

"She has worked for me for three years. She is still working for me."

"Still?"

"I asked her to take the papers from the Manoir."

"Did you tell her to hide them from me?"

He shrugged. "Sure."

"Why?"

He smiled. It was the old smile, but there was pain in it. He said, "You are a guy who can be trusted. I have always known this. You do . . . the right thing. I had done the wrong thing. I was ashamed."

Thibault had handed back the boat to me. I had come within an inch of forging an insurance claim and misappropriating his check. He was not the only one who was ashamed.

I said, "So Bianca knew where you were, all this time?"

"Of course."

"Does she now?"

"Of course."

I looked at him: the defeated slump of the shoulders, the

head hanging, the big brown hands on his knees. There was a small tattoo on his forearm. A foul anchor. Thibault was a seaman. One of the reasons he inspired loyalty was that he was reliable, as good seamen are. He was also naïve, as good seamen are. I could see him mixed up with clever Mr. Crespi in a bad loan, levered into a scuttle that went wrong, fighting to save his boats and his loyal team, the all-for-one-and-one-for-all spirit of Circus Kraken and the Équipe Ledoux shredding under the razor-sharp teeth in the piranha pool.

A gust of wind screamed in the rigging. Rain spattered the perspex dome, and *Arc-en-Ciel* shifted at her anchor like a horse on a long tether.

Something thumped against the side.

It could have been a floating log. But then there were feet on the deck. They had boots on. The boots had studded soles. I could hear them grinding and tearing at the dove-gray planking.

I was up, heading for the companionway. The hatch flew open. My eyes were used to the cabin lights. The engine in my head was still banging. It was black as a pig's innards out there, howling with wind.

Something grabbed me by the shoulders. I felt myself yanked out of the hatch. Wind and rain battered my face. I was yelling, wrenching away from them. They held on tight. There were two of them, and the dim shape of a semi-rigid inflatable alongside.

One of the men said, "Ah! Frankie's daddy. Well, you save Frankie some problems, *beau-papa*."

The voice was Jean-Claude's. I did not know what he meant. By the time I had worked it out, it was too late.

"Heave ho!" said Jean-Claude.

They heaved, both at once. They were strong. I had taken a smack on the head, and I was weak. I shot through the air, hit the lifelines that ran around the boat's side like a fence, slammed on to the deck with a bang that knocked the air out of me.

"Bye, bye," said Jean-Claude. His boot came out of the night, and shoved. I had no air in me. I was sliding under the bottom lifeline. My hands moved feebly on the deck. My left hand found a coiled rope. The boot came again. I had as much power of movement as a sack of Brussels sprouts.

I clutched the rope. The boot rolled me under the bottom lifeline.

Still hanging on to the rope's end, I went into the sea.

The water was black and icy cold. It knocked what was left of the breath out of me. I struggled back to the surface, and sucked air. I could see the masthead light of *Arc-en-Ciel* up in the black, waving as she rolled. I was still holding the rope. Panic bubbled up. Calm down, I thought. Hang on. Pull yourself in, nice and quiet, over the back end of the boat. And fix those little bastards.

The heart began to beat properly. I trod water, pulled in hand-over-hand on the rope. It came easily. I waited for the tension to come on.

What came was not tension. What came was the other end of the rope.

It had not been tied on.

A wave lifted me. I saw the masthead light, a good fifty yards away now. The tide was carrying me away, me and my stupid rope, into the big black sea.

I let the rope go.

Bianca had known where we were.

I began to panic properly.

24

Anyone who has gone a long way alone in a small boat on the big sea has thought about falling overboard. There will be the moment of shock, as the cold water comes up and smacks you in the face. There will be the panic, swimming at one knot after a boat that is drifting away at three. And there will be the hopelessness, as you wait to die.

I had worked it all out years ago, as a sort of mental vaccination against doing anything bloody stupid. I had been through the shock. I spat out the sea-water, kicked off my shoes, and shoved the panic firmly into the locked box in the mind.

And there I was, treading water in the black night. It was at this moment the hopelessness should have set in.

But it did not. What set in was determination to survive.

We had been anchored off Saint-Martin-de-Ré. The tide would be taking me down to the Île de Ré bridge. There was most of a gale blowing, but the sea in the lee of the island was still nearly smooth.

At least, it would have looked smooth from the deck of a boat. With only a head above water, it was already uncomfortably rough. All I could see were two-foot wavelets, some of them with foam on their crests, stretching into the dark like the backs of fighting animals. From the top of the waves, I could see the lights of Saint-Martin-de-Ré to the southwest.

Upwind.

I tried to swim for the lights. Three strokes had me blinded and choking. I turned away and trod water until I could catch my breath.

The chart was in my head. Up to the northeast, five miles downwind, was the bay of L'Aiguillon. Too far to swim, even in flat water. And the last part of it would be out of the shelter of the Île de Ré. The water would be far from flat.

Panic came back to nibble at the edges of my mind. I got another mouthful of water. Move, I told myself. There was only one way to move: into the big black emptiness ahead, where the waves would be breaking in the concrete mussel cages on the shore.

I started.

Swimming downwind is like sailing downwind: you lose all sense that the breeze is blowing. You move in a charmed circle of still air, with only the batter of the spray on the back of your head to remind you what will happen if you turn around. But taking a whack on the head from a pump handle and a severe kicking from a set of hobnail boots is not great training for a big swim. I was getting tired. I peered ahead into the dark, looking for signs of the shore.

There were none. But there was something else.

Away and up to the left a red light glowed and faded. My

heartbeat became solid and confident. The light glowed again, went out. I altered course, swimming up to where the light had been. That brought the wind on to my left ear. I stuck my face into the water, began a dogged breaststroke.

The trouble began.

All I could hear was the roar of my breathing and the bubble and crunch of water. My mouth was bitter with salt, my chest sore with inhaled spray. *Give up,* said a part of me. *Stay afloat, go downstream. Something will turn up.* But I knew that nothing would turn up except a couple of lungfuls of water. I could see the body, face down on the beach at Coup de Vague, water oozing from mouth and nostrils. Fell off his boat, poor bleeder. Not a mark on him.

Arthur Crespi and Jean-Claude would be happy as clams. They would tell Frankie all about it.

I began to get angry. The anger burned in my thickening blood. I swam again, hard.

In front of me, the red light cast gobs of blood on the waves, faded to black. It was a mortal distance up the sky, that light. It was so far up in the black that it could have been a star. It floated and shifted in the air. I swore at it, grinding my teeth. The grinding helped to keep the arms going, the legs moving in the frog-kick, the oxygen wheezing into the lungs.

I wondered where Frankie was. It was possible that she was in La Rochelle, ten miles away. No, I thought. Jean-Claude had escaped from police guard in a hospital bed in La Rochelle. He would have come back to the town furtively, with one thing in mind. To watch Thibault. Or follow me.

All I could hear was Thibault's voice.

Of course I trust Bianca.

My legs were aching. The muscles were trying to knot. The beginning of cramp. All you need, I thought. Tied up in a neat Turk's head. Sink like a brick to the bottom of the Pertuis Breton. Goodbye, world.

The red light pulsed again. It had sunk a long way down the sky. It was only just above eye level, now.

I swam.

Something was happening just below the light. There was a paleness against the black of the sea. I kicked toward it with legs that felt as if they belonged to somebody else. I was sick and light-headed, and I hurt from the soles of my feet to the crown of my head.

The red glow pulsed again. This time, it lit up vertical metal struts, painted red. There was a big white number, white as the water that roared against the base of the thing in the night. A big, beautiful, gas-powered port-hand buoy.

It took what felt like half an hour but was probably three minutes. It was full of the sob of breathing, and the roar of water, and it hurt. At the end of it, I slammed my hand into the slats of the buoy and clenched the fingers. I might have been crying. There was too much salt water about to tell.

The buoy consisted of a truncated cone of red metal slats with a lamp at its apex. Around the base of the cone ran a ledge, nine inches wide. I waited for a wave. Then I pulled myself onto the ledge.

That was wonderful. For some time, I reveled in the simple fact of being alive, and out of the water. But the wind was blowing hard out here. It was shoving the buoy over, dousing it with water every few waves. The red pulse of the light shone on my sodden clothes. The wind was sucking the heat out of me. I was standing on the ledge, gripping the slats. My fingers were losing sensation. The ledge was slippery, too narrow. As the buoy heeled over I was hanging from my hands, feet shuffling for a grip. The rain was going to come down, and I was not going to be able to hang on.

I heard a ticking in the water, a whirr of engines. I looked up. A set of navigation lights was bearing down, emerald to starboard, ruby to port, white up top. Fishing boat, I thought.

I could see the bulging wave of water under his bow, the comb of spray where it broke. He would be up there in the warm wheelhouse, clearview spinning the rain off, radar and radio and Decca gleaming their little green gleams in the darkness. And outside, lit by the red glow, there would be the spidery figure on the buoy.

He came abeam. The buoy heaved in his wake. He slid by, portholes and running lights blazing. There was no slackening of his engine note. I shouted. It came out weak as a kitten's meow. He hammered away toward the red lights of the Île de Ré bridge.

I stopped trying to shout. I concentrated on hanging on. I felt too weak even to be miserable.

Things were working out just as Mr. Crespi would have hoped.

Peculiar things started happening to my mind. A queue of people presented themselves, wearing rusty morning coats and summer dresses past their best, as at an Irish wedding. They took me by the hand. Instead of saying hello, I was saying goodbye. Uncle James was there, with his goggle eyes. He would not touch my hand. They all yelled at me, the whole queue. Goodbye was not the word, they shouted. Say *hello*.

It was a surprisingly vigorous shout. More of a roaring.

My head rolled around on my shoulders. Up there in the rain was a light. There had been no light last time I had looked. It was a white light, high in the air. Not a navigation light. An anchor light. Why would a boat be anchored in the channel?

The light moved. The boat was not anchored. So why the anchor light? And the roaring?

A wave tilted the buoy and crashed into my face. When I could see again, the white light was closer, high overhead. Underneath it was a white triangle. A sail. An unsheeted jib, flapping in the gale. Too much unsheeted jib for the wind.

The buoy's light pulsed blood across the waves and on the hull of the boat with the white light at the top of its mast. It reflected like a setting sun in the polished black hull of the boat, the way the setting sun had reflected in *Arc-en-Ciel's* hull a year ago. Not a year ago. Earlier this evening.

It was *Arc-en-Ciel*. It was *Arc-en-Ciel,* drifting. It was *Arc-en-Ciel,* about to drift within twenty feet of this shuddering iron buoy where I hung crucified.

A gust screamed in the rigging, and the thunder of the jib became a machine-gun rattle. *Arc-en-Ciel* started to turn away. The buoy-light bloomed again.

I dived into the sea.

I swam like a madman, head down crawl, at the last place I had seen *Arc's* hull. I could see red in the water, red from the buoy-light and from the blood thundering behind my eyes. My hand smashed into plastic. My head came out of the water. I saw the scoop of *Arc's* back end, at eye-level.

We were in the trough of a wave. It was as if the boat had waited for me. I laced my fingers around the backstay. Then the wave came under, and the gust wailed in the rig, and she was away with a surge of power that yanked my arms nearly out of their sockets.

I heaved myself on to the transom and into the cockpit, and fell on my knees. The hatch was open. I groped inside for the navigation lights. I put the cabin lights on, too. I was past caring who found me, or what I found.

That was what I thought, anyway.

The cabin sole was red. I blinked. It was all red, tonight. When I opened my eyes it was still red.

The reason it was red was by the galley stove, on the deck. The boat rolled. The thing on the floor slid. Once, it had been Thibault Ledoux. It was still Thibault's body, but the head was not Thibault's head. The head was a red ball of blood. The blood had gone everywhere. It was not coming out of Thibault anymore.

I went down the steps. Someone had hit him just under the left ear with something sharp and heavy. He was not breathing. There was no pulse. Whoever had hit him had hit him hard enough to kill him.

My old pal Thibault.

I turned away. The blood was sticky underfoot as I pulled out the chart. Water from my clothes dripped on to it. My hands were shaking so badly I could hardly unroll it. The numbers on the seabed ran around like ants. The bulkhead compass said the wind had gone around west, with some north in it. *Dead.* The number on the buoy pinpointed our position. *Dead.* We were heading for a wide, flat shore of mud, and oyster beds, and boulders. *Dead.*

I was heading. There was only me on board. Thibault was not there anymore. Only the outside of him.

Poor Thibault. Dead.

The autopilot seemed to be broken. I scrambled on deck, out of the eggy smell of a lot of blood, and into the cold blast of the wind and the rain.

The jib was still roaring up there at the front end, drawing at intervals. We were heeled hard over, driving northeast, across the tide. It was the wrong way to be going. I grabbed the wheel.

It spun loose in my hand.

I whipped the on-deck flashlight out of its clips, pulled the cover off the pedestal that housed the steering-gear's innards. There should have been a big, fat BMW motorbike chain in there on a pair of sprockets, linking to the steering.

There was no chain.

I was sweating, despite the cold. The aches had gone, submerged in a big, hot burn that filled my body and limbs. The emergency tiller lived in a special locker in the transom. I kicked off the clips, fumbled it out.

Arc-en-Ciel paused in her career, checked. I knew what the check meant. Eight feet underneath my feet, her keel had brushed the mud.

The seas were small, but they were steep and irritable. One of them came under with a sharp, petulant jerk. My fingers were swollen like balloons from hanging on to the slats of the buoy. The tiller jumped out of my hands, bounced once on to the side-deck, and went overboard.

The keel touched again. It tripped me on to my knees. There was a line of white water down to starboard. The jib drew, and for a moment all was quiet, except for the roar and whoosh of *Arc's* wake as she shot forward. No sound from the body of Thibault Ledoux in his blood on the cabin sole. No sound from me, semiconscious on my knees in the cockpit of the rudderless boat.

But from down to starboard, where the waves fell on the shore and smacked the white foam, there came a heavy, concussive roar.

I hit the ENGINE START button. No response. They had cut the anchor cable, and the steering chain, and the leads to the engine battery. They had snarled off in their Zodiac, left the boat on a lee shore. They had left the dead man to be washed clean by the waves, victim of a terrible accident, like his friend the Irishman, who must so tragically have been washed overboard earlier on. There would have been no survivors.

There still might not be any survivors.

Arc's keel touched, tripped, came free. It touched again and held fast. The noise came.

She was smashed over on her ear. Suddenly the world was full of the thunder of white water. Something parted with a bang. Against the lighter sky, I saw the mast fold lazily in half, plunge into the spume. I ran below, pulled my wallet out of my bag, shoved it in my pocket. I pulled one of the horseshoe lifebuoys off the transom and rammed it under my arms. Something was walloping at the hull like a giant hammer. There was a grinding, too, a long, horrible dragging from down in her bowels. We were in the breakers. A wave landed on my head. It drove me down, down. I felt the lifeline press against me like a cheese wire. I was yelling underwater. Then I was tumbling head over heels, and there was no boat anymore.

My head broke water. I got a breath, a glimpse of long, roaring lines of white foam running away into a general blur of white. Then a wave thundered down on top of me, drove me head and shoulders into something very hard. Ah, yes, thought a part of me detached from the rumble and crash of the waves. The concrete cages they use for storing mussels. Getting close to the beach.

Then the pain came, and I was hurled along, eyes and mouth wide open, head roaring like a well-beaten tam-tam. A wave picked me up, shook me in its crest, and slammed me down into a bank of stone-hard lumps. The water went away.

I was lying on a beach of boulders in the rain and the wind. I could taste blood on my face. I was mewing like a cat.

I made my hands and knees propel me over the rocks. Bits of oyster shell would have been digging into my palms, but the nerves had been out of action for a good half-hour.

I kept climbing. It was a kind of evolutionary instinct. Get above the water, as high as possible, out of reach of its violent, clammy hands. The boulders of the sea-wall were upon me. I scrambled up. On the sandy road that ran along the top, I looked back.

There was the dark beach, and the white breakers. Out in the breakers something long and black rolled, sluggish as a dead whale. And beyond, far toward the little lights of Saint-Martin-de-Ré, a little bloody spot bloomed and shrank in the ink-black sea. An eye, opening, sweeping the water, closing again.

Not seeing me.

I staggered to the inland side of the road, fell down the soft salt-grass of the bank. It was warm and windless, with a smell of new hay. I breathed it in. A car stopped on the road. There were lights and shouting.

I slept.

25

*L*ight was levering my eyelids apart. I kept them shut as long as possible. My body felt as if it had been beaten with clubs, and the ache in my head was a slow, blinding throb. There was grass against my face. I opened my eyes.

For a long time I could not see anything except a generalized white glare. Then it formed itself into planes. There was the green transverse line of the sea-wall, the blue-white dazzle of the sky. I started to crawl up the sea-wall toward the road.

The first movements seemed to take an hour each. After that, I began to remember how to move, and life got easier, but not much.

The road had emptied. The wind had dropped. The tide was out. *Arc-en-Ciel* lay out there on her side, in the middle of an oyster bed. Her black hull was dulled by the grinding of rock and sand. There was a gaping hole where her coachroof should have been, and the mud around her was scattered with fragments of mast and rigging.

I picked up a length of two-by-two driftwood to use as a walking stick, and began to trudge painfully south along the white road on the sea-wall.

It burned my eyes like a white-hot iron bar, that road. I could not seem to work out where I was going. I did not recognize anything except the sea to the right, and the flat green land to my left.

After what might have been twenty minutes, I came to a

collection of huts with cement water-tanks inside chainlink fences. Alsatians barked inside the fences. A couple of men were driving tractors loaded with sacks of oysters. They did not pay any attention to me.

I walked on. There was another shack ahead. There was something familiar about it. Stones rolled under my feet. There had been the smell of aftershave, the cold metal of a shotgun barrel on my jaw. And flames.

The muscles of my arms were full of flames. I staggered across the last ten yards of stones. There was still charring on the door. The door was locked. I picked up a stone and caved it in. I fell on to a pile of nets. The darkness came down again.

Some time later, there was a voice, cursing. I dredged around in my mind, remembered where I was. I said, "Christophe."

The voice said, *"Bon Dieu!"*

My mouth felt as if it was carved from stone, and my tongue would not do what I wanted. I said, "Thibault is dead. Don't tell anyone I'm here."

The words fell out of him in a torrent. He said, "You are both dead. Poor Thibault. I saw him. It was as if there was no blood left in him. One would have said a man of marble. It was me and some others who took him up the beach. They were saying that you were lost at sea. The anchor chain broke."

I could not cope with the words. I was sad. Very sad. The tears leaked out of my eyes, burned the side of my face.

His shadow fell across me. I could smell stale brandy and tobacco on his clothes. He said, "My poor friend."

He did things involving blankets and glasses of water, and brandy that I did not want. All the time, the words he had said played in my head like a loop of tape.

You are both dead.

I said, "I'm dead."

He said, "What?" His old brown face looked sad and worried.

"Don't tell anyone I'm alive. I must disappear. Like the *Résistance.*"

He said, "Ah!" His face shone with understanding.

I passed out again.

I must have been ill. The next chunk of time was a sort of blur. It was dark, and then it was light. Someone gave me soup, which I drank, and brandy, which I did not. After a certain number of darknesses and lights, there was no way of saying how many, the pain in my bones stopped being a fire, and became an ache. The headache faded, too, and the thoughts came unscrambled. It might have taken a long time. There was no way of knowing.

At a time when by the angle of the sunlight creeping through the blue shutters it was morning, Christophe came in. He had been in twice a day. This morning, I said, "Christophe, I want to thank you for everything."

He said, "Don't be stupid. You helped Thibault, Thibault helped me. It is correct."

I said, "Does anyone know I have been here?"

His face reddened behind the white bristles. "You should remember that I have been a *résistant*," he said.

I remembered. I said, "I am sorry."

He shrugged. "But of course you were quite right to ask."

I said, "Is Bianca Dufy still at the restaurant?"

"Dufy?"

"The dark woman. Pretty."

He said, "I'll ask." He pulled a supermarket bag from an inside pocket of his blue canvas jacket. "Here. Food." He left. I heard his key turn in the lock.

There was bread in there, and cheese, and a lump of cold fish, and a recorked half-bottle of white *vin de table*. I ate the lot, and drank the wine, and fell into a sleep that was an ordinary sleep, not a period of unconsciousness full of sweats and fever-dreams. I woke in the dark. The key was rattling in the door. He was back. His sister was with him, fists shoved firmly in her pockets.

"I have brought Giselle," he said. "She hears what happens in the restaurant."

Giselle looked as if she had been crying. "M. Thibault is dead," she said. "There have been many reporters."

"We know that, you bloody fool," said Christophe. "Tell him the other things."

"Mlle. Frankie has left, as you know."

"And Bianca? The dark one?"

"She left at the same time as you," said Giselle. "She

came back, one night only, last week. Then she left again. She asked for you." She began to look vaguely conspiratorial. "When she found you were not there, she cried. I think she is in love."

"You will do monsieur the honor of keeping your notions to yourself," said Christophe.

"And did she leave an address?"

"No," said Giselle.

My heart sank.

"Not a house, anyway," she said. "A poste restante."

"How do you know this?" said Christophe.

"M. Gérard," she said. "He is now in charge of the restaurant. He is not happy that he has the work of the restaurant."

I said, quietly, "Which poste restante?"

"Sainte-Jeanne-des-Sables," she said, promptly.

Sainte-Jeanne-des-Sables. "Thank you," I said.

That evening, I walked on rubbery legs back up the road on top of the sea-wall. *Arc-en-Ciel* had gone; the salvage people would have taken her. Near Esnandes, beyond the place where she had gone ashore, there was a café with a telephone. Christophe had brought in *Ouest-France*. There had been a big feature on Thibault and a picture of me. It was an archive picture, clean-shaven, wearing collar and RORC tie. Though Giselle had washed my clothes, they had not been improved by total immersion in the sea, and I had not shaved since Pulteney. I fitted in well with the café's clientele. Farming oysters is a muddy industry, and not one in which it pays to be well dressed. The man behind the bar had a blue-jerseyed café proprietor's stomach hanging over a pair of fisherman's trousers. He gave me a *café noir* and pointed me at the telephone. I dialed Mary Ellen's number.

She took a long time to answer. When she did, her voice sounded hoarse and ragged.

"Mary Ellen?" I said.

"Who's that?"

"Mick."

She said, "That's not funny." There was a click. A robot voice intoned: *The other caller has disconnected.*

I dialed again. Someone picked up the phone. "It's me," I

said. "Mick. In France. What have I done?" There was a pause. I waited for the click. What was it now? I wondered. She had hung up on me innumerable times. But not, for the love of God, tonight. I shoved in more money.

"Mick?" she said.

"That's right. Don't hang up. Just tell me what I'm supposed to have done, all right?"

She said, "It really is you." There was a sharp, crazy edge in her voice.

"Please," I said. "I'm in a call box."

"Mick," she said. The voice warmed up as if someone had lit a fire under it. "Mick, darling. How wonderful."

"What?"

"They said you were dead," she said. "Drowned."

I said, "Who said?"

"The French police."

"Does Frankie know?"

"She would have rung."

"Where is she?"

"I don't know. She sent a postcard from Montpellier. Passing through. She sounded fine."

It had been good to hear the warmth in Mary Ellen's voice. But my thoughts were moving on, and my stomach was tightening again. I said, "I'm going to go and look for her."

"How?"

"I know where she might be." I tried to keep it light.

Mary Ellen knew me well enough to know when I was trying. She said, "Is everything all right?"

"Fine," I said.

"So why are you bothering to go and look for her?"

I said, "I don't altogether approve of this Baragouin."

"Yes," she said. "I'm glad you're going." She sounded uncertain and tentative.

"Don't tell anyone you've heard from me," I said. "But could you call Justin?"

"Of course."

"Give him a message. Tell him I'm close to getting what he needs. Ask him to rent me a car, and send some money. I'll pick it up in the BNP at Rochefort."

She said, "Look after yourself, Mick." She hesitated. There was comfort in being connected to her, even by a tiny blink of fiber optics. I did not want to hang up, and nor did she. She said, "Thinking you were dead. It was . . . horrible. We don't see each other much, do we?"

I said, "No."

She said, "I'm so glad you're there."

I said, "I'll find Frankie."

She said, "It's lonely without her, isn't it?"

I said, "Yes." She had no idea how lonely it might get.

She said, "Thank you, darling."

I could imagine her there on her sofa in the flat, the lights of the river a constellation in the black water beyond the window. She would be smiling the confidential smile that came over her on the rare occasions we were really together, when she forgot that I was an irresponsible Irishman and she was Mary Ellen Soames, the most efficient underwriter in the world.

The money ran out. I hung up, paid for the coffee, and stumped into the night.

The legs were better already. Next morning I got a lift into town from Christophe, and caught the bus to Rochefort. In the BNP, I haggled for the money Justin had telegraphed, and picked up the Peugeot that was waiting at the Avis depot. Then I found Sainte-Jeanne on the road map, ate lunch with a fierce appetite, and began.

I stayed the night near Toulouse. The air was warm down there, scented with herbs, the morning light yellower and fiercer than the blue Atlantic glow of La Rochelle. The breakfast waiter's French was a sharp-edged language, as bitter as the coffee. The language of Crespi and Jean-Claude. I paid the bill with Justin's money, bought a straw hat in a noisy street market, and started for the coast.

An hour and a half later I was in big billboard country. The road was lined with a spiny vegetation struggling for survival under dun sand and graying newspapers. The billboards advertised wine and *appartements,* and villas and *appartements,* and sun oil and *appartements.* At eleven o'clock I drove under a sign that said SAINTE-JEANNE-DES-

SABLES—SON VIEUX PORT—SES CAMPINGS—SON PORT DE
PLAISANCE "LES DIGUES." There was an idealized picture of a
fishing village, red roofs, a church tower, palm trees on a
yellow sandspit sticking out into a blue, blue sea.

Sainte-Jeanne might have been like the poster once, but
the twentieth century had jumped on it and was still
trampling on the remains. I passed ten building sites between the town boundary and the first traffic light, each with
its plume of yellow dust rolling into the blue Mediterranean
sky. The place had a raw, anarchic feeling, very different
from the control and organization of La Rochelle. Toward
the middle of the town the sky became harder to see,
because of the high-rise blocks on either side of the road.
The tower blocks faded away, and suddenly we were in
Holiday France, old style. There was the pocket-hand-
kerchief Vieux Port with souvenir shops. There was the
square, with palm trees and cafés, and a little maze of
narrow alleys in which I got lost while looking for the post
office. And there was the deep, well-founded hatred felt by
the native inhabitants of the Mediterranean littoral for the
tourists who pay their rent.

Eventually, an old man showed me his remaining tooth
and indicated the post office. I raised my straw hat to him,
fought my way through a double busload of Germans, and
went in.

The men and women behind the windows looked hot and
unhelpful. They did not look like the kind of apple-cheeked
village postmistresses who would discuss the habits and
addresses of their constituents with unshaven strangers. I
shoved my hands in my pockets, and looked at the posters
on the walls.

There was a hollowness in my stomach. Sainte-Jeanne
might feel big and bustling, but it was the kind of place
where, to the trained eye, tall strangers with red beards
stood out like a bus in a swimming pool. The sweat was
beginning to run.

It froze.

There was a poster of a man in his sixties. He had a
senatorial quiff of white hair, a nut-brown face, laughter
lines carefully lit by the photographer, gazing out at the

crowd in the post office with an expression that managed to combine raffishness with paternal care. Under the poster, the message was brief, in large black type, VOTEZ POUR VOTRE MAIRE LE 16. Elect me mayor on the sixteenth. Across the bottom right-hand corner of the picture was an orange slash, on which was printed: COMME TOUJOURS! Like always.

I said to the woman in front of me in the queue, "Who's that?"

She had a shopping bag in each hand. She looked hot, and bothered, and irritable. When she saw the poster, she smiled. "Him?" she said. "That's le Patron."

"What's his name?"

She looked at me as if I were crazy. "Feuilla," she said.

She was dead right. The man on the poster was Thibault's sponsor and my benefactor, M. Feuilla.

"Next!" said the woman behind the counter.

I stood there with my mouth hanging open. The queue behind me started to mutter and groan. I walked out, into the blast of the sun.

If you want to know where the mayor lives, ask a barman.

26

I found one leaning on the *zinc* of the Café des Sports, watching the traffic and fiddling with the black hairs in his nostrils. I bought a black coffee and asked him where I might find the residence of M. Feuilla.

"Le Patron?" he said. "Villa Occitan."

"Where's that?"

He pointed in a vaguely westerly direction. "What do you want with him?"

"I'd like to meet him."

"Hang around long enough, and he'll come to you." The barman laughed. "And he'll know your name."

"What do you mean?"

"He owns the town. He built the town. He knows everybody in the town." The barman did not look happy.

I said, "Does this give you problems?"

He shrugged. "I lived in the republic of France, until I came to Sainte-Jeanne, and then I find I live in a monarchy." He caught the eye of a waiter with a drinks order, and mopped himself away along the bar.

I thought about Carthystown, and Uncle James. I knew about monarchies. I finished my coffee and wandered out into the square. The pressure of the eyes was still there. I found a room in a hotel a couple of miles inland. I took a shower, and eased the last aches out of my muscles. I was excited, nervous, dry-mouthed. I got the telephone directory from reception, called Feuilla's number. A butler answered. I asked if Feuilla was still away. No, no, he said, le Patron was at home. I asked if he could be seen. He was out, said the butler. And there was a dinner party this evening. But le Patron was always available. Could we make an appointment? I said not to worry, and rang off.

I spent the afternoon in my room and ate dinner, steak and salad and a couple of glasses of mineral water, in a quiet corner of the hotel dining room. The ache had gone from my muscles. I felt ready for anything. I went out, picked up the car, and drove back to Sainte-Jeanne.

There were strings of colored lights across the narrow streets in the old part of the town. Loudspeakers were pouring shockwaves of garlic disco down the canyons between the houses. People were drinking heavily at mobile bars set up on trestle tables. They were looking inward, preoccupied with each other. Nobody spared me a glance. I was only a tourist.

The road where Feuilla had his house was away from the old town, in what must until recently have been open country. I drove out there, parked the car in a side road and continued on foot, mooching along in the shadows of the palm trees. I was walking past little crescents of new houses, interspersed with open country. Crickets shrilled from the trees. The music of the town was a far-off jangle. Down toward the sea, a cluster of high-rise buildings stuck out of the foreshore like a jawful of floodlit teeth.

I came to a wall, high and beautiful, built of cut stone. There was a big oak gate with iron studs and hinges of Spanish-looking strapwork. There was no name. But there were no more houses in the road. This would be the one.

There was a big iron handle in the gate. I looked at it for a moment. Then I put out my hand and turned it. It was locked.

I shoved my hands in my pockets and walked on along the wall. After a couple of hundred yards it turned away from the road. I followed it around. There were trees inside now, holm oaks, black against the stars. Outside, where I was walking, my feet crackled on their dry leaves. It was dark in the shadow of the wall. That suited me fine.

After another couple of hundred yards, the wall turned again. There was the distant sound of voices. A little further on there was another road, little more than a lane. Roofs projected above the wall. Stables, maybe. I was at the business end of the house.

Where the lane touched the wall, there was another gate. This one was made of wrought-iron. I had been right about the stables. The gate opened into a paved yard. On the far side of the yard was the back of the house, cream-washed, with a light burning in a globe of moths above the door. The voices were closer. Faintly, as if from the other side of the house, I heard the mumble of conversation, the clatter of knives and forks on plates. A dinner party.

Someone else laughed. I stopped dead.

I recognized the laugh. I had heard it for seventeen years, filling out from a childish cackle into the voice of a woman. It was Frankie's laugh.

I was sweating properly now. She sounded happy and excited, the way a girl should sound when she is out to dinner in the south of France. I wanted to see her, get her directly under my hand, and keep her happy.

I pressed the latch of the gate. It opened smoothly inward. I could hear my breathing loud in my ears. I shut the gate behind me and walked into the yard.

It was empty. One side of it was occupied by a line of cars:

two Mercedes, a Ferrari, a BMW. There was a garden gate beside the back door. I walked around the side of the yard, under the eaves of the sheds. The cars gleamed like fish under the lights. I put out my hand for the latch.

A voice said, "Hey!"

I looked around. My mouth was dry as blotting-paper. A policeman was standing by the back door. His right hand was unbuttoning the flap of his holster. His left had just pitched away the stub of a cigarette.

I said, "I've come to see M. Feuilla."

He said, "Have you really?"

I did not want to be taken down to the station. At the station I would be charged with trespass, or burglary. In a town the size of Sainte-Jeanne, that kind of thing got into the newspapers. And Crespi and his friends would read the newspapers.

All of a sudden, I was deadly worried about Frankie. Bloody fool, I told myself. You've walked into the middle of it.

The policeman said, "Come with me."

I said, "Where are we going?"

He opened the kitchen door. "You are coming to see M. le Patron, of course."

"In private?"

He laughed. It was not a kindly laugh. He said, "It is not the habit of M. le Patron to involve his dinner guests with . . . tourists."

We were in the kitchen wing of the house. It smelled of frying garlic, boiled crayfish, rendered wine. He put me into a small room. There was no light. I caught a glimpse of boxes. The key turned in the lock.

I sat down on the cool concrete floor. The sweat grew clammy on my body.

I wanted to stay dead. I did not know if I could persuade Feuilla to let me. I did not know anything about Feuilla anymore, except that he had been sitting at the same table as Crespi at the Flotilla, laughing.

Above my head, perhaps eight feet off the floor, was a paler patch in the blackness. I fumbled for a box and kicked it against the wall.

The pale patch was a ventilator, a little window with an iron grille. Between the bars of the grille I could see slices of patio; not the little deck of paving stones that passes for a patio in England and America, but a real one, surrounded by the house, colonnaded on all sides, with a fountain in the middle, and torches burning in brackets on the pillars, their flames illuminating jasmine and roses growing from big terra-cotta pots, and a long table with silver candlesticks. There must have been eighteen people at the table.

Frankie was facing me. She was laughing. Her teeth were white in the candlelight, and the saddle of freckles over her nose was dark brown on her brown face. Her eyes were pussycat narrow. She had always been pretty. Tonight, she looked beautiful, and grown-up to a frightening degree. I had the sudden feeling that I was spying on something that had nothing to do with Mary Ellen or me. She was a stranger.

Bianca was there. The lights were winking in the collar of diamonds around her neck. Feuilla was next to her, at the head of the table, leaning over with his arm around her shoulders. It was a possessive gesture. I was shocked by it.

But that was not all that shocked me.

Down the table, a long way from Feuilla, next to a brown, brassy-looking girl wearing quantities of shiny makeup and not much else, was Arthur Crespi.

He laughed, an artificial guffaw that creased his porpoise jowls, and Frankie laughed along. Bianca did not. Feuilla smiled, a perfunctory smile.

A footman in a white coat bent and whispered something in Feuilla's ear. His smile did not flicker. Dinner was finished. He said something to the table. They all looked eager. They got up with a great squealing of chairs, and left. Maids came and cleared the table. Ten minutes later there was a sound of several car engines from the other side of the house. Then there was silence.

I got down from the window, and sat on the box. Crespi and Feuilla had sat at the same table at the Flotilla. Now Crespi was at dinner with Feuilla. If they were friends, I was in trouble, and so was Frankie.

I tried the door. There was no way out. After what seemed like a long time, footsteps crunched up to the door and a key rattled in the lock. It was the policeman. He said, "Le Patron will see you now."

27

I said, "Don't you usually take people to the police station?"

He did not smile. He said, "You should ask yourself who owns the police station." I thought of Jonzac, the policeman in La Rochelle. Nobody owned Jonzac but Jonzac.

He took me along stone-flagged corridors, through a door that in England would have been covered in green baize, and into a big room. Despite the heat there was a fire burning in the fireplace at the far end. There was a solid-looking Picasso nude above the fireplace. The floor was polished boards, with rugs that had the harmonious softness of extreme age. Bianca was sitting in an armchair on the right of the fire, reading a book. Feuilla was cutting a cigar.

The policeman cleared his throat, and saluted. My stomach was full of butterflies. Bianca had known where Thibault was hiding, and Thibault had died. And now here she was, all cozy with Feuilla, who was all cozy with Crespi.

Sorry, Frankie.

I said, "Good evening."

The policeman opened his mouth to tell me to shut up. Bianca looked up from her book. She dropped it on the carpet. She did not move. Her eyes were frightened, as if she were seeing a ghost. Which as far as she was concerned was precisely true.

She got up. She ran toward me across the beautiful carpets. She threw her arms around my neck, and kissed me on the mouth and leaned her head on my shirtfront.

"Ah." Feuilla had turned. A match was burning in his right hand, the cigar unlit in his left. His eyebrows rose, came down again. His eyes were dark slits. "Mick. How very surprising to see you."

At the sound of his voice, Bianca let go.

"So," said Feuilla. His voice was not quite level. "This is an unusual way of visiting us. Breaking and entering, *hein?*"

I said, "I was coming to see you."

"You could have rung the doorbell."

"Merde, Patron!" said Bianca. "Will you give him a drink?"

"Give him one yourself." Feuilla smiled indulgently, waved the policeman out of the room. "You must forgive my daughter. Fathers are never sufficiently welcoming. As I expect you know?"

I stared at him. "Fathers," I said, stupidly.

He shrugged. I looked at the short, hooked nose, the way the hair grew back from the forehead, the gypsyish good looks. Now he had explained it, I could not imagine why I had never noticed the likeness before.

I sat on a large sofa, opposite a cubist painting of bits of newspaper mixed up with a guitar. Bianca brought a bowl of nuts and a bottle of red wine. She smiled like the Queen of Sheba. She said, "We thought you were dead."

She was wearing a T-shirt made of some silky material, jeans and cowboy boots. It all went beautifully with the diamonds. She sat next to me, and hung on to my hand.

The Patron glanced at her quickly out of the side of his eyes. He said, "You will no doubt be asking yourself some questions." In La Rochelle, he had had the gift of taking control. Here, it was more than that. I had returned from the dead, but it was I who was surprised. I thought of what the barman in the café had said. *I lived in the republic of France. Then I find I live in a monarchy.* Feuilla had the head of a lion. A weary lion. There was a grayness about the eyes, a droop to the lower lids. He said, "What brings you here?"

"I was looking for my daughter."

He smiled. "Sure," he said. It was an old, knowing smile. "And what else?"

I wondered how much to tell him. He gazed at me with eyes innocent as a baby's. "Arthur Crespi," I said.

Something happened at the corners of his mouth. All of a sudden, the lion looked hungry.

Bianca said, in a voice of ice, "We don't talk about Crespi in this house."

"You had him to dinner."

Feuilla leaned back in his chair. He had lit his cigar. He blew a thin-stemmed tree of smoke at the Picasso nude. "Sometimes," he said, and stopped, a long pause. "Sometimes, maybe once in a lifetime, you do something terrible for the sake of your business."

I waited. The room was hot, and the fire was making it hotter. But there was a chill in the air that brought up the goose pimples.

The Patron raised his left hand, cigar between his fingers. "Maybe I should explain." Bianca turned her head away. "He came here ten years ago. In those days, he was quite a charming young guy. A live wire, you would say. He was wearing the silk shirt, driving his BMW *décapotable;* a discreet guy, very correct. My family have been here a hundred years, more. We made wine, not too good, we looked after the people in the town. Maybe a painter turns up, sometimes." He gestured to the painting over the fire. "That is Bianca's mother." He paused, looking at the picture. "It was a small town, in those days. There were some tourists. I had found a little finance, we had done a little development, not much. Everyone was looking east, beyond Marseilles, saying, why don't we have progress like those guys in St. Tropez, you know? But the beach here is marsh and oysters, mosquitoes, no shelter. Crespi came from the east. He started to give us advice. Build on the shore, he said, right up to the sea. Get the government to kill the mosquitoes. Make a marina, make apartments. Here are the figures, he says. The world is changing in such and such a way, people are getting richer, they can own their yachts, their apartments by the sea as well as their apartments in Paris. He shows us the papers. He introduces us to people in the government, not of the region, big government, who will get us the money. We give them dinners, there are bulls running in the town, beautiful women to make the government guys feel great. The money comes. He says to me, We divide. You build the buildings, I will look after the rest.

"So I build the apartments, start the marina. He puts his money into the launderettes, cinemas, offices, shops. He knows the right people to do finance, insurance, all the crap and bullshit you use to make a lot of small money. I trust him."

I said, "Why?"

Feuilla looked at me, then at Bianca. He said, "I have one daughter. This Crespi married her."

The silence deepened. Bianca was looking away, into the fire.

Feuilla said, "I am a man of honor. I made the foolish mistake of accepting M. Crespi as a man of honor also." He paused, blew another tree of smoke at the chimney. Then he looked up at me. "You must understand something," he said. "There is a difference between what is lawful and what is honorable. When we are talking about the law, we are talking about something stupid, without a face. It is the duty of an honorable mayor to look after his town, to have a face. There are those who will tell you I have bribed people." He shrugged. "Let them say it. In a lawyer's sense, a bureaucrat's sense, it may even be true. But it is my duty as a man of honor to care for this town."

Bianca said, "Papa." Her eyes were nervous, moving between us.

He said, "I am going to tell this guy the truth, because I have plans for him."

He reminded me of Uncle James, who had had plans for me too. I said, "So Crespi's not an honorable man."

He said, "I put this town on the map. I made it so guys who are catching sardines from rowing boats can send their children to university. Nobody likes tourists, but here we have little guys who amuse themselves, spend their money, go back to their little houses happy. Well, Crespi came to work for me, and I trusted him. Sometimes he went off to Marseilles, other places. This was no problem. A man has many businesses. For three years he worked quietly, made himself useful. Then he married Bianca. It grieves me to say this, but he married Bianca to become my son, because only a son of mine will have power in the town. And when he had the power, he started his . . . techniques."

I said, "Go on."

Feuilla said, "He understands very well this world in which he lives. I am like a farmer. If I see a field, I will ask myself: how can we make a little money here, and keep the field? If he sees that same field, he will say: how can I make a king's ransom here, and I do not give a damn if I burn the field, or that the smoke will choke the neighbors. It is the same with insurance. Of course, you can make money from insurance. But Crespi wants it all, quick, so he cheats, gets into fraud, kills to cover his tracks. He is an animal from the gutter, this Crespi, with brains but without feeling." He sighed, shrugged. "So," he said. "People are going bankrupt, old friends, because M. Crespi is lending them money, and they think this is a loan from the Patron, which is easier than other loans. But it is a loan from Crespi, and Crespi is a hard man."

I thought of what Thibault had told me, about loan repayments that had come unstuck.

The Patron said, "He has friends who are in the drug industry. So he will buy cheap money from them, dirty money, and lend it out, so that when it is repaid, it is clean money. And if people do not repay on time, they get hurt."

I thought of Thibault in his lake of blood on *Arc-en-Ciel*'s cabin sole.

"So," said the Patron. "The old people are frightened by all this. They leave, and new people, a lot of dirty shopkeeping people, are coming in. My wife was alive then. She had always been a friend of artists, and she loved Sainte-Jeanne in an artist's way. Mosquitoes, wind, marshes, the lot. She always said to me, don't touch it, don't hurt it. And I always said, it is necessary that the children are educated, that the young people have work, so they can stay in the village. Then people she knew in the town started to tell her what Crespi was doing. First, she did not believe it. Then she saw. Then she got ill. Then she died. They said it was cancer. But Crespi had broken her heart. Tell him, Bianca."

Bianca raised her eyes. The lenses were thick with tears. "I had been married to him for six months," she said. "On the day of my mother's funeral, he was drinking champagne. He was shouting at God, thanking him for getting the old bitch out of the way. The 'old bitch.'" The tears ran. "I told him I was leaving. He said, all right, go, you're not useful anymore."

The Patron broke his cigar in half, and threw it into the fire. "And there you are," he said.

There was silence.

I said, "Why are you telling me this?"

"Because you have become a friend of the family." He put his hands on his knees, and fixed me with his gaze. "You can help us. You would not help us unless you understood us."

The fire crackled. I took a sip of wine. I said, "So why was Crespi here tonight?"

The eyes were all of a sudden calculating. I had heard the hearts-and-flowers version. He was wondering whether to tell me the truth.

Bianca said, "Tell him."

The Patron said, "What have you discovered about M. Crespi?"

Bianca said, "Patron. Tell him."

The Patron waved a hand at her. He said, "What—"

"All right," said Bianca. She was angry now. "I'll tell you. Crespi is efficient, immoral, greedy like a wolf. My father is getting old. So my father, my *honorable* father will live in the same town as this bastard."

The Patron's lips were bluish. "Stop," he said.

"No. You wonder why I left home? Because I will not live in the place where you made me Crespi's whore."

The silence fairly crackled.

Bianca got up. The blood was in her cheeks. Her eyes were glittering with tears of rage. "So now I leave you in your filth," she said, and left the room.

Feuilla took a couple of steps after her, changed his mind, and sat down heavily on a hard chair. "Women," he said, with a frightful attempt at a smile. "So what will you do, here in Sainte-Jeanne?"

I said, "I have come to stop my daughter being hurt."

He smiled. "Your daughter," he said. "She reminds me a little of Bianca when she was that age. Beautiful, excited, knows everything." He shrugged. "So at the moment, she knows that she is having a delightful holiday with . . .

interesting people. And you could not persuade her different."

I nodded. It was easy to forget that the Patron was a man of insight.

"But the question is, how will you persuade her to come away?"

I said, "I have some evidence against Crespi. I'm collecting the rest."

He reached for his glass. His hand was clawed and shaking. "You have worked with insurance," he said. "I am told you make inquiries. I think you will find Arthur's activities . . . interesting."

I said, "So do I."

He said, "Good. I will show you. If they concern me a little, you will give me immunity. Yes?"

I made a noncommittal noise.

"I promise you, you will find them interesting. So then this is where we can cooperate." The eyes were sly again. "Perhaps you should look at a boat called *Laure.*"

"Why?"

"It is a . . . private venture of Crespi's. A friend . . . told me that it is interesting. A friend in Crespi's camp, but on my side."

I said, "How do you know I am on your side?"

The Patron gazed upon me with eyes that were less like a lion's than a lizard's. "Because you can help me destroy this man," he said. "Because you love your daughter. And because my daughter loves you."

28

I poured the last of the wine down my throat. It had been a professional performance. I said, "There is a problem."

He raised his eyebrows.

"I have a promise from some men who work for Crespi. If I am seen to be making inquiries about him, unpleasant things will happen to Frankie." I said it light as a feather. But here in the viper's nest, I had seen Frankie laugh. The knowledge of what Crespi could do made me feel physically ill.

Feuilla said, "We can protect your daughter."

I said, "How?"

"I have associates. The children of old friends."

"Thugs."

He shrugged.

I said, "If Crespi sees you are in his way, he will kill you."

The eyebrows went up again. The effect would have been comic, if the eyes had not been so cold. "He could try, perhaps."

It all rang false as a cracked bell. M. Feuilla might be the mayor of Sainte-Jeanne, sponsor of *Plage d'Or,* father to his townspeople, monarch of his sand and his swamp and his apartment buildings. But he was also old, and worried. He had asked a tiger into his camp. Now he could feel the tiger's hot breath on his neck.

But I was here to get solid evidence on Crespi, and Feuilla was the only ally in town.

He clapped me on the back. "You have helped me, with the Royaume des Phares. Now I offer to you and your daughter my protection."

I said, "Fine." I had a feeling that Feuilla's protection might be about as tangible as Uncle James's Egypt of the mind.

He said, "Tomorrow, we have a meeting, Crespi's men and my men, our regular monthly meeting, between partners. I'd like you to be an impartial observer. As I said, you will find Arthur's activities . . . interesting."

I said, "I'm sure. But I don't think he will be happy if I'm there."

"He won't know." He smiled, grandfatherly and absentminded as a parcel bomb. "Well, I am too old to be up all night." He heaved himself to his feet. He looked older. "You will stay in the house, of course."

I thought of my car, parked a long way away in the dark

streets. I thought of the hotel room, of walking through the streets of Sainte-Jeanne tomorrow in the daylight. In this house, it was in everyone's interest that I should stay dead. I said, "That would be very kind."

He said, "It is I who thank you."

A servant showed me up the stone stairs to a room with a crucifix above a big brass bed, and a shuttered balcony. I was leaden with the heat of the big room downstairs. I opened the shutters and the windows. There was a garden out there, gray and black under the moon. A big shape trotted from the cover of a bush. I could hear heavy panting, see the gleam of the slobber on its chops in the moonlight. Beloved father of his townsfolk the Patron might be, but he believed in trusting his personal security to at least one Rottweiler.

I took my shoes off and sat on the bed. I pulled off a sock, then another. I wanted Frankie safe, and a good case against the people who had destroyed my business and my friend. I did not want to get caught up in the power struggles of small-town big shots.

The door opened. I was sitting with my back to it. The sound made me turn too fast. It was Bianca.

She was wearing her jeans, but she had taken off the diamonds and the cowboy boots. She said, "So now you know." She padded barefoot across the tiled floor and sat down on the other side of the bed.

I said, "I have been told some things. Should I believe them?"

She looked down. "Most of them," she said. "My father is enthusiastic to have your help. He is a man of strong personality."

"Was it his idea you should marry Crespi?"

She said, "You have to understand life in this place. When I was a child, I had everything. My father thought it was everything I wanted. Actually, it was everything he wanted. I had a little dog. I said one day I did not like the dog, as a little girl, you understand; the dog had trodden on the house of my pet frog. And my dog disappeared. Someone told me it had been shot. So I learned not to say anything. Do you understand that?"

I thought of my parents, glum in the house in Carthystown, bowed under the edicts of my ludicrous but terrifying uncle. "Sure," I said.

"So when I was a kid, I went to the convent. The nuns could not make me behave. Then I was seventeen. Like your Frankie. And Arthur Crespi turned on me his . . . attention. He was the only person I had ever met who was . . . tougher than me. He had a big boat, a Ferrari. He was a terrific-looking guy, very hard, very sexy. I thought I loved him. He was pushing himself on my father, and my father was pushing me on him. We were all pushing in the same direction.

"I tell you the moment it happened. My father gave him a car, a Rolls-Royce, open-top. Crespi took me out in it. He got drunk. He drove it off the road. He got the jack, and he tipped it over a cliff, on to some rocks. It caught fire. We were above the beach. A beautiful evening, the car burning, this crazy guy. I made him make love to me, there by the road, with lorries passing, on a rock. I wanted the whole thing. I was in love."

"And then your mother."

She shrugged. "You do stupid things when you're seventeen. You grow out of them. That's why I went to sea, to help me grow out of them. Then I met Thibault." She ran her fingers through her hair. "I was still married to Arthur. I still am, in name. I call myself Dufy to remind me of my mother. She had an affair with Raoul Dufy, the painter. He painted Sainte-Jeanne, as it used to be. I loved it that way." She sighed. "Anyway. Arthur was mad jealous of Thibault. That's why he hated him so much. But there was nothing with me and Thibault. We had a little affair. Then he was a friend."

I said, "He was a good friend."

I saw the hair-fine lines that suffering had sketched around her eyes, the cynical droop of the full mouth. I thought of Frankie, seventeen years old, and Jean-Claude, the killer, who clonked her on the jaw. I thought of the educations of love.

"I came from what you would call a patriarchal tradition," Bianca said. "With Thibault, everyone did what they wanted, but everyone wanted the same thing. Le Patron sees life as the keeping of a balance between what he wants to do and what he should do. He has a sense of the greater good, you see. And he is not well."

I thought of the gray shadows under his eyes, the parchmentlike stretch of the skin. I did not answer.

"A patriarch who has got too old," she said. "It is a difficult thing to be if you are a proud man with no heir."

I remembered the night Crespi had brought *White Wing*'s crew into Chez Thibault. Bianca had shouted at Crespi, *You haven't managed to kill him yet?* I had thought she was worried about Thibault's safety. She had laughed, and told me Thibault could look after himself. She had been talking about her father.

I said, "You tried to keep the *Poisson d'Avril* papers out of my way in La Rochelle because your father was a director with Crespi of the chartering company. You were trying to protect him. Not Thibault."

"Sure," she said. She leaned back, resting against me. Her head was on my shoulder. "Hold me," she said.

I held her.

She said, "It's a bad thing when your father gets old. Lonely. I'm glad you came along."

I found I was kissing her. And I was glad I had come along, too. I put my hands in the hair at the nape of her neck. She shivered. "Come on," she said.

And she was up in the pale light of the window, pulling her T-shirt over her head so the stars shone on the skin of her breasts and back. She turned to me, unbuttoning her jeans. The skin of her groin was paler. "Come on," she said. "Cold as charity, aren't you. Englishman."

"Irishman," I said.

She stepped out of her jeans. "Take off your clothes," she said. "I've been waiting a long time for an Irishman."

So I did. It was curiously gentle, and companionable. Nobody burned any Rolls-Royces.

Afterward, she lay and hung on to me. She felt small and smooth. She made me feel large and protective.

I watched a gecko watching a fly. And I thought: Savage, there may be more corners to this battle than Crespi and Feuilla. There is you. And there is Bianca. Someone told Jean-Claude and Bobby that they would find *Arc-en-Ciel* anchored off Saint-Martin-de-Ré. Bianca knew. Nobody else knew.

She stirred, and looked up from behind her hair. Her face was soft, crumpled by passion. The mouth was not cynical anymore, and everyone has the beginnings of lines around their eyes.

She said, "I can't stay. Le Patron is an old-fashioned man." She bent and kissed me hard on the mouth.

I thought: Bianca Feuilla, how many shares do you hold in Atlas Industrien?

"Darling," she said. "Goodnight. Sweet dreams." The door thumped shut. I was alone again.

As usual.

29

*N*ext morning, I was woken by a rap on the door. It was early. Birds were singing in the shrubberies. A maid with thick legs brought in a tray of coffee and brioches. There was a note on the tray. "Carlo will show you," it said. Beside it was a small broadcast-quality tape recorder.

Someone had washed and ironed my T-shirt and jeans in the night. Downstairs a butlerine man in a white coat said, "Your hire car has been returned. Carlo will collect you in five minutes." I looked at the newspaper, and felt uncomfortable at having my life run for me. I had butterflies in my stomach. I wanted to know where Frankie was, and what she was doing. But there was nobody to ask.

Five minutes after the butler had left, Carlo came in. He was stocky, with black hair greased back from a heavily tanned forehead, a white smile and a rock-crusher handshake. He took me out to a black Mercedes. There was a replica of him already in the car. We drove at speed out of the lane, bounced through the building sites on the edge of town, along a road that skirted a dazzling lagoon pegged out for mussels. The driver hooted his horn at a flock of egrets. Beyond the windscreen, the Mediterranean rose white-hot silver to the white-hot sky.

"Les Digues," said Carlo, pointing ahead.

Across the line where the sky met the sea lay a line of white concrete tombstones. The smallest of them must have been a hundred feet high. The Mercedes turned on to a straight black road lined with infant palm trees and roared into a concrete square. Beyond the square was a sheet of water enclosed by white stone breakwaters. From the breakwaters projected a comb of short jetties, each with its white plastic yacht.

"Apartments all the way down to the water," said Carlo, with pride in his voice. "Boatyard. The lot."

The Patron had said Crespi had a boat I should look at. I said, "Is there a yacht by the name of *Laure* in the yard?"

"Fantastic thing," said Carlo. He had bright, eager black eyes. "Bought her a month ago. She's been sitting in Genoa, in a coal harbor somewhere. What I heard was that she looked dirty and bad, but inside, she is wonderful, beautiful, you know. She has mahogany, rosewood, paintings by, well, you know, all them guys. He got some guy to look at her, and the guy said, you've got a bargain there. All she needs is a coat of paint, she'll be worth two million bucks. So he's giving her one. She's nearly ready. Well?" he said, gesturing out of the window. "What do you think? Great place, eh?"

I grunted. The square was an eye-aching concrete pit, whipped by a wind like sandpaper. But Carlo and his colleagues were as hard and heavy as bowling balls and they looked as if they would be bad men to disagree with. That was probably why the Patron liked having them around.

"We go around the back," said Carlo. "Anonymous, you know."

I nodded as if anonymous was my middle name. The car turned off the square between two buildings. Les Digues was not much deeper than a stage set. The road became rutted, the buildings empty-eyed skeletons braced up with scaffolding. The track took us down to an assortment of sheds by the side of the marina. Along the roof of the biggest was a long banner that whipped and billowed in the breeze. CHANTIERS DU PALMIER—WEEK DU CUP, it said. There was a stylized yacht under a stylized palm tree. Chantiers du Palmier had been one of the Atlas companies.

Around the shed was the usual chainlink fence. There was a travel hoist in there, and a slipway. There was a huge yacht hauled up on the water, a 120-foot ketch with the long, sharp bow and endless counter of a 1920s ocean greyhound.

I said, "What's that boat?"

"That's *Laure,*" said Carlo.

I said, "Drive slowly."

We went past the chainlink fence at a crawl. They had already painted the port side. The reflections from the water of the harbor crept between the other boats, and wavered in the new-enameled wood.

Suddenly my mouth was dry. I said, "Has he been working on her long?"

"Nah," said Carlo. "She don't need it."

I said, "Can we take a look?"

Carlo looked at his watch. "Why not?" he said.

We drove around to the main gate. The security men waved us through. I slumped well down into the seat. My stomach was jumping with nerves, the way it does at the start of a big race, when you know you are going to wind everything up till it cracks. Except that today it was not a race. Today I was entering a yard whose owner's representatives had promised to mangle my daughter if I went near them.

"They're all working on the America's Cup boat," said Carlo. "Launch tomorrow."

The Merc stopped by *Laure.* I climbed out, went up the ladder on the blind side. She was big, and she was beautiful, and someone had spent a lot of money on paint and varnish, and elbow-grease for the brass. Below, there was a powerful smell of heavily scented French disinfectant.

There was a saloon, with four double staterooms forward. All of them were paneled in Honduras mahogany, the kind of timber nobody has been able to get for fifty years. There was more brass, and Turkey carpets, and books in the ship's bindings, with a pattern of laurel leaves on sea-green Morocco. It all looked like a million dollars.

Like two million dollars.

"Nice, huh?" said Carlo. "There's an owner's cabin aft, couple of bathrooms. We better move on, though."

"Sure," I said. I tried the door aft. It was locked.

"You interested in boats?" said Carlo.

"I work with them," I said.

"That true?" He did not look at all interested. The Patron had not told him who I was. That was at least part of his word he was keeping.

The Merc slid back along the white quay to the buildings around the square. I was not looking out of the window anymore. I had more to think about than the view.

Long experience had led me not to believe fairy stories about superyachts discovered in Genoa coaling docks, needing only a lick of paint to be worth more than two million dollars. The way the reflections from the harbor had behaved on *Laure's* side had made me deeply curious, and the smell of disinfectant had deepened the curiosity. After M. Feuilla's meeting, I was going to take a closer look.

The driver trod on the accelerator, then the brake. We drew up with the regulation squeal of tires on the concrete outside the tallest of the buildings around the square.

The building was only a shell, I realized. Carlo led me through the door. There was a lobby, a raw concrete box, unfinished, the openings for the lift doors gaping out of the wall opposite. I followed Carlo's big shoulders under an arch to a separate lobby with a single lift. This one was connected. A sign over the lintel said APPARTEMENT EXPO. Show flat.

"In," said Carlo.

I went in. Carlo put his thumb on 18. The doors closed. The little steel room smelled of hair oil and black tobacco, cooled by fierce air-conditioning. The lift whooshed into the sky, slowed, stopped. The doors hissed open. We walked out into a dazzling new world.

There was a football-pitch-sized room floored with Iznik tiles, a circular fountain with cushioned benches and a jet of water tinkling under a skylight. There were banks of tropical vegetation lurking in unlit corners, a swimming pool on a terrace. Beyond the terrace, sparkling in the morning sun, lay the big restless sapphire of the Mediterranean.

Carlo looked pleased. "Nice, huh?" he said. "Twenty million francs, and worth every centime." I liked Carlo. He seemed to take a proper pride in his boss's achievements. It was not his fault the achievements were flawed.

"So through here," he said. He opened a pair of Spanish chestnut double doors, and waved into a long cool room with Moroccan arched windows. The floor was silent with Turkish carpets. In the middle was a table with two chairs, an ice-bucket with a bottle of Le Montrachet and a bottle of mineral water. Around the walls were slatted doors of unpolished cedar. The room smelled like a cigar box. It was cool and dim; the perfect antidote to the bleached-out, salt-ridden glare of the square, eighteen stories below.

"So," said Carlo. "Somewhere in here, I think."

Some of the doors led to other rooms. Some were air-conditioning vents. But most of them were walk-in cupboards. Carlo found a folding chair at the sales desk in the corner of the big tiled hall, positioned it in the cupboard closest to the table. "For you," he said. He looked at his watch. "Better be quick."

It was not so much a cupboard as a pantry. There was a sink, and an elaborate rack for wine bottles, and a small fluorescent light. The door had a lock on it. I took the key from the outside, locked it on the inside, pulled the chair up against the slatted doors, took the tape recorder out of my pocket and sat down.

Sound from the room came undisturbed through the slats. I heard Carlo's footsteps in the tiled hall; then, faintly, the wheeze of the lift motor. The building below was an empty shell that amplified the sound like a guitar amplifying the resonance of a string. The lift doors clashed open. The penthouse filled with voices.

I could hear the Patron, and Crespi, blurred with the echoes of the tiles in the hall. Two other voices came into the meeting room: Carlo, and another that I recognized.

"Shit," said Jean-Claude. "Really nice, eh?"

It was cool in the cedar smell of the pantry, but I began to sweat.

"Too nice for a little faggot like you," said Carlo.

Jean-Claude said, "Shut your fucking mouth, Grandad."

"Try to shut it for me," said Carlo. "Go on."

It seemed that the two of them were getting on nicely.

Carlo said, "Search the room."

Jean-Claude said, "No need. I've been watching the place since midnight." I felt in my pocket for a weapon, found none.

"Ah," said Carlo, with what could have been an edge of sarcasm. "So that's all right, then."

"That's all right," said Jean-Claude.

And I realized that he had not been watching anything. What we had here was a simple case of one-upmanship. And Carlo was going to let him be caught out.

The door slammed. The Patron and Crespi came in.

They were talking minor shop about a building project that was behind schedule. They moved to the lunch table. There was the clink of a bottle on glasses. The escorts would be moving around the table, pouring. The talk was resolutely unbusinesslike, mainly about football. Crespi was thinking of buying a team. I sat in the folding chair, and kept my sweat-slippery thumb on the RECORD button of the tape recorder, and waited.

They took their time. Carlo had told me they had a couple of lobsters and a little salad. There were faint clatterings as people came and went from the kitchen. Their voices hummed like drowsy bees.

Finally, the Patron said, "Some coffee?"

Somewhere a Gaggia bubbled. The Patron said, "Business, then." Very gently, I pressed the RECORD button of the tape machine.

Crespi said, "We have some things to decide."

"Such as?"

Crespi said, "I hear you don't like my money."

The Patron said, "I can believe that you imagine you are doing what is right for these days." I could see him making a salaam with his cigar, the old ham. *Tempora mutantur nos et mutamur in illis.*

"What?" said Crespi.

"In my day, you could make money looking after your friends and buying the friendship of your enemies. Now, it seems you must be a big operator." The voice was smooth as silk. "But I think there is one rule. Do not make mistakes, because mistakes attract attention."

Crespi laughed. It was not a wholehearted laugh. "Mistakes?"

"There was some trouble in La Rochelle. I believe I am correct in thinking that you set up an insurance company as a vehicle for a . . . fraudulent claim. Agences Giotto?"

Crespi said, "Who told you that?" His voice was breaking up.

"I like to know what my partners are up to," said the Patron.

"Remedial action has been taken," said Crespi. "Things will be quiet up there from now on."

"But that ship," said the Patron. *"Poisson d'Avril.* Two men killed, and then the captain. I don't like to be connected with men killed."

Crespi laughed. It was a new laugh, coarse and full of authority. "Jesus," he said. "Listen to you. Feuilla, the man who bribed the whole bloody Ministry of Tourism."

"I only deceive deceivers. You have killed two innocent men."

"Two blacks," said Crespi. "A little local color. A cook and a deckhand, for Christ's sake. And a drunken Greek."

The Patron said, "In the war, I was a *résistant* to save the world from people like you."

Crespi said, "You bloody old fool, you have been dead since 1945."

The Patron's voice was filled with rage and wine. He said, "You killed Thibault Ledoux. You killed Mick Savage, the Englishman."

Irishman, I thought.

"Accidents," said Crespi.

"Accidents have a way of arranging themselves," said the Patron.

"Perhaps sometimes one must give fate a little push," said Crespi. His voice was silky as the edge of a chisel. "I feel we are in the hands of fate today."

The Patron plowed on. "Fate has nothing to do with this. We are partners. I cannot agree that you can behave in this clumsy way, and use murder to solve your problems. We have to work this out." Even through the intercom, I could feel the prickle of something new and nasty in the air. "So I am making a stipulation about our relationship. Sainte-Jeanne is a town that is for the benefit of its people. It is not the mouth of a sewer, through which you can pour into the world your dirty money."

"Dirty money?" said Crespi. "What do you mean?"

"Six weeks ago, Thibault Ledoux called me. He was confused. He said, 'Your partner Arthur Crespi came to me, offered me money from the partnership to build my boat. And I knew it was dirty money from drugs or whores or God knows what, so I said no. But since that time I have considered, and I have decided that money is money, and a boat is a boat. So I'll take it, please.'"

Crespi said, "Go on."

"So I told him," said the Patron, "I told him not to be a stupid pig. I told him I was your partner in Sainte-Jeanne for the good of Sainte-Jeanne, but I was not your partner in drugs and whores. And I told him that if he mentioned the words again, I would send him to the police."

"Hoorah," said Crespi. "Very upright."

Thibault had been lying when he said it was a government grant. It had been a loan for the purpose of laundering Crespi's grubby money.

"So he was late with the payments. And you killed him," said the Patron.

"He died because he was a very bad problem for us. He had corrupted an important deal with his private trading. The results could have been disastrous." That was *Poisson d'Avril*. "Also, he was not reliable with his payments, this is true. Furthermore, you had told him about our . . . difficulties in partnership, which was unwise, because he would have spoken about such things with the Englishman."

Irishman.

The Patron said, "And you were jealous, because Bianca preferred Thibault to you."

Crespi said, "You are a very stupid old man." There was something new in his voice. The air in the pantry had become suddenly cold, but despite the cold my hands were slimy with sweat.

The Patron said, "And you are a pederast."

Crespi said, "Patron, you have decided for me."

"Decided what?"

Crespi said, "The partnership is dissolved."

The Patron said, "Carlo, come here."

Crespi said, in his smooth voice, "Carlo knows also that the partnership is dissolved."

"Not possible," said the Patron. "Not without my permission. I am the senior partner."

"By forty years," said Crespi. I could hear the smile in his voice.

"What do you mean?"

"When one partner dies, there is no more partnership."

The Patron said something in dialect which sounded like a machine-gun shooting poison bullets.

Carlo said, "Your mouth, Patron."

The Patron started to cough.

"Lungs bad?" said Crespi. "Have a drink."

I heard the door open. The Patron said, "Carlo."

Carlo said, "Patron, I am sorry. Times have changed."

The Patron said, *"Merde!"* He started coughing again.

Carlo said, "Jean-Claude has overlooked an Englishman in the pantry."

The sweat squirted out of me. I shoved the tape recorder on to the top of the wine rack, high up, where it could not be seen.

There was a pause that crackled. Then Crespi said, "Get him out."

I pushed the key into the lock, half turned it. A key rattled in the other side, failed to secure an entry.

Crespi said, "Kick it."

Something crashed against the door. It held. Carlo's voice said, "Jesus, faggot, it's only matchwood. Allow me."

There was a *thump.* The door swung inward, admitting a flood of light from the room. Carlo was standing in the doorway. "Lunch over?" I said.

Carlo smiled. He had a kind, twinkling smile. "Forever," he said.

My stomach felt queasy, liquid with fear. I had heard a lot. They would kill me. I hoped that now I was here, they would think there was no point in killing Frankie.

The Patron was sitting at the table. His face was a bad, bluish color, and he was breathing in hoarse gasps.

Crespi was hiding his surprise nicely. He said, "Get rid of this."

I looked at his smooth face, his crinkly black hair. I said, "There are people who know where I am."

"Yes," said Crespi. "You have risen from the dead to snoop for your friend in the world of insurance. M. Peabody. I had thought that while your daughter is my guest, we don't have any problem. It seems I was wrong." He laughed. "OK, Jean-Claude. Accident, please. And this time a success?"

Carlo said, "Let me do it. He'll screw up."

Jean-Claude said, "Fuck off, Grandpa."

Crespi said, "He can do it."

Carlo made a noise expressive of professional mistrust.

The Patron said, "Bastards."

Jean-Claude took my arm. "Come on, *beau-papa,*" he said. "Accident time." There was a gun in his hand. The hand was shaking. He did not like being teased by Carlo. "Out of the door."

I walked out of the room, into the dazzle of the tiled lobby. The fountain tinkled away in front of the writhing blue Mediterranean. I hated the sound of the fountain, the color of the warm, tideless sea. I hated the sweat and the glare. I hated the idea that I was going to die.

Jean-Claude said, "I hope you're not scared of heights," and giggled, his high, stupid giggle. I hated that too. "Down the stairs," he said.

I walked down a set of stairs. At the bottom, the tiles and the glass and the marble vanished. Down here the world was raw concrete, dust, cables coiled like snakes, bags of cement.

And ahead, at the bottom of the stairs, a square black opening. The lift shaft, strung across with red-and-white striped tape. Seventeen floors. Better than two hundred feet.

"I don't think the lift works," said Jean-Claude. "Bad luck for you." He poked me in the back with the gun, hard. I lurched forward, toward the black mouth of the shaft. Oh, no, I thought. Not the big drop—

He shoved me again, over the kidney. My mouth was

bone-dry. My knees felt watery. Jean-Claude was watching me with his dark eyes, smiling a little, up on the balls of his feet, head sunk between his shoulders, like a boxer.

He said, "Jump."

I said, "Don't be bloody stupid." I hoped my voice sounded steadier than it felt. "You won't shoot me. This is supposed to be an accident. You'll need help." If I got him close enough, it would be a straight fight. "So why don't you ask Carlo?"

Jean-Claude's Greek-god smile stiffened slightly. He kept his eyes on me, bent down to the ground, holding the gun. He said, "I can do this myself." He was putting the gun down, not taking his eyes off me. All right, I thought. Now we are even Steven, no gun, and I will beat the hell out of you. I could feel the strength running back into my muscles.

The gun touched the concrete. Jean-Claude did something with his hand, down there on the ground.

My eyes caught fire.

Cement dust, I thought. He's thrown them full of cement dust.

I could not see anything.

Something hit me like a battering ram in the middle of the chest. I went backward, arms flailing. I felt the arms hit plastic tape. My vision was a red blur. I toppled back. I was leaning on the tape. The red-and-white tape across the gaping mouth of the lift shaft.

The tape gave. I plunged backward.

I fell.

30

Something hit me between the shoulderblades with an appalling crash. Bottom, I thought. I'm dead. But I was not dead. I was rolling, slithering off some sort of platform. My right hand was gripping the edge of what felt like a plank. My left had hold of a paper surface, paper stretched over something solid. A bag of cement. The bag moved, sliding over the planks. I moved with it. My eyes were beginning to work. My body fell over the edge of the platform. All my weight was on my fingers. I had fallen on to a cradle, two planks wide, suspended ten feet down the shaft. Now I was falling off it. I was holding on by my right hand. My left hand was on a hundred-kilo bag of cement, lying at its point of balance on the edge of the cradle.

I pulled the bag of cement. It pivoted, dropped. I jammed my left hand into the crevice in the boards. I hung, swinging above the abyss by two hands, blinking the dust out of my eyes, sobbing for breath.

Whoom, said the bag of cement, hitting the bottom 190 feet down. The echoes roared in the shaft.

A little voice above me said, *"Adieu, beau-papa."* Jean-Claude's voice. He would be looking into the shaft. It would be dark, after the blinding light in the lobby. He hawked and spat down the shaft. The grind of his hobnails receded on the stairs, ticked faintly across the tiles of the lobby.

Very carefully, I pulled myself up, got a heel on to the plank, and climbed aboard the cradle. I lay there, blinking, getting my breath back. When I could breathe and see, I looked at the cradle.

It was stopped opposite the boarded-up doorway of the next floor down. There was a winch at its right-hand end. I wound the handle. The cradle sank. I wound it the other way. The cradle rose. When it reached the next floor up, I stepped out.

Dust was still hanging in the air. I slapped at myself. Cement came off me in clouds. Moving slowly and quietly on legs that felt like columns of putty, I went up the stairs.

There was a noise at the top. A voice was bellowing; an old man's voice. The Patron's voice. It reminded me of the voice of my Uncle James, when he had been shut in his room with the whiskey, bellowing for someone to frighten. A blast of wind altered the tinkle of the fountain. There was a general sound of steps, and Crespi's voice. Three sets of feet, I thought. Crespi and Jean-Claude, and Carlo. The others had left during lunch.

The footsteps ceased. Carlo said, "Are you *sure?*" in a voice heavy with sarcasm.

"Of course I'm sure," said Jean-Claude, petulant.

Crespi said, "We need to be back at my house. Leave him for the builders tomorrow." They all laughed. A lift door opened. They got in. The lift sank away, humming loudly in the hollow building.

I went on up.

The fountain tinkled on. Beyond the window and the azure pool, the Mediterranean squirmed under the sun. The terrace was empty.

Something moved.

It was a flick of movement at the parapet of the swimming-pool enclosure. I remembered the blast of wind that had disturbed the fountain. I walked across the miles of tiles to the glass door and turned the handle. The wind hit me like the breath of an oven. The sweat burst from my body. I walked on, past the pool, to the parapet, and looked over.

It went down eighteen floors, a white concrete cliff that ended in a tangle of badly parked site machinery. There was a ledge six feet below the parapet. The ledge was maybe a foot wide, the top surface of a fat string-course running around the structure like a hoop on a barrel. A strong smell of drink rose from the ledge. It was coming from the Patron. He was standing on the ledge with his face to the wall. He was a small man. The top of his head came nine inches below the parapet. He did not look up.

I stood for a moment, watching him nine inches away from falling into the great spinning bowl of Les Digues, and the marina, and the endless yellow line of the beach meeting the endless white line of the surf. I did not want to do anything sudden.

He shouted something. The wind took his voice and smeared it into the concrete. He raised a hand, straight-armed, waving in an arc. It would have been the hand that had caught my eye from the lobby. At the top of the arc, the hand wavered away from the wall. His whole body was going with it, teetering out backward over the drop.

I grabbed his wrist. He roared with surprise. I pulled him up, hard. He came off the ledge like a cork from a bottle. We both landed on the concrete of the terrace. We both stayed there, on the good, solid concrete that went right down to the foundations deep in beautiful old terra firma.

I got up. The Patron did not move. His face was a nasty blue. He reeked of brandy. His lips rolled back in a sort of grin. One of his teeth was broken.

I remembered the taste of iron and gin.

I dragged him into the shade. There was a telephone on the sales desk. I ordered two taxis, one for the Patron and me, the other as a witness. The Patron groaned, vomited brandy on to the tiles. I made sure he could breathe. I went into the pantry off the meeting room, retrieved the tape recorder from the wine rack. Then I ran to the empty lift shaft, threw down bags of cement, boards, trestles, everything I could find to make life difficult for anyone who was looking for confirmation of the death of Michael Savage, an Irish tourist.

The service lift came up fast. I dragged the Patron in. By the time we were at the bottom, the taxis were waiting in the square. "Hospital," I said.

"Béziers?"

"Go."

I told the other taxi to follow us. We went.

It was more than forty miles to Béziers. The Patron lay slumped in the corner of the back seat, his eyes closed, sunk deep in his head. When I was sure we were not being followed, I told the driver to stop at a supermarket. I sent the spare driver home, and bought four bottles of Vichy water. I drank three-quarters of a bottle myself, without stopping, and used the rest to wash out my eyes, ignoring the yells the cabbie was putting up about his upholstery. Then I began to trickle another bottle into the Patron.

He coughed, and spluttered, and opened his eyes. I said, "You're on your way to hospital."

He said, "Pills." He patted his pocket.

I gave him two of the pills. He was suddenly a very old man. He said, "They made me drink a bottle of cognac. They left me on the ledge." He began to weep, the tears crawling in a confused manner across the lunar landscape of his cheeks.

I said, "Everything's fine."

He said, "Tomorrow. Arthur told me. They're taking out *Laure.* Look in the back shed at the Chantiers."

The pills made him look better. They wheeled him away on a gurney. The taxi-driver said, "Sainte-Jeanne?"

I said, "Leave me here."

He left me outside the hospital. I walked into the town, found a brasserie, ate a steak and drank a half-bottle of burgundy. Afterward I went to a hi-fi shop, waved my credit card, and got myself a twin-deck ghetto blaster. With the blaster as luggage, I repaired to a cheap hotel.

In my room, I took the cassette of Feuilla's conversation with Crespi out of my pocket. I slotted the original cassette in the left-hand side, taped over the anti-erase holes of a Charles Aznavour collection I had bought in the hi-fi shop, and shoved it in the other. Then I hit the DUB button. Aznavour began to disappear under Crespi and Feuilla. When it was finished I popped out the original tape, telephoned a courier service, and sent the original to Mary Ellen, overnight, with a note asking her to pass it on to Justin, and identifying the principal speakers. I ate another steak, bought a cheap camera and some film, and hired a car. Then I looked in the telephone directory for surveyors.

There were two in Sainte-Jeanne. One was a Charles Jamalartegui. His name rang no bells. The other was a M. Marcel Bonnard.

The survey of *Poisson d'Avril* in the folder Bianca had stolen from the Manoir de Causey had been signed by a Marcel Bonnard.

I went to bed, and fell asleep like a bag of cement falling down a lift shaft.

The alarm woke me at six. I put the car on the autoroute and headed west. The sun was up, a red-hot ball floating over a gray veil of mist as I crossed the lagoon and plunged into the high-rises on the outskirts of Sainte-Jeanne. The streets were quiet, except for a handful of bleary-eyed people threading their way through the building sites to the *boulangeries.* I drove straight to Les Digues.

The façades of the buildings were white as chalk in the early sun. I turned the car on to the track that ran around the back, and plunged into the desert of empty concrete shells and scaffolding.

The wind was picking up after the dawn calm. There was just enough of it to rattle the long banner on the roof of Chantiers du Palmier.

They had changed the banner. Today, it read JOUR DU LANCEMENT CUP. There were vans around the front of the shed, men milling about, the beginnings of a crowd. The big doors were open. Inside, in the early-morning shadows, there gleamed a long, lean hull. An America's Cup boat.

I was not watching America's Cup boats. I was looking at the slipway where *Laure* had been two days ago.

The slipway was empty. *Laure* was out there on the big-boat pontoon, sitting on the water like a swan.

I turned the car around, parked it behind one of the concrete skeletons, and walked back to the compound. The morning air smelled fresh and clean, but it could not mask the stink of dirty work rolling off Chantiers du Palmier.

In the back shed. It must have been important. The Patron had not had much breath, but he had still made the effort to tell me.

I walked down to the gate, head down, shuffling, mouth dry as dust. There was a PR man fending off a party of photographers, and a knot of bystanders, and a lot of efficient-looking people in hooded red boiler suits with LANCEMENT CUP—LES DIGUES written across the shoulders. There was a security man arguing with a gaggle of reporters and TV crews on the far side. He looked harassed and sweaty. I shoved my hands in my pockets and strolled through the gates.

I tuned in on the sound of the argument, listening for the first syllables of the shout that would be the end of me and Frankie. It did not come. I strolled on, followed the sign that said TOILETTES, dived into a maze of smaller sheds to the side of the main hangar.

People had been working all night. From around a corner came the tinny echo of voices and the crash of water on porcelain. In the lavatory block, people were having showers to wake them up.

I strolled into the shower room. The cabinets were all occupied. There were four red boiler suits hung above the bench. I picked up the one that looked the biggest, hopped outside and climbed in.

The suit was too short and too wide, but it was camouflage. I walked off down the side of the shed. Behind me, in the showers, someone started yelling. But the yelling was drowned by laughter. It was party day at Chantiers du Palmier. I pulled up the hood and turned in at a door in a corrugated iron wall.

I was in a lean-to annex to the main shed. There was a workbench, and a red door saying DANGER, that might have been the paint store. Behind it were shelves with cans of resin and hardeners. I went on through, and arrived at the back end of the lean-to.

The last shed was big and low. It looked like a kind of sump, in which all the potentially reusable junk of a working yard collected. Every yard has one. There were boxes of winches, a plastic dustbin full of brass cleats. And there was a stack of timber.

On the outside of the stack of timber was a run of paneling. It did not look like much. The polish was chipped and the edges ragged, as if it had been stripped out in a hurry. But the color was deep reddish gold, with a dark heavy glow. Honduras mahogany.

I pulled back the top layer of paneling. There was another layer behind it, and another behind that. It was heavy, the way modern mahogany is not heavy. It went back all the way to the wall.

It was going to look lovely, in whatever boat the parsimonious management of Chantiers du Palmier managed to install it. I knew exactly how lovely it would look, because I had seen some of it before, in the forward staterooms of *Laure*. The rest would have come out of the owner's cabin and the bathrooms. They had already started stripping it last time I had been on board. That was why the door had been locked.

I pulled the camera out of my pocket. I photographed the whole shed, frame by overlapping frame. Then I pulled up the hood of the boiler suit, picked up a paint tin for camouflage, and walked out of the shed and into the hard white light of nine o'clock in the morning.

The crowd at the gate had grown since I had arrived. Someone had slung a line of pennants across the gateway. The little flags rattled in the hot, dusty wind. There were two

TV crews out there. They had nothing to photograph, so they swung their lenses on me: a beanpole figure in an ill-fitting boiler suit, reddish stubble bristling out of the hood, slouching off down to the quay. Loads of laughs for the TV audience. *You folks out there may think the world of big-boat sailing is all suntans and racer-chasers. But what it still boils down to is a man with bare ankles and a bucket of paint. Some things never change.*

And some ways of stealing money.

I shuffled on down the glaring concrete of the quay, and swung myself up on to *Laure's* deck.

The planking was old, but recently belt-sanded to smarten it up. The pitch-caulked seams were drier and more cracked than you would expect in a two-million-dollar superyacht. There was a fourteen-foot Zodiac inflatable in a set of davits. I tried the hatches. They were locked. There were deck skylights. The middle one was open.

I put my mouth to the aperture and shouted, "Anyone there?"

Silence. Through the skylight I could see the paneling, the brass Argand lamp, a broad-bottomed decanter on the fiddled shelf next to the Morocco-bound books. A slight uncertainty began to nag at me. What if I had got it wrong?

There was only one way of checking. I pulled up the skylight and climbed down on to the table, bypassing the bowl of flowers.

Someone had cleaned up the disinfectant, but a faint whiff of it lingered, overlaid by the heavy smell of the flowers. There was jasmine in there, and stephanotis. I stood for a moment, buffing out of the table the marks my dusty feet had made, trying not to sneeze. I stood in the mellow glow of the decanter, feet in the deep Belouch rug on the floor, nose full of the smell of the flowers.

The smell of the flowers.

It was deep and musky, with the faint corruption of jasmine. And underneath it another corruption. Not rotting flesh: a mustiness, of the kind you smell in a house that has been sealed airtight for a hundred years. The flowers were to hide the mustiness.

There was a door, leading forward. I tried the handle. It was locked. It would be locked.

The lock was a stately looking object, made of brass. I knew all about such objects. I stood on the table, reached on to the deck, and brought down the paint can. The wire handle came off easily. I bent the end over at right angles, stuck it into the keyhole. The tumblers clicked over; one, two, three. I turned the handle and opened the door.

The smell hit me like the breath of a vault. I stepped in.

Last time I had been in here, there had been a paneled passageway, with elegant staterooms opening out, two on either side.

But someone had been busy with a screwdriver. Now, there were four shafts of light pouring in from four portholes. And absolutely nothing else. They had stripped out the interior back to the bare hull.

What was left of the bare hull.

It was like being in the belly of a whale. The frames stretched in their beautiful riblike curve on either side. In the inverted ogee of the keel's root, a runnel of black bilgewater reflected the portholes.

I put my hand on one of the frames. It was a slab of pine, six by four. Its surface was marked with a windowpane pattern of cracks. It crumbled under the thumb like stale cake.

The reflections down *Laure*'s side had waved because the curves of her planking were not smooth and fair. The reason they were not smooth and fair was that the metal of the bolts and rivets fixing them to her ribs had corroded and enlarged the holes in the ribs through which they passed, loosening the fastenings and allowing the planking to flex. So the water had trickled in, and in the voids behind the glorious paneling little spores swarming in the moist air had settled, and grown, and borne fruit, filling the air with the thick, fungoid smell of runaway dry rot. *Laure* was not so much a two-million-dollar superyacht as a couple of thousand quid's worth of wet firewood.

There was only one reason for giving a load of firewood a coat of fresh paint. That was to get her a superyacht insurance policy, and take her out for a sail.

And sink her.

I picked up the paint tin and stepped back through the

open door. I was looking forward to ringing M. Marcel Bonnard and having a long chat.

Something clanked on the deck aft. I froze. There were feet, and a lot of voices. The voices sounded cheerful. Someone rattled at the hatch, asked someone else for the key. I knew the voice. It belonged to Bobby, the bottle-blond who had poured gin down my throat on the pontoon at the Royal Flotilla.

And there was someone else up there, laughing, happy to be on holiday in the South of France, off for a sail on a big, beautiful boat, for a picnic and a sunbathe, to watch the launch of an America's Cup contender.

Frankie.

I was sweating. I went back through the door into the void where the forecabins had been, shut it, locked it with my piece of wire. I sat down on the rotten planking, in the stink of fungus and bilge. I listened to the slap of feet on the rotten deck, and the chug of a diesel starting, and the whine of mooring warps whipping aboard.

We were going to sea.

I clambered gingerly over the ribs to a porthole, and looked out.

Down there between the boats, the crowd was milling on the launching slip like ants. The sun was winking in the golden bells of brass-band instruments. Above the crowd towered a slim mast, dressed overall with strings of signal flags. The mast began to move, sliding, accelerating down the slipway through the empty lane in the crowd. There was a flare of white spray as it hit the water. My stripped-out compartment was suddenly full of the bray of a foghorn. A champagne cork popped. Frankie was stamping and cheering on deck.

Don't stamp too hard, I thought.

The porthole turned away from the slipway. The parked yachts began to slide by.

There was more stamping on deck, the roar of sailcloth, the clack of a halyard winch. Mainsail up. Then a series of lesser roars from further forward. Three foresails. The rib under my feet tilted. Timber groaned, the weary groan of a wooden boat that wants to die.

I was horribly worried. The longer *Laure* was around, the greater the danger of someone rumbling Crespi's little earner. Today could be the day she was going to sink. But if so, why bring Frankie along?

Be reasonable, I told myself. If they're going to sink *Laure,* they'll kid Frankie it's an accident. They'll want Frankie ashore as a witness.

But Jean-Claude was not reasonable. I remembered what Crespi had said about the dead men on *Poisson d'Avril. A little local color.* Two men dead, when they could have been warned and saved.

What better local color in the South of France than a pretty seventeen-year-old in a bikini?

31

Laure's heel steepened. When I looked out of the porthole I saw the Cup boat, leaning over on her ear, mainsail up, no jib.

Inside *Laure,* the chuckle of the bow-wave was up to a drumming roar. Big gusts were tearing across the sea. On the downhill side of her hull, where the big bolts of the chainplates came through the ribs, little jets of water were squirting in. The sides were shiny with water. Next time I looked through the porthole the spectator fleet was far astern, toy boats on a sapphire-colored sea. The sky was striped with long, sharply hooked mares' tails of cloud. The air was brilliantly clear, with the kind of clarity that is trying to tell you something. What it is trying to tell you, when you see it down here at the western end of the Gulf of Lions, is wind. Lots of wind.

There was nothing to be seen from the downhill portholes except flying blue water. A lake was forming in the turn of the bilge, and the rigging was groaning like a devil's orchestra.

Outside the uphill portholes, the land had sunk to a low line that came and went with the long roll of the wave crests. For an hour, there was only the plunge and roar of the bow, and the bubble of the water under the hull. The land went, and there was only the slow blue heave of the sea. I heard laughter from the deck. Picnic time.

Feet thumped down the companionway and into the saloon. I went aft, put my eye to the keyhole. I could see the gimballed table. Water had spilled from the bowl of flowers. A hand came on to the table with a cloth, wiped up the water. It was a brown hand, with black hairs on the back of it. The hand went away. It put something on the table.

My flesh crawled.

In the frame of the keyhole I could see a dial, with numbers from zero to 120. A kitchen timer. The hands came into frame, twisted the dial a quarter of the way around. I glanced down at the luminous hands of my watch. Twenty to one.

The timer disappeared from my field of view. I heard the rattle of a locker door. The feet went back up the companionway.

My heart was pounding, and my hands were slipping on my wire lock-pick. I fumbled with the latch. It took a good three minutes to get it open.

The saloon seemed dazzlingly bright after the cavernous forward regions. I closed the door quietly. *Laure* went up a wave, down the other side with a plunge and a whoosh of spray. I started looking in lockers.

It was under the deck, snuggled up against a moldering rib. It was a plastic sandwich box, connected by wires to the timer taped to its lid. I lifted it gingerly from its rotting nest and laid it on the cushions of the settee. It was emitting a brisk, cheerful tick. It brought to mind Mary Ellen's kitchen on a Saturday, the warm smell of baking, Islingtonians wheeling baby buggies outside the window, Frankie five years old, sitting on a hard chair with her legs sticking straight out in front of her, counting out glacé cherries. When the bell had rung, it had surprised her. She had jumped, and the cherries had rolled all over the floor like drops of blood in the dust. This time, it would have been more than cherries.

I did not want to pull any wires out, in case there was more to the machinery than met the eye. I twisted the dial clockwise all the way. An hour's grace. The locker next to the decanter was empty. It was small, but if you are choosing a locker for a bomb, you choose one where the bomb is not going to rattle. I put it in, gingerly, and refastened the door.

Then I went to the back end of the saloon.

There was another door there, past the curving companionway that led up to the deck. It led aft, to the owner's cabin and the two bathrooms, the crew's quarters and the cockpit. I shoved my wire into the lock.

Someone was coming down the companionway.

If I went through the door, they would hear me. Under the companionway was a kind of cubby-hole, where the steward might have kept a giant ice-bucket for the owner's champagne. There was no ice-bucket anymore. I squeezed myself in.

I could see the shadow of whoever had come down the stairs. The head door was opposite the bottom of the stairs. It opened, shut again with a bang.

The sweat was running off me.

The shadow had not moved. Whoever it was wanted the other people on the boat to think he was visiting the head. When all he wanted to do was have a reason for being below.

What reason?

I got up, quietly. I reached out, slapped a hand over the mouth, and yanked backward with a forearm around the throat. There was a moment of resistance. Then the body went limp.

I put my head forward. I said, "If you make a noise, I'll kill you." And I took away the hand that was covering the mouth.

Bianca said, "For Christ's sake."

My heart was knocking like an engine. I felt weak. I said, "What are you doing here?"

"No time," she said. "I think they're going to scuttle the boat."

I said, "How were they planning to get back?"

"They've got a rubber boat," she said.

"What makes you think they're going to take you?"

She said, "They wouldn't leave us."

I took a careful note of the *us*. I said, "They bloody well would. They tried to kill your father yesterday."

Her face was white and shocked. "But Carlo's here."

I said, "Carlo's changed sides. Why d'you think they brought you?"

She said, "I came to look after Frankie."

"At whose suggestion?"

"Nobody's."

"But nobody tried to persuade you not to come."

She said, "What do you mean?"

I said, "There's been a takeover bid. Your father is in hospital in Béziers." Her hand went to her mouth. I said, "He's doing well. But Arthur Crespi has reasons for wanting you out of the way."

The shock was leaving her eyes. She was thinking. She said, "I see."

There was not time for finding out what she was thinking. I said, "How many of them?"

"Jean-Claude. Carlo. Bobby."

"Where?"

"All aft. Soon, we go water-skiing." She opened the head door, banged it again. "I must go." She ran up the companionway at her springy lope.

There were noises from on deck: the slap of feet, the rattle of sails, the squeak of sheaves. The boat's motion changed. She had stopped, hove-to.

I looked at my watch. The minute hand said six minutes to big bang. I did not believe in water-skiing. I went to the locker and took out the plastic box with the timer. I clasped it to my stomach with sweating hands, clambered up the companionway and peered around the hatch coaming.

The seas were not water-skiing seas. They were steep and ugly, the color of blue-black ink. I had not realized how far the wind had got up. *Laure* was hove-to on the starboard tack, her enormous mainmast scrawling invisible messages in the sky. The Zodiac was on a set of telescopic davits, hanging out over the lee side. It was a big Zodiac, with a sixty-horsepower engine. It would be ashore in half an hour, to report the tragic sinking of M. Crespi's two-million-dollar superyacht and request a claim form. Jean-Claude was wearing shorts and a black singlet that showed off his brown, knobby shoulders. He was winding down the winch. Frankie was standing beside him, smiling, wearing a Chez Thibault sweatshirt, white short shorts and a lifejacket, holding a monoski.

There was a shout from the Zodiac. The davit lines went slack. It was in the water. Bianca was standing on the rail. Frankie stuck her nose in the air and said to Jean-Claude, "Ladies first."

He turned around to her. He smiled, his tender, spoiled-Greek-god smile. He took her by the shoulders, as if to kiss her.

He picked her up and threw her across the deck.

Her head hit the skylight with a sharp *chunk.* I had a frozen picture of her face, chalk-white eyes glazed with shock, mouth open in a scream that did not come out. Then I heard a sound.

It was Jean-Claude, laughing.

He jumped into the Zodiac and started to untie the knot in the painter. Carlo slapped him on the shoulder, and yelled, "Hurry up, faggot!" It was a full two minutes to big-bang time. Carlo's nerves were showing.

I should have been on the other side of the deck, out of sight. I was not. I had no idea how I got there, but I was standing over the Zodiac as it bounced below me on the ink-blue seas. The monstrous clarity was still with me. I saw the knot in the painter go, the Zodiac drift free, yawing down the wind. I saw my fingers go to the dial on the plastic box, twist it clockwise, eating up the minutes with a turn of the wrist, until I stopped it one precise click away from the final touching of the wires.

And I saw my hands make a throwing movement, a basketball throw. The semi-rigid was five yards away now. The box tumbled end over end into its bow, behind Jean-Claude's back, and rolled under the dodger. The laugh on his face congealed. He turned to rummage under the dodger. They were all shouting.

There was a brilliant flash, and a huge, flat bang, and something slammed me on to *Laure*'s deck so I was gazing at the big white sweep of the mainsail. It was not white any-more. From boom to peak there swept a long streak of red polka dots.

I pulled my eyes away from it.

Over the side the waves were scummed with a slick of petrol. A cloud of smoke was whipping away down the wind. I felt nauseous and empty. Fear was making my knees shake. I pulled myself up and lurched across the deck to Frankie.

She was lying with her eyes closed. Her face was slack, her mouth hanging open. Blood was flowing from her hair and on to the deck. A pulse was beating in her neck. She looked white and frightening. The pulse made her beautiful.

I picked her up and carried her aft to the cockpit. Then I went to Bianca.

She was crying. She wiped her eyes. She said, "Bastard."

I said, "I'm sorry." I had killed three men. I was sorry, all right.

"No," she said. "Clever bastard. You saved three." She stood up. She was laughing, a hectic laugh with too much edge to it. "Thank you, darling." She flung her arms around my neck, and kissed me hard on the mouth, there under the boom, with bits of Jean-Claude and Carlo and Bobby blown all the way up the white mainsail.

I felt suddenly sick, and tired, and disgusted. I pulled away. I said, "Let's get this thing home."

A gust came screaming across the water and pounded into *Laure's* sails. She went over on her beam ends. I thought of those rotten ribs, the planking streaming water down the inside. Home was a long way away yet. And there would be a lot to do when we got there.

We made Frankie a bed on one of the cockpit seats. There was a blanket in the saloon. I rolled her up in it, put her head on a cushion, and lashed her in place like a chrysalis.

The wind came on like gangbusters. Bianca was on the wheel. I went forward to reef the mainsail in a species of trance. The blood was drying brown and stiff. Half an hour ago, it had been part of three living men.

Who had wanted the same thing to happen to Frankie and me and Bianca.

I made a big mess of lashing the sail along the boom with my shaking hands, but *Laure* rode easier under mizzen and jib. Slowly, far too slowly, we rolled our way through the big easterly, toward the line where the flat yellow coast was rising out of the sea.

Frankie did not open her eyes.

Bianca said, "What is it with my father?"

"His heart," I said. "They're keeping him under observation."

"His heart," she said. She was looking down at her hands. "The heart has always been the problem." She looked up. "And you have enough to destroy Crespi?"

"Plenty," I said.

"How will you do this?"

I said, "It's done."

She stuck out her bottom lip. "Tell me," she said. She took my hand. Her eyes were trying to remind me about things that had happened in bedrooms.

I said, "I don't want you to get hurt." That was true. But there were things I had to find out, a few last things, before I could trust her.

She said, "The men who hurt are dead."

I said, "Not all of them."

"Who else?"

The wind screamed in the rigging. *Laure* lay far over on her side, creaking horribly. "Pumps," I said.

I went below. The water was over the floorboards. I worked away at the brass pump. The old machinery made a big, solid rhythm. It was a good background to bad thoughts.

Three men dead. Frankie unconscious.

And back in London, worse than that.

My shoulders were aching from the pump. There was a more immediate problem.

The water was coming in faster than I could pump it out. I went on deck. Frankie's eyes were still closed.

Over the bow, the white tombstones of Les Digues were the size of up-ended sugar lumps. There was a lot of white water on the ink-blue waves. The wind was up and roaring.

I said to Bianca, "We're sinking."

There was no radio. There were no flares. There was nothing but a rotten boat, and a big wind, and the sharp, inky sea. I said, "I'll hoist the mainsail."

Bianca said, "You'll open her up."

"She's opening anyway."

She shrugged. I walked forward to the mast, stuck the handle on the winch and began to wind. I was tired. The winch was sticky. The sail went up inch by inch, roaring and thundering in the big breeze. The breath came hoarse in my throat, and my heart tried to hammer its way out of my chest. And at last it was up, and we were on a broad reach, heeling horribly far over to port. The stripe of blood shone rusty in the sun, towering eighty feet in the air. *Laure* tucked her shoulder confidingly in the water and ripped her way northward through a cushion of foam. I went below. The noises were different, a succession of sharp, protesting creaks, as if things were too tight and being stretched too far, and were not going to put up with it for long. I ignored them, and stood knee-deep in water, pumping. Three hundred strokes made no impression on the water level, but plenty on me.

When I crawled back on deck, I could see the masts in the marina, and the windows of the glass-and-concrete shoeboxes reflecting the dazzle of the sun, and the breakwaters marked by the plunge and jump of spray along the white frontier between the concrete and the sea. Not far to go.

Down in the hull, there was a bigger creak than before. It became a sharp *crack*. Something tore with a sound like a tooth wrenched loose from its moorings. I looked forward. The arrowhead of *Laure*'s nose was moving diagonally toward the blue up-slope of a wave. It carved into the wave. White spray lifted, floated aft. I waited for the nose to rise.

It did not rise. It slid into the blue flank like a diving submarine. A couple of lorryloads of water sluiced back down her deck. They hit the skylight with a crash, poured green into the cockpit. I got Frankie upright. "Hang on," I said, in as near a normal voice as I could manage.

Bianca said, in a high, tense voice, "I'll look after her."

I took the wheel. We were moving up on the next wave. It was maybe half a mile to the entrance. The boat felt heavy as a truck with the power steering gone. I aimed at the gap between the breakwaters.

The wave came under the nose. Again there was the cloud of spray, heavier this time. Again the nose failed to lift, slid into the side of the wave like a submarine. This time it was not a matter of the wave coming down the deck. This time, the deck was underwater. When the crest passed over the doghouse there was a crash as the glass went, and a small roar as it flowed into the cockpit, and a vortex like a giant bathplug as a ton or so found its way down the companionway and into the saloon, to join whatever was sloshing around among the bookcases and the decanters and the paneling.

We were slowing. We were about half a mile off the breakwater. There would be people on the breakwater. They would be telling each other to look at that lovely great boat. *Now that's what I call a boat.*

She was still afloat.

Another wave. The bow tried to rise. I felt the drag as the tons of water below found their way aft, heard the groan as the ancient rigging took the strain. The wave came over us, lifted the stern, started to pour the water forward again. Another wave. The bow was tired. It did not try to lift. It stayed nose-down, the attitude left over from the last crest under the stern. As the sea heaved under the forefoot, the bow went down, and down, and down forever.

The blue Mediterranean tore up the deck. It sluiced around the mainmast, slammed into the skylights, poured down the hatch in a thick, continuous torrent. *Laure* went under clean as a sounding whale, half a mile off the breakwater.

Frankie went with her.

The masts leaned over sideways. The hull was a big, wavering shadow under the water. Bianca's voice was shouting. I could not see her.

I took a big breath, and dived. My hands found Frankie's body: slack, unconscious. The blue water stung my eyes. There was pressure in my ears. Big pressure. The boat was going down, and we were going with it. I fumbled at the blanket, looking for the knot. Found the knot. My ears were hurting like hell. The knot had gone hard as iron. *Go on,* said a voice. *Up, breathe, come down again, finish the job.*

I told the voice to shut up. You got one chance, and one chance only.

What if Laure *rolls, and you're stuck under?*

My fingers kept working. There was another voice, hard and grim. This is your daughter Frankie. That white blur in the water has been living between you and Mary Ellen all these years. It has kept you together. It has been the good and constant thing in both your lives. It is the thing you love . . .

The knot fell apart in my hands.

Her body was limp, weightless. What happens when you are unconscious underwater? Do you breathe? Is there a reflex that keeps the water out of your lungs?

I grabbed Frankie's arm. Her hair wrapped my face. My ears felt as if someone was driving six-inch nails into the drums. I started upward, for the place where the sun was making a thrashing mirror out of the surface of the blue Mediterranean.

It took a day, two days. The blue was turning red. My legs were stopping kicking. *Sink,* yelled the voices. *Drop the girl. Breathe in.*

I found my mind becoming quiet. This was my daughter. If someone had to die, I would die.

My head broke water. I breathed.

Frankie's face was bone-white. A wave slapped us in the face. I coughed, rose on to the blue flank of it. *Be alive,* I was thinking. *Please, Frankie, be alive.*

Someone was shouting. I turned my head. My eyes were stinging with salt water. I saw Bianca, hair slick to her head, lying on top of the water like a seal. "Here," I said. "Here." It was the best I could do.

Another wave hit me in the face. It was still hard to breathe. Frankie was a weight; not a big weight, almost neutral in the water. Frankie, I thought. Are you breathing?

There was something on the wave with us: big, brown, square, lying on the blue face of the swell. I started to swim at it, dragging Frankie with me. Ten yards. Five yards. It vanished. Faceful of water. Cough, splutter, swim. Frankie, are you there?

My hand touched wood. It was a grating, freed when *Laure* sank.

I pulled Frankie on, sat her up. Her head lolled sideways. I could not feel if she was breathing. I gave her mouth-to-mouth, with her head propped on my knee. It was all wrong, but it was the best I could do because our weight had shoved the grating underwater.

Her lips were warm. Live, I thought. Live. She slumped like a doll. I wanted to cry. There was no time for crying.

Something was snarling on the water. From the top of a wave, I looked up. I saw a speedboat, jumping from crest to crest in big, sporty blooms of spray. People were shouting, pulling us up, Frankie first. I was shaking. I did not know where I was. I said, gibbering like an old man, "She might be dead." We laid her on the floor. Water ran out of her. Then someone else was giving her mouth-to-mouth.

I said, "There's another one."

"We see her," they said. I was vaguely aware that they were pulling someone over the side: Bianca, dripping.

But I was watching Frankie with all my might, willing her to live. Things were turning out just as Crespi would have wanted.

Most things. Not all of them. The man doing the mouth-to-mouth straightened. He had a big black mustache. He was grinning. He said, *"Elle vit."*

She's alive.

I felt my own grin start at the soles of my feet and spread upward. I knelt, and I cradled her head. Her breath was a warm flutter on my cheek.

She was alive. But she was still unconscious.

The engine howled, a long tearing howl. We were alongside the breakwater.

We carried Frankie out of the boat. We laid her on the quay with a pillow of coats for her poor head. The concrete was hot. It smelled of lime and dust. There was a scream of sirens. An ambulance arrived.

The doctors took over. Then there was a hospital somewhere, cleaner than an English hospital, with flowers on the reception desk. A doctor shook his head and muttered about X-rays. They wheeled Frankie away. Later, the doctor came back.

"Fractured skull," he said. "Blood clot on the brain."

Oh Christ, I thought. Frankie.

"She must go to Montpellier," he said. "We operate."

"How soon will you know?"

He shrugged. "Hard to say," he said. "At least twenty-four hours."

I said, "Where is she?"

"They make her ready to move."

"I'd like to see her."

He nodded. I followed him through green corridors that smelled of antiseptic. People saw my drying clothes and bare feet, and gave me frightened looks, as if I were a bacterium.

She was lying on a gurney, unconscious. Her freckles stood out against the waxy pallor of her face. She was hardly breathing. Her eyelashes rested light on the curve of her young cheeks.

"Try not to worry," said the doctor. There were no guarantees in his voice.

I grinned at him, a grin that felt as if it would crack my face. I held her hand. It was warm and alive, but limp. "Good luck," I said. I was talking to her, not him. I went out of the hospital with my hand clenched on the warmth she had left in my palm, into a dry, dusty wind that stung the eyes and made it hard to see.

There was a bar down the road. I went in, drank a cognac. Crespi, I was thinking. This is the end of you.

I rammed money into the telephone, and dialed Bonnard, the surveyor. I told him I was working with Arthur Crespi. "Great surprise," I said. "*Laure*'s sunk."

"Oh," he said. His voice was a cynical Marseillais drawl. You could smell the cigarettes and pastis down the telephone. "Tragedy."

I said, "You'll stand by the survey?"

He said, "My children never stop eating."

And my child was on her way to Montpellier with a blood clot on the brain.

I said, "Are you in the office?"

"At home."

"We should meet."

"Sure," he said. "Café des Sports. Table by the telephone box."

I hung up.

32

A black Mercedes pulled up outside the café. The window slid down. Bianca was inside. "Get in," she said. "Where have you been?"

I got in. I did not speak.

"Where to?"

"Centre ville."

She drove slowly through the dust the wind was whipping out of the tarpaulins by the building sites. She said, "How is she?"

I told her.

She said, "I'm sorry."

I said, "It's not your fault."

She said, "About my father." She was formal, as if we hardly knew each other. "I would like to thank you."

I said, *"Je vous en prie,"* with the same formality. Then I put my hand on hers. I said, "And thank you for looking after Frankie."

She shrugged. "It wasn't a problem."

We were under the plane trees in the square. I said, "This is where I get out."

She said, "And later?"

There was one idea in my mind, and it had nothing to do with later. I climbed out of the door. She said, "I'll be at the villa."

I thanked her for the ride, and picked my way through the crowds to the terrace of the Café des Sports. The man at the table by the telephone box had the usual deep tan, stone-washed jeans, a long-peaked cap pushed back on his head. There was a glass of pastis on the table in front of him. I threaded my way through the tables of tourists and locals taking the evening air and sat down next to him. He looked up, took in my clothes. He grinned the kind of grin he might have practiced in the mirror. "So," he said. "Glug, glug, huh?"

"Glug, glug." I smiled right back at him with a face that felt as if it was pasted on the front of someone else's skull. He wore a gold bracelet, two gold rings, a gold Rolex, apparently genuine. He had a coppery, stupid face with a one-sided, artificial smile. I said, "When you did that survey, what was the name of the company you did it for?"

His glass was halfway to his lips. He put it down again. His big black eyebrows came down over his eyes. "Hey," he said. "Wait a minute."

I said, nice and quiet, "I'm doing an investigation into the fraudulent sinking of *Poisson d'Avril* and now *Laure* on behalf of Lloyd's of London."

The hand holding the glass rattled it violently against the plastic saucer. *"Non,"* he said.

"Not a dream," I said. "Not a nightmare. This is happening to you. Now. Here. There are seven people dead, because of your surveys. I am offering you limited immunity, if you talk."

"But M. Crespi—"

"M. Crespi has problems of his own. He is no longer in a position to cover up for you. Think about it."

The sweat popped out on his forehead like dew on a Krug bottle. He was too frightened to think, but he did his best. Finally he said, "What is this immunity?"

And I knew I had him.

He began to talk. When he had talked for five minutes, I got him a piece of paper from the bar. He wrote on it, and signed it; a full account, naming what names he knew. Crespi's was at the top of the list. I tucked the paper in my pocket. He was staring at the ice cube in the bottom of his glass as if it were a crystal ball, and he was seeing the end of the world in it. I left him to his thoughts.

There were taxis in the square, by the ice-cream hut. I climbed aboard one, and told the driver to take me to the Villa Occitan.

The butler let me in. The house was cool. It seemed to have a new echo, as if its emptiness had increased. I went up the stairs, showered and climbed into a clean shirt and trousers, and slipped the Charles Aznavour tape of the Patron's conversation with Crespi into my pocket. Then I rang Montpellier airport, and booked myself on to the London flight leaving in two hours.

The telephone was in the big room. The blinds were drawn against the sun. It was shady, almost dark. The big nude above the fireplace glowed blue and gold, shadow and flesh. I made one more call, to Crespi's office at Les Digues. I put on a strong English accent. I said, "Lloyd's here. We have a big problem with a surveyor in your part of the world. Absolutely crucial we meet at noon tomorrow. Usual office. Any problems, call this number." I gave the number of Mary Ellen's box at Lloyd's.

As I put the telephone down, a voice said, "Why are you going to London?"

Bianca's voice. She was standing in the doorway. Her skin was scorched with salt and wind. Her eyes were deep and somber.

I said, "I'm rolling up Crespi. I'm meeting him tomorrow."

She went to a cupboard, pulled out a bottle and a couple of glasses, filled me one. She said, "Thank you."

There was a pause. I could hear a fly buzzing in another room.

"Well, then." I raised my glass. "I'll be off." It was cognac, good and old. It bustled down the throat, stiffened the knees, chased fear into the shadows at the back of the mind.

She said, "I heard from Béziers. The doctors say my father is . . . finished."

"Finished?"

"He must never work again. His heart is too weak."

I said, "I'm sorry."

"Don't be," she said. "Le Patron is finished. Crespi is finished. So I am la Patronne." She took a step forward. Her lips were soft on my mouth. "Thank you," she said, again.

I said, "Are you a director of Atlas Industrien?"

She smiled. She said, "My father does not believe in women working. Not like you."

"What do you mean?"

"You have always thought I am making conspiracies."

I drank some more brandy. I said, "Just before he was

killed, Thibault said only you knew where he was. And Jean-Claude found him."

She said, "It was not me who told Jean-Claude."

Our eyes locked. Three weeks ago, she had been skittery as a young horse. Now, her eyes were calm and level. They looked through me, at what had to be done in the town of Sainte-Jeanne-des-Sables now she was la Patronne. They did not look like the eyes of a liar.

Not that it is sensible to judge the truth by simple eyeball contact.

I said, "I know."

My taxi hooted at the back door. I climbed in.

At Montpellier airport I rang the hospital. They said that Frankie was in the operating theater. Twenty-four hours, they said again.

I dialed Mary Ellen. She was not at work, and not at home. I climbed on to the airplane.

France crawled dusty brown under the window. I did not watch it. I was thinking about the lowest common denominator.

There had been a time when I had thought the lowest common denominator was Thibault. Then I had thought it was Crespi; after Crespi, Atlas Industrien.

But there was another one behind all that.

When I had visited Thibault the first time, he had disappeared. When I had found him the second time, Crespi's thugs had arrived soon afterward. When I had found him off Saint-Martin-de-Ré, they had managed to kill him.

The same with Captain Kallikratides. When I had found him, he had died.

The lowest common denominator was Michael Savage. And the people in whom Michael Savage had confided.

Not people.

Person.

I thought of the anonymous eyes, watching. They were not anonymous anymore.

The plane landed. The first-class passengers were a long way ahead. I saw a small, slim woman, with black hair in a French roll, wearing expensive-looking jeans. I was virtually sure it was Bianca. But I was on the bus behind, and by the time I got to the barrier she was long gone, if it had been her at all.

London was cold and gray and stony-hearted. I was tired. I still could not get in touch with Mary Ellen. I checked into the miserable Synge Hotel, stared at the flock wallpaper for twenty minutes, and fell asleep with the light on. Next morning I rang the hospital again. The operation had been a success, as far as they could tell, they said. Frankie was still unconscious. There would be no news for five, six hours.

I called Mary Ellen. This time she was in, and happy to hear me. I said, "Can I see you?"

"Later," she said. "Busy morning. How's Frankie?"

"I found her," I said. "I'll be over."

I ate breakfast. I went to High & Mighty and bought a suit, dark, a shirt, striped, and a tie, floral. I put them on, and brushed the hair back behind the ears. Nobody was going to mistake me for an insurance czar, but at least they would let me into the building.

At eleven, I climbed aboard the tube to Bank.

Leadenhall Street was crowded. But the pressure of the eyes was gone. I forged toward the corner of Lime Street, where the Lloyd's building towered above its surrounding office blocks like a greenhouse from hell.

I gave my name to the security man, and waited. I saw Mary Ellen coming a long way off, picking her way through the crowds. She was wearing a double-breasted suit, a shirt of heavy white silk with a gold chain inside the neck. She greeted a couple of people she knew. Her smile transformed the ascetic planes of her face. She looked happy. It was just another day, perhaps better than usual.

So far.

She kissed me on the cheek, quickly, dryly. She was at work. She led me back across the atrium. It towered twelve floors above us, a square well all the way up to the space frames of the barrel vault. We arrived at her box. She looked me up and down, finger on her chin, like an art critic in front of a forgery. "So what are you doing in London, dressed up like a dog's dinner?" she said.

"It's Frankie."

She turned around, and said, "What about Frankie?" Her face was suddenly white and drawn.

I said, "She's in hospital in Montpellier." I told her what had happened.

When I had finished, she said, "Oh." She was fiddling with a ballpoint. The ballpoint took on a light tremor. She looked around at the boxes, the glowing screens, as if she had woken up into a bad dream. She said, "Let's get out of here."

I said, "Stay in the box."

She looked at me sideways. Whatever she saw seemed to convince her.

Three brokers had drifted in. They were standing behind her empty seat. She gave them a tight smile. "Give me an hour," she said. The brokers wandered away into the jungle.

There were four men at other seats in the box, underwriters like Mary Ellen. They took no notice.

I said, "Ring the hospital." I dialed her the number.

There was still no news.

She said, "Why are you here?"

I said, "I want to talk to the person who put Frankie where she is."

"For goodness' sake," she said.

"The person's here," I said.

"Here?"

"At Lloyd's."

She stared at me. She said, "What have you been doing?"

I said, "You helped me find out about Atlas Industrien. Atlas is owned by Arthur Crespi, employer of Frankie's boyfriend, Lucas Baragouin, alias Jean-Claude Dupont. Crespi gets a lot of money that needs laundering. He does some of it via Atlas subsidiaries. I got the list of subsidiaries from Jon Green. A lot of them are insurance brokerages."

Her eyes were gray as cold lakes. "So?" she said.

I said, "They were selling a lot of insurance, cheap. And every now and then, they pulled a stroke. A scuttle, like *Poisson d'Avril*. Or *Laure*. What they needed was a wholesaler. Collect all the little policies, lump them into one big policy, flog it around the underwriters. The wholesaler would be party to the frauds, too. He'd know that if you made a lot of little claims, you wouldn't attract attention. He'd smooth things over if people started to ask awkward questions."

Mary Ellen picked up her telephone. Her businesslike

Canadian fingers moved over the buttons. Pager number. She put down the receiver. She said, "Are you telling me that there has been a systematic fraud?"

"That is correct."

"By someone inside Lloyd's?"

"Correct."

She was very pale. She said, "Oh my God."

"By the way," I said. "Did Justin tell you what was on that tape I asked you to pass him?"

"No," she said. "Should he have?"

The murmur of Lloyd's is like the murmur of a busy library. For a moment, it seemed to go quiet, so all I could hear was the blood, singing in my ears. "Yes," I said. "I think he probably should."

I placed complete trust in Mary Ellen. I had told her about my every movement.

And other people had found out.

The telephone chirruped. Mary Ellen picked it up. I looked at my watch. It was five minutes to twelve.

"Oh," said Mary Ellen. "I see."

"That was Justin," I said. "You paged him. He's got a meeting."

"How did you know?"

I said, "I think you should call the police."

She stared at me. She made no move toward the telephone.

"Central article of faith," I said. "At Lloyd's, the relationship between broker and underwriter is founded on absolute trust. Is that the problem?"

I got up, walked away. When I looked back, Mary Ellen was staring at the telephone as if it were a poisonous snake. I stepped aboard the escalator.

The Lloyd's escalators are made of perspex and white metal, and they zigzag into the cathedral heights of the atrium like stairways to heaven. The atrium itself is a rectangular crater surrounded by trading floors and offices opening on to it like galleries, under a glass barrel-vault roof. The barrel-vault rises from lumps of glass-and-steel offices. On the top, twelfth floor, shaded by passing clouds and illuminated by cinematic beams of sunlight, the President sits in his office, like Jupiter in a cloud.

Justin's office was on the fourth floor, in a boxy wing

tacked on to the side of the gallery, beyond a maze of boxes stacked with tottering files and lit by the green screens of a gaggle of motor insurers. The secretary sitting outside said, "Mr. Peabody's in a meeting."

I smiled at her. We had met before. It was the suit that was confusing her. "I am the meeting," I said, and walked in.

Justin was standing by the window, looking out at what would have been St. Paul's if there had not been fifty grimy office blocks in the way. He turned as he heard the door open. He was smiling. When he saw me, the smile faded. He turned a sudden, sick gray. He thought he was seeing a ghost. He recovered fast. He said, "Mikey, old boy. This is a surprise. Look, I've got a meeting. Might be all right for lunch—"

I said, "That little bit of bother with *Poisson d'Avril*. I've fixed it."

The light was behind him. He looked like a mountain with jug ears. He came toward me. He was a head taller than me. His face was on fire with sunburn. He said, "What do you mean, you've fixed it?"

"I've found out who organized it, who the beneficiaries were, how it was done. I've got statements from intermediaries, tapes of confessions between the principals."

There were ugly white circles under his eyes, like fish skin. His mouth was like a letterbox, and his pork-sausage fingers flexed and straightened at the seams of his pinstripe trousers. He said, "I don't know what you're talking about."

"You were following me about," I said. "While I was on the case, you were letting me lead you where you wanted to be. If I didn't tell you, Mary Ellen did. Absolute trust between broker and underwriter. Except that Crespi had hired you to be his wholesaler. Great rates, terrific prospects. Money for old rope, eh, Justin?"

He said, "I don't know what you're talking about."

"I suppose it was Mary Ellen who told you?" I said.

He opened the slot of mouth, shut it again. All the mateyness had gone from his face. It was cold, and hard, and vicious. "Don't you dare talk about Mary Ellen," he said.

I said, "I'm married to her."

He said, "You've wasted her time for, God knows, fifteen years. She could have made someone a proper wife."

"You."

He said, "Well, why not? I could have given her what she wanted. But she was always harking back, harking back . . ."

"So to get your hands on Mary Ellen, you decided to swindle underwriters, and endanger her daughter's life."

He did not answer that.

I said, "You're winding me up, sonny. You wanted money, is the reason. You've got expensive habits. You're a Member of Lloyd's. Maybe there were some losses to meet, a few open years you didn't like the sound of. Plus the boat, and the shirt bill, and the cars."

"I don't know who you think you are," he said.

"I'm the guy you hired to investigate you," I said. "The stupid Irishman. The one who was never going to rumble you. Is that what you told Arthur Crespi?"

He said, "Excuse me." He pushed me hard, with a hand like the bucket of a mechanical digger. I went backward over a chair. My head hit the wall. The door slammed. I got up, pulled the door open. Justin's big shoulders were heading for the escalator. He was walking fast, weaving through the men in their loose, expensive pinstripe suits.

I started to run. I ran in a loop, past a tangle of boxes, the screens flicking in my eyes. I got to the escalator first. It was one minute to twelve.

A man was coming up, looking at his watch. He had a dark face, and a dark suit, made of cloth shinier than the general run of suits at Lloyd's. I turned away, looked at a screen.

The face was the face of Arthur Crespi. It had lost its golden-boy cheerfulness. Now it was sallow and pouchy, and the eyes moved flat and watchful. Mr. Crespi was on his way to the meeting I had arranged for him with Justin Peabody. But he did not look like a businessman on his way to a meeting. He looked like a Marseilles gangster on his way to hurt somebody.

Justin was coming to the top of the down escalator. His face was shining with sweat. He saw me. His tongue came out, ran around his lips. He wanted the outside world, far away, somewhere quiet. He wanted it in a hurry.

I wanted him here, until the police came.

I blocked his path. I said, "There's nowhere to go. Don't make a fuss."

He was moving away, toward the thicket of boxes on the

gallery floor. I followed him. The crowd thinned out. We were coming to a backwater, toward the edge of the gallery, where the parapet overlooked the central well. Out of the corner of my eyes I could see Crespi's plump, shiny back heading in the direction of Justin's office.

"All right," said Justin. He had turned around. His back was to an empty box, the last one before the gallery's rail, its occupants gone to lunch. The sweat was running out of his yellow bristles, making dark patches on the eighteen-and-a-half-inch collar of his blue Turnbull & Asser shirt. "How much?"

"How much for what?"

Two men, making a deal by a box. One deal out of the five thousand deals being made in the Lloyd's building at this precise second.

The sun had crawled from behind a cloud. A ray shot through the bull's-eye of the semicircular window at the top of the vault, gilded the marble and the concrete. Justin screwed up his eyes against the glare. "Don't bugger me about," he said. "I'm in a hurry."

I opened my mouth to tell him to come along and meet Crespi, and start explaining. Then I shut it again.

Justin's face looked the same as ever. But the sameness was superficial. Usually, the neck and cheeks were relaxed, sleek as the chops of a dolphin. Now, there were big knots of muscle at the corners of the jaw, and the sinews of the neck were biting into the collar, and the laughter lines at the corners of the eyes had a quick, electrical tremor. It was the face of a man who had his back to a wall. He had stopped thinking. The adrenaline was screaming through his arteries, yelling *get out!*

My mouth was suddenly dry as blotting paper.

We were in the middle of the bustle of Lloyd's.

But I was in Justin's way.

His hand came out, fast, grabbed me by the coat. His other hand hit me in the neck, slammed me back against the blond-oak corner of the empty box. We were two men talking in a quiet corner. People do not kill people in Lloyd's.

His fingers were strong as car jacks. They began to close on my neck. I thrashed at him with my arms and legs. I could not reach. There was no air anymore.

The glass vault was full of red light. Outside, the sun rolled out of the clouds like an eye bulging with blood. There was a roaring of jet engines. There were no jets in this pit under its glass vault of sky. The jet was in my head, throttling up. And as it throttled up, the darkness was coming down, on me and Frankie and Mary Ellen.

I saw a face. It was behind Justin's left shoulder: a brown face, with crinkly black hair and deep pouches under the eyes. Crespi.

The face looked ancient and vicious. I had the ludicrous thought that I did not want the last thing I saw in the world to be the face of Crespi.

The teeth bared, as if Crespi were making a physical effort. Justin made a noise that penetrated even the roar in my mind. The iron grip on my neck slackened. His hands went behind his back. He lurched sideways, toward the parapet. He walked straight at it as if he could not see it.

I had my back to the box. My knees had lost the power to hold me up. I was sliding down to the floor. Crespi was standing over me. There was a knife in his right hand, a long, thin switchblade.

"Now you," he said.

The roaring faded. It was replaced by a roar in the mind. Savage, you bloody fool, it yelled. Justin's been silenced. Now all he has to do is silence you and Bianca, and he's halfway off the hook. There will be no absolute proof.

I tried to move my arms, to push myself up. They did not work.

You've blown it, I thought.

A drop of Justin's blood fell off the point of Crespi's knife. He smiled, a cold little smile. He was a man of honor, said the smile. Revenge was the icing on expediency. And since nobody knows me here, I will slide into the crowd, and be away . . .

And you will be dead.

A person materialized at his shoulder. A small person, slim, with black hair and a red mouth. Bianca. She stooped. She pulled off a shoe and brought it around, hard, so the sharp heel whacked into Crespi's right ear. Crespi clapped his hand to his head, turned away and dropped the knife. There was a lot of shouting now. Someone said, "Police!" I found some strength and pulled myself up.

Justin had his back to me. On the left hand side, just below where the heart should have been under the pinstripe, a patch was spreading. The sun in the vault caught the wet, turned it crimson. The crimson grew. In the middle of the crimson was a little knife cut, an unhemmed buttonhole in the wet superfine wool.

Justin staggered forward. He hit the parapet at waist height. His head went forward. His feet went up. He fell over the edge.

There was a small, dull crash. Up from the pit, like vapor from a crater, there drifted the sound of screaming.

I lurched away, and fell into someone's box with my head on a computer keyboard. A green screen winked to black.

A policeman said, "This one's hurt." People were lifting me up, asking me questions. Crespi was going away between two uniforms. There was a voice in the hubbub: a woman's voice. Mary Ellen's voice. It was not the calm, reasonable Canadian voice I knew. It was loud and commanding. It was shouting, "Get out of my way, you moron! I'm his wife!"

The crowd bulged and burst. She came through, hair on end, cheeks flushed, eyes glittering.

She sat down by me, and held my face. She was crying. She said, "Are you all right?"

I tried to talk. The sounds would not come out. So I winked, instead.

"You Irish bastard," she said.

Bianca was standing behind her. She was wearing a linen dress that looked as if it had been coach-built by Rolls-Royce. She was beautiful. The men around her, the leading underwriters in their loose expensive suits and their old school ties, kept glancing across at her with their bookie's eyes.

She said, "Everything I have done, I have done to protect my father."

I nodded. My neck hurt. I said, "I know that."

She said, "Including listening to your telephone calls." She paused. "Maybe you will come again to Sainte-Jeanne?"

"Maybe."

She nodded. She said, "Thank you." She pressed my hand and walked away, into the ghostly glow of the screens.

Mary Ellen was staring after her. She said, "Who on earth was that?"

"A friend," I said.

The police came down like starlings on a roost.

It took twelve hours to get rid of them.

I went up to Mary Ellen's flat. I sat on the sofa with her. I rang the hospital in Montpellier, and croaked at the girl on the switchboard out of my mashed larynx. I waited to be put through. Outside the big window a tug was towing a string of lighters against the tide.

"Hello?" said Frankie's voice.

I said, "Are you all right?"

"Bloody awful," she said. "What have you been doing to your *voice?*"

I handed the telephone to Mary Ellen. They talked. The doctor said she could come out in a week. Mary Ellen hung up. She said, "We'd better go to Montpellier."

"Yes."

She went to the kitchen. There was the sound of a cork. She came back with a bottle of burgundy and two glasses. She said, "I wasn't very clever about Justin."

I said, "Nor was I."

Neither of us wanted to talk about Justin. She said, "There's no flight to Montpellier until tomorrow." She paused. The long lashes hid her clear gray eyes. "Why don't you stay?"

The ceiling was dancing with the reflections of the sun on the river. There was a bowl of roses on the table. Next door was the cool bedroom, with the big bed. She took my hand.

I said, "Why not?"

Pocket Books
Proudly Announces

MAELSTROM
Sam Llewellyn

Coming in Hardcover
from Pocket Books
mid-November

The following is a preview of
Maelstrom . . .

We walked up the alley and along the street to Landsman's house. I hammered on the door.

A woman opened it, middle-aged and colorless in a blue-check apron. I said, "I'm looking for Mr. Landsman."

She said, "Mr. Landsman is not in."

I said, "Where is he?"

"He will be in the Mission," she said. "It's his night to be in the Mission." Her eyes shifted away, as if the word alarmed her.

I asked for directions. She pointed with a finger smoothed and stoutened by polishing furniture. We walked down the street, past painted houses, past the mouth of the alley leading to the quay, right to the end. It was eleven now, but the light was still strong. The streets were cobbled. The gables were steep and quaint. There were wooden buckets in the sheds, and a smell of new hay, and milch goats clanking their chains in the gardens.

Trevor was keeping very quiet, mooching along,

hands in pockets, staring at the ground. He said, "Like a bloody museum, innit? Watch yourself in this place."

I said, "What do you mean?"

He said, gloomily, "We came here last time. You'll see."

The building the woman had pointed out had a tall, steep-pitched roof and a Gothic door. It looked like a village hall, except that it was built out of big pine planks instead of corrugated iron, and the biting beasts carved on the timbers had cost someone a lot of time and trouble. Above the door was a plaque covered in Norwegian writing. Around the plaque was coiled the double loop of the serpent tattooed on the skinheads' arms, perpetually devouring its tail. A dull roar of voices came from inside.

I twisted the door handle. We went in.

Seamen's Missions are usually dour spots upholstered in vinyl and Formica, with a couple of sets of dominoes, an understocked bar, and a chaplain hanging about next to the fruit machine. This one was different.

The room occupied what must have been the whole of the building. Big iron chandeliers hung from the purlins, illuminating a dozen or so long wooden tables full of men and a few women. There were the remains of food on the tables, forests of beer bottles, the taller necks of vodka and aquavit. Broad blond girls moved between the tables carrying trays of more bottles and glasses. The air was thick with cigarette smoke and wood smoke and sweat. Through the haze I could see at the far end of the room a sort of dais, with a table twice as long as the ones on the floor.

It was Vikings in Disneyland. I walked down between the tables. A Rhodesian ridgeback snarled at me. Its shaven-headed master swore at me in German. There was a good sprinkling of skinheads, a lot of tattoos on necks and arms.

Landsman and Gruskin were on the dais. Gruskin's face was almost luminous in the dim light. *Watch out for a White Russian.* Hugo was next to Gruskin. He was laughing at something Gruskin had said. He had been hard at it already: his head was rolling about, the way it rolled about when he had drunk a lot. Kristin was next to him, her hair hooked behind her ears, her heavily made-up eyelids drooping. Landsman's protuberant eyes rested on us. He raised a hand in the air. "Welcome!" he bellowed theatrically. "Come hither!"

Trevor muttered, "Not on your nelly," and found himself a place on one of the benches. I climbed up the steps to the dais.

Hugo said, "All *right!*" Kristin rolled her eyes up, and smiled a deep, beatific smile at an invisible person a foot to my right. Her pupils were enormous. Her sharp nose was running, but she was not bothering to sniff. I guessed that she shared Hugo's weakness for pharmaceuticals.

"Drink!" roared Landsman, pulling a chair up for me and shoving a glass and bottle at me. I sat down in the chair, tipped a small measure into the glass, and did not drink out of it.

Landsman leaned forward and caught his weight on the table with his elbows. There was vodka on his breath. He said, "You worry about the man Olaf. You are not used to our ways." He jabbed a forefinger at the crowd.

I followed his finger into the sea of heads. In the

middle was a yellow blob, swathed in a white turban. Olaf, his missing ear bandaged, drinking vodka from the bottle.

"Hard man!" bellowed Landsman, spitting in my ear. "What you saw was natural justice. The man offended his leader, so he must lose a part of his body. He understands this. He will make no complaint to the police. These people are like hunting hounds. You control them so much, but the wild part of their nature is the useful part of their nature, so you do not interfere with it. You give them meat and alcohol and women if they want them. And they will serve you till death."

I nodded. I was thinking of Hugo's terror. Landsman was frightening, all right. He was also crazy.

His eyes were glittering like ice under a grubby sea. He raised his head. He shouted, *"Sieg!"*

There was a brief flutter of silence. Then the crowd roared, *"Heil!"* There was a forest of right arms, blue with tattoos. The shouting died gradually away. "On their arms," said Landsman. "The Jörmungandr, the Midgard serpent that eats its own tail. Perpetually regenerated by consuming itself." His voice was a low, dangerous hiss. "The serpent encompasses the world. Its movements produce storms in the world of ordinary men. We of Midgard produce storms that will rock this civilization out of its soft bed." He smiled. His teeth were brown. "I tell you, there is a time coming when Europe will be sorry it forgot its clean, primitive power. It is drowning in its own fat and softness. It must be reminded. Mr. Hope, tonight Midgard has reminded *you.*"

The smile showed his teeth all the way back to the molars.

I looked at him. I wanted to laugh. Then I thought about the ear and the gulls and the stink of sweat and fear. And I wanted to be sick.

Someone nudged my right arm. Hugo's face was at my shoulder, yellowish, gleaming with sweat. He raised his eyebrows. I knew he was saying: are you seriously intending to sabotage these people's whale hunt?

I smiled at him. I said, "We promised Helen."

He closed his eyes. He was terrified. He said, "Oh, Christ." The last word rang in a sudden silence. The roar of talk had faltered and died. I looked around, and saw why.

There was an empty area among the tables in front of the stage. In a nightclub, it would have been the dance floor. Here, they probably used it for bite-the-head-off-the-live-chicken contests. In this empty area arrived a little boy.

He was maybe nine years old, with a pudding bowl of yellow hair and a wide, pointed face. He was wearing a pair of sloppy jeans and a Snoopy T-shirt; nice liberal clothes that stuck out a mile among the Fair Isles and seaboots of the fishermen, and the studs and tattoos of the Midgard fun-Nazis at the tables. He arrived on the dance floor suddenly, as if someone had thrown him there. There was a laugh like a kennelful of rottweilers barking. For a moment Landsman looked surprised, even shocked.

The child stood as if dazed, looking around him, his face stiff and anxious. Then he tried to walk back down the aisle between the tables, heading for the exit.

An enormous skinhead was sitting in the front row. He grabbed the child by the arm and threw him across the dance floor. The crowd roared, "Stroh!" The skinhead raised his tattooed arms above his head. A skinhead on the other side caught the child. There was a cheer. The second skinhead flung him to a third skinhead. Landsman stopped looking surprised. "That Stroh," he said. "A lion!" He started to cheer, woodenly, without conviction. There was a lot of laughing. The child was not doing any of it. The anxiety on his face had become misery.

Landsman was leaning back in his chair, hands on his thighs, eyes narrow, his goatee jutting horizontally. I noticed that the seat of the chair was higher than any of the others, to make up for the fact that he was shorter. He said something to me, but the noise was so big now that I could not hear. I said, "What?"

"My grandson," he said, pointing to the boy. "God knows how he came here." One of the skinheads fluffed his throw. The boy skidded on hands and knees on the rough wooden floor. He stayed there, trying not to cry. Stroh lumbered over, picked him up, and threw him again.

I said, "That's not fun."

"Puppies must play with the dogs," said Landsman. "So they will learn to hunt."

He looked at me with pebbly, drunken eyes. I found I could not stand any more. I got up and walked off the dais.

The child flew across the dance floor, a spray of tears sparkling in the jaundice-yellow candlelight. The skinhead who had caught him grinned the no-teeth Todsholm grin, looking for someone to throw him back to. I went up to him and said, "I'll take him."

The grin emitted sour beer and spirits. He yanked the child out of the way. I hit him hard on the nose. I felt bone crunch under my knuckles. He went backward off the bench with a crash. Then there was a silence, into which fear rushed like the tide into a rock pool. The boy stood looking at the floor, hoping that what was happening was not happening. I said to him, "Come on. We'll find your mum."

The child was breathing fast. He looked up with eyes the size of TV screens. I put my hand out. Whatever he saw in my face, he preferred it to skinhead grins. He put his hand in mine.

I looked for the way out. I found hundreds of eyes, all centered on me. My knuckles hurt. The silence continued. My stomach began to jump with nerves. Bloody fool, I thought, you shouldn't have hit him. Any minute now, this quiet is going to break like a wave, and you and this child are going to be right down there under a pile of boots and fists and Bowie knives they cut people's ears off with.

I glanced at the dais. Gruskin was watching with his black-hole eyes in his lard-colored toad face. Landsman's chin was still up, but he looked as stiff and uncertain as his cheering. Landsman was having second thoughts.

I gave the hand a squeeze and began to walk down the aisle between the tables. The back of my neck was crawling, waiting for the flung bottle or the baseball bat. Out of the corner of my eye I saw Trevor stand up, blushing deeply. His right hand was in his coat pocket, where he kept the big shackle. Footsteps fell in behind me. "Nice one, Fred," said his voice. "Keep walking. I'm behind you." There were more footsteps. Out of the corner of my eye I saw a good-sized group of fishermen. One of them nodded and said, "That's right."

Trevor said, "These lads didn't like it either."

I said to the child, cheerful and natural as possible, "That's Trevor. Very tough guy. Good mate."

"That's right," said Trevor. "Don't like bastards."

We were past the last of the tables. The fishermen were around us. The door was ahead. I put out my hand, turned the handle, pulled it open, and walked into the midnight daylight.

Back in the hall, someone started shouting. The hairs on my neck bristled. A couple of the fishermen started to run away, their boots crashing on the cobbles. Trevor's hand came out of his pocket, wearing the shackle like a knuckle-duster. There were more shouts, a scraping of benches, the thunder of boots on a wooden floor. Then over the top of it all a harsh voice cried, "Halt!" and added something in German. Landsman's voice.

The boots stopped drumming on the floor. Landsman said something else, and began to laugh, the big hollow laugh with as much humor as a cough, the laugh of a little man kidding himself that he was a Viking chieftain.

Hands began clapping—a lot of hands, roaring like surf on the beach. A group of harsh voices were bellowing *"Sieg Heil!"*

I shut the door. The fishermen nodded and grinned. We stood in a knot in the long midnight shadows. The sweat was running off me like water from a shower.

I said to the fishermen, "What did he say?"

One of them looked at me with a face that was fair,

but not friendly. "He said not to kill a hero. A hero will find his own way to Walhalla." He chucked the child under the chin, and walked away.

I said to the boy, "Where do you live?"

He was still holding my hand, the way a nervous parachutist might hold the D-ring of his ripcord. His face was losing its strained look. He said, "Here," and tugged me back down the street. I went with him quickly, before the Midgard storm troopers could change their minds.

We arrived in front of another of the painted wooden houses. This one was less stark than the others. It had a clematis growing by the door, and a larch tree in a yard at the back, and tubs of alyssum and begonias. The boy reached up and opened the door on to a pine-paneled hallway. I said, "Is anyone in?"

"Mama," called the boy. A woman came into the hallway.

The boy stepped forward. The woman looked down at him, then at us. "What do you want?" she said. She had shortish blond hair, high cheekbones and cold, suspicious eyes. She was Karin Landsman.

I said, "Your son was in the Mission. I thought we should bring him home."

The boy began talking fast in Norwegian. His voice became higher. It had sobs in it. He buried his face in his mother's blue-check shirt, and began to cry. Karin spoke to him sharply, but her arms were around him, and she was smoothing his yellow hair. Her face had softened. She said, "I am sorry. Please come in." She was not the boss's daughter anymore. She was a mother who had had a bad shock, and her face was full of worry and anger.

Women made Trevor more uneasy than skinheads. He said, "I'll get back to the boat, then."

I said, "Watch out for that lot. Get ready for sea." He nodded and shambled away down the road.

Karin gave me a stiff bow. She said, "Thank you. Sverre, my son, he's a wanderer, specially when the nights are light. He got used to it when he was young. When Hanno . . . my husband . . . was alive, he would not have permitted this kind of thing. They would not have tried it, these people. And my father would not have let them." She sounded formal, but flustered. "But now, it's, well, I don't know what it is. I hope you will drink some coffee? But first, please excuse me, I must put Sverre in his bed."

She left me in what looked like the living room. It was a normal room. It looked as if a family lived in it and did normal, everyday things, not the kind of things that had been happening in Todsholm today. The furniture had the well-used, faded look that family furniture develops. There was a television and a model ketch and a narwhal's tusk, and a lot of black-and-white photographs of rocks and boats and people. On the wall was a Russian icon of the Virgin and Child. On a sycamore table was the only color photograph in the room. It was a man with a square face, a chin with a dimple, blond hair sticking out from under a blue peaked cap. He was grinning a competent, affectionate grin. He was on a ship of some kind, leaning against the wing of the bridge. There was blue sea behind him, a couple of stern trawlers trawling.

The door opened. Karin came in with a tray of coffee. She said, in her cold, shut-off voice, "My husband. In the spring. Just before he was killed. He was fishing in the Lofoten Islands. Do you take cream?" She raised her eyes from the tray. There was a little of her father's blue mixed with the green: the color of a northern sea. She said, "Fishing is a dangerous trade." She was not the uppity charter guest anymore. She was trying to make amends for her distance.

I fingered the clean-shaven chin behind which Hope the saboteur was hiding. I wondered whether her new civility was real, or whether she had heard me talking to Hugo on *Straale*.

She said, "Are you going to stay in this madhouse?"

I grinned at her. "My job is to go where I'm sent. And I've got to look after Hugo."

She said, "I guess you're good at looking after people." She said it quietly. She was looking down at her lap. Something dented the brown surface of the coffee. She was crying. I decided that she could not have overheard me and Hugo. Trevor would not have accepted this as a sensible conclusion; but according to the Hope Code, if someone cries you have to believe in them. It would have brought a cynical glint to Ernie's eye, too. Charles Draco, on the other hand, would have understood perfectly.

She said, "It was brave of you to rescue Sverre. But it could have been a bit stupid, couldn't it? You must be careful." She pulled a handkerchief from the sleeve of her jersey, and blew her nose firmly.

"I wasn't on my own. There seem to be some guys from the village who don't like watching children being tortured."

"Bunch of fishermen," she said. "Nobody leads them."

I said, "What are those lunatics doing here?"

"They're pilgrims." She sipped her coffee. "If you can believe that."

"What's the attraction?"

"My father." She shrugged. "He is the godson of Hermann Goering. My sister went to Germany. She's proud of it, stupid girl. She told a lot of people in Germany about my father and Goering. They told other people. They started to turn up here, like it was a shrine. So Papa thought he was a big shot, and started his organization."

"Midgard."

"Honestly," she said. "It's like the wolf cubs from hell. But not funny. They think they're the real people and nobody else matters. You should hear them talk. One minute you think they're just here to drink, have a holiday. Then . . . well, some of them have killed people. *Gastarbeuer,* Turks. It's so . . . *peculiar.* You see it on the TV; you think it couldn't happen here. But here it is."

Sverre's voice floated down the stairs. "Mama!" he yelled.

She stood up. "First day back from school," she said. "I must say goodnight to him."

I said, "I ought to be getting back."

"No," she said quickly. She smiled at her eagerness. "It's nice to talk," she said. "Five minutes."

I waited, wandering around the room. The model ships were of good quality. The Russian icon was good and powerful. The Madonna's eyes were wells of Byzantine calm, and the infant Jesus looked as if he could not wait to bounce off her lap and start saving mankind.

I was still looking at it when Karin came back. "He thinks you're terrific," she said. "He thinks the whole thing was a rugby match, and you were the hero." Her eyes went to the icon. "Hanno brought that back," she said. "Trip before . . . his last one. He bought it from a Russian in Nordland."

"It's a beauty," I said. Either Hanno had been rich, or he had gotten a bargain.

She said, "I'd rather have Hanno." It was a very small joke, but a joke nonetheless. She looked as if she might cry again. For a moment I saw the bleakness of her eyes and the tautness of the skin over her cheekbones. I caught a glimpse of a lonely world walled in with mountains, where Fascist thugs brawled in the streets.

She said, "Do you have a wife?"

I nodded.

She smiled. She said, "Look after her."

I said, "I have to. She's quadriplegic."

"I'm sorry."

I shrugged. Helen was perfectly good at talking about herself, and she did not like me to do it for her.

Meanwhile, I was in Todsholm, and it would be a good idea to get back to *Straale* before they came out of the Seamen's Mission.

I said, "I must go."

She lifted her chin. She said, "I am most grateful." The doors of intimacy had opened a crack and slammed again.

I got up. I said, "Bring Sverre onto my boat."

She said, "He'd like that." She shook my hand. Her grip was warm and firm. "Mr. Hope," she said formally on the doorstep. She blushed. "It is good to have a friend."

The street outside her house was a ravine of shadow, not friendly at all. A confused roar came dully from the direction of the Mission. I walked quickly, fists clenched in the pockets of my coat.

As I turned down the alley to the quay, a figure stepped out of a doorway and blocked the way. It was a big man, with wide shoulders and a black watchcap. My stomach lurched. I thought: here we go.

Look for

Maelstrom

Wherever Hardcover Books Are Sold
mid-November